The Book Of Wars : Legend of the Prophetess

ISBN: 978-1-955531-18-4 [Paperback Edition]
978-1-955531-19-1 [eBook Edition]

Table of Contents

Dedication

I dedicate this book to my wife!

Like Deborah, my wife is a woman of visions, and a true warrior! In my times of greatest despair, she is always a voice of reason for me, and a beacon of faith. She continues to inspire me to face my greatest battles with supernatural optimism.

A Word from the Author

This novel initiated as one of my screenplays for my Master's Thesis in Professional Screenwriting back in 2014.

Thus far, I have yet to win any competitions with the screenplay of this story. However, I wanted this story to have a life beyond collecting dust as an obscure, unrecognized screenplay, so I wrote this novel based on the screenplay.

I put a great deal of research into this story, doing my best to make it both entertaining, and also retaining a degree of historical substance. To that end, I did my best to mold this story to fit the narrative given in the Book of Judges, chapters 4 and 5. However, I also used creative license.

Note: Before reading this book, please take a 5 minutes detour to read the Book of Judges in the Bible, chapters 4 and 5. It is a very brief narrative, probably fitting on a single page, and this narrative of the prophetess and judge, Deborah, is the raw material from which I constructed this story.

My initial inspiration from the Book of Judges quickly grew to encompass other books in the Bible, but I also consulted sources outside of the Bible, such as the Book of Enoch, Bible commentaries, archeology, history, mythologies, and much more.

I used anything I could find that provided information about ancient Israel, Israeli culture, and additional details regarding the account of Deborah and this story that took on a life of its own as I began to write it.

I flexed the use of creative license for many elements in this story, but the governing principle I did my best to adhere to was not to put anything in this story that actually refuted, or contradicted the Biblical narrative.

For example, the Scriptural narrative states that Deborah was a judge and prophetess, and that she ordered General Barak to lead Israel into battle.

This story follows that narrative. However, there is very little information in the Biblical narrative explaining...

- Deborah's rise to power
- Whether or not Deborah was friends with or even knew Barak or Jael on a personal level
- How Deborah was able to convince Barak to go to battle against insurmountable odds
- What caused Barak to insist on Deborah's presence on the battle-field
- How Deborah was able to accurately predict a storm, and use that prediction as the primary ingredient for an overwhelming victory
- The extent of Deborah's prophetic abilities
- If Deborah used her prophetic abilities in her role as a judge
- The back story of the antagonist, Sisera

The narrative of Judges 4 and 5 is actually very sparse, and it leaves a great deal of "what if" speculative wriggle room between the lines. It is in this area of speculation where I asked some of the questions listed above, and many more, and daydreamed about possible answers to those questions.

Why did Barak obey Deborah's command? We don't know for sure. Remember, this story dates to 1200 BC in the land of ancient Palestine. Women were generally regarded as property, and in some places in the Middle East they still are.

Whatever Deborah's backstory truly is, we may never know, but one thing is for certain; it had to be absolutely fantastic, if not other-worldly.

Scripture is very clear that Deborah was a prophetess. Only a person with unyielding confidence, charisma, and amazing clairvoyance would be capable of orchestrating a battle strategy with thousands of lives at stake, based on a freak storm resulting in a river overflowing its banks and wiping out the enemy.

The Biblical narrative includes this detail, which opens the door to question, what other prophetic abilities might Deborah have demonstrated? What exactly gave her the position and authority she wielded? Again, we do not know for sure, but I suspect the answer has to be fantastic, if not otherworldly.

Perhaps the biggest question addressed in this Biblical narrative is why would General Barak not go to battle unless Deborah was with him? Women in ancient times were often considered a prominent acquisition as the plunder of battle. Knowing this, Barak's request for Deborah to go with him to the battlefield was completely over the top.

On this point, I speculate that Deborah was a warrior who knew how to handle herself on the battlefield. Scripture does not state this explicitly, and many Rabbis and commentators would argue against this.

However, observing Barak's request for her presence on the battlefield, and Deborah's masculine response, regarding the glory of battle belonging to a woman; to me, this indicates Deborah was a woman who understood a warrior's mentality from an insider's perspective.

Furthermore, Israel has a long standing history of women serving in combat roles that dates back to WWII. Could it be that this progressive stance on women in combat has an earlier precedent?

This question led me to research Israel's military, where I was delighted to learn about Avivit Cohen, one of Israel's leading Krav Maga military instructors. Avivit's YouTube segments from the show, The Human Weapon, transported me back in time to the Valley of Megiddo, where I could envision her kicking, punching, and hacking through Sisera's forces like nobody's business.

In summation, Deborah was probably not an experienced warrior, however, I do not think the possibility should be completely ruled out. And I also say the same about many of the other examples of creative license I used in this story.

I did my best to stay true to the main points of the narrative. And to be thorough, I also included notes that document my sources of inspiration and all the research I conducted to create this story. In these notes, I list areas where I explored creative license issues, and why I thought some of these aspects of creative license might be more plausible than others.

Chapter 1

An Unprovoked Attack

א

A shapely young woman struggled up a rocky slope lugging a massive jar of water in her arms. It should have been two trips, or perhaps even three, but no, that would take entirely too long for this impetuous young lady.

Deborah approached the rock fence that encircled her home, relieved that she finally made it, or so she thought. Her pet goat Caleb had other plans.

Caleb had his eyes on her since she was at the bottom of the hill, and he had since been intently planning his attack with exuberant anticipation.

Just as she entered the opening in the fence, Caleb lunged forward with a hearty head-butt to her thigh. Wham! She instantly stumbled and twisted, trying to recover from Caleb's fiendish ambush, but to no avail.

The bottom of the jar hit the ground first, catching Deborah in her lower abdomen. The end result was an awkward pole vault over the jar ending with her face in the mud.

Fortunately she was able to break the fall somewhat with her hands, but then the jar gushed its contents all over her.

As icing on the cake, Caleb leaped on top of her back, claiming victory over his defeated foe. No doubt, this was a brilliantly executed strategy, an unparalleled triumph of which there was no equal!

But Deborah was not one to flee a battle like a yelping pup. No, this brutal manifestation of cowardly malfeasance must be countered by an earth shattering show of force! Deborah was actually a bit peeved at her pet this time; he was taking these border skirmishes too far. That jar of water was no kidding, really heavy. Now she was going to have to heave another load back up the hill again. Caleb was going to pay a hefty price for this one.

Summoning the pent up rage of her counter strike, Deborah spun over on her back, instantly interrupting Caleb's victory dance. The moment he stumbled off of her, she leaped toward him, grappled his neck and torso and wrestled him down.

Caleb squirmed to free himself, but she locked her arms around him, squeezing him in a death grip. Then she rolled over on top of him and successfully pinned him to the ground.

"Are you feeling it now? Have you had enough yet?" Deborah growled at the unruly beast. Caleb squirmed another feeble kick with his back leg, to which Deborah responded with another hearty squish. "You're not going anywhere!"

Interrupting the final vestiges of this battle, a young man cleared his throat from behind, standing near the opening of the fence where Deborah was ambushed.

"Ahem, hello?"

Deborah glanced over her shoulder and was immediately stunned to see an extremely handsome young man with a beaming smile aimed directly at her. A subtle breeze tossed his hair.

Who was this beefed up guy with the long, flowing hair, chiseled jawline, twinkling eyes, and a ridiculous grin? Did she see a sparkle in his teeth?

Game over; Deborah released Caleb, and he quickly sprang to his feet and retreated with a few disgruntled bleats.

Deborah then stood up and took a not-so-subtle deep breath to elevate her chest while tossing her jet black hair. Her chest didn't need elevating; that added flare was entirely unnecessary.

This was especially the case with a soaking wet dress, which she was oblivious to until she noticed a queue in the young man's eyes. When she glanced down, she suddenly realized a couple of her perky friends were saying hello.

The young man was not prepared for such a cosmic explosion of splendor blasted into his mortal eyes. His seared retinas would never recover from this magnificence.

Oy! She jerked around quickly, pealed her dress away from her skin, instantly aired it out then folded her arms up high and spun back around.

Let's smile and pretend that didn't happen. It was an accident; no harm, no foul.

This exotic young beauty had the straw infested fizzy hair of a feral child, and a side order of dirt with a thick smear of mud on her chin. But that couldn't hide her intense, captivating eyes, and the flawless symmetry of her face.

As for the exquisite combination of curves in her voluptuous, athletic form, she was no stranger to every young male in her village.

Deborah had many suitors since she came of age, but none met with the approval of her father. Haran didn't know exactly what he was looking for in all these young tomcats meowing around his house, but none of them had it, whatever it was.

"Your name must be...*Deborah?*"

Deborah nodded and smiled, then brushed away a few clumps of mud, though it was a bit slimy and had little effect. So much for a grandiose first impression with this new guy, who was clearly not a local; she would have noticed a bray from this young stallion.

Ironically, she thought she blew her first impression, but in reality, it couldn't have been improved upon.

"How'd you know my name?"

The man paused momentarily, gawking at her. "I'm sorry," he giggled, light headed. If there were a female specifically designed to fit the exact specifications of this man's definition of perfection, Deborah exceeded it.

"The instructions I had were to look for the prettiest girl in Ramah. Her name would be Deborah, and her father has a batch of arrows for me."

Deborah blushed, and her smile was utterly bedazzling; if anything, her frazzled straw mingled hair and playing with a goat only added to her appeal, if that was even possible. She was a fun person, utterly delightful; he could tell.

He stepped through the opening in the fence and nodded toward her. *"Glory..."* he whispered, marveling, trying to collect himself.

Was this how Adam felt? How did God do that with a rib?

"To see you up this close is..." he chuckled, almost unable to speak. "You are...profoundly..." gulp, *"shockingly beautiful."* He touched his fingertips to his lips; his mouth opened slightly.

How was this even possible? A twinge of drool was itching to escape the corner of his mouth. Perhaps that's why his fingers were nearby, prepared to address it.

She wondered if he was referring to her wet dress.

He was, but that wasn't all. Deborah was beyond words. Only a face like that, was worthy to compliment such a body. As for the addition of a playful, youthful joy, and that resplendent smile; this is what God meant when He created something and said *it was good*.

"Oh brother, I'm a mess," Deborah laughed. "And I'll have you know, Caleb attacked me!" she pointed at her devious pet who was eyeballing them from the corner of the yard.

"Look at him, he's planning his next attack right now. You better keep an eye on him, or you'll be next."

The young man stepped a little closer to Deborah, perhaps a little too close for social norms. "I might do the same thing if I were him, except I wouldn't squirm to get lose. How your goat is not paralyzed is a mystery to me."

"Who are you?" Deborah finally questioned this stranger who invaded her personal space, though the intrusion was not entirely unwelcome. "How long have you been watching me?"

"Not long enough," he paused, allowing a brief silence to pass between them while he gazed deep into her honey brown eyes. He was not a shy man.

"Barak is my name," he bowed to her and reached out his hand, hoping she would bequeath him the honor of her own hand. Was this going a little too far? At least they were outside.[1]

Deborah glanced around her yard, making sure she wasn't being spied on by anyone other than Caleb. Her father wouldn't like this, oh no, he most certainly would not. Her smile morphed into the grin of a rebel. Okay, so it is, the hand I shall present.

Deborah bestowed her hand in Barak's palm, and the warmth of her touch sent a shiver of delight into Barak's hand, up his arm and straight into his chest. His heart rate accelerated with the thumping of a horse's hooves as he gave the back of her hand a simple kiss.

Returning to his erect posture while attempting to inhale her scent, the only scent he caught was that of a goat. But setting that silliness aside, the gravitas of this first encounter with Deborah etched a marvelous memory he would cherish for the rest of his life.[2]

There was no way he was ever departing this female's presence without every full intention of meeting her again—just no way.

Deborah, likewise, liked this man right away, partly because it was obvious that he was quite taken with her. But unfortunately, like so many others, he would most likely join the ranks of her father's rejected minions; the aimless, forlorn tomcats wandering in nearby hills, kicking stones and grumbling to themselves.

"Oh my," came a gruff response from the corner of Deborah's home, "what have we here?" Deborah's father Haran swiftly rounded the corner of their home with the curt question.

Barak was quick—a smooth operator, sneaking this extent of a masterful greeting in with his daughter, and wrapping it up just in the nick of time.

"Hello sir, you are...Haran?"

"That I am," Haran approached. "Your father didn't come? No other men; you can't be the only one?"

"Just me" Barak nodded. "It's quicker that way."

The two greeted with a customary kiss on the cheek.[3] Deborah wasn't expecting this at all. Any response from her father other than

"Scram!" was mildly shocking.

Barak had thus breached the first round of barriers to this fair maiden.

Impressive.

"We knew if you had business with us, it was going to take you further than you usually go, and we're new customers. Far be it from us to put you through all that extra effort for just one new customer."

"It won't be a problem, just a minor change of our usual route is all. It's far too dangerous these days for you to constantly travel down here all by yourself."

"I'm light on my feet," Barak shrugged.

"Please join us for a meal," Haran invited Barak into their home.[4] This was a most pleasant, unexpected surprise.

The moment Haran turned to enter their home, Barak stole a flirtatious glance toward Deborah, flicking his eyebrows; almost as devious as Caleb. Such audacity—how fantastically appealing.

Deborah nearly tripped over her own feet following them in the house, but Haran spun around and pointed his rigid finger at her. "You have other matters to attend to young lady."

What was this? Was she celebrating too soon? She should have known, he detected too much joy in the area, too much young excitement.

"Finish what you started," Haran pointed at the jar on the ground and the muddy mess in the yard. "You better tie him up this time," he motioned toward Caleb.

Deborah was so distracted, she forgot all about the water.

Beautiful wild flowers and a few stray bees adorned a primitive stone altar overlooking the Jordan River. A haunting flute melody carried softly in the breeze as the first light of dawn pierced the morning mist, splashing color on the flowery, rocky terrain.

Deborah, the source of the melody,[5] and her father, carried oversized backpacks with all manner of wares attached. They meandered in a ravine nearby.

Haran shared his daughter's taste with regard to his frazzled hair, though he fancied himself in the likeness of the magi from the east, complete with white beard and gnarled staff.

The way Haran walked, slightly bowlegged, hobbling along with his staff, passersby often underestimated him, because he was much stronger and agile than he appeared. This illusion was dispelled, however, when he was wearing a backpack the size of a small house.

Haran suddenly stopped and lifted his hand. "Put that away," he motioned to her flute while scanning the area. Deborah stopped playing, slightly annoyed with her father's paranoia.

"It's dangerous around here, we have to be quiet."[6]

Several hundred yards up a slope to the left, they both spied the previously mentioned ancient stone altar, illuminated in a beam of sunlight. Observing it momentarily, they both glanced at each other and smiled, each perceiving what appeared to be a divine invitation.

"Honey Bee, do you remember this place?"[7-8]

"Should I?" Deborah was confused, wobbling to a halt. She puffed out her cheeks with a labored breath, sweat dripping off her brow.

"The altar of Ebal?"[9] Haran grimaced, irritated. "When are you going to remember your lessons?"

Deborah squatted down, then fell backward on her pack, relieving herself of the load. "Why don't we get a donkey," she panted.

The strain of their journey was wearisome, but these frequent trips through the wilderness blessed her with an amazing physique. Her strong shoulders, powerful legs, and exceptionally firm posterior were the envy of every girl for miles around.

Deborah gazed up at the altar and spotted something next to it. "What's that thing next to the altar?"

Haran squinted but couldn't make out what she was pointing at. While he was straining his eyes, Deborah suddenly burst into a sprint up the hill. Her recovery rate was notable, though on this occasion, annoying her father.

"Get back here!" Haran chided her. *Too late.*

As soon as Deborah reached the altar, she rubbed her hands across the roughhewn stone, inhaling the fragrance of pungent weeds and wildflowers.

When Haran finally approached, he found Deborah fixated on the statue of a Canaanite fertility goddess. "What is it?" she asked her father as he scowled at the stone fixture.[10]

"Heathen idol. Now come on, let's get out of here."

Deborah turned to go, but then suddenly whirled around and impulsively side-kicked the idol in the head, knocking it over the ledge.

Haran's eyes lit up like saucers as the idol instantly busted in half, then its two halves proceeded to tumble down the hill, smashing into rocks and debris as it went.

Oops. Haran snatched his wide-eyed daughter's arm and forcefully yanked her back to the trail. "Run!"

Later in the afternoon, fatigue was setting in again as they skirted a hillside on a narrow, rocky path. Deborah reached for her flute, but Haran noticed and tapped her arm with his staff. "No."

"But there's absolutely nobody out here!"

"Keep your voice down," Deborah's father growled.

"That guy that came by our house the other day," Deborah fumed,

"he made this trip all by himself, no big deal."

"Well that guy isn't just anybody," Haran replied.

"Seemed normal enough to me," Deborah replied.

"Hmph," Haran snickered. "What did you think of him, anyway?"

"I was surprised you invited him in for dinner."

"You didn't answer my question."

Deborah smiled, self-conscious, not very successful at holding her cards close to the vest. "He seemed...nice enough."

"That all? He was nice?"

"Why do you ask? You're acting strange."

"Buying a few arrows wasn't the only reason he came by."

Deborah's ears perked up. "What do you mean?"

"Well, I suppose you could say it was sort of an interview," Haran babbled, barely audible.

"A what?"

"He came...*to see you*."

Deborah halted, alarmed, eyes bulging.

Haran approached a large boulder, and using its shade for a small break area, he lowered his pack.

"The last time we went up to Shiloh, General Abinoam was there. He actually approached me and spoke with me when you were setting up our stand. His son saw you in the market there, and he asked me about you; asked his father if we could arrange for him to meet you."[11]

Deborah's eyes grew wider as Haran spoke. "Barak?"

Haran nodded.

"He was *that* Barak? So you're telling me, you invited that man to our home to meet me, and you didn't even tell me?"

Haran shrugged as if it were no big deal.

"You have got to be kidding me!"

"What do you mean? You always complain about me chasing off all these boys, so now I finally introduce you to a real man, and you're all upset about it?"

"Had I known he was coming, don't you think I might have been slightly more prepared? But no, you'd rather having me dressed like a peasant, wrestling a goat in the mud!"

Deborah released her backpack and dropped it to the ground. "A most splendid first impression, yes indeed. And this was...General Abinoam's son you say?"

"Yes."

Deborah was lost in wonder. Every girl in Israel knew about Barak by name, but she had no idea what he looked like, so she never put two and two together.

Sure, that guy that came to their home was a very handsome young man, but a celebrity? Barak was the closest Israel had to a prince; a kind of royalty. Now way. A lot of guys were named Barak.

Deborah finally laughed, thinking her father was joking. "Good one. You had me."

"I'm not kidding, that was really General Abinoam's son," Haran continued.

Silence.

"So...the son Israel's Commander in Chief, came to see me, and I was wrestling with a goat in the mud."

"It's just as well. He came thinking he was checking you out, but I was actually the one checking him out. You present me with a difficult challenge," Haran gazed at his daughter inquisitively, hoping she understood the importance of his words.

"I don't want just any farm boy from Ramah to be your husband. For you, I am searching for the cream of the crop. I reach for the fruit at the highest branch, because I am searching for a champion.

"I want someone who will care for you; respect you like no other, and protect you and my grandchildren in these dangerous times. Nothing short of a champion will do."

"And you think this Barak might be the one?"

"I'm not sure yet. The problem with a guy like that is, he probably has women fawning over him all the time. Who knows, he might even have a wife or two already, and perhaps even a few concubines. Maybe he's just itching to add you to his collection," Haran teased.

"Would you like that? He comes from a family of means; it's certainly a possibility."[12]

"If that's the case, then no, that way of living goes against the Lord's commands, and it disgusts me."[13]

"Excellent, we agree."

"I will share my man with no other woman, but I didn't get that impression from him."

"We'll see," Haran hummed to himself.

"I don't want any part of being the wife of some old, fat, dopy turd looking guy, either. If there isn't a spark, it's not going to happen."

"That's a lesser concern," Haran replied. "Nobel character is more important."

"Well I am concerned, and you should be! This is my life we're talking about! I'm not getting married to a stinky, ugly slug, even if he's rich, has a heart of gold, and he's superbly faithful.

"You might think that's shallow, but it's not, because that's a big reason why people are unfaithful. They settle for less, and pay for it later on. When there isn't any chemistry, even if everything else is right, it all goes to crap.

"I'm really worried about Jael, too. That Heber, he's just the kind of guy I'm talking about. He's nice and he's wealthy, but the story ends there. Don't even think about bringing Heber over to our house."

"Not to worry Honey Bee; Heber already inquired about you, and he offered me a fortune of a dowry for you, but I know you well enough and I told him no."

"And when were you planning on telling me that?" Deborah shot back.

"What does it matter? You just got through telling me not to even think about..."

"This is my life!" Deborah interrupted. "I'm the one to say no, not you!"

Haran gushed out a belabored sigh. "Okay, calm down," he smeared his hand down his face.

After a brief pause, Haran continued, "So Barak, correct me if I'm wrong, but this all-important chemistry thing you speak of...I'm pretty sure I detected a few stray sparks."

Deborah shrugged. *No comment.*

"That's what I thought. But what about him, do you think *you* are *his* type?"

"Oh, I'm his type alright, but you certainly didn't do me any favors. I thought I ruined my first impression, but amazingly, he seemed to like me anyway, goat stink and all."

"I'm sorry about that. You know, I need to make this up to you, get you some new clothing, or maybe one of them fancy Egyptian mirrors so you can fix yourself up.[14] We'll invite Barak over again, and this time you'll be more prepared."

"I don't need a fancy mirror."

"But didn't you just say..."

“I have more mirrors than I ever wanted,” Deborah elaborated. “Every time I walk past a guy, it’s pretty ridiculous lately. Sort of embarrassing actually. They can’t seem to keep their tongues in their mouths, salivating all over themselves.

“I used to think there was something wrong with me, but Jael set me straight. She’s right, it makes sense.

“I never changed the way I dressed, or acted, or even fixed myself up. All that changed was I got a little older, and a little more...”

Deborah held her hands in a gripping motion, hovering over her breasts, to which Haran looked away, disturbed.

“Oy!”

“Sorry,” Deborah giggled. “But honestly, I think I’m Barak’s type without saying a word.”

“You’re probably right,” Haran sighed. “You have grown, and I’ve put this off for too long.”

Deborah kept giggling, then she started laughing so loud, Haran chastised her.

“I said be quiet, it’s not safe around here!”

While Deborah was wheezing in laughter, she lost her footing and started skidding down a patch of loose gravel near a steep ledge. In the last instant, Haran whipped out his staff for her to latch onto, and she snatched it without a second to spare.

“You need to be more careful.”

“Well I wouldn’t be tripping all over the place if we walked on the main road like normal people,” Deborah exclaimed, exhausted from the burden of her heavy pack.[15]

“Shhh!” Haran pointed, then he scurried up to the nearest boulder. Deborah crept up and peeked from behind him. She peeked just in time to see a man scurry off the main road down below, drop into a gully and scan the hillside in their vicinity.

Commentary Notes

††

1. Rick Meyers, "Equipping Ministries Foundation, e-Sword Bible software, version 12.2.0," downloaded Nov 20, 2020, http://www.e-sword.net; *David Guzik Commentary* on Judges 4:1-24, Note C, 3, b, i. In ancient Israel, it was a breach of etiquette for a man who was not an immediate family member to be in a tent alone with a woman. However, conversing in the front yard out in the open may have been acceptable.
2. Scripture says nothing about Deborah and Barak knowing each other before Deborah summons him in Judges 4. However, the possibility exists.
3. Judah David Eisenstein, "Greetings, Forms Of:" Jewish Encyclopedia, http://www.jewishencyclopedia.com/articles/6873-greeting-forms-of, (Last Accessed December 2, 2020). A kiss on the cheek was widely common in ancient Israel, and still is. Also see Romans 16:16; 1 Corinthians 16:20; 2 Corinthians 13:12; 1 Thessalonians 5:26; 1 Peter 5:14.
4. Rick Meyers, "Equipping Ministries Foundation, e-Sword Bible software, version 12.2.0," downloaded Nov 20, 2020, http://www.e-sword.net; *Fausset Dictionary*, definition of Dinner: "'Supper' was the later meal, and that to which friends were asked as to a feast (Luke 4:12)."
5. Jesse Lyman Hurlbut, *Hurlbut's Handy Bible Encyclopedia*, (Philadelphia, PA: The John C. Winston Co., 1908), p. 239. "Musical Instruments, III. Wind Instruments, (5) The flute ('halil,' meaning 'bored through'), a pipe perforated with holes, originally made from reeds, but afterward of wood, bone, horn or ivory. It was chiefly consecrated to joy or pleasure. (6) The flute, alluded to in Daniel 3:5; probably a kind of double flageolet." The Bible does not explicitly state that Deborah played a musical instrument, however, she is the most likely author of The Song of Deborah documented in Judges 5, indicating a musical inclination, similar to King David, one of the authors of the Psalms.
6. See Judges 5:6, "highways were abandoned"
7. Kenneth Barker, *The New International Version Study Bible*, (Grand Rapids, MI: Zondervan Bible Publishers, 1985). pp. 334-338. The name Deborah, listed in Judges 4:4, means "Bee," or "Honey Bee"

8. in Hebrew. In this story, Deborah's father uses the pet name "Bee" to commemorate this.
9. J. E. Cirlot, *A Dictionary of Symbols*, (United States: Dorset Press, 1991), pp. 23-24. "Bee. In Egyptian hieroglyphic language, the sign of the bee was a determinative in royal nomenclature, partly by analogy with the monarchic organization of these insects, but more especially because of the ideas of industry, creative activity and wealth which are associated with the production of honey... In Orphic teaching, souls were symbolized by bees, not only because of the association with honey but also because they migrate from the hive in swarms, since it was held that souls 'swarm' from the divine unity in a similar manner."
10. William G. Dever, *What Did the Bible Writers Know & When Did They Know It? What Archeology Can Tell Us about the Reality of Ancient Israel*, (Grand Rapids, MI: William B. Eerdmans Publishing Co., 2001), pp. 98, 115-116. Altars were frequently built on mountain tops as depicted here in this story. An ancient installation has been found on Mount Ebal in Israel. Also see Exodus 34:13; Deuteronomy 12:3, referencing altars and idols placed on mountain tops.
11. Jonathan M. Golden, *Ancient Canaan & Israel*, (Santa Barbara, CA: Oxford University Press, 2009), p. 182. "Canaanite divinity, patchwork 'pantheon' is difficult to sort out. Perhaps the most intriguing of these female deities is Asherah, who over the course of many centuries fulfilled a variety of roles. She was a mother figure in the divine family, associated with fertility and warfare. Bronze statuary dating to the fourteenth to thirteenth centuries E.C.E. from Syrian sites such as Ugarit (Ras Shamra) features a goddess widely thought to be Asherah."
12. Ken Anderson, *Where To Find It In The Bible, The Ultimate A to Z Resource*, (Nashville, TN: Thomas Nelson Publishers, 1996), p. 317. Arranged marriages were common in ancient Israel, sometimes with the daughter's consent, sometimes without. See examples with Genesis 24:58; 1 Samuel 25:19-43; Joshua 15:16.
13. Carol R. Ember & Melvin Ember, *Cultural Anthropology, 6th Ed.*, (Englewood Cliffs, NJ: Prentice Hall, Inc., 1990), pp. 187-190, bracketed comments added. "Although it [Polygyny] is not permitted in Western and other highly industrialized societies, polygyny is found in many societies throughout the world. *Murdock's World Ethnographic Sample* reports that over 70 percent of societies allow it, and there is ample evidence for its existence in our own cultural background. The Old Testament has many references to it: King Da-

vid and King Solomon are just two examples..." Deuteronomy 17:17 forbids polygyny for kings, and the New Testament is much clearer on this prohibition for church leaders, 1 Timothy 3:2, 12; Titus 1:6. Most every instance of polygyny in the Bible is rife with extreme conflict, as in the case with Jacob's wives, Leah and Rachel, King David's wives, and King Solomon's wives, who led him astray into idolatry, even though he is considered one of the wisest men who ever lived. In this story, Haran has objections about his daughter being one among many wives, because the conflict in such marriages was common knowledge.

14. Deborah sees no reason why the prohibition on multiple wives, outlined in Deuteronomy 17:17, shouldn't be applied to every man, not just Israel's future kings. Her father agrees.
15. Ken Anderson, *Where To Find It In The Bible, The Ultimate A to Z Resource*, (Nashville, TN: Thomas Nelson Publishers, 1996), p. 331. We see the existence of mirrors in Exodus 38:8, when Israeli women dedicated them to the Tabernacle. It is likely they could have acquired them while in Egypt.
16. See Judges 5:6, "the highways were abandoned, and travelers kept to the byways." [ESV]

Chapter 2:

Caleb's Advice

ב

"Back," Haran pulled Deborah behind him as he cautiously peeked around the boulder. "This doesn't look good."

"You gotta be kidding me," Deborah blurted out.

Haran growled, "Be...quiet!"

Unfortunately for the two of them, there were actually three bandits, and one of them was busy flanking from behind.

"Over here!" he called out to one of the others.

Haran whipped his head around and shoved Deborah. "Run!" He then lifted his staff and scanned the area in all directions.

Instead of running, Deborah quickly snatched a small pouch off her backpack and loaded a leather sling with a small stone from the pouch.

"I said run!" Haran yelled at her again while shaking his staff at her.

"Father!" Deborah protested.

"Do as I say!" Haran then stepped forward and pushed her again.

Deborah trotted away, but rather than the direction Haran wanted her to go, she trotted up the hill, taking the high ground about twenty feet away. She then spun around and searched for a target.

Meanwhile, one of the men hoped to distract Haran by engaging him directly with two daggers, while another flanked him from behind with a club. The tactic would have worked were it not for a painful shot thudding into his ribs, curtesy of Deborah's sling.

Thump!

The man stumbled to the ground, holding his side. Where did that come from? He then looked up and saw Deborah fumbling for another stone from her pouch.

Leaping to his feet, he instantly sprinted her direction, fully intent to reach her before she could fire another shot.

By now, Deborah's cavalier attitude was long gone, and she realized more than ever that she should have kept her stupid mouth shut. She and her father were in a very grave situation.

By now, Haran was deflecting dagger attacks with his staff with relative ease, but the first bandit they saw was armed with a sword. He finally made his way to their location, charging from behind and screaming like a madman.

Haran was overwhelmed, this time without backup, until a stranger burst through a patch of brush and blocked the man with the sword.

Where did this guy come from? Was he hiding in that brush the whole time, listening to Deborah and Haran's conversation? Where were all these people coming from in such a desolate location?

"Ha!" yelped the older, bald, dark skinned stranger with wild eyes hinting at insanity. The powerfully muscular, bearded Phoenician grinned with delight as he hunkered low, facing off with the bandit. "Make you move..."

The man lunged with his sword, but the contrast was clear that Adonia, the bald Phoenician, was a skilled warrior who could run circles around this petty thief.

In that very first attack, the man overextended himself, and before he knew it, snap! Adonia busted his arm and snatched the sword away from him in one fluid motion. "Ah!" the man squealed and dropped to his knees in anguish.

A short distance up the hill, Deborah wasn't sure if the cries of pain were her father's, or someone else's. In fact, she was so distracted with the man wielding a club sprinting toward her, she fumbled and dropped her stone.

Defenseless and out of time, instincts took over, and she suddenly bolted straight toward the man running toward her. This was the last thing he expected.

As she sprinted toward him, she faked to the right, then instantly jerked to the left, and sped right past him as he stumbled and tripped trying to catch her.

Haran was steadily blocking the man with his daggers until he finally caught the upper hand, and smacked him across the skull so hard, he busted his staff. The man instantly thudded to the ground, out cold.

As for the bandit who tried to catch Deborah, he saw that they were outnumbered by now and decided to retreat. Haran spun around just in time to see Adonia throwing his sword at the man's back.

Gasping at the violent display, Haran didn't think such an attack was warranted; after all, the man was retreating. But he was relieved to see that Adonia's intent was not to kill.

The hilt of the sword smacked the man on the back of his head, sending him sailing to the ground and tumbling down the hill with a painful reminder that the life of a bandit wasn't always easy pickings.

"Go away!" Adonia ordered the man with his deep, authoritative voice, speaking Hebrew, but with an odd accent. "Beat it," he ordered again and tossed a rock at the heap of flesh moaning on the ground.

The man finally rolled around and staggered to his feet, stumbling away as Adonia marched toward him. "Go earn honest live, and these thing not happen you," Adonia rebuked him as he limped away.

The man that Haran knocked out was sprawled on the ground at Haran's feet. While Haran observed him, he noticed something familiar about the dagger in his hand.

He picked it up and after a brief observation he replied to Adonia, "This is stolen. I know the rightful owner." He then fetched the other dagger. "This one too," Haran kicked the man's foot, annoyed.

The man finally came to, gripping his skull. He quickly looked around to see if he was still in danger. Haran loomed over him.

"This was my favorite staff!" Haran then spun his half-staff like a baton in his left hand, threatening another strike.

The bandit scurried a few feet away, then he reached for one of his missing daggers.

"Looking for this?" Haran held up the dagger in his right hand, then he flipped it around, caught it by the blade and acted as if he were going to throw it. "Want it back?"

The man staggered to his feet and trotted away. Haran tossed the blade in the air with a spinning twirl, caught it by the handle then gracefully re-sheathed it with a spin.

"You okay?" Adonia asked.

"I'm fine, thanks to you," Haran nodded.

"Young lady?" Adonia asked Deborah.

"Where did you learn to fight like that?" Deborah quizzed him.

Adonia nodded and held up his right hand with the fingers together, pointed upward and facing forward; an unusual official greeting neither Haran nor Deborah were familiar with.

Haran reciprocated the gesture, then Deborah held up her hand as well. "That's an unusual greeting, where are you from?"

"Ah, this Khamsa," Adonia proudly proclaimed, "the sign of Tanit, patron goddess of capital city Carthage."

"Oy," Deborah dropped her hand. "Well, let's say for us Hebrews, we'll call it the Hand of Miriam," Deborah nodded enthusiastically. "She was a prophetess, and sister of the famous Prophet Moses who led us to this land."[1]

"Okay, Hand of Miriam sound good. Adonia my name. I am Phoenicia, travel very far from here."

Haran smiled; surely he meant he was *from* Phoenicia. "I'm Haran, and this is my daughter, Deborah. And she's right, I've never seen a fighting style quite like that."

"From such a skill warrior as you, I take comply the mint. I no tell what hand is strong hand...eh...fast, eh...better hand," he shook his right hand, frustrated that the word he was searching for wasn't quite there.

"Tribe of Benjamin; we train with both hands," Haran nodded with a smile.[2] "What brings you so far?"

"I was avenger of blood, but that over now.[3] I was traveling north," Adonia pointed north in his animated manner of speaking, "but I see these men here, so I hide the bush," Adonia pointed to the patch of bushes he sprang from.

"We think same, you, I, avoid main road," Adonia pointed to the main road. "I know to fight, but I not look for it; avoid when possible. I apologize, intrude on you privates, I mean no."

Haran took a moment to process what Adonia just said. *He probably meant privacy.*

Haran nodded.

"We were very fortunate that you were right here, and if you're free, I could certainly use someone of your skill. Merchants are easy targets in these hills, because our best weapons were confiscated by Sisera.[4] Many of these bandits are probably his men."

"Sisera? I hear of him; he dangerous. I no think he this far south."

"He usually isn't, but that may be changing."

"Hm. What you have in mind?" Adonia queried.

"You could train me for a start," Deborah chimed in.

Haran and Adonia both looked at Deborah, then at each other. Adonia chuckled, but Deborah wasn't laughing.

"What would've happened if he didn't show up?" Deborah addressed her father while motioning to Adonia.

"Oh, so now all of a sudden you're concerned about how dangerous it is out here? If you would've just kept your mouth shut, none of this would have happened.

"Aside from that, I shouldn't have brought you in the first place. This route is too dangerous."

"But you say it's dangerous everywhere these days."

"It is."

"And you think going on these trips alone will make you safer? We need more people with fighting skills, not less!

"When you told me to run, how do you think that made me feel? If anything ever happened to you, I could never live with myself, running away like a coward. I need to know how to fight!"

"You did really well Honey Bee," Haran complimented her, "but it would've been better if we didn't have to fight at all."

"She have skill; good shot," Adonia chimed in. "And only a warrior would charge opponent unarmed like she. That instinct...cannot be train. You either have, or you not."

"Well?" Deborah questioned her father.

Deborah's home was one of a few permanent structures made of adobe and stone; the majority of the dwellings were tent structures. A stray pigeon was perched in a tree nearby, observing the scenery in Deborah's yard.

There was a rock fence surrounding her home that served as an enclosure to allow Caleb and some domesticated pigeons to wander freely in the yard, though its necessity was debatable.[5] The pigeons and Caleb weren't going anywhere.

Just inside the gate, Deborah was training with a half-dozen young men under the tutelage of Adonia. Similar to the men, Deborah was wearing leather armor, but with a few female modifications, especially in the chest region.

Adonia was teaching them to spar with a staff in slow motion, starting with the basics of Adonia's special brand of mixed martial arts that he picked up from his extensive world travels.[6-8]

A group of village gossip girls in their late teens, Gavriella, Tamar, and Sarai, passed by, observing Deborah with envy. They snickered to each other and giggled, making a show of their mockery.

Interrupting their training session, Deborah's mother Miriam, an attractive spitting image of Deborah in her early fifties, exited their home with a platter of food for the trainees.

Following her was Deborah's petit young friend Jael.[9] Jael was only fifteen years old, but in some ways she exceeded Deborah's knowledge in the ways of the world. She waddled behind Miriam, struggling with a large jar of water.

"Come inside, this is foolish," Miriam snapped at her daughter, self-conscious of the undue attention she was getting from the pass-ersby.

"Let 'em laugh, I don't care."

"But I do. You look like an idol of Asherah wearing that thing," she frowned at Deborah's battle attire.[10-12]

"Oy!" Deborah fumed, then threw her staff to the ground.

Haran approached from behind and snatched some food off of Miram's platter. "There you are, thank you!" he replied while taking a bite.

Miriam shoved the plate into Haran's stomach. "Did you see that?" she pointed at the girls giggling down the road. The other trainees paused in their training, taking note of the fuss.

"We'll talk later," Haran calmly spoke to his wife.

Miriam spun around in a rage just as Jael stumbled up behind her, tripped and fell on the jar, smashing it to pieces.

"Jael! I told you not to take that one!"

"Are you okay?" Haran asked her.

At all this commotion, the gossip girls paused in their stride and turned to observe them while laughing. Completely incensed, Miriam made a beeline toward them, to which they immediately disbursed.

"Oh no, this is the third one," Jael lamented over the broken pottery

"What are you doing struggling with that big thing?" Deborah chastised her while helping her up.

"Father's going to be so angry," Jael whined.

"Don't worry. Come by the well tonight after story time. When I'm done with my chores I'll bring you one of ours; he won't know the difference.

Later that day, following their training, Deborah was conducting her daily chores. While pulling grain out of a jar next to the house, Caleb approached from behind.

"Any advice?" Deborah questioned him while he stared at her. Caleb let out a casual bleat.

"I appreciate it. Do you want some of this feed?"

Caleb bleated and scraped his hoof in the dirt.

"Okay. And what do you think about my training, should I quit?" Deborah pointed to their training area.

Caleb bleated again.

"Does that mean yes, or no?"

Caleb suddenly seized up, stiff as a board, then fell over on his side. His legs jutted outward like rigid, wooden pegs.

Deborah cupped her chin. "What's that supposed to mean?"

When all her chores were done, and evening set in, Deborah was apprehensive about going in the house. She shouldn't have thrown that staff on the ground like she did. When she entered, she was quiet as a mouse.

Deborah's home was built in the pillar-courtyard style, usually seen in larger towns. On the bottom floor were three banks of cobble-floored rooms grouped around a central courtyard room that served as a combination kitchen, dining, and living space.[13]

The kitchen area featured a deep cistern cut into the bedrock, a clay oven and hearth for cooking, and a table surrounded by chairs. Stone pillars that surrounded the central room supported the second story of the home.

Normally, the rooms on the bottom floor of similar homes were used for animals, and people would sleep upstairs. However, Haran preferred to use the downstairs rooms for sleeping. He and Miriam took one room, Deborah took another, and Caleb and the pigeons took the third room.

The remainder of the home, including the entire upstairs, was filled with all manner of trinkets. Jars, sacks of grain, clothing, and leather cases filled with various items were scattered all about. Haran was a

merchant, and his home was a make-shift trading post; a popular pit-stop in the hill country of Ramah.[14-15]

Miriam was cleaning some vegetables, preparing dinner when Deborah entered the home. She switched to washing a few dishes when Deborah approached from behind.

"Sorry," Deborah mumbled.

Miriam paused, then continued washing a dish with a stoic countenance. Deborah picked up a cloth to dry it off when she set it down.

"Do I really look like Asherah?"

"Yes," Miriam replied dryly.

"Jael made it. She even carved the commandments in it. Do you want to see..."

"I want you to stop training with those men," Miriam blurted out. "It's not right."

"I already told you I need to know how to defend myself, and father too for that matter. We had a close call, but I hit that guy with a sling-shot. You should've seen it. Father said..."

"Then wear the cursed thing! Look like an idol for all I care."

"My love, I don't think she's violating the law," Haran interjected as he entered the home. "Her heart is in the right place."

"I prayed to the Lord for a daughter, precisely to avoid this! Now that we have a daughter, you raise her like a son! Why?"

And such was this evening at home, and others that followed, regarding Miriam's discontentment about her daughter's battle training with men in the front yard of their home.

Miriam saw the way those men looked at Deborah, or rather, the way they couldn't stop ogling her the instant Haran's attention was diverted.

Where did Deborah get this bizarre notion to want to fight like men on the battlefield? Haran insisted this was her idea, not his. Was she spending too much time out in the wilderness observing birds with strange matting practices to get ideas like this?

From the looks of the men in their yard, that was a distinct possibility. Half the time they were shoving each other around because of

Deborah rather than their training. Miriam imagined her daughter was the gossip of every dwelling in Ramah, wherein any female resided, and to a certain extent, she was right.

Deborah already stood out as arguably the most beautiful woman in Israel, even attracting the attention of General Abinoam's son.[16] She already had Israel's attention, without routinely hanging out with all the guys in town, as if to rub it in the face of every girl for miles around.

Miriam was also correct in singling out Deborah's fancy battle outfit as a source of scrutiny. It was a very well made outfit. When she hung out with the men, she was literally hanging out. Every time she bent over, every time she stretched, every time she arched her back; every eye was on her.

A slightly baggy outfit could've hidden a little of Deborah's body, especially her cleavage, but this battle suit was perfectly tailored to accentuate her flawless physique.

Deborah's excuse for the outfit's design was purely utilitarian. Baggy clothing can snag in a battle; a potential vulnerability.

Additionally, Deborah was often uncomfortable with this excessive attention; it was simply an annoying side effect of the desires of her heart.

She just wanted to know how to fight, so she could better defend herself and her father. On that account, her father was right, her heart was in the right place. But that made little difference to the overall outcome in Miriam's opinion.

Every so often, the villagers of Ramah would gather at an arranged location for an evening of storytelling, or putting on a play, show and tell with the children, animal tricks, talent show activities, or whatever anyone would think up.[17] This evening was storytelling, hosted at Deborah's house.

Haran sat at the head of a large bonfire in his yard. Behind him, leaning against their stone fence, was the busted wheel of an Egyptian chariot, though the origin of the wheel was not yet divulged. It was one of the many wares of interest in Haran's trading post residence.

The amber glow of firelight sparked with a mystical aura in Haran's eyes, and his voice carried the enchantment of an oracle. About two dozen people were gathered, with the children sitting up front.

"For forty years, we wandered in the desert," Haran pointed east. "It would've only been eleven days if we listened to Caleb and Joshua."[18]

Upon hearing his name, Deborah's goat Caleb bleated, and all eyes turned to see him; the children laughed hysterically.

"Not you!" Haran howled.

Deborah's mother scowled at Deborah, "I told you to tie him up."

"I did. He chewed through it," Deborah moaned.

Haran tried to rescue his story, but it was difficult to salvage the mystical mood following Caleb's bleat bomb.

"For forty years we wandered in the desert, guided by a cloud at day, and a column of fire at night," Haran grabbed a burning stick in the fire and waved it to the sky. "And as I said, that forty years would have been eleven days..."

"They afraid of Anakim," Adonia piped up. "That what I hear; entire race of people big like Sisera.[19-20] Who could blame?"

"If the Angel of the Lord can part the Red Sea, can He not defeat the Anakim?" Haran responded.

"Then why He not?" Adonia questioned. As a foreigner, Adonia was able to get away with openly voicing such a brazen, borderline sacrilegious question to this people of faith, because he was simply ignorant.

Many had similar questions echo in their minds from time to time, but they would never dare to speak them out loud.

"Adonia!" Haran countered him.

"My uncle doesn't believe that story," Jael indirectly joined the underdog, using her absent uncle to do so. Her uncle was most likely going to hear about this at some point. Nothing new; Jael had a propensity for getting herself into trouble.

In response to Jael's comment of her uncle's lack of faith, Haran stood up, took a step back, and placed his hand on the large wheel resting against the stone fence.

"My grandfather took a raft out on the Red Sea. This is what he found on the bottom of the sea."[21-22]

Oohs and Ah's whispered throughout the gathering. The children chattered excitedly, and a few jumped up and ran over to the wheel, touching it and observing it up close.

"This is the wheel of an Egyptian chariot."

Jael continued to voice opposition, even though Adonia remained silent. "Maybe that fell off a boat, transporting it to the other side?"

"Grandfather said these are scattered all over the bottom where he was at, far more than any stray article dropped off a ship. Egyptian chariots are a work of high level craftsmanship; very pricey," Haran waved his hand over the wheel.

"I can't imagine Pharaoh transporting an entire shipment and losing the entire ship. No one has ever heard of that happening. But we have heard, and continue to hear to this day, an amazing story about a humbling experience between the mighty nation of Egypt, and our people.

We were slaves in Egypt for four hundred years, but we are free today. Egypt is still licking its wounds."

No one dared to contradict Haran by publicly questioning the integrity of his grandfather, not even Jael. She quietly nodded and took the queue to fade into the night.

Commentary Notes

††

1. Linda Heaphy, "The Hasma (Khamsa)", Kashgar Website, https://kashgar.com.au/blogs/ritual-objects/the-hamsa-khamsa, (Last Accessed December 2, 2020). "The Hamsa, also known as the Khamsa, the Humes hand, the Hand of Fatima and the Hand of Miriam, is a popular symbol found throughout the Middle East and northern Africa, particularly within the Islamic and Jewish faiths... The first known use of the symbol can be traced to the civilization of Phoenicia that spread across the Mediterranean between 1550 – 330 BCE. The Phoenicians used an image of the hand to represent Tanit, patron goddess of their capital city Carthage and controller of the lunar cycle... The symbol was adopted by the ancient Sephardic Jewish community of the Iberian Peninsula, who named it the Hand of Miriam after the sister of the biblical Moses... It also symbolizes the fifth letter of the Hebrew alphabet, "Het", which represents one of God's holy names, and further reminds Jews to use their five senses when praising God." For fun, I suggest Deborah was the redeeming source for this hand greeting, redirecting its use away from the foreign Phoenician goddess, and giving honor to a famous prophetess in Israel. It is likely Deborah would have known a great deal about, and admired Miriam, for two reasons. As a judge, Deborah would have known about the laws of Moses, and Miriam was Moses' sister. Secondly, Miriam also inspired the Song of Miriam, Exodus 15:20-21, the oldest song in the Bible with a woman's name attached to it for authorship. With Deborah being the most likely author of The Song of Deborah, Judges 5, she might have had a particular affinity for Miriam.
2. Byod Seevers and Joanna Klein, "Genetics and the Bible: The Curious Case of the Left-Handed Benjamites", Communication, The American Scientific Affiliation, https://www.asa3.org/ASA/PSCF/2012/

PSCF9-12Seevers.pdf, (Last Accessed December 2, 2020). "The mention of left-handed Ehud is one of only three places where left-handed people appear in the Bible. All of these left-handers appear in military contexts, and all, curiously, come from the tribe of Benjamin. In addition to the left-handed Benjamite Ehud, Judges 20:16 refers to 700 Benjamites who could use the sling with great accuracy ("Everyone could sling a stone at a hair and not miss") and all were left-handed. Finally, 1 Chronicles 12:2 states that some of the Israelites who came to support King David when he ruled in Hebron included some two dozen ambidextrous warriors who could use either the bow or sling "with either the right or the left hand; they were Benjamites." Some researchers propose the possibility that the Tribe of Benjamin may have had an unusually high genetic predisposition for left-handedness. However, for this story, whether they were born left-handed or not, a unique feature of Benjamite culture was to insist on developing ambidextrous fighting skills to attain a superior fighting advantage.

3. Avengers of blood served as executioners in an ancient system of law. They were the next of kin of a murdered family member, whether the murder was purposeful, or on accident, i.e. manslaughter. Scriptures where discussed include Numbers 35:19-37; Deuteronomy 19:6-12; Joshua 20:3-9; 2 Samuel 14:11.
4. Kenneth Barker, *The New International Version Study Bible*, (Grand Rapids, MI: Zondervan Bible Publishers, 1985), pp. 334-338. Judges 5:8 indicates Israel may have been disarmed by weapons confiscations. A clearer example of this in Scripture is outlined in 1 Samuel 13:19-22. This tactic, commonly employed by occupying forces, is actually the reasoning behind the right to bear arms as established in the 2nd Amendment of the United States Constitution.
5. Jesse Lyman Hurlbut, *Hurlbut's Handy Bible Encyclopedia*, (Philadelphia, PA: The John C. Winston Co., 1908), p. 264. Domesticated pigeons were common in ancient Israel, and used in sacrifices, see Leviticus 1:14, 12:6; Numbers 6:10.
6. Mark Cartwright, "Phoenician Colonization", Ancient History Encyclopedia, https://www.ancient.eu/Phoenician_Colonization/, (Last Accessed December 3, 2020). The Phoenician people are most popular for their contributions to language; the Phoenician alphabet served to further develop both the Hebrew and Greek alphabets. Part of the reason for this is because the Phoenicians were a

sea faring people with colonies throughout the Mediterranean, as well as Great Britain and India. For this story, it is from India where Adonia would have acquired his unique martial arts skills.

7. Shikha Goyal, "Top 10 most famous Martial Arts in India", https://www.jagranjosh.com/general-knowledge/top-10-most-famous-martial-arts-in-india-1467440667-1 (Last Accessed December 3, 2020). Kalaripayattu is frequently listed as one of the oldest, if not the oldest form of martial arts, originating from India. Silambam is a specialized form of martial arts using staffs.
8. Krav Maga Worldwide, "The History of Krav Maga", https://www.kravmaga.com/the-history-of-krav-maga/, (Last Accessed December 3, 2020). Israel's modern form of mixed martial arts, known as Krav Maga, was actually initiated by Imi Lichtenfeld. "Born in Budapest in 1910, Lichtenfeld grew up in Bratislava, Slovakia where his father was a police officer and self-defense instructor... As a young man, Imi fought and competed on the national and international levels. In the late 1930's Imi used his experience in boxing, wrestling, and gymnastics to help defend Jewish neighborhoods from anti-Semitic riots, which were flaring up in Bratislava."
9. The Bible does not say that Deborah and Jael, the heroines of Judges 4-5, actually knew each other. While it is likely that Jael at least knew about Deborah, and may have been inspired by Deborah, whether they knew each other or not is unknown.
10. Jonathan M. Golden, *Ancient Canaan & Israel*, (Santa Barbara, CA: Oxford University Press, 2009), p. 182. According to archeological evidence, Asherah had direct associations with warfare. In this story, Deborah's mother makes the connection with Deborah's battle attire and female warrior persona, as getting very close to a form of idolatry regarding Asherah.
11. Ibid, p. 252, Archeology suggests that some Israelites straddled the fence, worshipping both Yahweh and Asherah simultaneously. "Important discoveries concerning early Israelite religion come from a series of inscriptions discovered at the site of Kuntillet 'Ajrud, a station, or caravanserai, in the eastern Sinai, dating to the ninth and eighth centuries B.C.E... Archeologists found a number of inscribed vessels... One of these inscriptions, probably a poem or psalm, includes both El and Baal as venerated gods. The most well-known of the Kuntillet 'Ajrud inscriptions, those pertaining to Asherah, come from the sherds of large store jars. In these examples, the phrase

'YHWH and ... his a/Asherah' appears no less than three times, once as '...I have blessed you by YHWH of Samaria and by his a/Asherah' and twice as '...I have blessed you by YHWH of (the) Teman and by his a/Asherah.' It has been suggested that the 'Asherah' here refers not to the goddess but to a cult figure or symbol. Many scholars have understood this phrase to mean that the goddess Asherah belongs to YHWH, that is, she is his consort."

12. Carolyn Trickey-Bapty, *Martyrs & Miracles: The Inspiring Lives of Saints & Martyrs*, (Owings Mills, MD: Ottenheimer Publishers, Inc,, 1994). pp. 121-122. In this story, the issue of Deborah's female battle attire creating a rift between her and her mother was inspired from a combination of Scripture and reading accounts of Joan of Arc. Deuteronomy 22:5 lists a prohibition on women wearing men's clothing, which is likely to prevent sexually deviant behavior that warranted the death penalty according to Leviticus 18:22, 20:13. This is why Deborah makes the point in this story, that her armor has distinct, female modifications. Regarding Joan of Arc, part of the reason why Joan of Arc was burned at the stake, is because she refused to stop wearing men's battle armor. "Jeane la Pucella (better known as Joan of Arc) was born in 1912 in the region of Champagne, France, to a young peasant farmer and his gentle wife. As a young girl, Joan witnessed the invasion of Normandy by Henry V. of England and the overthrow of the French king, Charles VI. When she was fourteen years old, she began to hear the voices of Saint Catherine of Alexandria, Margaret of Antioch, and Michael, the archangel, which revealed her mission to save France. She finally took her message to the Dauphin, the eldest son of the king of France, and convinced him to listen to her. At her instruction, troops led by Joan herself were sent to Orleans, and a great victory resulted. The Dauphin was crowned King Charles VII with Joan by his side. But Joan had disturbed the men at Charles's court, and soon she found herself kidnapped by the Duke of Burgundy and sold to the English. She was sent to an ecclesiastical tribunal at Rouen, where she was questioned day and night. Finally, she admitted to hearing voices, and she was told to stop wearing men's armor. Joan soon disregarded this admonition, was recaptured, declared to be a lapsed heretic, and burned at the stake. She had not yet reached her twentieth birthday. Four hundred fifty years later on May 16, 1920, she was solemnly canonized. In France today, the

Fete de Jeanne D' Arc is celebrated on the second Sunday in May."

13. William G. Denver, *Who Were the Early Israelites and Where Did They Come From*, (Grand Rapids, MI, William B. Eerdmans Publishing Co., 2003). p. 103-104. Houses in ancient Israel "were of a distinctive type that we may call 'pillar-courtyard' in style... In a typical example, three banks of rooms are grouped around a central courtyard, usually set off by a row of pillars. At Raddana (and elsewhere), two or three of these individual houses are usually grouped together to form a sort of 'family compound.' This turns out to be significant because it reflects the biblical ideal of the 'mishpaha,' or 'extended multiple-generation family,' as for instance in the narratives in Judges and Samuel." These houses "have been called 'four-room' houses because the plan of the ground floor features a large open courtyard around which are grouped three banks of adjoining rooms. Stone pillars set the rooms off from the central courtyard and also supported the second story... The courtyards often feature a deep cistern cut into the bedrock, clay ovens and hearths for cooking, and space for storage or simple industrial installations. The living surfaces here are of tamped clay. The side rooms, often with pillars for tethering animals and cobbled floors that could have been more easily 'mucked out,' are best interpreted as stables. Excavations at Raddana and elsewhere suggest that these houses originally had only two bank rooms, though after a time most were built with three... The several rooms of the upper story could easily have accommodated up to two dozen people, with ample space for eating, sleeping, and other domestic activities. And the flat roof would have been an ideal area for drying foodstuffs or for additional storage." These homes were "spacious enough (with up to two thousand square feet of living and working space) to have served a typical large, multi-generational farm family, together with their several animals."
14. The Bible does not say what occupation Deborah's father had, however, a merchant seems feasible, for merchants traveled throughout the land, and Deborah could have gained exposure to more of Israel than a typical Israelite female. Judges 5:6-7 also describes how travel and village life ceased, which would have heavily impacted commerce.
15. Rick Meyers, "Equipping Ministries Foundation, e-Sword Bible software, version 12.2.0," downloaded Nov 20, 2020, http://www.e-sword.net; *Preacher's Homiletical* on Judges 4:9. Deborah may

have come from an affluent family, "if we are to believe the Chaldee paraphrase, who tells us that she possessed palm-trees in Jericho, parks (or paradises) in Ramah, and productive olives in the valley, a house of irrigation in Bethel, and white dust in the king's mount."

16. Scripture makes no mention of Deborah's appearance, however, some interpretations state she was married, so she probably wasn't homely.
17. Rick Meyers, "Equipping Ministries Foundation, e-Sword Bible software, version 12.2.0," downloaded Nov 20, 2020, http://www.e-sword.net; *Easton Dictionary*. The ancient Israelites were a culture rich with oral tradition. The Pentateuch was often transmitted via oral tradition. "In the time of Moses there existed certain oral traditions or written records and documents which he [Moses] was divinely led to make use of in his history." Also, speaking of translated versions, the Easton Dictionary states of the Targums, "After their return from the Captivity, the Jews, no longer familiar with the old Hebrew, required that their Scriptures should be translated for them into the Chaldaic or Aramaic language and interpreted. These translations and paraphrases were at first oral, but they were afterwards reduced to writing, and thus Targums, i.e., 'versions' or 'translations,' have come down to us."
18. See Deuteronomy 1:2.
19. Anakim are mentioned in Deuteronomy 1:28, 2:10, 2:21, 9:2; Joshua 11:21-22, 14:12-15.
20. Scott Alan Roberts, *The Rise and Fall of the Nephilim*, (Pompton Plains, NJ: 2012), pp. 210-211. "The Old Testament mentions several occurrences of 'giants' and 'Nephilim' appearing, specifically the giant races of Canaan: The Rephaim, the Emim, the Horim, the Zamsummim, and the Anakim." According to Deuteronomy 2:10-12, "The Kingdom of Og was ruled by the King of Bashan; this was the 'land of the giants.'" According to Joshua 12:12, "Anak and his seven sons of the Anakim were also giants, along with the famed Goliath and his four brothers." Other accounts of giants are listed in 1 Samuel 17:4-7, and 2 Samuel 17:16-22.
21. Ron Wyatt, "Red Sea Crossing" videos, https://anchorstone.com/red-sea-crossing-revealing-gods-treasure/, (Last Accessed December 4, 2020). Those who visit Ron Wyatt's website, might be amazed by what he found. His claims are extraordinary, and what's

more, he provides video evidence of his findings. Unlike professional archeologists, Rom Wyatt was an anesthesiologist by trade, but with a curiosity to see if the stories in the Bible were true. Rather than spending years in universities to obtain official archeological credentials, he just went all over the Middle East, and using scripture as his guide, searched for clues. He claims to have found many amazing things, like the massive anchor stones that belonged to Noah's Ark, many artifacts on the bottom of the Red Sea, and massive stone pillars that marked the Red Sea crossing.

22. "Fake News in Biblical Archeology", Bible Archeology Report, https://biblearchaeologyreport.com/2018/10/11/fake-news-in-biblical-archaeology/ (Last Accessed December 4, 2020). This website has an article that mocks Ron Wyatt's research, attacking his lack of credentials, his propinquity for ignoring the rigorous paperwork and requirements involved in government sanctioned archeological research, and his lax academic attitude. The article's author states that Ron Wyatt has no idea what he's talking about when he interprets his findings. However, I find it interesting that not one word is mentioned in this article to provide any explanations for any of Ron Wyatt's findings. Instead, the article mixes Wyatt's findings with findings of other blatant hoaxes that were easily disproven by exposing Photoshop edited graphics. Nothing actually refutes any of Ron Wyatt's findings. For example, exactly who placed those ancient, massive stone pillars there at the Red Sea? One pillar is on each side of the Red Sea, marking something significant for that location. Those pillars are there for something, but not one word is said to explain them. Why? His videos certainly show what appear to be chariot wheels covered in coral on the bottom of the Red Sea, so what are they? The same goes for the massive anchor stones Wyatt found, leading to what he claimed was Noah's Ark. Wyatt's detractors simply state his findings are bogus, because he's not a "real" archeologist.

Chapter 3:

Checkmate

ג

Cargo falls off ships all the time; it happens!

Jael pouted, sitting on the edge of an isolated well near the center of town. The three gossip girls from earlier that day manifested from the shadows.

"Where's your other half?" Gavriella prodded Jael.

"You mean her new mother," Tamar added a mean spirited jab.

"More like her father," Sarai heaped on another serving of insult, this time taking aim at Deborah.

"Shut your mouth!" Jael shot to her feet and fired back.

Gavriella stepped forward, about to lash out with a slap, but a voice from behind shot a chill up her spine. Her ambush was out flanked by a master strategist who already predicted this encounter the moment Jael left the fireside.

Deborah approached with a large jar and set it down. This was the jar she promised Jael earlier.

"Ah, there she is, as always," Gavriella struggled to contain her composure, in spite of her full scale inner panic. Deborah could practically hear the thumping of Gavriella's heart, racing like the heart of a field mouse clutched in the talons of a falcon.

Even in the dim light of the full moon, Deborah saw Gavriella's hand twitching, and she also detected a nearly imperceptible waiver in her voice.

The other two girls banded close to Gavriella, hoping to morph into a larger organism. The amorphous blob of this amoeba only amplified the fear that emanated from them.

"What's going on here?" Deborah questioned them.

"Nothing I can't handle," Jael replied defiantly, still stinging from their insults about her feeble dependence on Deborah, her "new mother."

"You're little friend has a big mouth," Gavriella stepped up her game, summoning every ounce of courage to double down. Deborah could easily take her out, but the backlash she would receive for doing so was the chess piece Gavriella was playing.

"Not as big as some I know," Deborah replied back while stepping forward. This was her game; she was the queen on this board, facing down a pawn.

Paying the price of additional gossip, or even further criticism from her mother, was a bargain price to pay if any of these girls laid a finger on Jael.

As far as the venomous insults they spit in her direction, their words were meaningless waifs of ether fluttering in the wind.

"One of these days you're not going to be around to defend her."

Overplayed.

Whap!

Deborah socked Gavriella in the face. She thudded to the ground, out cold, blood spattered across her face. Threatening Jael right in front of her was close enough to doing the real thing, and Deborah wasn't going to tolerate it.

The other girls gasped and jumped back, utterly shocked.

"Might want to check that. Probably broke," Deborah casually replied while flicking the pain out of her knuckles and simultaneously thinking, damn, there'll be hell to pay for this.

Miriam was already angry about the gossip, so Deborah would hear no end to this if she caught wind of it. But Gavriella was way out of line. Hack and slash chess was messy, but Gavriella took it there, and Deborah was done playing.

Checkmate.

"What's wrong with you?" Tamar blurted out, though profoundly terrified in the face of this unpredictable force standing before her.

Deborah stepped forward, to which Tamar and Sarai immediately spun and bolted, abandoning their friend to this savage beast.

Meanwhile, Jael stood motionless, eyes bulging out of her skull, hands cupped over her mouth while gawking at Gavriella.

"I...can't...believe...you just did that."

"What else could I do, she threatened you right in front of me. If I just stood here and let her do that, how do you think it would play out later on when I'm not around?

"You think she wouldn't make good on that threat? I know she would. She's mean, a very mean spirited person. Vitriol and hatred; a total vindictive piece of shit."

Jael sucked in a gasp. "You shouldn't talk like that."

"Me? I'm just telling the truth. They're the ones that should be ashamed of the cesspool of vile filth pouring out of their mouths."

"I wish I knew how to fight like you."

"We shouldn't be fighting each other. We have enough enemies out there, to be dealing with this."

Jael giggled a little, still cupping her mouth; then Deborah starting giggling too. Their giggling grew in amplitude until they were both howling and cackling uncontrollably.

"Oh...look at her," Jael wheezed and pointed at Gavriella on the ground, then doubled over, barely able to stand.

Gavriella finally started to come to, blinking her eyes in a daze. She rolled her and stared at Jael, confused, not sure of what she was looking at.

Jael laughed so hard, she fell to her knees, and Deborah snorted; then they both started laughing about how funny their laughing sounded.

"What's all this," Haran's voice emerged from the darkness. His eyes suddenly dropped to Gavriella, shock setting in. His eyes widened to such an extent, they were competing with the moon.

He knew this was eventually coming; he just didn't know when, or exactly how bad it was going to be. Gavriella finally got what she was begging for.

Fortunately, Haran was also a master tactician, and he was on excellent terms with Gavriella's parents. This was going to test the boundaries of that relationship. Hopefully her nose wasn't broke.

Upon seeing him, Deborah and Jael instantly ceased their laughing, but the needle on their pressure gauges quickly started jiggling near the red.

Deborah and Jael looked at each other, then to Haran, then back to Gavriella's dazed and confused expression. She wasn't even bothering to move; just laid there wobbling her head around like a broken puppet.

Jael couldn't hold it anymore, and she suddenly exploded with a gut wrenching cackle, tears shooting out of her eyes.

Deborah's gauge also busted, with the needle flying in Haran's direction. She bent over howling, slapping her knees, then she squatted to avoid falling.

Haran cupped his mouth and chuckled quietly, thinking, *I sure hope nobody's watching me*. His paranoid moonbeam eyes scanned the area like a flashing beacon.

I'm just here with my beastly daughter, laughing at a girl on the ground with a busted nose. No big deal, move along...

The next day, Adonia and Deborah were training with staffs. Flipping his staff around his back, Adonia blocked Deborah's attack as they sparred at a much faster pace than before. Other young men from Ramah and a nearby village had also joined in, swelling their ranks.

Deborah was, by some gossiping accounts, a shameless recruiting strategy for these young men. Who wouldn't want to get in an opportunity for a hand full of flesh, and blame it on a training accident?

Miriam continued in her complaints, pointing out how the men were behaving on several occasions.

To minimize their shenanigans, Haran made a ruling that Adonia was Deborah's dedicated sparring partner. That put an end to *accidental groping*, but it still wasn't enough to allay Miriam's discontentment.

Haran also had other plans for his daughter. He arranged for Barak to meet her again, and just like before, he didn't inform her about it. However, for this next encounter, it was Barak who would be ill prepared.

"Men, this is Barak, son of General Abinoam."

"My friends call me Lapidoth, or Lapi for short," Barak replied.[1-4]

Deborah's instant reflex of a beaming smile was suddenly overcome with a jolt of self-conscious embarrassment and she quickly looked at the pigeon sitting on the rock wall observing them. She then glanced around the yard as if she heard someone call her name.

He noticed her brilliant smile and grinned at her until she stole another glance, then she closed her eyes; full bloom blush. Utterly marvelous; Barak couldn't take his eyes off of her.

The men were immediately impressed with Barak's pedigree; a little less relaxed, sucking in their guts, improved posture, almost as if someone called them to attention.

"What he learns with us, he will take back to his father's command at Mount Tabor."[5]

Barak bowed, though he was a trifle confused at Deborah's presence among the men. He was hoping to see her alone; he certainly wasn't expecting this. What was she doing? Adonia quickly discerned Barak's distraction and addressed him.

"Greeting," Adonia held up his hand. Barak stared at this hand, confused.

"This Hand of Miriam. What, you not know this greeting? Everyone use Hand of Miriam," Adonia's eyes darted toward Deborah for an instant—a minute twitch on the corner of his mouth.

"Uh, no, but okay," Barak lifted his hand to return the gesture.

"She train with us."

"She what?" Barak laughed. Indeed, Deborah was fun. She heard that he was coming, and this time she prepared with an elaborate prank, complete with female warrior battle attire. "Nice," he complimented her outfit.

"No estimate her," Adonia replied in a serious tone. Barak was confused a little more now.

"Uh...," Adonia stammered, "*under...estimate*, yes, the under, that the word, do not under...estimate," Adonia bopped his finger up and down for each half of the word.

"She is like the bee," Haran chimed in, "sweet as honey to her friends, a deadly sting to her enemies."[6]

Barak's eyes widened, partly in shock, partly disturbed. Were these two men taking this prank to the next level, or were they actually serious?

"You don't mean she actually...*trains*..." Barak craned his neck.

Deborah bit her lower lip and squinted at him with undivided attention. Now it was Deborah's turn to interview *him*. How would he react to this female warrior business?

Haran was also curious. His gut told him that Barak would completely reject the notion of a female warrior. A woman's place was as far away from the battlefield as possible.

Why?

First and foremost, Haran knew Barak was acutely aware that losing in battle was worse for women than it was for men. When battles were lost, men were killed, but women became the spoils of war.

In Barak's opinion, that would be worse than death. The harshness of that reality was the kindling that fueled the fierce rage of every warrior he knew.

What Barak underestimated was the depth to which Deborah also contemplated this harsh reality, following the ordeal with those bandits. She wasn't kidding about being scared to death, when terror welled up in her to such an extent, part of her consciousness dissolved into pure instinct.

Deborah had just a small taste of what a warrior experiences on the battlefield; staring death in the face, and allowing that fear to transform into action.

In psychology, they say dangerous confrontations result in three instinctual responses: fight, flight, or freeze. Deborah was a fighter. Time slowed down, and the degree of clarity she experienced was utterly exhilarating.

In an instant, just looking at that man with a club running toward her, she knew she could outmaneuver him. And there was more. She had a keen sense that much more potential was at her disposal, and that was much preferred over helplessness.

Furthermore, Deborah knew these trips that she and her father were taking up north were going to become more dangerous in the days ahead. Knowing that, she didn't want her father leaving and never returning home; she was going with him.

Therefore, it was common sense that she had to prepare for the next time they encountered bandits.

She might not be as strong or as fast or as skilled at fighting as many men, but she was absolutely going to pursue her fullest potential, and see just exactly how far she could take this business of self-defense.

Barak just stared at her, slightly troubled. Was a dark cloud brewing over Deborah's previous enchantment? Where was his good natured grin?

"What, you don't think a woman should learn how to defend herself? Would you rather have your harem back home huddle together like helpless, sniveling crybabies?"

"Harem?" Barak chuckled. "Listen, basic self-defense is one thing, but the training I was told we would be conducting is *offense*. This is serious business; multiple opponent attacks using various weapons. War.

Vicious brutality. That's a completely different scenario than..."

"So I want to be a little more advanced in my fighting skills, what's that to you?" Deborah interrupted him.

"Then maybe you should have another female sparring partner. The way I train with my men, we can get pretty rough. I could never hurt you..."

"From now on," Haran interrupted their dispute, "Deborah will be your sparring partner. If you don't like that, you can leave."

"Wha...?" Barak gasped.

"Part of fighter skillset is restraint," Adonia chimed in. "If you no can pull punch, hit with flat of blade, or strike with hilt of dagger or sword when you throw, then you practice alone."

"I can do all that, but..."

"You have your choice," Haran interrupted him again.

"That's not necessary father," Deborah protested. "I was doing just fine before he showed up."

"This goes for you too," Haran rebuked her. "If you don't spar with Barak here, then your training here is done."

Deborah's jaw dropped. What was this? "Father! All this training started here because I..."

"We're not arguing, *daughter*. You have your choice as well."

Haran was already planning to make this decision when he invited

Barak to join them, and this decision had nothing to do with their current spat.

Haran didn't like the way these men were acting around his daughter, not one bit. He was in full agreement with Miriam about that.

He exercised every ounce of the restraint Adonia spoke of, every single day. He chased off half of these men at one time or another in the past, but now here they all were, clustered in their yard like a veritable tomcat convention.

Making Barak her sparring partner was a strategic move on multiple counts. First, setting aside the much older Adonia, Barak was the alpha male, and the younger men would respect him.

They bickered and pushed each other around in their minor skirmishes over Deborah, but that would all come to an end with a seasoned warrior in their midst. Deborah was assigned to Barak, and that was that. A few of the men might even stop showing up, because she was the only reason they showed up.

Secondly, pairing up Deborah with Barak would certainly add to their chemistry. Getting all worked up with each other, blood flowing, adrenaline pumping, was a guaranteed recipe for passion.

If there was going to be any *accidental groping*, it would be these two. This, ideally, would lead to a marriage with a family held in high regard throughout all Israel.

Haran also noticed how quickly Deborah brought up the issue of a potential haram at Barak's disposal. This was exactly the sort of banter he hoped for. They could work out their differences while literally working out.

Last of all, if anyone was a match for Adonia's fighting skill, it was Barak. He brought his own skillset to the table, so Deborah would benefit from the tutelage of the both of them.

"So what's it going to be?" Haran addressed the two of them.

Deborah hoped more than ever that Barak would just get over himself. She tilted her head sideways, eyebrow raised, a slight frown smile creased on her gorgeous lips. Who could resist her?

"Who greatest warrior among Canaanite?" Adonia interjected.

Quiz time; Barak pipped up, "Most would say General Sisera."

"I agree, he very large. He throw horse on battlefield," Adonia replied. To this statement, a few of the men exchanged nervous glances. Throwing horses? Did they hear that right?

A big guy was one thing, but throwing horses? They all heard the term "giant" bandied around, but exactly how big was a giant? Stories circulated, but there were more questions than answers for many citizens in Ramah.[7-8]

"What you think matter most fighting someone like that, size and strength, or speed and skill?"

"If Israel depends on women to free itself from Sisera's yolk, then we've already lost," Barak blurted out.

Oops. Restraint applied to the tongue as well, perhaps more-so in dialogue than maneuvers in a sparring match.

"The day may be here sooner than you think, young man, when King Jabin decides to make his move, and take everything we have," Haran countered Barak.

"If Sisera's men start overstepping their bounds even more than they already are, we may be forced to mount a defense. If that happens, and his men break through your lines, what comes next?"

"We won't allow that," Barak replied.

"Barak, son of Abinoam, surely your father has taught you that sound strategy requires us to face all possibilities. King Jabin's forces number four times what we have up north, and their weaponry, and massive fleet of war chariots completely out match us.[9] We have garden tools. You know this, so I will answer your question, what happens when they break through your lines?

"Israel's women may be all that remains. I for one, would much prefer my daughter facing them on her feet, and dying honorably, than to be ravaged by those depraved, uncircumcised pigs!

"I very much agree with her about that. Here you have an opportunity to help her, and any other young ladies in this village that have her foresight to join us.

OR...you can get back on your horse and go back home."

Barak stood quietly, contemplatively, then he finally nodded and smiled. "Okay," he replied. "I understand, and that makes sense." He then turned to Deborah. "I just pray to God I don't accidentally hurt you. I wouldn't be able to forgive myself."

Deborah sighed with relief. "Don't worry, I'm pretty tough."

The Israelites had much to contend with in their Promised Land. Not only were they dealing with an oppressive pagan king ruling from the city of Hazor, they also had division among themselves.

The primary source of this division was a creature of legend, rumored to serve King Jabin.

Giants were once very numerous in the Promised Land. Their ancestors knew it was promised to the descendants of Abraham, so they populated the area with every intention of invalidating that promise.

But this strange group of people who wandered the desert, following a mysterious cloud in the sky that transformed into fire at night, swept in from the desert one morning, and crossed the Jordan River on dry ground.

Who were these nomads with their peculiar golden box? Over a half million of these people somehow survived in the desert for forty years. How did they do that?

And they claimed among themselves that they were once slaves in Egypt. How were they able to get out of that situation?

After crossing the Jordan, they circled the walled city fortress of Jericho for a week, all the while blowing ram's horns. How odd, the activities of these people, yet suddenly that towering fortress transformed into a brittle pile of a rubble, dissolving like a sandcastle struck by the ocean's tide.[10]

These people, known as the Israelites, then moved up north, clearing out cities and villages as they went. Even the giants, Anakim they called them, could not withstand these mysterious desert people. But how could this happen?

The Anakim were descendants of the gods.[11-13] Their immense stature, extensive longevity,[14] and extraordinary abilities, were a testament to this.[15]

Some of these six fingered, six toed Anakim[16] were even worshipped, and surrounded with all manner of otherworldly mystique. Who was like unto the Anakim, equal in size, strength, and power, to drive them out from this land?

And yet, the Anakim were defeated, one city and village after another, as the Israelites abandoned their nomadic ways and settled down in the land of their inheritance, the land flowing with milk and honey.

The only Anakim who survived the Israelites were those who fled. While many simply left the area and traveled far away, some remained close and simply went into hiding in desolate regions of the wilderness.

Their defeat was so swift and resounding, by the time Deborah's generation came along, many among the Israelites had never even seen one of these legendary beings. Exactly how big were they?

Each generation of Israelites recalled their parent's and grandparent's stories from early childhood, and as they grew into adulthood, they often wondered if these stories about so-called giants were the mere product of exaggerated legends. Could someone please point out one of these giants, and put all of this talk to rest?

In the southern hills of Ramah, a few families, such as Jael's family, doubted there were ever any giants at all. A tall race of people, perhaps six to six and a half feet tall, that was most likely the extent of it.[17-18]

Some of these families were second and third generation inhabitants of the Promised Land who had never seen anything out of the ordinary in their entire lives, so they commonly dismissed these stories as fables.

However, recent reports of a mysterious giant in the city of Hazor, who lived in a temple of Baal, started spreading throughout Israel. At first, many people in Ramah laughed at these stories, but then the reports became more numerous.

Some even claimed to have went, saw this giant for themselves, then reported back to Ramah what they saw. These stories grew with more details. This Giant of Hazor also had a brother who wielded a seven foot battle axe.

Even so, some in Jael's family, and a few other holdouts, continued to believe these reports were exaggerated accounts.

But to residents in the northern city of Hazor, the existence of giants was now common knowledge. A descendent of the Anakim was among them. And no, he wasn't a mere six and a half feet tall.

Sisera arrived only a few years ago, and completely shocked everyone in Hazor when he simply wandered into the city one day, as if he were an ordinary person. But he was not ordinary; he was a six fingered, six toed, ten foot tall musclebound freak! [17]

Commentary Notes

++

1. Arthur E. Cundall & Leon Morris, *Judges & Ruth: An Introduction & Commentary*, (Downers Grove, IL: Inter-Varsity Press Leicester, England, 1968). pp 81-101. For this story, a romantic development between Deborah and Barak obviously makes for a more interesting story, but could there be any substance to this possibility? Commentators Cundall and Morris believe the idea "rests upon very flimsy evidence." However, I disagree, because there are several arguments that support the notion that Deborah and Barak may have been married. 1. To begin with, the narrative in Judges 4 describes a bold order issued from the Lord through Deborah to General Barak. To issue this order, Deborah would certainly find herself in a more comfortable situation if she were in fact arguing with her husband, or husband to be, about something the Lord was insisting on, rather than confronting a complete stranger, and a powerful man in authority at that. In a sense, Deborah and Barak both seem to be on very familiar terms with each other, for Deborah to issue the order in the first place, and then for Barak to one-up her with his audacious condition that she go with him to the battle field. 2. If Deborah was the author of Judges 4 and 5 as most suspect, as a godly woman, she would not want to shame her husband. Using another name to refer to her husband would be a way around that. 3. The names Lapidoth, and Barak, have interestingly similar meanings. In Hebrew, Lapidoth means "torches" and Barak means "lightning." Could this be a crafty literary ploy hinting that they may have the same person? Is Lapidoth a proper noun, or an adjective? The answer to that question might be "Yes." The similar meanings of these names has been noted by multiple commentators. Deborah would not want to elevate her own station at the expense of her husband's humiliation, and I also add that the New Testament author of Hebrews 11 may have felt this way as well. Barak is ironically listed as a hero of the faith in Hebrews 11, and Deborah is completely absent, when in fact Barak refused to go to battle unless Deborah was with him, (Judges 3:8), and the glory of the battle went to a woman (Judges 4:9). 4. Lastly, according to the Preacher's Homi-

letical on Judges 4:4, and according to other commentators, one possible way to interpret the sentence, "the wife of Lapidoth" is "a woman of torches" or "a woman of fire," because the Greek word "gune," pronounced goo-nay, can mean either woman, or wife. So depending on how the word for wife is interpreted, Lapidoth could either be a person, or an adjective to describe Deborah's character. Again, the crafty wording of this sentence may be an ingenious literary ploy of ambiguity, used to blatantly state that Deborah was married to Barak, but it also says something else, leaving a hovering question mark for the ages.

2. *The Great Courses, Religion, The Old Testament, Part Two, Lecture 13, The Book of Judges, Part 1*, DVD Series, Taught By: Professor Amy-Jill Levine, (Chantilly, VA: The Teaching Company Limited Partnership, Vanderbuilt University Divinity School, Copyright 2001). Most translations render 4:1 "wife of Lappidoth," but no such character appears in the narrative. The phrase could be translated "woman of flames," which complements the name of her general, Barak ("lightning")
3. Rick Meyers, "Equipping Ministries Foundation, e-Sword Bible software, version 12.2.0," downloaded Nov 20, 2020, http://www.e-sword.net; *Preacher's Homiletical* on Judges 4:4, "She was commissioned to act both as judge and as prophetess. The name Deborah signifies 'a bee;' and she is described as a burning woman—'the wife or a woman of Lapidoth,' torches—a woman of a torch-like spirit. She was a person of fire-bearing character and intense enthusiasm. Some say she was the wife of Barak, which signifies lightning. [Edersheim.]"
4. Rick Meyers, "Equipping Ministries Foundation, e-Sword Bible software, version 12.2.0," downloaded Nov 20, 2020, http://www.e-sword.net; *Strong's Enhanced Lexicon*, Wife: "G1135. γυνή gunē *goo-nay'* Probably from the base of G1096; a *woman*; specifically a *wife:* - wife, woman."
5. Judges 4:6 lists Mount Tabor as the strategic location where Yahweh commands the assembly of 10,000 Israelites. It would make sense for General Abinoam's forces to have a military presence in this area, because it lies at the intersection of three tribal lands; Naphtali, Zebulun, and Issachar.
6. Rick Meyers, "Equipping Ministries Foundation, e-Sword Bible software, version 12.2.0," downloaded Nov 20, 2020, http://www.e-sword.net; *Fausset's Dictionary* describes Deborah as "a honey bee to her friends, a stinging bee to the enemy (Cornelius a Lapide)." Deborah's sting in Fausset's definition, is part of the inspiration for Deborah's desire to learn how to fight in this story.
7. "How Tall Was Goliath?" Apologetics, WordPress, https://bibleapologetics.wordpress.com/2011/01/30/how-tall-was-goliath/ (last accessed April 9, 2016).
8. Bethania Palma, "Did U.S. Special Forces Kill a Giant in Kandahar? False. Snopes.com. "https://www.snopes.com/fact-check/u-s-special-forces-killed-a-giant-in-kandahar/" (Last Accessed December 6, 2020). Like usual, Snopes labels

the claim that a remnant survivor of the Nephilim "giants" was discovered and killed in a brutal attack, in the Kandahar province of Afghanistan, false. Snopes most likely did not even read author L.A. Marzulli's full account, because he stated that his source informed him that the military whisked this creature away in secrecy. Military authorities also made everyone involved in this incident sign non-disclosure agreements, and they classified the incident out of existence. So when Ms. Bethania simply called the Department of Defense (DoD) and asked about this fantastic incident, of course the DoD laughed and told her the claim was false. That is the extent of Snope's exhaustive research to declare this claim is "false." Like L.A. Marzulli, I have also conducted research on the Nephilim, and I have been in many radio interviews over the years, talking about books I have written. During one of my interviews, a caller identified himself as a former Army sniper, (I still have his email address), and his account of shooting a Nephilim "giant" in Afghanistan carried with it a high degree of authenticity in my opinion. The Nephilim he witnessed, was so large, he said it was carrying a full grown cow under its arm. He estimated its height at about twelve feet tall. This creature lived in a cave, and kept company with the Taliban. Some may consider it wild speculation, but I think there might still be surviving Nephilim living in the remote areas of Afghanistan.

9. Land of the Bible, "Hazor", https://www.land-of-the-bible.com/Hazor, (Last Accessed, December 7, 2020). The ancient city of Hazor "is the largest tel (archaeological mound) in Israel today, at almost 200 acres, and at one time was a thriving Canaanite fort-city of 20,000 to 40,000 residents, just north of the Sea of Galilee." The estimate of Sisera's forces numbering to 40,000 given in this story, (four times Barak's force of 10,000), was based off the estimate of 40,000 in the city of Hazor, and the 900 chariots under Sisera's command listed in Judges 4:13.
10. See Joshua 6:20, "the wall fell down flat..."
11. According to the Bible, Genesis 6:4, the Nephilim (aka Anakim, Raphaim, etc.) "giants" were descendants of the "gods," (with a little "g," denoting the sons of God, aka Bene Elohim, aka Watchers. sons of God sounds good, but Genesis 6:5 states that these beings were the progenitors of purely wicked offspring.
12. Rick Meyers, "Equipping Ministries Foundation, e-Sword Bible software, version 12.2.0," downloaded Nov 20, 2020, http://www.e-sword.net; *Preacher's Homiletical*, Genesis 6:1-8, bracketed comments added. "That these [sons of God] were angels [that sired the giants], is a view which, it is well-known, has been held from ancient times, both by Jews and Christians. Of the latter class may be named Justin and Tertullian among the ancients, and Luther, Stier, Baumgarten, Kurtz and Delitzsch among the moderns." While most ancient commentators believed the giants mentioned in Genesis 6 were the progeny of fallen angels and the daughters of men, (i.e. human-angel hybrids), most modern commentators, (though not all), reject this interpretation for two reasons: 1. Angels do not marry, (Matthew 22:30; Mark 12:25; Luke 20:34-36), and sex should only be conducted within the confines of marriage. 2. Many modern commentators also tend to downplay the supernatural elements spoken of in Scripture, finding natural causes to explain many miracles and events, and dismissing accounts of giants as symbolic, metaphorical, or exaggerated legends. The idea of angels inbreeding with humans seems too strange to have actually happened, so these modern commentators simply dismiss it. To explain what happened in Genesis 6, they propose that the sons of God who sired the Nephilim were not angels, but rather human, from the godly

line of Seth. However, this "Sethite Theory" fails to address six major inconsistencies: 1. Angels that conducted this activity were not faithful to God; they were disobedient. Scripture does not say that angels cannot have sex. It states that they do not marry; there is a difference between "do not marry," and "cannot have sex." It should not be assumed that fallen angels would obey any mandate for celibacy or the avoidance of fornication. This leads to the second inconsistency. 2. In the New Testament, Jude 1:6-7 and 2 Peter 2:4 speak of the angels that sinned. Jude 1:6 in particular immediately connects these angels that sinned with Jude 1:7, the events of Sodom and Gomorrah and the surrounding cities. What happened in Sodom? Genesis 19 states that the people of Sodom tried to rape the angels that went there. Is this not telling? Additionally, the entire book of Enoch, (from which Jude quoted in Jude 1:14), describes in vivid detail, that fallen angels, also known as "Watchers," were not humans descended from Adam. Rather, according to Enoch 7:7, they descended from the heavens, landing on Mount Armon/Hermon, roughly fifty miles north of the city of the city of Hazor. 3. The exact same phrase used for the sons of God in Genesis, is also used in the book of Job, chapters 1 and 10. The sons of God in Job 1 and 10, were reporting to God's throne, and Satan was among them, so they were obviously angels, and at least some of them were probably fallen angels. Why would these two sources of ancient literature, Genesis and Job, use this same exact term, the sons of God, to refer to natural people in one instance, and angels in another? 4. The Bible emphasizes the unnatural size and strength of the giant races, pointing to a blatantly obvious, highly unusual genetic profile. If simply being six feet tall made someone a Nephilim, then why wasn't King Saul, taller than all those around him according to 1 Samuel 9:2, considered a Nephilim? 5. There are two Scriptural references of a perfect distribution of six fingered, six toed giants: 2 Samuel 21:20, and 1 Chronicles 20:6. While this may be two accounts of the same individual, it is noteworthy that polydactylism as a birth defect is usually not perfectly symmetrical. In most cases, it only affects either the hands or feet, or one hand or one foot. A perfect symmetry is indicative of a species characteristic, rather than a defect. 6. Last but not least, in the very next verse following the introduction to giants in the Earth, Genesis 6:5 states that all of mankind descended into such vile wickedness, that "the thoughts of his heart was only evil continually." Why would the sons of God have such wicked children in a uniformly unanimous fashion? There is a common joke about the preacher's kids, but that is a stereotype, and not a 100% descent into unbridled lust and violence that nearly destroyed all of human civilization. Does not a narrative of angels rebelling against God, better match the progeny characteristics of the Nephilim, rather than the godly line of Seth, from whom the godly man Enoch descended according to Genesis 5:6-22?

13. Bruce Fessier, "Did 14-foot giants exist? Did they differ from humans? Author explores these ancient beings", Desert Sun, "https://www.desertsun.com/story/life/entertainment/people/brucefessierentertainment/2019/05/23/annunaki-nephilim-and-denisovans-contact-desert-explores-ancient-giants/3700717002/" (Last accessed March 7, 2021). This is a fascinating article with a long list of archeological research conducted into the field of "Giantology." Believe it or not, there are some reputable scientists that delve into this scientific research. They focus on empirical evidence, and provide insight into why the existence of giant humans

has been systematically attacked and obscured.

14. Richard Laurence, *The Book of Enoch the Prophet*, (London: Kegan Paul, Trench & Col, 1883), obtained at https://archive.org/details/bookofenochproph00laur, (Last Accessed December 8, 2020). All my references to the book of Enoch came from this source. According to Enoch 10:14, the Nephilim had lifespans of five hundred years. This extensive longevity may be derived from giants having a lineage connected with immortal angelic beings. However, this reference in the book of Enoch predates the flood of Noah, when humans also lived a very long time, prior to God reducing humanity's lifespan to 120 years in Genesis 6:3.
15. Scott Littleton, *Mythology: The Illustrated Anthology of World Myth and Storytelling*, (London: Duncan Baird Publishers, 2002), pp 49, 84, 140. Genesis 6 states that the progeny of the sons of God and the daughters of men were "men of renown, of which many legends are told." Indeed, there are hundreds of ancient religions/mythos to choose from around the globe that describe otherworldly beings crossing with humans and animals. The entities described in these mythologies fit the description of the Nephilim, i.e. men of renown in Genesis 6, for four main reasons: 1. They descended from among the stars, i.e. the heavens. 2. They corrupted the human population, as well as other species. 3. They were incredibly wicked, filled with unfettered lust and violence. 4. They were extremely powerful, wielding supernatural abilities, and many were worshipped as deities. Enoch 7:10, 8:4, and 9:6, state that the Watchers, aka angels, taught sorcery. The Watchers named Armers, and Samyaza, were chiefly credited to this by name. In Egyptian mythology, Seth turned into a ram on one occasion, and a bull on another occasion. In Greek mythology, Medusa could turn people into stone by looking at them, and Hercules had supernatural strength. In Babylonian mythology, Marduk "dates from second millennium B.C. He was mighty in every way; he had exceptional powers of hearing and sight, and he breathed fire."
16. See 2 Samuel 21:20; 1 Chronicles 20:6
17. Michael S. Heiser, "*Clash of the Manuscripts*," Bible Study Magazine, October 31, 2014, http://www.biblestudymagazine.com/extras-1/2014/10/31/clash-of-the-manuscripts-goliath-the-hebrew-text-of-the-old-testament (last accessed December 6, 2020). When it comes to Goliath's height, there is considerable debate among scholars concerning variations in ancient manuscripts. Heiser claims that most scholars believe Goliath was six and a half feet tall rather than nine and a half feet tall. I disagree; I believe the nine-and-a-half-foot-tall manuscripts are accurate. King Og's bed was about thirteen feet long according to Deuteronomy 3:11, yet multiple websites I found with scholars downplaying Goliath's height leave out this reference to King Og. It also seems absurd that 1 Samuel 9:2 makes a big deal about King Saul being head and shoulders taller than everyone around him, but he was no "giant." Saul also refused to fight Goliath, so why would Scripture make such a big deal about Goliath being a giant, if Saul was just as tall as Goliath?
18. Kenneth Barker, *The New International Version Study Bible*, (Grand Rapids, MI: Zondervan Bible Publishers, 1985), p. 334. Scripture does not state that Sisera was a giant, however, representing his character in this story as a giant is cinematic, and it was also derived from three sources of inspiration: 1. Sisera's specific mention in Judges 4-5 seems to overshadow King Jabin, highlighting him as a notorious man of renown. Genesis 6:4 states that the Nephilim, aka giants, were

men of renown. 2. Sisera's unusual name is not Canaanite, so he was a foreigner with unknown origins. 3. The Nephilim were still in the land of Canaan during Deborah's time, though probably not nearly as numerous as when the Israelites first entered the Promised Land. We still see references to these giants at later dates, during the times of the Kings, such as in 2 Samuel 21:16-22; 1 Chronicles 11:15, 20:4-8; Numbers 13:32-33.

Chapter 4:

Sisera's Audacious Plan

ד

Devils, or demons as the Greeks called them, were once living beings of flesh and blood who walked among people.[1-2] Many were wildly popular, even to the extent that they were worshipped as gods. Exactly how did these freakish beings gain such popularity?

Sisera's rise to fame and fortune might have seemed like an overnight sensation, but it was actually a meticulously orchestrated plan, years in the making.

Early one morning, Sisera, a humongous, demon-spawn monstrosity, casually strolled down Main Street carrying an ox under his arm.[3-4] People stopped in their tracks, mouths fell open, children dropped their candy, and yapping dogs suddenly shut up.

Most heard legends of these beings, but no one had ever seen one.

Everyone just stared at him as he walked by with thudding footsteps; he weighed close to a ton. He also radiated a mysterious aura. When he stared at people, they would sometimes grow feint and pass out.

He stopped at the largest outdoor merchant shop in Hazor, and set down his ox, along with several large sacks of gold, silver, and bronze.

He then hired a tailor to fashion for him an extensive wardrobe to replace his aged, weathered strips of leather that barely covered his herculean body.

When he spoke, his voice was mesmerizing; exotic, like the deep rumblings of a distant thunder.

He bought enormous quantities of silk, skins, and various other goods, and he inquired about hiring metalworkers, artisans, and skilled craftsmen of every kind. These were to report to a mountain where he was establishing a new temple of Baal, the pagan god of which he claimed ancestry.

No one doubted him.

Everyone marveled after this unnatural creature. Where did he obtain all this wealth? And where did he come from? Many people of Hazor concluded that the legends of old must be true; he was one of the gods among them.

He emanated power, which he offered to anyone who was interested.

While he spoke, he would perform random magic tricks, causing objects to move telekinetically with a flick of his fingers or a wave of his hand.[5] He confused people. He would ask, "What is your name?" and they couldn't remember.[6]

He fascinated them, demonstrating how he knew things about them that no one else knew. Playing mind games was one of his many talents. He was an extremely charismatic, charming trickster; practically a walking carnival of entertainment.

Excited whispers and gasps echoed throughout the city, and by that evening, this otherworldly entity was the most popular *thing* in town. Such was the grand entrance of Sisera, but this was only the beginning of his plan.

Hiding in the desolate wilderness, Sisera and his brother were among those who fled their village over one hundred years earlier.

This was shortly after the Israelites crossed the Jordan River. In the eyes of all the Anakim who knew them, they were deserters; cowards deserving of death, but they fled nonetheless.

Sisera and his brother made their home in a cavern in the mountains. As the centuries passed, their only solace was to one day exact revenge on these insolent Israelites,[7-8] but how?

If their entire race was nearly wiped out by these Israelites, or rather, higher powers allied with them, how could two lone Anakim manage such a feat?

Through the years, the only tactics Sisera and his brother employed in their revenge were ambushes on small caravans or isolated travelers, only when they were sure there would be no survivors. In this manner, they quietly amassed wealth.

However, their plans did not fully develop until they entered *telesphoreo,*[9] a kind of spiritual puberty among the Anakim, when manifestations of supernatural power begin to emerge.

This power was the source of Sisera's ability to do magic tricks and mind games. This power also opened up his and his brother's senses to receive visions.

Sisera and his brother Lahmi[10] starting having dreams of a vast city not too far away that was once a mighty civilization predating the great flood, when the ancestors of the Anakim once ruled the world. All that remained of this place now were ruins buried beneath a mountain.

However, this ancient place was a central hub of activity for their species at one time, and untold secrets of awesome power resonated there.

Then came the voices.

The formless voices of their ancestors started calling out to them in the night. At first, Sisera and his brother wondered if they were going mad. Who, or what, was speaking to them?

If these whispers were from the Anakim who were slain by the Israelites, were they seeking their blood?

They were filled with terror at first, yet the most powerful among these voices eventually became clear. His words, much to their surprise, offered hope.

This master of the deep was a wellspring of sacred knowledge,[11] and if Sisera and his brother heeded his instructions, he promised them fabulous wealth, honor, and untold glory.

This mysterious voice first instructed Sisera and his brother how to move large quantities of earth underground, and fashion and manipulate monolithic stone blocks weighing thousands of pounds.[12-16]

This sacred knowledge, long forgotten among the peoples of Earth, was once commonplace among the Anakim.

For roughly forty years, Sisera and his brother quietly extended their cavern through an expansive tunnel system that stretched for miles to a mountain overlooking the Valley of Megiddo. Their destination centered on uncovering the ruins of that ancient city they first saw in their visions.

In this hidden dwelling, they uncovered some rare materials and exotic artifacts that they planned to use in their quest. These would add to their power.

The voice also instructed them that their audacious plan to come out of hiding required three primary objectives:

1. They must keep their activities a secret until the time was right, else they would likely be killed by the Israelites.
2. To overcome the Israelites, they needed to make allies among the enemies of the Israelites.
3. Finally, if possible, they needed to seduce the Israelites into abandoning their God; the one they called Yahweh. If the Israelites abandoned their God, then they could be defeated.

Addressing their first objective, after they excavated the ruins beneath the mountain, they then worked their way to the surface, slowly hollowing out portions of the mountain from inside. Finally, they constructed stone archways that opened it up, overlooking the Valley of Megiddo.

This was their crowning achievement; a temple of Baal, bringing glory to their defeated ancestors. This place would also serve as a defensible fortress if needed.

For their second objective, Sisera, the older brother, was the first to come out of hiding, but not until he learned more about the current generation of Canaanites living in the area. This was an easy enough task now that the building project was complete.

The first curious visitors to investigate their building complex were captured and imprisoned. Sisera learned their customs, manners of speech, and especially their interests with entertainment.

Sisera studied these prisoners for several years, until the day finally arrived when he entered the city of Hazor, roughly sixty miles north east of his temple. There, he successfully seduced the pagan population of Canaanites, as well as a number of exiled Israelites.

He lured them up to his plush palace of pleasure. In a short matter of time, temple prostitution and a selection of interesting herbs and potions with intoxicating effects, were among the many services and products available there.

The Canaanites Sisera hired were expert interior decorators, completing the final touches of his elaborate temple.

As for the previously captured prisoners that taught Sisera what he needed to know, they outlived their usefulness, so he and his brother executed them to tie up loose ends.

Sisera's brother Lahmi remained at their temple of Baal, in charge of the activities there. He also served as the Chief Executioner in charge of temple security.

Meanwhile, Sisera secured a position with King Jabin, whose throne resided in the city of Hazor. Sisera was King Jabin's personal champion.[17] What king could resist such an offer?

So the people of Hazor skipped with joy at the sight of Sisera, greeting him, bowing to him, and offering him various goods for free, as he smiled and walked by.

Sometimes he tossed gold coins at them in return. He no longer needed to ambush travelers on deserted roads; these people now routinely gave him offerings in his temple.

Today, Sisera was in a good mood, dressed in his pseudo-military garb. He had the appearance of warrior cleric with full plate armor adorned with shamanistic religious artifacts, symbols, animal skulls, and a lion's pelt with its head serving as his cap.

A spike-wheeled war chariot with a skittish warhorse pulled over to make room for him to pass by. That horse didn't want to be anywhere near him.

Sisera was on his way to King Jabin's royal palace. This grandiose structure was a combination of adobe and large stone blocks.

Sensual, bare breasted idols of the female goddess of Asherah, about the size of Sisera, flanked each side of a massive set of gold plated, intricately carved double doors.

The doors in this palace were among the select few of any structure, where Sisera did not have to duck and squish his way inside.

Sisera paused in front of one of the stone statues of Asherah while cupping his chin. "I love these statues; they remind me of the good ol' days.

"You know, the real Asherah didn't have a twin. I need to find out who made these statues, because they actually might be *my* twin sisters," Sisera commented in his profoundly deep voice, to the military officer in front of the temple.

"I wish one of them was still around, what a woman," Sisera chuckled and gripped a breast on one of the statues. The guard started laughing.

Wait, was Sisera lusting after his own sister?

"Aren't any Canaanite women around here can handle a guy like me," Sisera gripped and squeezed his crotch, and a few other men walking nearby started joining in the laughter of this carnal creature. Festive music that was playing in the streets started making its way to their location.

"Hell, the only thing around here that can take a guy like me is that horse!" Sisera slapped his knee while pointing at a passing warhorse.

Unlike normal horses, warhorses were trained for battle and usually immune to loud noises and sudden movements, but this warhorse met her limit, and she instantly burst into a sprint.

The charioteer shouted vehemently, pulling back on the reigns, but to no avail. *That horse was out of there*.

"A guy like me got to be careful about that kind of stuff. Unlike you Canaanites, we actually get results," Sisera raised his eyebrows.

"Next thing you know, you'd be having a bunch of strange creatures running around here; maybe a few looking like Baal,"[18-19] he glanced over at an ox strapped to a cart full of vegetables while pointing to a bull-headed humanoid pendant on his right shoulder.

"There's only room for one Baal in this land!" Sisera started laughing hysterically, until his laugh morphed into a demonic cackle, gleeful and proud of his depravity. Hoots and hollers ensued from the town folk, pointing at the steed fleeing in panic.

"Yes, what a woman," Sisera returned to the statue and reminisced, tracing his finger under the idol's jawline. "Both of them together was a nightmare," Sisera pointed his thumb to the other statue.

"When she found out her boyfriend cheated on her with my other sister, she killed him...*and ate him*."[20-24]

The guard's laughter became a little nervous, then Sisera lowered his voice even more and he grinned. "She was a good cook."

Sisera howled again with demonic gurgling, and the guard was no longer laughing. He smiled uneasily and nodded, and the passersby resumed course when Sisera looked at them and licked his chops. "Tasty," he flicked his eyebrows, as if joking, *but not*. His dark humor was for real.

"And you know, I honestly don't even think that guy knew that was my sister's twin he was with. I mean really, she was her twin. If you're going to cheat, why cheat with a twin?" He shook his head, and the guard continued to smile and nod.

"They both ate that guy together," Sisera smiled, almost in a joyful recollection. "Pretty strange, don't you think? Why wasn't she angry with her sister? But no, she was just angry at her boyfriend, for cheating with *her twin*.

"Maybe that guy was some sort of game they liked to play with their boyfriends, who knows. You Canaanites all think you have psycho girls around here, but you don't even know. *Anakim women...*" Sisera continued to laugh at his own morbidity.

As such, were some of the awkward conversations with Sisera, but the people of Hazor loved him nonetheless.

Inside the palace, a white haired King Jabin sat enthroned in his royal court, flanked by several guards on each side of his throne.

General Arad, his chief advisor, clad in decorative military attire, stood before him. Next to him was Heber, a balding obese merchant in his mid-thirties, dressed in colorful silks and gaudy jewelry.[25-28]

"I'm glad you brought these things to my attention," King Jabin replied to his chief advisor. Interrupting their conversation, they heard Sisera's thudding footsteps echoing in the outer hall.

"Speak of the devil," King Jabin replied with a smile, but General Arad didn't share King Jabin's enthusiasm. Instead, he and Heber soberly moved to the side of King Jabin's throne. The closer those thudding footsteps approached, the closer Heber scrunched next to General Arad.

Sisera finally entered the room, completely filling the archway of the royal court. "My king," he replied, nodded his head, then he glared at General Arad and Heber.

His deep voice was particularly cavernous in the echoing halls of King Jabin's palace. "Your highness, I will dispense with idle conversation. I came to ask for more men."

"You just received your command. What do you need more men for?" questioned the king.

"The Israelites threaten your kingdom with slaughter. As we speak, they forge weapons against you."

"Your majesty, if I may?" Heber replied to the king, and King Jabin nodded toward him.

"You have amassed great wealth from these Israelites. They practically serve you as slaves. Why kill them?"

"Who said anything about killing them?" Sisera interrupted the question. "There's a lot you can do before killing them."

General Arad cleared his throat and addressed Sisera directly. "General Sisera, we know your intentions. Many people revere you as a god, but that does not mean you are one. Set aside your grudge against these Israelites; they are harmless."

"We confiscate their weapons routinely," Sisera responded.[29-30]

"King Jabin," Heber rebutted, "I am a Kenite, chief metalworker among my people. I assure you, whatever his men have confiscated is not for war. They are crude implements for hunting."

Sisera looked at Heber, and Heber responded by quickly diverting his eyes to a bird sitting on a nearby window sill. A strange dizziness started swirling around in his head.

"You may continue to confiscate their weapons, but I have no intention of starting a war with them," King Jabin made his ruling.

"Your highness, they defy you. Their temple in Shiloh is a mockery

of your throne."

"Are you sure you're not speaking of your own little throne you have established in your temple of Baal?"

General Arad was one among a very few who dared speak to Sisera in such a bold manner. Interestingly, he was also immune to Sisera's ability to manipulate people's minds.

"Sire, these people breed like flies, they will be your undoing if you do not eradicate them."

"I thought you said you weren't talking about killing them?" General Arad questioned again.

"Eradicate, enslave, take everything they own, destroy their temple, force them to bow down to you; what does it matter? We're not doing enough."

Sisera gripped a fist in one hand, and punched it into to palm of his other hand. "They need to be put in their rightful place."

Sisera's plan to seduce the Israelites was the long game. In the meantime, using the Canaanites as pawns to do his bidding to make their lives absolutely miserable, was his most enjoyable pastime.

"I do not think the king is interested in your ambitions," General

Arad continued to blatantly contradict Sisera's requests.

"Allow the king to speak for himself," Sisera spoke sternly to General Arad, restraining the overwhelming impulse to rip his head off with his bare hands right then and there.

Did Sisera' eyes literally glow red for an instant? General Arad blinked several times, then dismissed it.

Needless to say, Sisera hated General Arad almost as much as he hated the Israelites. Sooner or later, he was going to kill him, but not today.

"General Sisera," King Jabin calmly replied, "I respect your opinion, but the Israelites are no threat."

"They have skilled warriors; they train to fight against us," Sisera persisted.

"Before I invade, I need more reason than the mere existence of crude weapons," King Jabin finally concluded.

While King Jabin was stifling Sisera's ambitions, Israel was in its formative stages, waiting for Deborah to fulfill her destiny. And that destiny paired her up with Barak, the man who was currently testing her resolve.

Isolating themselves a little further from the others each week, Deborah and Barak sparred high atop Mount Ephraim, amidst some stone ruins overlooking the valley below. The other warriors were sparring nearby, just out of visual range.

As usual, Barak was sparring slowly, this time with a staff. Deborah knocked his staff out of his hands without hardly any effort. "Stop being easy on me, I know you can fight better than this. I can't improve if you're moving so slow," she complained.

"Well you're pretty fast," Barak commented while fetching his staff. "The faster we go, the harder it is to maintain control."

As they started to spar again, Deborah almost instantly knocked his staff out of his hands again. As he turned to fetch it, Deborah tripped him over a ledge, and he fell about four feet, thudding on his back. Poof, she knocked the wind out of him.

"What was that for?" he questioned when he finally caught his breath.

"Try harder!" Deborah yelled at him.

He laid on the ground and marveled at her angry expression. Even when she was angry, she was breathtakingly beautiful, literally in this case.

"Get your stupid staff," Deborah chided him, annoyed that he wasn't taking their training seriously. *I'll get my staff alright*.

Barak stared at her and cracked a smile; his tongue was on the verge of blurting out those words, but fortunately he harnessed it. Restraint of the tongue; Haran's words of wisdom rang true.

"What's so funny?"

"Nothing," he smiled.

On another day, Barak faced Deborah standing waist deep in a creek, shivering. Other warriors were scattered nearby. "Everything different in water," Adonia instructed them. "The deeper you are, the less secure you feet. This change rule."

As the dozen warriors sparred with wooden swords, shivering uncontrollably, Deborah continued to block Barak's feeble attacks. "Is this how you fight Sisera's men?" she questioned him impatiently.

"Sorry, I'm having a hard time focusing. The last time I saw you like this," he referred to all of them being soaking wet, "well, I just keep thinking about your dress."

Deborah smiled at the recollection. He still remembers that? Oy, he's probably replayed that introduction countless times.

No, not going there! We need to train, focus!

"Try not to get distracted, this is serious, focus," Deborah took the moral high ground, though her request to focus was as much directed toward herself as it was to Barak.

The chemistry had grown so thick between these two, it was affecting the environment; spring would be arriving a few weeks earlier.

"I am focusing, just on other things," Barak stared at Deborah's chest briefly. "Sorry," he shook his head, then he swung his wooden sword at her. Deborah smacked it out of his hand, flinging it to the shoreline.

"Please," Deborah's patience was wearing thin.

"I told you, the faster we go, the harder it is for me to maintain control," Barak defended himself.

Adonia tossed the sword back to him, and the next time he swung it at Deborah, she blocked it again, then countered with a strike so hard that she snapped his wooden sword in half.

"You're not helping either of us. Just treat me like one of them," Deborah pointed to the other men.

Barak shook his head negatively. "You're already better than most of them, but you're still leaving yourself vulnerable," Barak explained.

A few of the men cast smug expressions in Barak's direction, but he ignored them; his attention was focused entirely on Deborah, for more reasons than one.

"Almost every time you kick with your left leg, you're slightly off balance. Every time you take a side swipe with that sword," Barak swung his sword, "and when you're jabbing with your left fist," Barak punched the air, "you're overextending yourself."

"I have perfect form, Adonia said so," Deborah defended herself.

"It's true that you're getting much better, and you're certainly a lot faster, but that's the problem. You're so damn fast, it's hard to see those flaws, and I have to move even faster than you to exploit them.

"That's just too damn fast to pull a punch or block your sword without accidentally hurting you. I think even Adonia would agree to that." Barak looked at Adonia, but he made no comment.

"You have to trust me, you don't know what you're asking," Barak warned her again. "You've reached a point in your training where this can get downright painful, if not dangerous."

Commentary Notes

++

1. Rick Meyers, "Equipping Ministries Foundation, e-Sword Bible software, version 12.2.0," downloaded Nov 20, 2020, http://www.e-sword.net; *Companion Bible Appendix 25, E. W. Bullinger*. One of the words translated as giant in the Bible is Rephaim. This same word is also translated as ghosts in other Scriptures, connecting living giants with their deceased counterparts, demons/devils. Commentator Bullinger states, "As Rephaim they were well known, and are often mentioned: but, unfortunately, instead of this, their proper name, being preserved, it is variously translated as 'dead,' 'deceased,' or 'giants.' These Rephaim are to have no resurrection. This fact is stated in Isaiah 26:14 (where the proper name is rendered 'deceased,' and v. Isaiah 26:19, where it is rendered 'the dead'). It is rendered 'dead' seven times (Job 26:5; Psalm 88:10; Proverbs 2:18, 9:18, 21:16; Isaiah 14:8, 26:19). It is rendered 'deceased' in Isaiah 26:14. It is retained as a proper name 'Rephaim,' [referring to giants] ten times (two being in the margin). Genesis 14:5, 15:20; Joshua 12:15 (marg.), 2 Samuel 5:18, 5:22, 23:13; 1 Chronicles 11:15, 14:9, 20:4 (marg.); Isaiah 17:5. In all other places it is rendered 'giants,' Genesis 6:4; Numbers 23:33, where it is Nephilim; and Job 16:14, where it is gibbor (Ap. 14. iv)." In summation, the Bible mixes these words translated as giant, with the lost spirits of the dead. This explains the origin of demons/devils; they are the ghosts of the Nephilim/Rephaim/Anakim giants.
2. Rick Meyers, "Equipping Ministries Foundation, e-Sword Bible software, version 12.2.0," downloaded Nov 20, 2020, http://www.e-sword.net; *Strong's Enhanced Lexicon* provides definitions for H7495,Rapha/Rephaim,anditscounterpart,H7503,Rapha,asshown:
   רָפָה רָפָא

   râphâ' râphâh

   raw-faw', raw-faw'

   From H7495 in the sense of *invigorating*; a *giant*: - giant, Rapha, Rephaim (-s). See also H1051.

   Total KJV occurrences: 21

   רָפָא

   râphâ'

   raw-faw'

From H7495 in the sense of H7503; properly *lax*, that is, (figuratively) a *ghost* (as *dead*; in plural only): - dead, deceased.
Total KJV occurrences: 8

3. Tim Chaffey, "Giants in the Bible", Answers in Genesis, https://answersingenesis.org/bible-characters/giants-in-the-bible/, (Last Accessed December 12, 2020). This website provides a wealth of research regarding the existence of giants in the Biblical accounts.
4. I took the image of a giant carrying an ox under his arm, from a former Army sniper I once spoke with during a radio interview. This sniper claimed he personally witnessed a living Nephilim in Afghanistan, carrying an adult cow under his arm. He estimated this being to be about twelve feet tall, more than double the height of any of the Taliban members he was keeping company with. He actually shot this creature with his 50 calibur rifle, but that didn't kill it. He said it dropped the cow and ran for cover.
5. Rosemary Ellen Guiley, *Harper's Encyclopedia of Mystical & Paranormal Experience*, (New York, NY: HarperCollins Publishers, 1991). pp. 478-481. Telekinesis and tricks of the mind, can be categorized as forms of psychokinesis, (PK) "The apparent influcnce of mind over matter through inivisle means, such as the movement of objects, bending of metal, and the outcome of events. The term 'psychokinesis' comes from the Greek words psyche, meaning 'breath,' 'life,' or 'soul,' and kinein, meaning 'to move. '..Psycokinesis has been observed and scientifically studied since the 1930s. Rudi Schneider, for example, was a medium 'whose materializations and telekinetic movement of objects was intently studied by psychical researchers during the first part of the twentieth century... The most famous Soviet PK subject was Nina Kulagina, a housewife from Leningrad, born in the mid-1920s, whose abilities were revealed to the West in 1968. Kulagina was observed by Western scientists, who witnessed such phenomena as the movement of many different sizes and types of stationary objects; the altering of the course of objects already in motion; and impressions upon photographic film."
6. Ibid, 606-607. Telepathic hypnosis (also hypnosis-at-a-distance). "A combination of telepathy and hypnotism, in which a person may be induced into a hypnotic trance by the projection of thought over any distance. The term was coined in the late ninteenth century by Frederic W. H. Myers, one of the founders of the Society for Psychical Research in London." The former Sovient Union was heavily involved in this research. "Beginning in 1924, Russian

scientists conducted extensive experiments with telepathic hypnosis, much of it under cover during the repressive Salinist regime. The experiments focused on manipulation of behavior and inducement of pain, and were led by L. L. Vasiliev, who said he successfully hypnotized a subject more than 1,700 kilometers away to fall asleep and awaken on command... In the 1978 world chess championship, held at Baguio, the Philippines, Victor Korchnoi, a Soviet defector who was challenging champion Anatoly Karpov, claimed he was the victim of 'telehypnosis.' Korchnoi said he was hypnotized to lose the game by a Dr. Vladimir Zoukhar, a Russian hypnotist and parapsychologist, who sat in the fourth row of spectators and stared at him throughout the match."

J. Pritchard, *Ancient Near Eastern Texts and the Old* .7 Princeton: University Press, 1969),) *Testament, 3rd Edition* Bible Encyclopedia, quoted in Christian Answers Network s.v. "Nimrod: Who was he? Was he godly or evil?" by Dr. David P. Livingston, http://www.christiananswers.net/dictionary/nimrod.html, (Last Accessed December 10, 2020). The giants in Scripture were filled with hatred, which they eventually directed toward God, following the example of their rebellious, fallen angel parents. After the flood of Noah, they wanted revenge against God for wiping out their ancestors. In Genesis 11, shortly following the flood of Noah, we see this desire for revenge in the account of Nimrod, whose name in Hebrew means "rebel." The citizens of Nimrod's city were sinful for following Nimrod's mandate to build a giant tower. They met with God's judgment for doing this, and their languages were jumbled up as a result. This destroyed the foundation of their civilization, and they dispersed from the region afterward. The only clues in Scripture pointing to Nimrod being a bad guy are the association of his name with rebel, and the fact that God destroyed his tower and confused everyone's language. Scripture does not clarify why building a tower was such an offence to God, however, the Epic of Gilgamesh is the Summerian version of this same story. While it is a twisted perspective of the same account, it fills in a few gaps. The Epic of Gilgamesh describes Gilgamesh as a hero who defied the "evil entity" that brought about the flood of Noah. Building a massive tower was Gilgamesh's way of defying that so-called evil entity to escape any future flood. This same defiance against God and his chosen people, the

Israelites, was continued by all the successive generations of giants, aka Nephilim. The other races of giants were named after their ancestors; Anakim were descendants of the giant Anak, and Raphaim were descendents of the giant Rapha. Part of the reason these entities populated Canaan, is because they knew this was the land God promised Abraham, so they intended to invalidate God's promise with a preemptive strike by populating the area while God chosen people, the Israelites, were temporarily enslaved in .Egypt

8. The Epic of Gilgamesh, trans. Robert Temple, Biblioteca Pleyades website, http://www.bibliotecapleyades.net/serpents_dragons/gilgamesh.htm (Last Accessed December 10, 2020). p. 382.
9. Rick Meyers, "Equipping Ministries Foundation, e-Sword Bible software, version 12.2.0," downloaded Nov 20, 2020, http://www.e-sword.net; *Strong's Enhanced Lexicon* provides definitions for G5052, telesphoreo, a Greek word meaning "maturity."

    Τελεσφορέω
    telesphoreō
    tel-es-for-eh'-o
    From a compound of G5056 and G5342; to *be a bearer to completion* (maturity), that is, to *ripen* fruit (figuratively): - bring fruit to perfection.
    Total KJV occurrences: 1
10. See 1 Chronicles 20:15, Lahmi is the name of a Philistine giant, one of Goliath's brothers.
11. Richard Laurence, *The Book of Enoch the Prophet*, (London: Kegan Paul, Trench & Col, 1883), obtained at https://archive.org/details/bookofenochproph00laur, (Last Accessed December 8, 2020). One of the themes listed in the book of Enoch, especially in Enoch 8, 9:5-6, is that the Watchers, i.e. fallen angels, taught people "all the secret things which are done in the heavens." God considered this accelerated accumulation of knowledge a very bad idea, for it was part of what caused the world to become so corrupt in Noah's day. Shortly after the flood, history repeats with a rapid accumulation of knowledge in Genesis 11:6, "Behold, they are one people, and they have all one language, and this is only the beginning of what they will do. And nothing that they propose to do will now be impossible for them." [ESV].
12. Rick Meyers, "Equipping Ministries Foundation, e-Sword Bible software, version 12.2.0," downloaded Nov 20, 2020, http://ww-

w.e-sword.net; *Companion Bible Appendix 25, E. W. Bullinger*, "The Nephilim, or 'Giants'." Ancient structures composed of megalithic stones span the globe, and they have baffled scientists for years, about how they were created. Even with today's modern machinery, the task of moving large objects is daunting. According E. W. Bullinger's Bible Commentary on the Nephilim, he states "Their strength is seen in 'the giant cities of Bashan' today; and we know not how far they may have been utilized by Egypt in the construction of buildings, which is still an unsolved problem. Arba was rebuilt by the Khabiri or confederates seven years before Zoan was built by the Egyptian Pharaohs of the nineteenth dynasty. See note on Numbers 13:22. If these Nephilim, and their branch of Rephaim, were associated with Egypt, we have an explanation of the problem which has for ages perplexed all engineers, as to how those huge stones and monuments were brought together. Why not in Egypt as well as in 'the giant cities of Bashan' which exist, as such, to this day?"

13. "Golan Heights (Biblical Bashan)", BiblePlaces.com, https://www.bibleplaces.com/golanheights/, (Last Accessed December 12, 2020). Ancient stone structures are found throughout the Golan Heights, which is the location of ancient Bashan. "Hundreds of dolmens have been found in the Golan Heights. Used for burial in the basalt areas where grave digging is difficult, dolmens were used for burial during both the Early Bronze I and Intermediate Bronze periods. The dolmen was most likely intended as a burial chamber for the chief of a clan, or another member of the nomadic elite. A dolmen is constructed of two large vertical stone slabs capped by a horizontal stone, which can weigh up to 30 tons (27 T)."
14. Hassan Ammar, "Solved! How Ancient Egyptians Moved Massive Pyramid Stones", NBC News, https://www.nbcnews.com/science/science-news/solved-how-ancient-egyptians-moved-massive-pyramid-stones-n95171, (Last Accessed December 12, 2020). Many theories have been postulated how the ancients transported and built structures with massive stone blocks in ancient times. "The ancient Egyptians who built the pyramids may have been able to move massive stone blocks across the desert by wetting the sand in front of a contraption built to pull the heavy objects, according to a new study... Physicists at the University of Amsterdam investigated the forces needed to pull weighty objects on a giant sled over desert sand, and discovered that dampening the sand in front of the primitive device reduces friction on the sled, making it easier to op-

erate... To make their discovery, the researchers picked up on clues from the ancient Egyptians themselves. A wall painting discovered in the ancient tomb of Djehutihotep, which dates back to about 1900 B.C., depicts 172 men hauling an immense statue using ropes attached to a sledge. In the drawing, a person can be seen standing on the front of the sledge, pouring water over the sand, said study lead author Daniel Bonn, a physics professor at the University of Amsterdam." Note, this theory is postulated, but only tested with very small-scale models. The size and quantity of the blocks constructing the great pyramid is so outlandish, it is difficult to conceive how it could have been achieved using any ancient methods, even if taking hundreds of years to do it.

15. PBS Nova, "Pyramids: How Heavy?" https://www.pbs.org/wgbh/nova/pyramid/geometry/blocks.html#:~:text=How%20Heavy%3F,-metric%20tons%20(2.5%20tons)", (Last Accessed December 12, 2020). "More than 2,300,000 limestone and granite blocks were pushed, pulled, and dragged into place on the Great Pyramid. The average weight of a block is about 2.3 metric tons (2.5 tons)."
16. Bedford Astronomy Club, "Moving Large Stone blocks in Ancient Times", https://www.astronomyclub.xyz/easter-island/appendix-2-moving-large-stone-blocks-in-ancient-times.html, (Last Accessed December 12, 2020). This website goes into an excellent analysis, including mathematical and engineering details of many modern examples of moving very large, heavy objects. "Moving one-off extra-large loads a distance is, even today, a tricky matter..."
17. See Judges 4:2.
18. Ray Vander Laan, "Fertility Cults of Canaan", That The World May Know, https://www.thattheworldmayknow.com/fertility-cults-of-canaan, (Last Accessed December 12, 2020). The Canaanite god Baal, fit the same description as the Greek Minotaur; a man's human body with a bull's head.
19. Jeffrey H. King, "Connecting the Dots; The Book of Enoch, Part 7", Jeffrey H. King's Blog, May 27, 2017, https://jeffreyhking.wordpress.com/2017/05/27/connecting-the-dots-the-book-of-enoch-part-7/, (Last Accessed December 8, 2020). The Bible describes how the sons of God corrupted all species, (Genesis 6:12, "all flesh"). This led to God destroying all life on Earth in the flood of Noah. Additionally, Enoch 7:14 states that the Nephilim began to "injure," or "sin against" birds, beasts, reptiles, and fishes, to eat their flesh one after another, and to drink their blood. These accounts of Scripture agree with many examples of bestiality in ancient mythologies.

Otherworldly beings capable of shape-shifting into animal species, brought into existence a large collection of bizarre hybrids. These hybrids included "Centaurs (half-human, half-horse); Cerberus (three-headed dog guarding entrance to Hades); Chimeras (part-lion, part-goat, part-snake); Gorgons (snake-haired and snake-bodied humanoids; Medusa was a Gorgon); Griffins (lion body, tail of a snake, head and wings of an eagle); Mermaids (head and torso of a woman and tail of a fish); Minotaur (head and legs of a bull, torso of a man); Pegasus (winged horse); Satyrs (half-man, half-goat, wild and lustful; Pan was one of these beings); Sphinx (half-human, half-lion; answer his riddles or die); and Unicorns (magical horse with a single horn on its forehead), to name a few. Today, we have modern-day chimeras. "Research has progressed far enough that laws regulating it have already been enacted in the United States and Europe. It is now a felony to produce mixed species hybrids. It's only a misdemeanor to simply have one you bought, say from England, where it's legal."

20. C. Scott Littleton, *Mythology: The Illustrated Anthology of World Myth and Storytelling*, (London: Duncan Baird Publishers, 2002). pp. 41-42, 48-49, 117, 133. Ancient mythologies are filled with examples of horrendously wicked behavior among the mythological gods. They committed adultery, rape, incest, bestiality, murder, and cannibalism, among other things. According to the legend of the Egyptian god Seth, "One day as Seth was walking by the Nile, he came across the goddess Anat, bathing in the stream. He changed himself into a ram and raped her..." Seth also "turned himself into a raging bull and trampled Osiris into the dust." Osiris was Seth's brother. "Pegasus, the entrancing winged horse, had monstrous origins. He was born from the neck of the snake-haired Gorgon, Medusa, when Perseus cut her head off. Perseus' father was Poseidon, who had slept with Medusa before she was transformed into a Gorgon by Athene, for thoughtlessly defiling her sanctuary." The Egyptian god "Anat, a deity of battle, was in a twist of the Isis myth, both sister and husband to the Middle Eastern god Baal, who was worshipped in Egypt as an aspect of Seth." Mythologies blend into fact concerning the existence of Gilgamesh, who was no literary invention. "The hero of the epic was based on a real king who ruled Uruk c. 2600 B.C., and whose prowess was the subject of tales circulating centuries before the poem was written. The Sumerian King's List records him as the fifth ruler in Uruk's First Dynasty and

provides him with the customary divine antecedents; his mother, it is said, was the goddess Nisun." Just like his mythological counterparts, Gilgamesh had little respect for human life. There is a "long list of his companions, including his wives, his concubines, his musicians and entertainers, and even his valet. He makes offerings to the gods of the underworld to persuade them to accept the new arrivals. In this list of names and rituals, we are probably reading an authentic description of a mass human sacrifice. The retinue that followed Gilgamesh on his final journey may well have been slaughtered in order. Archeology supports this grim interpretation. When Sir Leonard Woolley excavated the royal tombs of Ur, he found not only the bodies of Ur's rulers, but around them scores of retainers who had been killed so that they could serve their masters beyond the grave."

21. Scott Littleton, *Mythology: The Illustrated Anthology of World Myth and Storytelling*, (London: Duncan Baird Publishers, 2002), p. 41. "Baal was infamous in the Old Testament, because he killed and devoured human beings." This excerpt is likely taken from the references of Israelites sacrificing their children, causing them to "pass through the fire," (2 King 16:3, 21:6).
22. Richard Laurence, *The Book of Enoch the Prophet*, (London: Kegan Paul, Trench & Col, 1883), obtained at https://archive.org/details/bookofenochproph00laur, (Last Accessed December 8, 2020). The giants were cannibals, Enoch 7:12-13 "These devoured all which the labor of men produced; until it became impossible to feed them; When they turned themselves against men, in order to devour them..."
23. Robert Fitzgerald, *The Odyssey, Homer*, (New York, NY: Vintage Books, Random House, Inc., 1990), pp. 155, etc. Giants are mentioned in multiple places in Homer's Odyssey. These creatures, Cyclops, also referred to in other sources as the Laistrygones, were vicious cannibals.
24. Heather Burton, *Cannibalism in High Medieval English Literature*, (New York, NY: Palgrave Macmillan, 2007). Beowulf is the hero of a 6th century Scandinavian account of a cannibalistic giant known as Grendel.
25. See Judges 4:17, "there was peace between Jabin the king of Hazor and the house of Heber the Kenite." The peaceful relations between Heber and King Jabin is first established here in this story.
26. John H. Walton, Victor H. Matthews & Mark W. Chavalas, *The IVP Bi-*

ble Background Commentary, Old Testament, (Downers IL: InterVarsity Press, 2000), p. 249. "Hazor is mentioned as an important city both in the eighteenth-century Mari texts and the fourteenth-century El Amarna letters. Hazor (Tell el-Qedah) stood at a strategic point in northern Galilee (ten miles north of the Sea of Galilee) on the road between Damascus to Megiddo. Joshua 11:10 describes it as 'the head of all those kingdoms.' In both Joshua and in Judges, its king Jabin that is defeated (Joshua 11:13; Judges 4:24, and 1 Samuel 12:9)... Archeological investigations do show a major destruction level in the thirteenth century, which could be the result of attacks by either the Sea Peoples, the Israelites, or some other group. Subsequently the city was refortified by Solomon (1 Kings 9:15) and remained a major center of commerce and a key to Israel's northern border until the Assyrian conquest (2 Kings 15:29)." In this story, the idea to make Heber's character a wealthy weapons merchant sided with the enemy, was inspired by two main variables. 1. Heber was a member of the Kenites; a tribe associated with metalworking. 2. Heber severed ties with his fellow Kenites, who were allied with Israel, dating back to Moses. He then moved north to be closer to the city of Hazor, a major trading hub in the ancient Middle East. A logical motivation for doing this that directly relates to his Kenite heritage, was a better compensation for metalworking than the Israelites could offer.

27. Kenneth Barker, *The New International Version Study Bible*, (Grand Rapids, MI: Zondervan Bible Publishers, 1985), pp. 334-338. "Judges 4:11, Heber the Kenite. Since one meaning of Heber's name is 'ally,' and since 'Kenite' identifies him as belonging to a clan of metalworkers, the author hints at the truth that this member of a people allied with Israel since the days of Moses has moved from south to north to ally himself (see Judges 4:17) with the Canaanite king who is assembling a large force of 'iron chariots.' It is no doubt he who informs Sisera of Barak's military preparations."
28. Kenneth Barker, *The New International Version Study Bible*, (Grand Rapids, MI: Zondervan Bible Publishers, 1985), p. 334. "Hazor. The original royal city of the Jabin dynasty; it may still have been in ruins (Joshua 11:10). Sisera sought to recover the territory once ruled by the kings of Hazor."
29. See Judges 5:8, which hints at weapons confiscation, "Was a shield or spear to be seen among forty thousand in Israel?"
30. Arthur E. Cundall & Leon Morris, *Judges & Ruth: An Introduction & Commentary*, (Downers Grove, IL: Inter-Varsity Press Leicester,

England, 1968), p. 95. “They had been deprived of their weapons (1 Samuel 13:22), although it may be unwise to accept this as an absolute statement. If it were, the battle at the Kishon could hardly have been undertaken. Probably the meaning is that these weapons dared not be displayed publicly.”

Chapter 5:

Now You Can Smile

ה

"Enough of your stupid warnings!" Deborah shouted at Barak, thoroughly frustrated. "I don't even think you're afraid of accidentally hurting me. I remember what you said on that first day you saw me in training."

Deborah then mocked Barak's deeper voice, adding a twinge of cognitive impairment for exaggerated effect.

"'If Israel depends on women to free itself from Sisera's yolk, then we've already lost,' So you see," Deborah pointed an accusatory finger at Barak, hoping to provoke his ire, "that's the crux of it. You're holding back because the *mere thought* of a woman stealing your glory is so humiliating, you can't bear it."

"Sure, that's it, *I'm afraid*," Barak nodded with a retaliatory mock of his own.

"Wipe that stupid smile off your face for once!" Deborah was incensed. Seeing that Barak no longer had a sword to spar with, she tossed hers to the shoreline. "Hand to hand, come on!"

"Oh boy," Barak sighed.

"What?"

Barak looked around the area to double-check if Haran was anywhere around, but he wasn't. However, Adonia was watching.

"What if I touch or grab you somewhere I'm not supposed to?"

Barak cautioned her with a raised eyebrow.

This issue was subtly alluded to several times during their training, when Barak's hands would hover over a forbidden zone of Deborah's succulent body.

Thus far, unlike the other trainees that had a few groping incidents with Deborah in the past, Barak respected Deborah and worked around these limitations. However, he never directly stated this dilemma until now.

Deborah had a quick response, somewhat telling of her overall disposition. "As if you don't want to," she replied, halfway inviting him to grope at will; *accidents happen*. She then briefly flicked her eyebrows, presenting the welcome mat.

Adonia grunted, mildly uncomfortable, but he still wasn't saying anything. Perhaps Haran told him to drop the leash with these two?

"Got a point there," Barak was very pleased with this solution. More hand to hand sessions were definitely getting added to the syllabus!

Noticing that Barak and Deborah were demanding more of Adonia's attention, the other warriors became curious, paused in their training and subtly migrated to the area. What was this escalation of Deborah and Barak's repartee?

Did they hear that right? Did Deborah say something about hand to hand?

To Barak's point-blank statement about the potential for invading forbidden zones, was Deborah's response nothing short of *'go for it'*? Barak was indeed a lucky man!

"Hey, focus on training!" Adonia addressed them. Barak nodded toward Adonia, then he returned his attention to Deborah.

"Well hey, if we're going hand to hand, that changes things a bit. No need for this leather armor slowing me down." Barak then tossed the hilt of his broken sword to the shoreline, and proceeded to release the leather bonds on his leather top.

Deborah's eyes lit up. Wait, don't tell me you're taking your top off. No. Stop... please, don't...do...that...

The thumping in Deborah's chest started to sway her body as the verdict was confirmed. Barak indeed peeled off his top, and he casually tossed it to the shoreline.

The tables were turned; he was now exploiting the male's socially acceptable practice of going topless without creating a scene. Why that underhanded, conniving, low down, dirty rotten...

Now, when her hands touched him, every touch would be against his glistening, smooth, bare skin. If they grappled, she might find her face pressed up against his wet, bare chest, or elsewhere...

Deborah's expression transformed the moment she saw sparkly beads of water dripping down Barak's massive chest, then weaving through the glistening, rippled lumps of muscle in his eloquently formed six-pack.

Oh my.

Taking Deborah's queue from their first encounter, Barak stretched his arms back while sucking in his gut, then he pulled them back forward and puffed up his powerful chest, adding a not-so-subtle complete torso flex while clenching his teeth in a grin.

Barak's traps nearly tapped his ears. Were those twenty inch biceps? This guy was a massive hunk of solid muscle; not an ounce of fat on his perfectly sculpted body.

Oy.

An expert in micro-expressions would have detected Deborah's instantly dilated pupils, raised eyebrows, deep breathing, and the pulsating vein in her neck. Barak was emanating so much testosterone, she was about to become pregnant just looking at him.

Deborah finally couldn't contain herself. Those micro-expressions were blasted off of her face with the humming force field of Barak's flex. She gasped, opening her mouth slightly and then audibly sighed, "Oh."

Wow, this dude was awesome, just absolutely awesome! Deborah's open mouth then formed into a smile that continued to grow wide and magnificent.

Deep breath. Another sigh.

She then glanced over at Adonia, who was pursing his lips, hand cupped on his chin; he was shaking with corked giggling. A quick glance at the other men revealed similar expressions. Somewhere nearby, a teapot was whistling.

Deborah's brilliant smile then compounded with utter humiliation. That audible gasp was absolutely inexcusable. She would never hear the end of this!

Deborah suddenly exploded with a horrendous cackle, pointing at Barak, barely able to breathe. She then bent over and staggered, coughing and laughing hysterically. The cork was blown; everyone burst with howls of uncontrollable laughter.

This was seriously embarrassing.

"What are you doing?" Deborah finally bellowed at Barak, then covered her hands over her face.

Barak soaked it all up, placing his hands on his hips, thoroughly amused.

"That's my pre-battle-stretch-flex," Barak blurted out a lame impromptu excuse for his shameless machismo display, then he buzzed through a few other stretches and poses as if he were posing for a sculptor.

"Almost every fighter has a little prep routine like that. Why do you ask? Are you having a little trouble...*focusing*?" Barak teased her, then bounced his pecks up and down a few times while grinning.

"Stop it!" Deborah howled at him.

"Okay, enough," Adonia gurgled out, choked, then he quickly reissued a corrected copy. "Enough. Stop this..." he waved his hands, "whatever you doing; get to train."

"Exactly," Deborah agreed, as if she were the model of composure. She conveniently did not request Barak put his top back on. Instead, she cautiously moved forward. In response to her advance, Barak moved backward into deeper water.[1]

"If too deep, best weapon is water. Palm strike chest. Attack throat if underwater. That will force opponent to breathe," Adonia continued to instruct them.

The two finally grappled, and Deborah's hands immediately slipped on Barak's slick skin. That was the plan.

Before she knew it, Barak had her in a bear hug with her face squished between his meaty pecks. "How you doing in there?" he taunted her. "I could probably break your back if I went full force."

Deborah twisted to break free. In the midst of their struggle, Barak accidentally grabbed her right breast. *Oops*. The instant he was delightfully distracted, Deborah struck him in the throat with her elbow and repelled him back in a fit of coughing and choking.

"Good one, don't get distracted, your lives depend on it," Adonia chimed in. "Again."

The two grappled again, and this time, Barak grabbed Deborah's hair and yanked her head back. An instant later, she nailed him in the crotch with the back of her heel. He immediately released her, cheeks puffed.

"Now you can smile," Deborah grinned.

Joining in another round of contentious training on another day, Barak and Deborah were using weapons in a barren desert area. Deborah was swinging a wooden tent peg tied to a thin rope, and Barak had a donkey jawbone in one hand, farm tool in the other.[2-3]

"What first rule of combat?" Adonia questioned them.

"There are no rules," Barak answered.[4]

"Good," Adonia answered.

"Except that's a rule, making it an oxymoron," Deborah added.

Adonia grunted and asked another question. "What best weapon?"

"Whatever you can pick up,"[5] Deborah responded. Then facing Barak, she questioned him, "You ready? Or is today another hollow victory for the Honey Bee?"

"I keep telling you, be careful what you ask for," Barak warned her.

Spinning her spike, Deborah whipped it out like a grappling hook. The cord struck Barak's spear and the spike spun around it and instantly locked into place. Deborah then snapped the spear out of Barak's hand and into her own hands.

"Pathetic," she reprimanded him while dropping his spear to the ground.

"That was kick ass!" Barak was truly impressed, never having seen such an odd makeshift weapon used in such an extraordinary manner.

Deborah practiced that move hours on end, but she still didn't believe Barak was impressed by it.

"I am begging you, *begging you*," she pleaded, "you have to treat me like I'm a guy! I'm never going to get any better if you don't. Do you think I want to get raped the next time I'm in the middle of nowhere with my father? Do you?"

This was perhaps the most upset Barak had ever seen Deborah.

"You are my only hope. You said I have vulnerabilities, well then, prove it! If you don't, I'm dead, or maybe even worse. Is that what you want? Is it!"

Fine.

Barak clenched his teeth, hoping against all odds that he could move quick enough to exploit her vulnerabilities, and simultaneously pull his punch. He suddenly rushed forward.

Deborah kicked, overextended and missed. Barak dodged, then taking advantage of that nanosecond vulnerability, he slugged her in the stomach, dropping her to her knees.

The other warriors instantly stopped fighting, appalled at Barak.

"Damn it!" Barak was furious with himself. "Sorry, damn it! Deborah, you have to believe me...*I didn't...*"

"What's wrong with you?" one of the other men yelled at him. He stepped forward and took a swing at Barak. Barak ducked and took a defensive posture.

"Hey!" Adonia shouted at them.

"I didn't mean to!" Barak defended himself.

"Stop," Deborah finally replied to all of them, still holding her gut. A tear trickled down her cheek. That slug in the gut hurt, *really bad.*

Deborah felt like vomiting, but instead, she brushed the tear away and struggled to her feet. The other fighter yelling at Barak dropped his attack, confused and disgruntled.

Barak couldn't take seeing her in such terrible pain; her cheeks were a bit puffy. He quickly gripped her shoulders, steadied her, then he embraced her.

"I'm sorry, I'm sorry, I'm sorry," he whispered repeatedly. "My whole life, I was taught to never raise my hand against a female...*ever*, no matter how much I am provoked, no matter what the situation is.

You've been yelling me all this time for not taking this training seriously, but every day, *every...single...day*, it's a struggle, and it pains me to... I *do not* want to hurt you. I..."

Barak's comforting had an immediate effect.

Transported beyond the threshold of intense pain, Deborah's breathing steadied, then slowed, then deepened as Barak stroked her luscious, thick, wavy black hair.

A warm tranquility swept over her as Barak gently rocked her, then cupped her head with his hand. He washed his face with her glorious hair; those delicate strands soaking directly into his soul through his face.

An amber ray of God's glory surely strayed from His throne, and slipped through the veil unnoticed, for that intoxicating emanation struck them both in an overwhelming jolt of pure ecstasy.

An angel's embrace would have had less effect.

Barak kissed Deborah's cheek repeatedly, inhaling her. He captured a few strands of her hairs with his tongue and slipped them into his mouth for a taste.

Then a few more. What compelled this desire, to feast on her hair? So strange it was, and yet, he couldn't get enough.

Then one of those tongue clutching maneuvers to apprehend a few more strands touched her ear. What was that? Deborah's ear? Now he wanted to chew on her ear.

Something was happening...

Deborah was paralyzed like a lizard stroked on its tummy. Every fiber of her being wanted to remain immobilized in this perfect location, trapped in a bubble of time for all eternity. The moment was perfect, pure and simple; this was heaven.

She impulsively nuzzled him and opened her mouth for a deep inhalation of his scent. Without thinking, she ran her fingers up his back and then wrapped her arms fully around him, squeezing him tightly.

If it weren't for his leather top, she would've licked his chest.

Yes, this was going somewhere, and the rate of acceleration was increasing.

Then they both suddenly felt that vibrational energy of being watched. Did a trans-dimensional portal open above them? Did a silent cloud of witnesses lean forward for a better look?

Deborah apprehensively cracked opened an eye to peek outside the confines of Barak's fortress of comfort.

Indeed, once again, these two were in the spotlight, center stage. The curtain was closed behind them, and all of the men were staring at them, waiting for their bow.

Embarrassed, Deborah begrudgingly pushed Barak away and cleared her throat. The instant she did, she gripped her abdomen; it was reminding her of something. Oh yea, she was still in extreme, unbearable agony!

Shake it off.

Barak conducted an expedited version of his pre-battle-stretch-flex, flopping and twisting his tree trunk arms around. Okay, here we go.

"You're right, I've been asking for it," Deborah finally spoke. "And you finally gave it to me. That's all I wanted. Now I know I have vulnerabilities to work on.

"That was the most wonderful thing you've done for me yet. I know it was hard for you, but I deeply appreciate it. From now on, I expect nothing less."

Deborah then sucked in a gulp of air, fighting back the pain, and ignoring the acidic taste in her mouth. She still felt like she might vomit at any moment.

Summoning every ounce of concentration, Deborah resumed her previous composure, and with her foot, she kicked Barak's spear back over to him.

"Now come on!" she yelled, then winced. Simply yelling ached her abdomen. Barak started laughing as Deborah resumed her spinning tent peg.

"You're insane, I know that hurt!"

Deborah grinned, fiercely determined, still seething in pain. Barak picked up his spear. Deborah whipped out her spike again, this time striking sand on the ground. A spurt of sand shot up into Barak's eyes.[6]

Then in a swift maneuver, Deborah swept a back kick to Barak's heel, flipping him to the ground. This time, she was very careful not to overextend!

The instant Barak fell on his back, she spun the spike and slammed it into the ground with a thud between his legs, nearly impaling his crotch.

"Hah!" one of the other men yelled and pointed with glee.

"Are you mad? That nearly got me!" Barak yelled at her.

"The glory of this battle is yours!"[7] The other man pointed at Deborah while shouting his declaration. Everyone instantly cheered for Deborah as she smiled, then suddenly dropped to her knees and gushed out a blob of vomit.

No problem.

After spitting a few times, she wiped off her mouth then presented a thumbs up while grinning ear to ear. A tear trickled down her cheek.

Back in Ramah, kicking and punching in an obscure location behind a nearby tent, Deborah's friend Jael was shadow sparring by herself, mimicking Deborah's movements.

Jael kicked high in the air, then stumbled over a garden tool and fell in front of a much older man dressed in expensive silks. He was intently observing her.

"Oh, hi there!" Jael greeted Heber while she stood up and dusted herself off.

"Jael, how have you been?" Heber asked her.

She smiled bashfully, clearly pleased to see him. "I was wondering if we would see you again."

Interrupting their conversation before it fully started, Haran approached from behind to fetch Heber and introduce him to the warriors in training.

"Everyone, this is Heber, a chief metalworker among the Kenites." The warriors paused in their training and nodded to Heber, giving him their undivided attention.

"Is that your white donkey?" one of the men asked him, pointing at the unusual steed. Who else but this over-dressed guy would have brought such an unusual animal to Ramah?

"Indeed it is," Heber replied.

Ooh, a white donkey. Jael was extremely impressed with this creature and immediately rushed over to pet it.

"We Kenites make the best spears. Here, try these, I offer fair trade,"[8-9] Heber pointed to a collection of spears leaning against a nearby tree.

One of the men grabbed the spears and distributed them. Heber's attention was keenly directed toward Deborah as she was handed a spear.

"You train with these men?" Heber questioned her. Deborah pretended not to hear him. She then suddenly spun the spear at lightning speed and flung it at a tree twenty feet away, impaling it expertly, center mass. Her training was paying off.

"We should get one, I like that spear," she commented to her father.

Heber was abundantly aroused with this powerful display. This young, athletic woman could handle herself. Heck, a wife like that could double as a secret body guard!

"Young lady, are you engaged?" Heber questioned Deborah directly in front of Haran. Deborah glanced at her father with an annoyed expression. Haran smile-frowned and shrugged.

Did Heber increase his dowry offer, or what? Time to put this to rest.

"Yes," Deborah answered Heber.

"You are?" both Haran as well as Barak questioned her at the same time. Deborah didn't realize it, but Barak overheard Heber's question, as well as Deborah's answer.

"To whom?" Haran asked.

"Not you," Deborah pointed her finger at Heber. She then wondered if her father took her earlier comment about being the one to say 'no' a little too far.

Some of the warriors chuckled at this somewhat humiliating interaction, but Heber accepted it lightheartedly, shrugged, then turned toward Jael, who by now was observing them.

"What about you, are you engaged?"

Jael blushed, speechless.

What was going on with Heber? Every time he came to Ramah, he piddled around all the homes with young females making inquiries. Now he was cutting straight to the chase.

As Jael strolled away conversing excitedly with Heber, Deborah stared at them, puzzled. Barak then approached her and asked, "She likes him?"

"You really think so?" Deborah grimaced.

"Sort of looks like it to me, but hey, none of my business. Let's say we take these spears and do some target practice out back?"

"Sounds good." Deborah snatched a spear from Barak, and the two approached Barak's horse.

"You are such a splendid steed," Deborah addressed Barak's horse while petting his face and inspecting her own reflection in his large almond shaped eyes.

"You are a good horse, a very good horse," she wrapped her arms around the horse's neck, hugged him and ran her fingers through his mane. Barak's horse whinnied softly, soaking up the affection.

Barak watched Deborah with deep admiration, seeing how she had a way with animals. His horse truly loved her; he would always get very excited and make horse noises whenever she greeted him.

Of course, part of that was because she occasionally offered him a carrot, but she was the only person aside from Barak that would give him that degree of affection.

Deborah equals carrot. Carrot good; Deborah awesome! Such were the contemplations of Barak's steed.

"Should I be jealous?" Barak questioned her while she hugged his horse.

"What can I say, I have a thing for studs," Deborah patted Barak's chest with a flirt. "Come on, let's go."

Commentary Notes

1. Rick Meyers, "Equipping Ministries Foundation, e-Sword Bible software, version 12.2.0,"
2. Human Weapon, Krav Maga Israel, https://www.youtube.com/watch?v=bt8w92ilbVM, (Last Accessed December 12, 2020). Part of the inspiration for Deborah's warrior persona comes from watching video clips of Israel's top ranking Israeli Krav Maga instructor in the world, Avivit Cohen. In this clip, she exhibits some of her deadly skills, tough personality, and warrior mindset. This video shows water training at 20:16.
3. Lawrence O. Richards, *Bible Reader's Companion*, (Colorado Springs, CO: Cook Communications Ministries, 2004), p. 163. "In Old Testament times, taking down and putting up the tent, including driving tent pegs in hard ground, was the job of nomadic women." For this story, I was searching for a unique "signature weapon" for Deborah's character. Indiana Jones had a whip, King Arthur had Excalibur, and many comic book characters have unique weapons. What was Deborah's unique weapon? Analyzing the details of this Biblical narrative, from Judges 5:8, we see that weapons were limited, so what might have been a make-shift starter weapon that Deborah could have readily obtained? Something not normally used as a weapon, but was used as a weapon in this Biblical narrative, was a tent peg, Judges 4:21.
4. The Human Weapon, Krav Maga Human Weapon Israel, https://www.youtube.com/watch?v=UpyoYuTW_V8, (Last Accessed December 12, 2020). Adding to Deborah's signature weapon, in this video clip, we see the famous Israeli Krav Maga instructor Dr. Dennis Hanover at 28:25, spinning a knife around, attached to a cord. This is highly unusual; people don't normally spin knives around on cords! Seeing this inspired the idea of a tent peg attached to a cord, because tent pegs are often attached to cords under normal circumstances. Deborah therefore might have thought of something like this to practice with. Such a weapon could have various uses, serving as both a spike, as well as having whip-like properties.

5. The Human Weapon, Krav Maga Israel, https://www.youtube.com/watch?v=bt8w92ilbVM, (Last Accessed December 12, 2020). Adonia uses one of Avivit Cohen's statements about Krav Maga, 17:07, "There are no rules."
6. Ibid. Avivit Cohen says at 16:58, "...you see something, you pick it up," describing the intense level of improvising involved in Krav Maga martial arts.
7. Ibid. Avivit Cohen explains with a hand full of dirt at 14:07, any instant of vulnerability might be met with dirt in the eyes.
8. See note 10 for Chapter 23.
9. It is likely that Heber regularly interacted with both the Canaanites, and the Israelites, which supports that the idea that he could have been a weapons merchant.

Chapter 6:

Prayers to Yahweh

ו

Flinging her spear through the air, Deborah struck a tree above the target she marked; about one foot too high. Barak took his turn, hitting a little closer to the mark for his tree.

"You're just as good as any of us," Barak gave Deborah a genuine compliment. "And really, you should accept what I say for once and not force me to punch or kick you, just to get you to believe me."

"Not to worry," she replied as they strolled together to fetch their spears.

"So uh," Barak stammered, lacking his usual bravado, beaming confidence. "I'm pretty sure you've noticed by now, the way Adonia and even your father have been giving us some breathing room. I mean look, here we are, all alone. Your father saw us leave together."

Deborah nodded, smiling at the ground.

"Do you have an idea what that means...*what all this means*?"

"My father likes you," Deborah was still smiling at the ground as they walked.

"You don't think it means a little more than that?"

"Maybe," Deborah teased.

"You want me to tell you what it means?" Barak spoke softly, almost in a whisper. Deborah remained quiet, allowing the silence to permeate the air.

The two stopped walking and faced each other.

Barak touched the tips of his fingers beneath her chin, trying to lift her gaze to his eyes. When their eyes met, he slid the back of his fingers down her cheek. Her honey brown eyes sparkled in the crimson sunset.

He brushed away a wisp of her hair, lightly cupped her face in his fingertips, and simply stared at her. He was in no hurry, focusing on one eye, then the other, etching the image of this glorious creature into his soul.

"It means you're the one," he whispered in a low tone.

Misty eyed, Deborah opened her mouth slightly, allowing his words to pour life into her being, flowing throughout her body with intoxicating ecstasy.

He moved his fingertips to her lips, marveling at her perfection. This woman was created by God...*for him*. He had no doubt of this, because everything about her, absolutely everything, he adored incomprehensibly.

At times, during his prayers in the night, he sometimes confessed that he feared the overwhelming captivation she held over him.

Was he treading in dangerous territory? She was not his God; by no means should he ever worship her, yet he fashioned an idol of her in his mind nonetheless.

Dear God, please do not become jealous, and forgive me when I stray; when the earth melts away, and all that remains is her image in my mind. Give me a strength greater than Adam, that I would obey your voice over hers, if ever it comes to that.

"I better not kiss you," Barak gasped while stroking her hair, soaking in her presence. He then gripped her shoulders and replied, "There's nobody around to stop us."

"And I don't trust myself to stop you," Deborah heard herself speaking with unfiltered honesty. Who was that talking? She felt the wag of her tongue, the movement of her lips, but she had little control over them. She lost that the moment Barak touched them.

They continued to gaze into each other's eyes and slowly move closer to each other, but then the familiar sound of a horse's hooves tromped in the distance.

Ah, perhaps this was a welcome distraction, for soon, someone else would be in their midst, so they surely couldn't take this too far in this deserted location.

Seizing the moment, Barak pulled Deborah in for a passionate kiss, focusing on her upper lip, tasting its delicate texture, feeling the heated exhalation of her nostrils against his cheek. They gripped each other fiercely with savage hunger.

Again and again, he kissed her lips, then her cheek, followed by her neck, but now those thudding horse hooves were close behind, just in time to cease their unveiling.

After one final kiss, they both stepped away from each other, light headed, searching for something to grasp for stability.

A warrior dressed in full battle attire, Gabriel, trotted up to the two of them. "I'm glad I found you. Your father needs you back at your post. Your training here is complete."

Barak's jaw fell open. Deborah did a double take at Gabriel, then looked back at Barak. "What?" she asked, though she heard exactly what the man said.

"Just like that?" Barak questioned.

"Haven't you heard of the increased aggression up north? It's looking like a battle could break out any day. This harassment is getting out of control. We're hoping a show of force will help stabilize the situation. We need all the men we can get."

Barak looked into Deborah's eyes. Separating at this point was utterly unbearable. "I have to go," he sighed, "but you and I have unfinished business," he tapped the tip of her nose.

Deborah nodded in return with tears trickling down her cheeks.

"They always send a detachment to the festival at Shiloh. I will be there."

If Deborah were crying blood, the capillaries of her tear ducts were transforming into arteries.

"Don't cry; warriors don't cry," Barak whimpered while wiping away one of her tears. Seeing her weep was far more painful than any wound received in the heat of battle.

Barak finally broke down; a few tears started streaming down his own cheeks. Deborah laughed and cried at the same time, wiping the tears from his cheeks.

"Look at you," she was amazed, never having seen a man in tears before.

The man on the horse sat there grinning at them until Barak finally addressed him. "What? You can go now."

Shortly after Barak left, Deborah didn't return home right away. Instead, she wandered through town, gazing at the stars and mumbling to herself, until she ended up near two large palm trees, side by side.

This well-known landmark was a symbol of their town, marking the east entrance of Ramah.

At least these palms were blessed with companionship. Staring at the palms, Deborah recounted the two trees where she and Barak were at earlier in the day, before that devastating news arrived. They were enjoying a simple round of target practice.

Deborah's leather armor was fashioned with a series of sheaths, which she filled with sharpened tent pegs. She pulled out one of the tent pegs and flung it at one of the trees.

Thump; the peg sunk deep into the tree.

A bead of sap formed beneath the tent peg and oozed down the tree. That was an excellent throw; it landed exactly where she intended.

Deborah eventually opened a dialogue with the God of Israel; the one whose name they all knew, yet never mentioned in casual conversation. Yahweh.[1]

What's the point of all this? And what about Adonia's question, Lord? If you parted the Red Sea, then why do you continue to allow these Anakim to torment us? Why can't we be in peace? I apologize if it is wrong for me to ask such a question, but wouldn't it be foolish of me not to be honest with you?

Please don't get me wrong, I don't want to sound like a whiner. But a guy finally comes along that is just...so amazing, and now he's gone. Job was right, the Lord gives, and the Lord takes away, but if that's

what you do, then you must know how it makes us feel. Or do you?[2-3]

If you've never been one of us, dealing with all of our limitations, with our lack of knowledge, our lack of power, our lack of everything compared to you, then how could you know?[4] *It's one thing to have knowledge, but to experience life as we do, now that's knowing.*

Compared to the lowest of your holy ones, we're just a bunch of feeble mortals down here, blind, deaf, and crippled. They say you're all-knowing, but how could you know what it's like to be one of us; to experience a divine gift like the love of another soul unlike any other we've encountered, just to have that soul snatched away?

How could you know?

As these thoughts ran their course through Deborah's mind, she suddenly shouted to the starry sky, "Have you ever considered not giving to us in the first place? If I didn't know what I lost, I for one think I'd be a heck of a lot better off!"

A dog started barking in the distance.

"I'm sorry, but I have to say it, because I can't help thinking it, and you already know what I'm thinking, right?

From where I'm at, it looks like you're on your throne, completely disconnected from us. I'm sorry, you know I don't mean to offend you. I just... I guess that's all I have to say for now."

Deborah sighed, wiped her tears and tried to shed the external evidence of all of this sorrow before she reached home. As she meandered through the gate to her yard, she encountered Caleb blocking the way to her door, challenging her to a battle.

"I'm not in the mood Caleb," Deborah moaned. The zest of life was wrung out of her like an old dish cloth, but Caleb didn't care. In fact, he actually interpreted this as a greater opportunity for success. She was in a weakened state, and he wasn't going to pass this up.

Caleb charged across the yard, leaped in the air and slammed Deborah in the abdomen with the most powerful head butt he could muster.

Deborah skid backward about a foot, but she remained on her feet. Caleb thought he had her this time, even adding that leap to his full force attack, but it wasn't enough.

Ever since Barak punched Deborah in the gut, she allowed Caleb the luxury of head butting her in the abdomen on a regular basis, to serve as additional training. Caleb's lessons were paying off; her rock hard abs were pretty much immune to him by now.

Caleb was frustrated to no end, and he reared up on his back legs, preparing for yet another head butt, but Deborah instantly tackled him, landed on top of him and pinned him down.

"Okay, enough!" she immobilized him. Just then, the front door opened. Deborah looked up, dirt smudged across her face, straw in her hair.

"You're late for your lessons," her mother chided her, "and you let the pigeons out again. They're all over the house!"

"Sorry mother, I'm coming," Deborah replied. As soon as the door shut, Caleb finally bleated for mercy and she released him. As soon as he jumped up, he stared at her momentarily, contemplating yet another attack, but then he let it go and walked away.

Another day, our paths shall cross...

Later that evening, Deborah was sitting with her mother at the kitchen table with a velum scroll partially unrolled on the table.[5-7] Miriam was quizzing Deborah on Mosaic Law. "If a man shall steal an ox, or a sheep, and kill it or sell it, how much shall he restore?"[8]

Deborah stared at the flickering candle on the table.

"Deborah?"

"I'm leaving to Mount Tabor," Deborah blurted out.

"You'll do no such thing!" Miriam corrected her. Just then, Haran approached from the other side of the room.

"What brings you to this?"

"There are no questions, the answer is no!" Miriam interrupted with a resounding declaration.

"But Israel needs warriors, people who are willing to fight!" Deborah insisted.

"I told you where this would lead, all this...*training*," Miriam hissed at her husband.

"Deborah, when all the men leave for battle, who will defend Ramah?" Haran brought up an intriguing point Deborah never considered.

Rather than telling her to stay away from battle, he instead appealed to her usefulness as a warrior protecting their home.

"Stop it! She is a woman!" Miriam yelled at Haran. She then turned to Deborah and bellowed at the top of her lungs, "You're place is not on a battlefield!"

Haran and Deborah briefly looked at each other, both thinking the same thing. Miriam was showing her warrior spirit to both of them, somewhat invalidating her own point, because their house was turning into a battlefield.

Miriam was getting so upset, she was about to flip the kitchen table.

Deborah tried to reason with her mother, though she knew it would be of little use. "How can you say that? I can fight."

"Yes, at the expense of making a mockery of our family! Don't you realize what they say about you?"

"Who cares?" Deborah fired back.

"Enough," Haran jutted out his hand to halt the argument. After a brief pause, he finally broke the silence.

"I've seen enough of the way you and Barak interact with each other. If he should ever ask for your hand, I would give my consent. But he doesn't want you on the battlefield any more than we do."

"Have you asked him?" Deborah challenged her father's assessment.

"What are you trying to prove? Why do you have to draw such attention to yourself?" Miriam was now pleading in desperation.

"This was never about me mother, it never was!" Deborah countered. "This is about father, when we travel to other towns. It's about you, if ever danger should come here to Ramah.

"It's about...everyone in Israel! You said yourself, our people wandered this desert for twenty years because they were not willing to fight."

"It was forty years!"[9] Miriam cried out, now incensed that Deborah was so lax on her lessons, her head was totally in the clouds.

"I said enough!" Haran yelled. After a deep breath, he then tried to deescalate the argument by speaking calmly. "Honey Bee, I wanted you to know how to defend yourself, but not go to battle. If you go, it is without my blessing."

"Who needs your blessing?" Deborah roared, then suddenly leaped up from the table, flipping it over in the process, then she stormed across the room and slammed the door on the way out.

Oy.

Haran quickly picked up the candle on the floor before it caught anything on fire. He then carefully rolled up the vellum scroll and stood next to his wife and they both quietly stared at the door for the next minute or so.

As they both accurately predicted, the door slowly creaked open. Deborah re-entered and picked up the table, set the chairs back in place, then sat down.

Another slice of humble pie, please...

"Seven," Deborah replied.

"What?" Miriam asked.

"He shall restore five oxen for an ox, and seven sheep for a sheep."

"Actually it's four sheep. And next time, how about not flipping the table?"

"It was an accident. Wait, four? Everything else is seven. Who cares? Why do we study the law? I'll never need to know it. Sisera rampages all over the place, and no one ever does anything. Just because we're so far south doesn't mean we're not part of Israel."

"You're tired, go to bed," Miriam replied.

Deborah pouted in the chair, refusing to budge.

"Do it," Haran agreed with his wife.

As the long night passed that evening, it was time to try to return to life's routines before this chapter of warrior training transpired, but there was no going back.

Most of the men were gone now. A week had passed, and Deborah was dressed in her full battle attire, standing alone in her yard where they usually trained.

All the young men with their newly honed skills left with Barak, recruited with glowing recommendations from him to join their forces at Mount Tabor. Even Adonia was leaving soon, though he said he would return in a few months.

So all this training in Ramah, which was a movement inspired by

So many conversations she had with this goat; she shared everything with him. He listened, and he responded with a profound, eerie comprehension. He knew what she was saying. She knew he knew.

While Deborah sobbed uncontrollably, clutching her beloved friend, she heard one of her neighbors sobbing as well. "Murderer!" her neighbor screamed.

"Life for a life!"[10] The woman screamed again while pointing in the direction they left. She then saw Deborah in her yard and started to stumble in her direction.

"They murdered my husband!" she bawled, tormented in agony, overcome with inconsolable grief. She then vented her rage on Deborah.

"I've seen you out here training with those men! What are you going to do about this? Or are you just like they all say around here, a harlot putting on a show?"

Deborah trembled in sorrow, then rage; then outright fury. Tremors in her hands shivered up her arms and into her face.

What just happened?

Who gave these sick, vile cretins the right to ride into town on a senseless, murderous rampage, all the while laughing about it? Was there no one willing to take a stand?

Now, even Caleb was gone. She convulsed with Caleb's lifeless body in her arms, then she set her eyes on his severed head. Utter madness.

Snap!

Deborah, mobilized all the young men in town, and then sent them all away. Only Deborah remained, bereft of her father's blessing to join them.

And now Deborah's popularity among the young ladies in town was beyond redemption, for they all blamed her directly for the multiplied anguish of heartache they were all going through.

Yes, this was all Deborah's fault. Like a succubus from the pit, she lured all the young men in town into a lair in her yard, beguiled them, and then sent them all away to get killed.

Nice. Thank you Deborah, much appreciate that...

Throughout Ramah, there was an eerie silence, like a calm before the storm. So strange, the sounds of sparring in the yard were so fresh in her ears, Deborah almost thought she heard something, but then she realized, that wasn't an echoed memory.

In the distance, there really were the trampling hooves of horses, but other sounds accompanied those hooves; an unfamiliar rumbling.

Deborah walked through the opening in the wall around her home and tried to see what the commotion was.

Over near the east entrance of Ramah, four of Sisera's mounted war chariots rolled into Ramah single-file. One of the four chariots stopped at Jael's home.

A soldier dismounted the chariot, approached the door, and without warning, he kicked it open. A great deal of angry shouting ensued inside the house.

Haran opened the front door; Miriam was behind him. "Get over here," he called to Deborah, and Deborah returned to the house.

"This is strange, they never bring chariots down here," Haran commented, concerned.

"It's only been one week with most of the men gone up north. Do you think someone told them?" Deborah asked her father.

"Quiet, here they come," Haran motioned for Deborah to come inside their home. "Whatever you do, don't do anything stupid!" he warned her.

A few minutes later, one of the soldiers was pounding on their door. Haran answered, and the second he cracked it open, a soldier forcefully shoved it open all the way and he and two other armed men barged into their home.

Immediately, one of the soldiers spotted Heber's two spears that he recently sold them, leaning against a wall. He snatched them up, and the Captain in charge gripped Haran's cloak in his fist at his chest and gave it a hearty jerk.

"Where did you get these?" he questioned him.

Deborah instinctively took a defensive stance, but Harran motioned to her with his eyes to stand down.

One of the men eyed Deborah lustfully with a twisted grin.

"We use them to hunt," Haran calmly replied.

The Captain shoved Haran against the wall; Miriam gasped in response. The soldier eyeing Deborah then tried to grope her, but Deborah blocked his hand reflexively. "Don't touch me," she snapped at him.

"Hunt? Right; hunt without them," the Captain replied gruffly. He let go of Haran's cloak, glared at each of them momentarily, then walked back outside. The other men followed him out, and Miriam sighed with relief.

Outside, the men were laughing, then suddenly there was the grisly sound of a sword hacking through flesh and bone. "Damn animal," one

of the men shouted.

Deborah's eyes widened in horror. She instantly bolted to the door, but Haran leapt in front of her to block the way. She tried to shove her way past him, but he gripped her in a bear hug and struggled to hold her back.

"Let me go!" she shouted, but the two struggled until they finally heard the chariot riding away. "Stop!" Haran tried to arrest her rage, but she continued to struggle until she finally succeeded in breaking free and slipping out the door.

There on the front lawn, Deborah collapsed on Caleb's decapitated corpse, howling in anguish. She then let out a gut wrenching scream. All that sorrow of Barak leaving rushed back, and now combined with the loss of her longtime childhood friend.

What did Caleb ever do to anyone, to warrant this brutal slaughter?

Deborah was there the day he was born. She cared for him when he was sick. She used to sneak him into her room at night when it was raining outside. And he never tired of their rough housing games. He chased her; she chased him.

Caleb was always there to cheer her up, without fail. He greeted her early in the morning, and late in the evening.

He could tell when she needed a distraction from life's agonies, whether life altering or minor. He held no grudges; his love was a simple joy and affection, pure through and through.

While most people had dogs as hunting companions, Deborah had Caleb. He routinely went hunting with her, and they climbed the rocky hills together outside of town.

Commentary Notes

++
++++++++++++++++++++++

1. Scott Alan Roberts, *The Rise and Fall of the Nephilim*, (Pompton Plains, NJ: 2012), p. 171. The Hebrews regarded the true name of their tribal God, Yahweh, as far too sacred for common use, and they usually called Him simply "Lord" (Hebrew Adonai or sometimes Lord).
2. See Job 14:1, in her prayer, Deborah echoes Job's sentiments about how difficult life is as a human being, "short-lived and full of turmoil."
3. See Job 1:21, being familiar with Job, Deborah quotes his lament and acceptance of God's rule, however painful it can be, "The Lord gives, and the Lord takes away."
4. The Next Faithful Step, "The Self-Emptying of Christ", Fuller Seminary, https://www.fuller.edu/next-faithful-step/resources/kenosis/, (Last Accessed, December 12, 2020). This article is about Kinosis, which explains what it meant for God to become fully human in the person of Jesus, setting aside his omniscience and omnipotence, and taking upon Himself the limitations of humanity. In this New Testament, this is best expressed in Philippians 2:5-11, however, there are hints of this in the Old Testament as well. King David wrote in Psalm 8:4-5, "what is man that you are mindful of him, and the son of man that you care for him? You have made Him a little lower than the angels..." Here, King David is speaking of God, then he states that He [God] made him [Jesus?] a little lower than the angels, which speaks of God lowering himself below His angels. This prophecy of King David's was confirmed in Hebrews 2:7-9 as a reference to Jesus. Both King David and Deborah had many similarities. They both had prophetic anointing, a military authority and perspective, and they were both psalmists, so their prayers may have been similar. Deborah's prayer in this story, for God's understanding to be in her shoes and experience life from a limited human being's perspective, is similar to King David's Psalm, pointing to a future Messiah; one who would be an advocate for humanity, understanding from experience what it is like to be a fail, limited

human being.

5. Rick Meyers, "Equipping Ministries Foundation, e-Sword Bible software, version 12.2.0," downloaded Nov 20, 2020, http://ww

6. w.e-sword.net; *Sketches of Jewish Social Life, Synagogues: Their Origin, Structure, and Outward Arrangements*. Speaking of the vellum (leather) scroll, "At present the vellum, on which the Pentateuch is written, is affixed to two rollers, and as each portion of the law is read it is unrolled from the right, and rolled on to the left roller. The roll itself was fastened together by linen wrappers or cloths ('mitpachoth'), and then placed in a case' ('tik,' the Greek 'theke')"
7. Rick Meyers, "Equipping Ministries Foundation, e-Sword Bible software, version 12.2.0," downloaded Nov 20, 2020, http://www.e-sword.net; *History of the Christian Church (Philp Schaff)*, Vol. 4, Ch. 13, pp. 134-139. For a family to own a vellum scroll may be an indicator of wealth. "Many ancient libraries were destroyed over the centuries, by ruthless barbarians and the ravages of war. After the conquest of Alexandria by the Saracens, the cultivation and exportation of Egyptian papyrus ceased, and parchment or vellum, which took its place, was so expensive that complete copies of the Bible cost as much as a palace or a farm." Deborah's time predates the conquest of Alexandria by about 1,800 years, so many existing vellum scrolls and papyrus had not yet been destroyed by invaders. However, a scroll of the Mosaic Law might still have been very valuable in Deborah's time. Deborah likely did have access to a written copy of the Mosaic Law during her youth, because she was a judge. One must have studied the law in order to be an effective judge. Deborah was also an accomplished academic, familiar with reading and writing, hence, she authored Judges 4-5. In this story, making Haran's character a merchant, one of the wealthier members of her town, enabled him to afford academic luxuries that he used to invest in his daughter's education. The decision to make Deborah an only child also played a part in her character development. Deborah's character is highly unusual in the ancient Biblical narrative, because she exhibits a high level education, and she commands with authority, in a patriarchal society that often treated women as property. If Deborah was an only child, then it makes more sense for her father to invest more of everything he has into his only child,

regardless of whether that child is a female.

8. Rick Meyers, "Equipping Ministries Foundation, e-Sword Bible software, version 12.2.0," downloaded Nov 20, 2020, http://www.e-sword.net; *Preacher's Homiletical*, Judges 4:9. (Bracketed comments added). Regarding the wealth of Deborah's family, "Her [Deborah's] influence arose not from her social status, though that was considerable, if we are to believe the Chaldee paraphrase, who
9. tells us that she possessed palm-trees in Jericho, parks (or paradises) in Ramah, and productive olives in the valley, a house of irrigation in Bethel and white dust in the king's mount. But her peerless distinction was that the Spirit of the Lord spoke by her." This reference to Deborah's wealth from the Chaldee paraphrase, indicates her father would have been wealthier than depicted in this story, however, this story begins with Deborah in her youth, and not after forty years serving as Israel's judge and prophetess with the authority of a governess. So Deborah could have started out much as she is presented in this story, but became much wealthier over the years. It was because of her and Barak that Israel entered into a new season of prosperity.
10. See Exodus 22:1, "If a man steals an ox or a sheep, and kills it or sells it, he shall repay five oxen for an ox, and four sheep for a sheep." [ESV]
11. See Numbers 14:33-34. Israel wandered the desert for forty years.
12. See Deuteronomy 19:21, "Your eye shall not pity. It shall be life for life, eye for eye, tooth for tooth, hand for hand, foot for foot." [ESV]

Chapter 7:

Life for a Life!

ג

Gone was all manner of reason; all that remained was pure impulse. Deborah leapt up and sprinted to her neighbor's horse. Commandeering the steed, she leapt on him bareback and bolted out of town after those chariots.

Haran ran out of the house, but she was already zipping out of town.

"Life for a life!" the woman screamed at Deborah again, demanding justice.

Just outside of Ramah, the terrain was hilly and full of rocks, not advantageous for chariots.[1] That was the main reason they never saw chariots in the region, but these men might not have been down south enough to know that.

Deborah soon caught up to the last chariot, pulled out her trusty tent peg with cord attachment, then started whirling it around, intent to use the same maneuver she used on Barak's spear.

She rode up to the eight o'clock position, which was an essential location for this trick to work while on horseback.

The peg was zipping around so fast, it made a humming noise.

The moment that sensation of *locked on target* rushed through her veins, she released it toward the man in the last chariot, while simultaneously navigating her horse to the six o'clock position.

By now, Deborah had experimented with her makeshift tent peg cord enough to customize the peg with a particular shape that made it conducive to locking in place like a bullwhip. She also added a barb on the end of this particular peg.

The peg whirled through the air with an arc. The cord then passed over the throat of the soldier, and it spun in tight circles around his neck until it smacked the back of his head and locked in place.

Pulling back hard, Deborah's horse skid to a halt, yanking the charioteer off of his feet and out of the back of his chariot.

Wham!

The charioteer slammed to the ground with a booming thud. Deborah then gripped the cord with all her strength, and ordered her horse with a slight jab, "Yah!"

Ridding in the opposite direction, she drug the man through the rocky terrain, pummeling him senseless, and choking him to death. He flailed momentarily, but not for long.

Her first kill.

Deborah hopped off her horse and approached the man to untie her tent peg.

This was the same soldier who was sneering at her earlier. As she bent down to untangle her tent peg, the other charioteers finally realized what happened.

The lead charioteer tried to turn his chariot around, but he hit a large rock going too fast and his chariot flipped over, knocking him to the ground.

The other soldiers in their chariots stopped, leaped out of their chariots and started racing toward Deborah.

Deborah barely had enough time to untangle her cord, but not enough time to get back on her horse. Sword drawn, the first man reached her charging with a swing.

Deborah instantly ducked, then sprung up with a fist full of sand and threw it into his eyes. He took a blind swing and gashed Deborah's cheek.

These weren't wooden swords. Barak's words; his constant badgering and warnings that she complained endlessly about, echoed in her mind. This was why. A mistake at this point could cost her life.

Taking advantage of the soldier's blinded state, Deborah was able to leap back on her horse before another other soldier reached her. She

then galloped up to a hill further outside of town. "Come on!" Deborah yelled at the men, daring them to come near her.

By this time, the Captain in the lead made his way to his slain comrade and was infuriated that this girl, this village peasant, had the audacity to strike back at one of his men.

"Burn down the whole damn village!" he barked at his men.

"No!" Deborah bellowed back. "You want me, here I am!"

Thump!

An arrow suddenly sank into the Captain's eye socket. He dropped to the ground mid-stride, dead. Whoever shot that arrow was nowhere in sight.

Thump!

Another solider was pierced in the chest with yet another arrow. He only had time to look down at the arrow and acknowledge its presence, then fall over dead.

Three men down, a sniper nowhere in sight, and all of them were sitting ducks in the open.

The remaining soldiers quickly assessed the situation and sprinted back to their chariots, leaving their fallen comrades and two of the chariots behind.

From the top of the hill where she sat, Deborah scanned the area and finally spotted her father with Adonia; each had a bow in hand.

"Great shots!" she yelled in their direction. "Look at them go! We did it!"

"For now," Haran replied. "They'll be back."

While Sisera's men were getting trashed in Ramah, Sisera was blissfully unaware, enjoying his creature comforts, literal in this case, in his decadent temple of Baal.

No place was more popular among the residents of Hazor than Sisera's temple.

This imposing fortress, carved out of solid rock, adorned a mountaintop overlooking the Megiddo Valley. Its massive stone pillars towered over one hundred fifty feet above the valley floor, contrasting with the vast expanse of dry, desolate, mostly flat terrain below, extending to the far horizon.

Magnificent arches opened up this architectural wonder, with its polished stone floors, intricate carvings in the walls, crown molding, plush tapestries and gaudy artwork to tantalize the senses.

Sisera sat enthroned between two flaming cauldrons. Before him, robed figures were bowed around a magic symbol embedded in the floor. They quietly chanted in harmony with dreary, mystical music.

A scantily dressed temple prostitute wearing a wolf pelt danced lasciviously before him.

Sisera's equally large brother Lahmi stood next to him, adorned with a silver plated ox-skull helmet. He rested his six fingered hands on the hilt of a seven foot long battle axe.[2]

A Chief Hooded Figure emerged from a dark cave-like corridor at the far side of this spacious chamber.

Was he walking, or floating?

His hood obscured his face, and he drifted with a perfect forward momentum; no upward or downward variation as one would expect with footsteps. He must have practiced this walk for hours on end to perfect it.

His robe was more ornate than the others entranced in their mindless chanting. Its folds glided across the floor, serpent-like, silent and smooth.

"Your liege, I have seen it. The heathen of Ramah have attacked us," hissed the Chief Hooded Figure.

"Excellent," Sisera's deep, rumbling voice reverberated in the open chamber.

"Those of Ramah will soon attend a festival at their beloved temple. If we strike there, we can also destroy the ark of their God," the Chief Hooded Figure advised.

"I will not destroy it," Sisera replied. "I will use it; I will harness its power."[3-4]

"My lord, the ark is not just an artifact. It is the throne of their God. It serves its master."[5]

Sisera stood up, and for a brief instant, his eyes pulsated red as he spoke. The flames in the cauldrons flanking him popped and sparked with emphasis.

"I will be its new master! I will dedicate it in this temple, to myself, with the blood of Israelites!" Sisera declared with a growl.

The Chief Hooded Figure dropped to his knees, trembling. "As you wish, master" he hissed.

Sisera then walked over to the open archway and out onto the balcony. The Chief Hooded Figure rose to his feet and hovered after him.

"My lord, there is something else. I see a young woman, a scar on her cheek. Something about her..."

"What?" Sisera asked.

"A warning perhaps."

Sisera's intelligence reports were well beyond what King Jabin or General Arad could fathom.

The Chief Hooded Figure, Malchus, was Sisera's first official disciple. He was also an Israelite; or at least he used to be before he was exiled for practicing sorcery.

The High Priest before Elias ordered the people of his town to give him the death penalty, but they refused. The High Priest then visited his town in person, accompanied with an armed warrior.[6-7]

Malchus fled into the wilderness, and settled in a camp of Canaanites and other disenfranchised Israelites that had been cut off for disobeying the Mosaic law.[8]

Among the Canaanites and the Egyptians, Malchus studied their sorcery and magic. In time, he became a high priest of several pagan gods.

When he witnessed Sisera for the first time, he saw greatness in him. He also saw an opportunity to join forces with someone who hated Israelites as much as he did, so he swore his allegiance.

In return, Sisera richly rewarded him, adding even more power to what he had already attained through years of practice in the dark arts.

The cancerous tumor of Sisera's temple was a spiritual blot on the landscape, spreading its tentacles in the bowels of the earth.

Idols of Baal were now competing with idols of Asherah, Molech, and other pagan gods.[9] Even idols of Sisera were starting to appear in various homes throughout Israel.[10]

Rumors spread throughout Israel about the worldly Israelites up north, flocking to Sisera's temple. Most were lured there by prostitution, psychedelic herbs, and money.[11-12]

Young women could make a lot of money in Sisera's temple, quick and easy, and young men enjoyed spending it there.

Sisera's temple also offered young ladies, including the prostitutes, a convenient service to brush unwanted pregnancies under the rug.[13-14]

Rather than face the wrath of angry parents, for a modest fee, young pregnant teens could sneak off to the temple and dispose of their un-

Still, she needs to get out; break the routine. I think the festival would help; there's music and dancing, delicious food..."

"Food?"Deborah's eyes suddenly lit up. "You're right! The festival! I can't believe it's here again! I completely forgot, Lapi's going to be there!"

"He is?"

"What am I going to wear?"Deborah fretted while gripping Jael's shoulders. "Do you still have that...?"

"Yes," Jael answered excitedly, "I'll let you borrow it!"

"My mother's perfume; do you think that...?"

"Of course! It's lovely," Jael was brimming with excitement for her best friend.

Later that night, Deborah gazed into a small flat piece of polished silver, but her distorted image left much to be desired. The most she could tell with it, was the cut on her cheek was probably going to turn into a scar, but Deborah actually didn't mind.

It was a battle scar.

"Wow, you are absolutely amazing! I have never seen you so beautiful!" Jael was thrilled and brimming with excitement for her friend, and she was right. Deborah was never so dressed up in all her life in Jael's highly ornate, colorful dress.

in all her life in Jael's highly ornate, colorful dress.

The dress was a gift from Heber to Jael. Fortunately for Deborah, Heber had several dresses designed for Jael with extra material in the inseams, allowing for future growth in areas where he hoped she would fill out as she matured.

Jael was an excellent seamstress, so she allowed Deborah to pick out one of her dresses, and she tailored it for her. The results were stunning.

In addition to the dress, Jael added some beaded sandals, a cloak covering, and a gold colored rope for a belt.

And so it was, in the bowels of Sisera's lavish temple of Baal.

For the two men in Ramah who claimed to have gone to Sisera's temple of Baal, and saw Sisera for themselves, they each purchased an idol of Sisera in the temple gift shop. They wanted to show it off to their friends back home.

They didn't take these idols seriously, but there were a few elders in Ramah who were extremely upset about those stone statues when they saw them.

Jael's cousin was one of the two men in question who bought an idol of Sisera. When her cousin brought it home to show to his father, they laughed about it, but Jael's father wasn't pleased with his brother at all. Just keeping that thing in their home created a rift in the entire family.

Jael's father was not a faithful Israelite; he practiced very little of his faith, but for him, that idol was disrespectful to their community. Not believing the legends of old was one thing, but openly mocking them was uncalled for.

As for Jael, she was on the fence. When she was at home, she was exposed to her father and other members of her family, some of who-moutright ridiculed the Israeli faith.

However, when she was with her best friend Deborah, she was exposed to Deborah's wandering thoughts about the God of Israel.

Deborah had faith; she believed, though she often admitted that she sometimes didn't understand her God very well.

Jael admired this honesty.

Deborah's God loved the Israelites, and He rescued them in times past, but where was He now? Who understood His ways? And why did they have so many rules to follow?

The Mosaic Law seemed endless. But of course, most of that opinion stemmed from Deborah's lack of interest. She didn't think she'd ever need to know the bulk of the Mosaic Law.

Why bother memorizing the consequences of stealing oxen or sheep, when she didn't own any, nor did she want any?

wanted pregnancies on Sisera's clean, polished altar.

Sisera's priests were very discreet, and highly skilled in the art of human sacrifice. They could safely remove the contents of any womb with specialized herbs and sanctified temple instruments before anyone ever even knew they were pregnant.[15]

For Sisera's priests, these inconvenient accidents were always welcome in the temple. They were considered holy sacrifices, passing through the sacred fires at the altar of Baal.

The glamor, glitz, and pleasures of Sisera's temple were many.

The first level of bed chambers below were polished and pristine, reserved for high paying customers. This first level was the rebuilt city complex of ancient times, now modernized with gift shops.

Sisera sold standard items, such as musical instruments and furs, but more common were psychedelic herbs and associated paraphernalia, occult trinkets, scrolls, and ingredients for sorcery. There were also countless games for gambling.

As for the chambers further below, they decreased in quality the further down they went.

Most customers were not even allowed to go to the deepest chambers, until they obtained a certain level of trust with Sisera. Needless to say, the customers, contents, and activities of the deepest chambers were not advertised to the public.[16]

Near the bottom, the prostitutes were slaves, diseased and addicted. They resembled corpses writing in agony; self-loathing; suicidal. These were a pitied, wretched lot to look upon, which is why they were kept in the dark.

And other chambers were reserved for the depths of depravity; places to which the most corrupt minds could explore their deepest, darkest fantasies.

These often involved blood or other fluidic concoctions, entrails, sacrifices of all kinds, incomprehensible, twisted fetishes, and all manner of sexual deviance.[17-18]

Unlike most others in Ramah, Deborah wasn't afraid to voice her questions from time to time, often to her mother's annoyance. Miriam was insistent, Deborah was going to learn or else! But Deborah was always full of questions, often difficult to answer.

While Miriam was often annoyed with Deborah's questions, it was that inquisitive aspect of her personality that made her faith more genuine in Jael's opinion.

In the very least, Jael thought Deborah's God was more intriguing than the god of nothingness in her own family. Yahweh was also more meaningful than the disgusting associations surrounding the pagan gods.

Jael and Deborah frequently spoke with each other about anything that came to mind, and issues of faith often entered their conversations.

Jael was Deborah's only female friend in town at the moment, and now with Barak up north, Jael was selfishly happy that he was out of the picture for the time being. For the past few months, Deborah was spending much more time with her.

"Well I don't know, I wasn't really thinking," Deborah whispered to Jael. "But I believe the Lord delivered him into my hands, because I've never been so accurate while riding a horse. Everything happened so quickly," she explained.

"When are you going to give me some more lessons?" Jael pestered her.

"Did you ask your parents yet?" Deborah reminded her.

"Okay, I'll ask, but if I can get them to agree, will you?"

"You know I will! I don't know why every female in Ramah isn't asking me the same thing. It's only a matter of time before they come back, and it's going to be worse when they do. Now quiet down, I think he's just right over there," Deborah whispered.

The two were about a mile outside of Ramah, tracking a fallow deer.[19] Jael was taking Caleb's place, keeping her company for the hunt.[20]

As they crept up to a small mound, they both spotted a fallow deer and Deborah gave a hand signal to hunker down.

As Deborah was aiming an arrow, Jael accidentally stepped on a twig, causing the fallow deer to panic. Deborah instantly shot it in the heart, dropping it with a single shot.

"Wow!" Jael leaped up, "I thought I messed it all up; you're so quick!"

Deborah flung her cord-bound tent peg around a tree branch. They both then hoisted up the fallow deer. Deborah splayed it open with a sharp stone knife to remove the entrails and drain the blood.

"I wonder how Naomi's doing," Deborah pondered. "I can't image what she must be going through. At least there was justice, thanks to Adonia, but that still won't bring back her husband."

"I heard her sister is living with her now. I hope she convinces her to go to the festival; she is still young enough to get married again."

"It's only been a few months; I'd give it at least a year," Deborah replied.

"Still, she needs to get out; break the routine. I think the festival would help; there's music and dancing, delicious food..."think it's too much."

"You're right about that, but that has nothing to do with this outfit. Any guy who lays eyes on you, whether you're wearing this or battle armor, think's you're too much, but that's not a bad thing. I know Barak will like this, trust me."

"But he's never seen me like this. What if he laughs?" Deborah fretted.

"Oh he won't laugh. You should take my necklace too."

"Where did you get this?"

"Heber gave it to me. He says it was made by some famous master craftsman."

Deborah took the necklace and analyzed it up close, marveling at the details. "This is incredible. Heber must want to marry you."

Jael beamed with delight. “He does; he already asked. Father hasn’t given his blessing yet, but I think he will.”

“Congratulations!” Deborah hugged her, sharing in her joy, and simultaneously concealing her bewilderment.

Heber...*seriously*? The guy was afraid of bugs; a most unimpressive man of soft living.

Sure, he was wealthy, and dressed to impress, but even with age and obesity set aside, would he last a day in the wilderness without abortion services for profit under this guise.

14. The Old Testament refers to the Israelites adopting the pagan practices of their neighboring nations. They caused their children, particularly their firstborn, to “pass through the fire” as human sacrifices to pagan gods, 2 Kings 16:3, 17:17, 21:6, 23:10; 2 Chronicles 33:6; Ezekiel 20:26, 31, 23:37; Jeremiah 32:35, etc. A common interpretation of “passing through the fire” was thought to include living children capable of walking. However, that may have not been the case. Later scriptures, such as Isaiah 57:5 and Jeremiah 19:5, speak of the Israelites murdering their children, and offering them as “burnt offerings.” It is therefore likely that a pagan temple would offer abortion services for profit, not much different than the modern day abortion industry.

15. Rick Meyers, “Equipping Ministries Foundation, e-Sword Bible software, version 12.2.0,” downloaded Nov 20, 2020, http://www.e-sword.net; Didache, The Teachings of the Twelve Apostles, Ante-Nicene Fathers, Volume 7, chapter 2. Around the 2nd century A.D., there are specific references to abortion in the Didache; abortion is included in a list of forbidden gross sins, “though shalt not murder a child by abortion nor kill that which is begotten.”

16. Rick Meyers, “Equipping Ministries Foundation, e-Sword Bible software, version 12.2.0,” downloaded Nov 20, 2020, http://www.e-sword.net; Hippolytus - Refutation of All Heresies, Book 9, Chapter 7. Around the third century A.D., there are more specific references of pagan practices integrated with abortion services. “Whence women, reputed believers, began to resort to drugs for producing sterility, and to gird themselves round, so to expel what was being conceived on account of their not wishing to have a child either by a slave or by any paltry fellow, for the sake of their family and excessive wealth.”

1. itual elements of shamanism, shamans use powerful, dangerous halluci
2. nogenic drugs, which are integrated with their practices, both due to their hallucinogenic properties, and also for healing purposes. Because of this, various forms of ancient shamanism are linked to modern day equivalents of the legal and illegal drug industry. Mr. Brown describes a scene, when Yankush, the shaman he knew, "entered into a trance by inducing a bitter, hallucinogenic concoction he had taken just before sunset (it is made from a vine known as ayahuasca)." The antics associated with the hallucinogenic drugs are part of what stage the dramatic presentations of the healing ceremonies. Since these drugs are in use and available to shamans, it is likely they would also be available for recreational use as well, for the right price.
3. An obvious link between drugs and sorcery is evident in scripture, with three translations of the English word for sorcery deriving from the Greek word for pharmakeia, where medication and magic are used interchangeably. See Galatians 5:19-21; Revelation 9:21, 18:23

   G5331

   φαρμακεία

   pharmakeia

   far-mak-i'-ah

   From G5332; *medication* ("pharmacy"), that is, (by extension) *magic* (literal or figurative): - sorcery, witchcraft.
   Total KJV occurrences: 3
4. Isidore Singer, George A. Barton, "Moloch (Molech)", JewishEncyclopedia, http://jewishencyclopedia.com/articles/10937-moloch-molech, (Last Accessed December 16, 2020). The Old Testament refers to the Israelites adopting the pagan practices of their neighboring nations. They caused their children, particularly their firstborn, to "pass through the fire" as human sacrifices to pagan gods, 2 Kings 16:3, 17:17, 21:6, 23:10; 2 Chronicles 33:6; Ezekiel 20:26, 31, 23:37; Jeremiah 32:35, etc. "As to the rites which the worshipers of Molech performed, it has sometimes been inferred, from the phrase "pass through the fire to Molech," that children were made to pass between two lines of fire as a kind of consecration or februation; but it is clear from Isaiah 57:5 and Jeremiah 19:5, that the children were killed and burned. The whole point of the offering consisted, therefore, in the fact that it was a human

17. The obvious examples of inspiration for the description of Sisera's temple are Las Vegas, aka "Sin City,"and Los Angeles, a central hub of human trafficking, rampant drug addiction, and sexual immorality.

18. These explicit details are provided, to illustrate the reasoning behind God's intense hatred of idolatry and everything associated with it, expressed throughout the Bible.

19. Jesse Lyman Hurlbut, Hurlbut's Handy Bible Encyclopedia, (Philadelphia, PA: The John C. Winston Co., 1908), p. 118. "Fallow deer. This is uncertainty as to what animal is meant by this name.

four armed escorts wherever he went? He always had guards pampering him, catering to his every whim. He was the antithesis of Deborah's type.

"I especially like the belt," Deborah replied while spinning it. The material was tightly woven; a better quality than the cord attached to her tent peg.

While Jael was distracted with Deborah's low quality mirror, Deborah slipped on a dark leather shoulder strap full of sharpened tent pegs, draped across her chest. She then started to tie the belt rope to one of her tent pegs.

"What are you doing?" Jael finally noticed and gasped. The contrast between the leather strap with tent pegs and the colorful dress was ridiculous.

"You're not going to training! Show him another side of you, take that off!"

One early afternoon, a group of roughly forty villagers from Ramah traveled the main road to Shiloh, accompanied by four armed escorts. The guards were somewhat distracted, periodically ogling Deborah.

Deborah was adorned in Jael's eloquent outfit, and her hair was stylized unlike ever before, adding an aura of splendor. At any moment, a wild bird might perch on her shoulder and sing of her beauty, keeping harmony with her flute.

Deborah wasn't the only musically talented member among them. A number of other musicians brought their instruments as well. They practiced for the festivities ahead, filling everyone's ears with a cacophony of disjointed harmonies.

"I heard Heber might be there," Jael quipped enthusiastically.

"That's fantastic, maybe we can all dance together," Deborah paused her flute melody to respond, then stumbled. "I'm still not used to this dress," she stopped and fumed with her leg.

"What are you doing?"

"Just...adjusting my gown," Deborah grunted, trying not to draw attention.

All four guards stopped their horses and observed her, perhaps waiting to see if she would bend over. Every twist, every turn; their eyes were on her. Your sandal's loose, you know you have to check it...

They periodically looked at each other and giggled. There would be conversations later on, no doubt.

Before long, the travelers started seeing signs of civilization; Shiloh was near.

Commentary Notes

††

1. Arthur E. Cundall & Leon Morris, Judges & Ruth: An Introduction & Commentary, (Downers Grove, IL: Inter-Varsity Press Leicester, England, 1968). pp 87. Chariots did not operate effectively in the hill-country, whereas in the valley, they were supreme.

2. See 2 Samuel 21:20 and 1 Chronicles 20:6. Polydactylism with a perfectly equal distribution of 6 fingers on each hand and 6 toes on each foot, might have been a common characteristic among the giants.

3. The idea that Sisera might have wanted to capture the ark for his own use, was inspired from 1 Samuel 4-5. Years later, when the prophet Samuel was the judge of Israel, the Philistines thought they could benefit from the Ark of the Covenant, but after they captured it in battle, they discovered they were very wrong!

4. In the future, according to 2 Thessalonians 2:4, the Antichrist "takes his seat in the temple of God" [ESV]. Since the mercy seat is the only seat mentioned in the Holy of Holies where God's presence rested, it is suspected that the Antichrist will seek out the Ark of the Covenant to use it for his throne.

5. Carol R. Ember & Melvin Ember, Cultural Anthropology, 6th Ed., (Englewood Cliffs, NJ: Prentice Hall, Inc. 1990), p. 281. Sisera's idea of capturing the Ark of the Covenant to use it as a weapon, was based on his animatism philosophy. "Anthropologist R. R. Marret suggested that animatism, a belief in impersonal supernatural forces, (for example, the power of a rabbit's foot), preceded the creation of spirits." In this story, the Chief Hooded figure was familiar enough with the Israelites that he knew that Moses heard God's voice above the ark, Numbers 7:89. Because of this, he was afraid of the ark and its close association with Yahweh.

6. This is a speculation, that armed warriors may have served the Levite Priesthood to enforce the law when there were major violations and no family members kept it in check. In this story, this was what the Levites resorted to, because the residents of the town were unwilling to stone anyone to death to enforce the Mosaic Law. It makes

sense that Israel would have gone through stages of apostasy like this, when the Levites were still holding to the Mosaic Law, while others had abandoned it. A similar situation occurred in Numbers 25:7-9, when Phinehas, grandson of Aaron the High Priest, executed and man and a woman for flaunting their sin in public and nobody was willing to do anything about it.

7. See Deuteronomy 18:10, 20. Sorcery was forbidden. Using sorcery, then proclaiming false prophecies or prophecies in the names of other gods, was a death penalty offence.

8. Scripture has many examples of sins or offences that were banned among the Israelites, and failing to comply resulted in banishment, i.e. getting "cut off." See Exodus 12:15, 19, 30:33, 30:38, 31:14; Leviticus 3:9, 7:20-27, 17:4, 9-10, 14, 18:29, 19:8, 20:3, and many more. In this story, it is a speculation that many of the cut off Israelites might have formed into sub-culture groups within the surrounding nations.

9. While there were many pagan gods among the Egyptians and other nations Israel contended with, the Old Testament primarily focuses on three of them: 1. Molech, Leviticus 18:21, 20:2-5; 1 Kings 11:7; 2 Kings 23:10, etc., 2. Asherah, Deuteronomy 16:21; Judges 5:25, 28, 30; 1 Kings 15:13, 16:33, 18:19, 2 Kings 13:6, 17:16, etc., and 3. Baal, Judges 6:25-32, 8:33, 20:33; 1 Kings 16:31-32, 18:19-40, 19:18, 22:53, etc.

10. Since the Nephilim giants of old and their fallen angel progenitors were the origin of the pagan gods, it would make sense that living Nephilim would be highly venerated, and perhaps even worshipped. Such veneration could come from claims pointing back to their "divine" ancestry.

11. Elvio Angeloni, Anthropology, 92/93, 15th Ed., (Guilford CN: The Dushkin Publishing Group, Inc., 1993), p. 167. The attainment of wealth via drugs, prostitution, and human trafficking, are problems that have plagued humanity since the cradle of civilization. Anthropologist Michael Forbes Brown speaks of the dark side of shamanism, which is far from a quaint and colorful bit of traditional lore. "Shamans, who are found in societies all over the world, are believed to communicate directly with the spirits to heal people struck down by illness. Anthropologists are fond of reminding their students that shamanism, not prostitution, is the world's oldest profession..." Regarding the dark side of

shamanism, for starters, there is a blurry distinction between shaman healers and evil sorcerers inflicting harm, because they both interact with the spirit realm. Shamans can sometimes be accused of sorcery, which is an accusation that can carry the death penalty. Setting aside the spiritual elements of shamanism, shamans use powerful, dangerous hallucinogenic drugs, which are integrated with their practices, both due to their hallucinogenic properties, and also for healing purposes. Because of this, various forms of ancient shamanism are linked to modern day equivalents of the legal and illegal drug industry. Mr. Brown describes a scene, when Yankush, the shaman he knew, "entered into a trance by inducing a bitter, hallucinogenic concoction he had taken just before sunset (it is made from a vine known as ayahuasca)." The antics associated with the hallucinogenic drugs are part of what stage the dramatic presentations of the healing ceremonies. Since these drugs are in use and available to shamans, it is likely they would also be available for recreational use as well, for the right price.

12. An obvious link between drugs and sorcery is evident in scripture, with three translations of the English word for sorcery deriving from the Greek word for pharmakeia, where medication and magic are used interchangeably. See Galatians 5:19-21; Revelation 9:21, 18:23

G5331

φαρμακεία

pharmakeia

far-mak-i'-ah

From G5332; medication ("pharmacy"), that is, (by extension) magic (literal or figurative): - sorcery, witchcraft.

Total KJV occurrences: 3

13. Isidore Singer, George A. Barton, "Moloch (Molech)", JewishEncyclopedia, http://jewishencyclopedia.com/articles/10937-moloch-molech, (Last Accessed December 16, 2020). The Old Testament refers to the Israelites adopting the pagan practices of their neighboring nations. They caused their children, particularly their firstborn, to "pass through the fire" as human sacrifices to pagan gods, 2 Kings 16:3, 17:17, 21:6, 23:10; 2 Chronicles 33:6; Ezekiel 20:26, 31, 23:37; Jeremiah 32:35, etc. "As to the rites which the worshipers of Molech performed, it has sometimes been inferred, from the phrase "pass through

the fire to Molech," that children were made to pass between two lines of fire as a kind of consecration or februation; but it is clear from Isaiah 57:5 and Jeremiah 19:5, that the children were killed and burned. The whole point of the offering consisted, therefore, in the fact that it was a human sacrifice." With these human sacrifices of children being a common practice, it is not unlikely that a pagan temple would offer abortion services for profit under this guise.

14. The Old Testament refers to the Israelites adopting the pagan practices of their neighboring nations. They caused their children, particularly their firstborn, to "pass through the fire" as human sacrifices to pagan gods, 2 Kings 16:3, 17:17, 21:6, 23:10; 2 Chronicles 33:6; Ezekiel 20:26, 31, 23:37; Jeremiah 32:35, etc. A common interpretation of "passing through the fire" was thought to include living children capable of walking. However, that may have not been the case. Later scriptures, such as Isaiah 57:5 and Jeremiah 19:5, speak of the Israelites murdering their children, and offering them as "burnt offerings." It is therefore likely that a pagan temple would offer abortion services for profit, not much different than the modern day abortion industry.

15. Rick Meyers, "Equipping Ministries Foundation, e-Sword Bible software, version 12.2.0," downloaded Nov 20, 2020, http://www.e-sword.net; Didache, The Teachings of the Twelve Apostles, Ante-Nicene Fathers, Volume 7, chapter 2. Around the 2nd century A.D., there are specific references to abortion in the Didache; abortion is included in a list of forbidden gross sins, "though shalt not murder a child by abortion nor kill that which is begotten."

16. Rick Meyers, "Equipping Ministries Foundation, e-Sword Bible software, version 12.2.0," downloaded Nov 20, 2020, http://www.e-sword.net; Hippolytus - Refutation of All Heresies, Book 9, Chapter 7. Around the third century A.D., there are more specific references of pagan practices integrated with abortion services. "Whence women, reputed believers, began to resort to drugs for producing sterility, and to gird themselves round, so to expel what was being conceived on account of their not wishing to have a child either by a slave or by any paltry fellow, for the sake of their family and excessive wealth."

17. The obvious examples of inspiration for the description of Sisera's temple are Las Vegas, aka "Sin City," and Los Angeles, a central hub of human trafficking, rampant drug addiction, and sexual immorality.

18. These explicit details are provided, to illustrate the reasoning behind God's intense hatred of idolatry and everything associated with it, expressed throughout the Bible.

19. Jesse Lyman Hurlbut, Hurlbut's Handy Bible Encyclopedia, (Philadelphia, PA: The John C. Winston Co., 1908), p. 118. "Fallow deer. This is uncertainty as to what animal is meant by this name. It was permitted to be eaten as food (Deuteronomy 14:5), and was included among the beasts daily slain for Solomon's table. Many writers think it was the 'Alcelaphus bubalis,' a hollow-horned antelope-like mammal, well known to the ancients. R.V. gives Roebuck, q.v."

20. Kenneth Barker, The New International Version Study Bible, (Grand Rapids, MI: Zondervan Bible Publishers, 1985). p. 335, commentary on Judges 4:19, Jael's name means "Mountain Goat." Here in the story, Jael is taking the place of a mountain goat.

Chapter 8:

Wish I had an Apricot

ח

Herbs, spices, and incense filled the air. Excitement grew among the travelers as they entered Shiloh.

The village of Shiloh consisted of several thousand tents and a few permanent structures. There were many tables prepared with food, decorated with colorful tablecloths, menorahs, and other elements of Israeli culture.

No one set out an idol in this place, though some had them in their homes. Israel was a polarized nation at this time, but at least in this place, the fear of God was still tangible with the Ark of the Covenant so near.

However, unfortunately for many, that fear was quickly forgotten the moment they set foot outside of Shiloh.

While the legends of old remained, and the customs and rituals of faith were intact, over half the nation made excuses for those who passed their children through the fire.

They indulged in pagan practices. Theft was common, and integrity was waning. Yet in this place, at least on this day, those who were faithful flocked together.

People were eating and carrying on with animated conversations. A priest was speaking to a group of travelers, reading from a scroll, and several elders were verbally sparring over the interpretation.

If there were ever a national sport in Israel, it was having civil, yet often heated arguments.[1]

Children were playing games, and jugglers and street performers of all kinds interwove the vast encampment, adding to the festive ambiance. Music played in all directions; claps, cheers, dancing, and shouts of celebration were everywhere.

A kind of holy excitement, sacred and pure, could still be felt in the air of this joyful place. Anything could happen here. The Ark of God, that holy relic containing the Ten Commandments, given to Moses by God Himself, was right up the hill.[2]

The courtyard of the Tabernacle was visible up ahead, at the top of a hill on the northern side of Shiloh. It was enclosed by a rectangular white linen fence, supported by brass poles interconnected with silver rods, and held upright with ropes tied to brass tent pegs.[3]

This structure had one gate on the east side, and just inside the entrance was a massive cube shaped bronze altar in the courtyard.

Near the back of the courtyard was a silver fountain about twelve feet in diameter. Behind that was an enclosed rectangular badger skin tent, known as the Tabernacle, and also the Tent of Meeting.[4]

About twenty priests and several women dressed in white gowns continually washed themselves at the fountain, bowing, and praying.

No one went near the Tent of Meeting.

The High Priest, Elias, was in his eighties. His flowing robes, staff, and long gray hair and beard distinguished him as a wise man among the elders. "Ah, you're here!" he was relieved to see Barak enter the Tabernacle with several of his men.

"I'm so glad your father finally saw the wisdom of my request. The ark must be protected at all cost, it cannot fall into enemy hands."

"We'll guard it with our lives," Barak nodded. He then exited the Tabernacle and pointed out several key defensive positions to his men, then he sent out several lookouts. Others were busy carrying supplies around the perimeter of the Tabernacle.

It didn't take long before Deborah spotted Barak and cautiously made her way to him, feeling strangely self-conscious about her appearance.

A few months had passed without seeing him. Was he possibly distracted with other women she didn't know about? He never did answer her jibe about having a harem.

How well would Barak's memory serve him regarding this small-town girl from Ramah? Was she overly confident before, thinking he was definitely attracted to her, when in fact maybe that was a false impression? Were his words about her being "the one," a line he used with other girls?

When Barak finally saw Deborah, he did a double-take; saucer eyed, mouth agape.

Okay, so he remembered, but what of this expression? Deborah started kicking herself over Jael's outfit. It was definitely too much. He was going to fall on the ground howling in laughter any second.

But wait...

Barak's bewildered expression of astonishment finally formed into an ecstatic, beaming smile, overflowing with uncontainable joy.

He immediately sprinted over to her, gripped her waist in his hands and lifted her up high over his head, then he pulled her into a tight embrace, smothering her with kisses.

"Oy, heaven's glory! Look at you, just look at you!" He shouted and backed up, opening his arms to survey the entirety of this delicious feast for his eyes, profoundly delighted beyond words with her womanly transformation.

"Wow, you are...astonishing!" he gasped, barely able to speak. "I can't...I can't believe this, who...what...?" he could no longer articulate himself, and instead, he started giggling, teary eyed.

"Don't laugh, oy, I knew it, this is too much," Deborah looked down, slightly embarrassed, though she knew Barak's compliments were genuine. However, his reaction was drawing considerable attention, and the threat of embarrassment loomed.

"Oh no, no, no, this is *not* too much, please, please, I pray..." he clasped his hands as if in a prayer, "don't be upset. I just don't know what to say," he cupped his hands over his nose and mouth.

"You have no idea how much I've been thinking about you. I can't think; I can't sleep; I've been...an absolute wreck..."

"I was going to go with you. I told my parents I was going," Deborah sighed.

Before Barak could respond, they both suddenly heard a loud bang, followed by a clamor emerging from the festival. Whatever was happening, it didn't sound good.

Panic broke out in Shiloh; shouts and screams echoed in the distance.

"Stay right here!" Barak instructed Deborah, then he quickly spun around and ran toward the clamor.

Naturally, Deborah immediately ran after him.

Several armored war chariots blazed into Shiloh from the east, plowing through the festival in a destructive rampage. Their large wheels had eighteen inch blades cutting through everything in their path, including a number of citizens.[5]

Even small children weren't spared; they simply couldn't get out of the way fast enough.

As they hacked their way through Shiloh, the charioteers unleashed a stream of arrows at helpless victims.

Sierra's brother Lahmi was one of the charioteers, riding in a specially crafted oversized four-horse chariot. He leaped out of his chariot, pulled out his titanic battle axe, and started swinging wildly in all directions.

Lahmi didn't like shooting arrows; he preferred a front row seat to his carnage, severing heads, and hacking people completely in half. He craved the splatter of blood.

Deborah's mother Miriam was among Lahmi's first round of victims. She tried to dodge his attack, but her throat was gashed open in the process, killing her instantly.

Haran was not very far away, but a few feet too short might as well have been the span of the cosmos.

The previously jovial atmosphere in Shiloh was immediately malformed into complete chaos. Sisera's soldiers started torching tents and firing flaming arrows.

But not every fire initiated from Sisera's men.

Barak's men ignited a wall of oil-soaked kindling spread around the courtyard of the Tabernacle. It created a wall of fire, shielding the Tabernacle from attack.[6] As for Barak, he rushed into battle, sword ablaze, fiercely clashing with Sisera's men, one after another.

Barak's sword was busted in half with his first attacker, but he flung a dagger into the man's chest and acquired his much higher quality sword immediately afterward.

Upgrade!

The instant battle broke out, Deborah's fancy dress no longer served its purpose. Besides, Barak saw it; that was good enough.

Rip!

Deborah revealed what all the fuss was about with her leg while traveling to Shiloh. Concealed beneath her dress, she had several tent pegs strapped to her leg. One of them was secured to the golden belt rope for her dress.

Would anyone expect anything different?

She quickly had that tent peg whirling through the air, and her first order of business was stopping one of those mad charioteers wreaking havoc.

She let fly her instrument of death, and rather than wrapping around the neck of the charioteer, it pierced through his neck, then hooked him with its barb.

When the cord sprung taut, he flew out of his chariot backward, smashed through a tent and landed on top of a fire pit, adding to the menu of a leg of lamb. Two olives settled perfectly on top of his eyes.[7]

Seeing the high quality of her victim's sword, Deborah took a page out of Barak's notebook and went to fetch it. When she reached for it, she was almost beheaded, when...

Clank!

Barak blocked an attack from behind. No more warnings; he might not be able to save her skin the next time. No time for thank you, either; these two were in the center of savage combat on all sides.

Deborah's senses were activated like the flip of a switch, even more so than what she experienced with the bandits. An intense focus seized hold of her as the sounds around her drowned out, and the sands of time delayed their descent.

Every tactic, every movement; every weapon she ever touched; every skill in her arsenal was at her immediate disposal.

A sword swung from the right. Deborah ducked below it, then sprung up with a kick, several blocks and a few swings; she was on fire!

Barak caught glimpses of her in action, and if ever there were any doubt about her being ready for the battlefield, it was forever vanquished at the sight of her intense ferocity.

These were her people; she was mobilized in their defense, fighting with a speed, strength, and stamina beyond her means. Was this pure adrenaline, or perhaps something more?

Not too far away, Lahmi continued to make mincemeat of helpless villagers. They screamed and panicked in terror as he hacked them to bits.

The moment Deborah saw Lahmi, she had him in her sights as a weapon of mass destruction that had to be eliminated.

As Deborah fought her way toward him, she made it just in time for

Lahmi to slash his massive battle axe toward Gavriella. Deborah barely deflected the attack, saving her life, and Lahmi's axe plunged into the ground.

Lahmi let loose a deep gurgling cackle, then he stood erect, towering over everyone around him; taller than most of the tents in the area. His silver-plated ox skull helmet flickered red with reflections of fire round about them.

The pause for that laugh was all Deborah needed. Before Lahmi finished his needless cackling, Deborah flung a tent peg at his face, slamming it into his eye socket.

Lahmi roared in anguish and swung his axe while gripping his eye and fleeing toward his chariot.

"Laugh at that!" Deborah yelled at him.

By then, Barak made his way to her. They were both out of breath, exhilarated with the moment. "You're as good as me," Barak huffed.

"I was caught off guard back there, thank you," she replied, equally out of breath. Barak nodded.

Just then, they heard Jael screaming inside a tent. They both turned and sprinted into the tent where they witnessed Sisera's hand clamped around Jael's throat, holding her helplessly about five feet above the ground.

Jael kicked and flailed, using both of her hands to try to release herself from his grasp. Sisera was on the verge of crushing her windpipe.

One of Sisera's men jumped in the way, and Deborah blocked the attack, then pierced him in the chest. Barak charged passed Deborah, running straight toward Sisera. Seeing his advance, Sisera tossed Jael and spun around to swing his enormous sword.

Barak was close enough to escape the blade, but not his boulder sized fist. Wham! Barak was airborne, flung into the tent wall. He ripped half of the tent down as he flew through it, thudding to the ground.

Jael, meanwhile, was on the ground, unconscious.

Sisera turned to face Deborah and flexed with towering rage. Even the eyes of his lion pelt cap appeared animated, glimmering with wickedness.

"What is this, a woman?" Sisera growled as if insulted. He then noticed the small scar on her cheek. At that, he puffed out his chest and opened his arms in a mocking challenge. "Here I am."

It worked with the other giant; why not this one?

Deborah flung a tent peg at his face, but Sisera was much quicker than his brother. As large as he was, it was a mistake to think his size would slow him down, because it didn't; he was incredibly fast.

Sisera effortlessly jerked his head and dodged the attack. Then at lightning speed, he spun his sword around and jutted it forward.

Whack!

It stuck Deborah center mass, followed by the grisly sound of bone, gristle, and flesh. Deborah's mouth gaped open; she gurgled as a fountain of blood started oozing past her lips and down her chin.[8]

Deborah dropped her sword as Sisera lifted her from the ground by several feet, cackling with macabre madness. As he lifted her in the air, she slid further down his sword, fully impaled, through and through.

"I was warned about you," Sisera laughed as he pulled his arm back to get a closer look at her face while she gagged, skewered like a roasted lamb. "I wish I had an apricot for your mouth," Sisera laughed with a hideous, demonic zeal.[9-10]

"No!" Barak screamed uncontrollably when he saw Deborah in the air, impaled on Sisera's sword. He charged into the fray with a half dozen warriors trailing behind him.

Sisera quickly threw Deborah off of his sword, then blocked Barak's attack and kicked him in one fluid motion. Barak smashed through a table and was knocked to the ground. Immediately afterward, the tent burst into flames.

One of Barak's men rushed toward Sisera from outside, and Barak joined him. Sisera saw both of them charging and instantly pulled a jeweled dagger off of his hip and threw it.

The dagger was headed straight for Barak's chest, but the man next to him dodged in front of it. The dagger struck him in the shoulder with such force, it threw him backward, pummeling Barak.

Several other warriors, including Barak once again, swarmed Sisera all at once, repelling him back. The fighting ensued, but the sounds of battle dissolved into an ambiguous hum.

Deborah, meanwhile, used what little life remained in her to crawl away, amidst the flames and debris, leaving a trail of blood behind her.

She didn't know how much time she had left, and quite frankly, she was astonished she wasn't dead yet.

Or was she?

Quivering in shock, Deborah managed to stand up, wondering how this was possible. When she looked down, she saw the torrent of blood still pouring from her mouth and even more from her abdomen. Her tiny fragment of life was quickly diminishing.

What to do?

She couldn't see Barak anywhere, and her blurred vision was fading. About the only thing big enough and bright enough to see, was the brilliant white linen of the courtyard Tabernacle a short distance away, illuminated by a wall of fire.

Ah, the Tent of Meeting.

The Ark of the Covenant. Yahweh's Mercy Seat was just right over there.

Under normal circumstances, everyone considered it a death sentence to enter the Tent of Meeting, though many throughout Israel wondered in awe what that must be like for the High Priest.

It was probably a bit nerve wracking, attaching the little bells around his ankle before going behind the veil and into the presence of the Mercy Seat, over which the Creator of heaven and Earth reside.

Never mind the bells, what about the rope? If the other priests no longer heard those little bells of the High Priest, that's when the rope came into play. They could drag his lifeless corpse out of there, without going inside and adding to the death count.[11]

A lot of Israelites didn't take the issue of ceremonial cleanliness very seriously, but the High Priest certainly did if he wanted to live.

The God of Israel was loving beyond what human reasoning could comprehend, but His power was so truly awesome, that disrespecting Him in His very presence could be fatal.

He defined the consequences for disobedience ahead of time, and always, without fail, He gave ample warnings.

And even while enduring the consequences of disobedience, Yahweh was lavish with forgiveness, and He would often show mercy at the first sign of repentance. But there were still consequences.

Such was the case with this massacre at Shiloh, which never would have occurred, were there not such rampant sin throughout Israel.[12]

Hopefully this was the worst of it, or was it?

The High Priest wasn't disrespectful in the Lord's direct presence, but many throughout Israel were beyond disrespectful with the extent of their shameful ways.

Some Israelites were in Shiloh on this very day, putting on a show of external appearances. They were celebrating in the very city of God's throne on Earth, all the while, planning to stop by Sisera's temple of Baal directly after the celebration. They did this and thought nothing of it.

These were a provoking lot, to say the least.[13] Most of the worst offenders were known by name, yet there was little effort to dissuade them from attending the festival. Complacency was the norm.

The very God who humbled the entire nation of Egypt; the same God who split the Red Sea; He whose presence made Moses' face glow with power and glory from on high, was, by many accounts, a visitor to that Tent of Meeting, just right up yonder.

But where was He now?

Was He actually sitting on His Mercy Seat right this very moment, while all of this mayhem was occurring just outside?

Would He possibly consider turning His attention to His wayward children? Would He forgive them? How much was enough?

Deborah was intent to raise these questions to Yahweh in person, before His Earthly throne, as humbly and respectfully as possible, if she had enough life left in her body to make it there.[14]

After all, at this point, what did she have to lose? Could there ever be a better reason to die? Everyone dies.

Dying from an accident, a sickness, old age, or a battle wound; those are common. Imagine being the person to say, I died because I saw the face of God. Could there be a more content way to die?

Such was Deborah's limited reasoning with her few cognitive faculties remaining.

And so she stumbled toward the courtyard of the Tabernacle as the mayhem continued around her. She bumbled as the bee, her father might say, tripping past swords, arrows, flames; strikes and counter strikes between friend and foe.

At one point, a warhorse reared up, and she stumbled beneath his hooves. He didn't drop back down until she plodded past.

She wove her way through a small breach in the wall of fire surrounding the courtyard of the Tabernacle, then she finally collapsed near the entrance.

Every fiber of her being; the fullness of her spirit; the eternal essence of her soul, demanded that she make it to the courtyard of the Tabernacle before giving up the ghost.

Crawling desperately, convulsing in agony with each movement, she pressed forward until she was finally inside the courtyard of the Tabernacle.

And there it was; the Tent of Meeting! That glorious place, was just right there; she could see it with her fading vision. Even in this state, she finally felt relief at the sight of that tent.

Whether she lived or died, the entity who visited that tent had the power to meet her if He was so inclined.[15] She knew He had to be looking upon her at this very moment.

With her dying breath, she strained with her arms stretched toward the Tent of Meeting. Her arms finally dropped. She stopped breathing.

Her eyes remained fixed on the tent until they glazed over, frosty; lifeless.

Deborah died.[16]

Sisera and his men eventually retreated, and Sisera's brother Lahmi lost his eye. But the death toll was much higher for Israel; mostly civilian casualties.

General Abinoam would later regret not having sent more than triple the number of warriors he sent.

Darkness fell on Shiloh as the evening set in with a moonless night. Wails could be heard throughout the city all night long. The grief stricken residents could not be consoled.

Where was their God?

Commentary Notes

++

1. My Jewish Learning, "Conversation and Debate", (Last Accessed December 17, 2020). "Although Jews have excelled in many different sports, only one sport truly has a claim as being the Jewish national sport. Soccer? Dreidel? No. The Jewish national sport is... arguing! ... Jewish texts, insofar as they seem to have personalities, are almost always either engaged in argument or perceived to be so. Some texts, such as the Mishnah, use the explicit language of dispute ("... these are the words of Rabbi Y. But Rabbi Z says...") as their primary mode of expression. The Bible retells stories of disputes (such as the rebellion of Korah against Moses and Aaron), includes stories that contradict each other (the first chapter of Genesis says plants precede people but the second chapter says people precede plants), and dares to include writings that are at odds with the tone of most of the rest of the Bible."
2. Just before the time of the judges, in Joshua 3:8, the Israelites crossed the Jordan River with the Ark of the Covenant. The ark is again mentioned in the Promised Land in Judges 20:27, but its exact location is not listed. Judges 21:19 states that the yearly "Feasts of the Lord" were at Shiloh, which is an indication that Shiloh was the center of Israel's priesthood at that time. The festivals included animal sacrifices, which were most likely conducted in the courtyard of the Tabernacle, and the Tabernacle housed the Ark of the Covenant. The next reference to the ark is in 1 Samuel 4:3, which states directly that the ark was located in Shiloh. So it is likely that the Ark of the Covenant ended up in Shiloh not long after the Israelites crossed the Jordan River and took the city of Jericho, because Shiloh is only about twenty miles away from Jericho.
3. Tabernacle construction supplies are listed in Exodus 35, the assembled components of the Tabernacle and all the Tabernacle artifacts are listed in Exodus 36-39, and the final design of the Tabernacle with its surrounding courtyard are described in Exodus 40.
4. In Numbers 4, the Tent of Meeting is made of a type of skin, though different translations vary widely, from badger skin [KJV], [YLT] to goatskin [ESV], to leather dyed skin [ISV], to sealskin [JPS], to dugong skins [MKJV]. Obviously there are many ideas about the

meaning of the animal in question for the Hebrew word tachash. Strong's Enhanced Lexicon might be more accurate in terms of this being a generic word, i.e. "a (clean) animal with fur" rather than a specific species.

5. James M. Volo, "Did war chariots ever actually have blades on the wheel hubs?", Quora, https://www.quora.com/Did-war-chariots-ever-actually-have-blades-on-the-wheel-hubs, (Last Accessed December 19, 2020). "War chariots had limited military capabilities. They were strictly an offensive weapon and were best suited against infantry in open flat country where the charioteers had room to maneuver. The scythed chariot was a modified war chariot. The blades extended horizontally for about 1 meter (3 feet) to each side of the wheels... Chariots with iron scythes were recorded in the Hebrew Scriptures at both Joshua 17:16, 18 and Judges 1:19, in direct reference to the Canaanites."
6. "Olive Oil in Biblical Times and Later", Israel Olive Bond, https://israelolivebond.com/olive-oil/olive-oil-history/, (Last Accessed December 19, 2020). "In the heroic battle of the Jews against the Romans, the Jews used oil as a weapon. In the battle of Yodfat, Joseph, son of Matthias, commander of the revolt in Galilee, ordered boiling oil poured on the Romans as they attacked the walls of the city."
7. Jan Cashman, "Origin of Species of Corn, Potatoes, and Tomatoes - and Some Other Interesting History", https://cashmannursery.com/gardening-tips/2012/origin-of-species-of-corn-potatoes-and-tomatoes-and-some-other-interesting-history/#:~:text=Tomatoes%20are%20native%20to%20South,tomato%20was%20small%20and%20yellow, (Last Accessed December 19, 2020). I originally mentioned tomatoes for this scene, but according to this research, tomatoes find their origin in South America, so I switched to olives.
8. The Bible says nothing about Deborah ever encountering Sisera in battle like this. However, it makes for good story telling to foreshadow a final confrontation with an earlier event.
9. Jesse Lyman Hurlbut, *Hurlbut's Handy Bible Encyclopedia*, (Philadelphia, PA: The John C. Winston Co., 1908), p. 19. (Bracketed comments added) "Apple, mentioned only six times [in the Bible]. Cannot apply to the apple as known to us, which produces but a poor fruit in hot countries. Fairly applies to the apricot, a delicious and common fruit in Palestine. [Apple] - of the eye, Deuteronomy 32:10; Psalm 17:8; Proverbs 7:2; Lamentations 2:18; Zechariah 2:8." In this story, the scene has Sisera referring to Deborah as if she were a

skewered animal ready to serve as a meal. Most modern depictions of whole skewered animals show an apple in the mouth, but that doesn't work in this case, so the apple was swapped for an apricot.

10. Analida, "Moroccan Lamb Tagine with Apricots", https://ethnic-spoon.com/traditional-lamb-tagine-with-apricots/, (Last Accessed December 19, 2020). Tagine is an Israelite dish of lamb served with apricots.
11. Kenneth Barker, *The New International Version Study Bible*, (Grand Rapids, MI: Zondervan Bible Publishers, 1985). p. 129, commentary note for Exodus 28:35, "According to Jewish tradition, one end of a length of rope was tied to the high priest's ankle and the other end remained outside the tabernacle. If the bells on his robe stopped tinkling while he was in the Holy Place, the assumption that he had died could be tested by pulling gently on the rope." It also goes without saying, if the High Priest was dead, that same rope could be used to pull out his body so no one else would need to go into that forbidden location.
12. See Judges 4:2, "And the LORD sold them into the hand of Jabin king of Canaan..." The reason the Canaanites were allowed to dominate Israel and oppress them, is because the Israelites had fallen into rampant sin.
13. The Old Testament refers to Israel as "stiff-necked" five times, Exodus 32:9, 33:3, 5, 34:9, 2 Chronicles 30:8. The word "provoking" is listed 16 times, and "provoked" 18 times; all these references are Israel provoking God to anger.
14. During the time of the Judges, God searched Israel for those whose hearts cried out for their nation. Again and again, when the Israelites sinned, Moses interceded for them, begging God for mercy. See Exodus 32:30-33, 33; Deuteronomy 9:13-14; Numbers 12, 16, 21:7. Deborah exhibits this same characteristic of an intercessor.
15. According to Hebrews 11:19, the patriarch Abraham reasoned that God had power over life and death. In this story, Deborah holds this same understanding as she makes her final appeal to Yahweh before dying.
16. Scripture says nothing about Deborah dying, however, whatever Deborah's backstory is, I suggest it has to be fantastic to warrant the vast attention, popularity, authority, and universal respect she held in the eyes of all Israel.

Chapter 9:

A Mysterious Entity

י

Infamy had its day in Shiloh, but the shadow of death finally departed, and a stillness settled over the courtyard just before dawn.

Sorrow became silent. No birds issued a peep, nor the chirp or trill of a cricket was heard. The wind ceased altogether, and all anyone living could perceive was the ringing sound of air in the ears.

And in the center of this perfect serenity, within the Tent of Meeting, just over yonder, something began to happen. Behind the veil in the most holy of holy places, wherein the Ark of the Covenant reside, *something was happening*.

The top of this golden chest was adorned with two cherubs flanking each side of the Mercy Seat, and just above that Mercy Seat, an amber glow manifested. What, or better yet who, was this amber glow, if not the author of mercy Himself?

The amber orb grew in size; it elongated above the ark, then draped down the front of it. This amber light then began to take shape. The form of a luminous humanoid figure materialized in front of the ark.

A moment later, a billowing, luminescent cloud flowed from the Tent of Meeting, and from the midst of it, a Mysterious Entity emerged. He was wearing full plate battle armor, and radiating rippling waves of sparkling, amber light.[1]

A glowing scarlet hooded cape draped down to his ankles, and in His hand was a double edged sword.[2] He had a mustache connected with His small, neatly trimmed beard.[3]

His eyes were like flames of fire, and His shimmering white hair flowed in an ethereal wind.

He approached Deborah, paused before her lifeless body and stared at her a moment. Though the area was deftly silent, He tilted his ear as if He heard something. Were these Deborah's last words He was hearing, or words yet to be spoken?

Okay.

He gracefully flipped His sword into a backhand position and stuck it in the ground at his feet. He then knelt down next to Deborah, gently grabbed her shoulder and rolled her over on her back.

Deborah was a blood-soaked mess; that beautiful gown was now spattered crimson from top to bottom. He placed His hand on her cheek and stroked her scar a few times with his thumb while smiling.[4]

Then removing His hand from her face, He spread out His fingers and held His hand over her abdomen.

A dazzling rainbow of liquid light poured out of His hand, seeped into her wound, then flowed over her body, saturating her entire form in a blazing brilliance.

Leaning forward, He lowered His hand until it rested directly on top of her wound, injecting life force back into her body. Then adding the final ingredient, He blew into her face.

Deborah's body suddenly convulsed as she inhaled His breath of life.[5]

When she finally cracked open her eyes, she rolled her head just in time to catch a glimpse of the back of this Mysterious Entity re-enter the luminous cloud at the entrance to the Tent of Meeting.

The mist then receded, and the sounds of the night slowly resumed with the chirping of crickets and the distant hooting of an owl.

Deborah's eyes slowly closed; this time, not with the sleep of death, but rather a restful sleep, and peaceful dreams of happier times.

A short while later, Haran was among the first to awake. Raw, gut wrenching pain reverberated in his voice as he cried out his wife's name, "Miriam!"

He bawled, drenched in blood, cradling Miriam's body in his arms. He witnessed her death just a few feet away, but immediately afterward, he was trampled by one of Lahmi's warhorses and knocked unconscious.

As he looked upon her precious face soon after he awoke, he could not process that she was gone. She was his inspiration; his motivation; his ultimate companion for life. Deborah would soon cling to another, and depart on her own journey.

After that, the longest chapter of his life would remain with Miriam. They were partners; an excellent team! Through thick and thin, they always had each other's backs. Haran could not fathom that even death could part them.

In fact, he could hear her speaking in his mind as he held her face in his hands. He knew her so very well, more than half of his thoughts spoke in her voice.

What was she saying?

"Deborah? Where is she? Is she okay? What are you doing with my dead body, I'm not here anymore! Go find our daughter right this instant!"

Haran nodded, hearing her loud and clear, and he agreed. Search for Deborah, and hope and pray she is still among the living.

"You rest," he gently stroked Miriam's hair, covered her up, then he began his frantic search, rolling over one dead body after another.

Each body he inspected was an agonizing experience.

That one! She looks like she could be Deborah; about the right height; similar proportions from the back side. Did her dress look like that? Please no! Roll, gasp; sigh of relief, cringe, repeat...

He checked a number of bodies that did not match Deborah's proportions, but that was because he was profoundly distraught, trembling, eyes blurred with sobbing.

Some of the bodies he inspected were grotesquely mutilated; heads crushed, eyes gouged out; dismembered; gray matter spilled onto the face.

Seeing a dead animal was somewhat of a natural occurrence from time to time, but one does not see so many dead human beings so horribly disfigured, and simply brush it off.

This was especially the case for dead children. Even seasoned warriors were wise to limit their exposure to such brutality if possible. Failure to do so could potentially affect them in many unpleasant ways.

Haran finally found Deborah in the courtyard of the Tabernacle. She was still drenched in blood, but her skin was not the pale shade of a corpse, and the serene expression on her face was that of an angel. Haran collapsed next to her.

"My Lord, why, why, why?" he coughed; tears mixed with mucus and spit drooling from his mouth as he sobbed, completely broken. How could this happen?

She was the pride and joy of his heart; such a glow about her, so radiant and full of joy all her life. That pure innocence never left her. She had much the same smile, and clearness of conscience in her eyes as a young woman that she had as a ten year old.

The wisdom of age comes with pain, and it dulls the glimmer in one's eyes, but even the incident with losing Caleb did not steal that glimmer in Deborah's eyes.

They buried Caleb, and held an official service in the yard, complete with ceremony, a grave marker, words of remembrance; flowers.

But standing up to those men gave Deborah a source of confidence, and sense of purpose that she didn't have before. That unfortunate incident strengthened her heart, and the brightness in her eyes still beamed with the life force of an infant.

Deborah's conscience was clear, held intact with a natural sense of justice that resonated within her. Contrary to her parents' perception, much of what they taught her about the law was part of her being. Life for a life, made perfect sense to her.

So how could this be, this daughter of promise, gone at such a young age? She was even reaching toward the Tent of Meeting when she died. How could Yahweh allow this to happen?

"Why?" Haran sobbed, staring at the Tent of Meeting. It was not really a question, but rather an attempt of *suicide-by-God*. Perhaps that unyielding temptation to die in God's presence ran in the family.

"What did she do? Why did you punish the just with the unjust?[6] What sin has she committed to deserve this?"

Haran was no longer in his right mind. He wanted more than anything for God to strike him dead on the spot. That was the only solution to terminate this madness, and it wasn't a half bad idea in his opinion, because he might even get to see his wife and daughter right away.

If God was truly merciful, this request would be granted.

Haran trembled with grief, gripping the Earth in his hands, then he stood up on his feet, facing the Tent of Meeting.

"I know Israel has sinned, but my daughter lives and breathes your justice," Haran jutted his finger at Deborah on the ground. "If you don't bring my daughter back, then please just strike me down, so I can be with my family again."

Haran started marching toward the Tent of Meeting when he suddenly became aware that someone was speaking behind him.[7]

"Father?" Deborah spoke, wondering why her father was screaming so violently at the Tent of Meeting.

Haran paused, saucer eyed with shock. He saw her. All that blood, her dress ripped to shreds; she had to be dead!

Sitting up, Deborah called out to her father again, "Father?"

Haran finally spun around. When he saw her sitting up, propped up on her arm and looking at him, he wobbled, buckled, dropped to his knees, then fell forward, face first into the ground.

Deborah scrambled over to him and shook him, but he was out cold.

Then Deborah paused to assess her situation.

She instantly jerked her head down and saw her blood-soaked dress. She felt her abdomen, wiped away some of the caked-on blood, and felt a scar beneath, completely healed up. Whipping her hand behind her back, she felt a scar there as well.

How?

She recalled the realization that she failed to block Sisera's attack. That was a mistake, and it was to be her last, so she thought.

She also clearly remembered his hideous cackling in her face, and his wise crack about an apricot.

So that wasn't a dream? Or was it? Her present moment felt more like a dream, than those horribly vivid memories from yesterday.

Wait, where am I? This is the courtyard of the Tabernacle. Oh yea, uh...

Was that...?

Deborah eyed the Tent of Meeting, and her eyes slowly opened wider and wider. She vaguely recalled seeing a glowing figure entering a luminous cloud of mist at the opening of the tent.

And just prior to that, she remembered her last waking moment before slipping beyond the veil. She was reaching for the Tent of Meeting, and her last breath was a desperate plea for Israel.[8]

What does this mean?

Just last night, she was crying out to Yahweh, asking Him how He could allow such an injustice to occur just outside the Tabernacle. Now she was wondering why He spared her.

She was no one of noble birth; an obscure female from a small town. If anything, she was an outcast widely frowned upon in her community.[9] How many were not spared, that she should live?

Confusion set in, as it often does when one uses an infinitesimally limited capacity to contemplate the mysterious ways of an omniscient, eternal Supreme Being.

"Thank you," Deborah humbly whispered, nodding toward the Tent of Meeting.

Haran finally revived after Deborah rolled him over and lightly slapped his cheek a few times.

His mouth fell open as he stared at her, overwhelmed with everything passing through his mind, similar to the way the brain will shut off pain receptors for a severed limb.

He looked at the scar on her abdomen, exposed through the gaping hole ripped in the front of her dress. He then glanced over at the Tent of Meeting, then back to Deborah.

"My God, He heard me!" tears poured from Haran's eyes once again-but this time, they were tears of joy. He immediately gripped Deborah's shoulders and embraced her, nearly squeezing the life out of her.

"He heard me!" he shook with rapturous wonder, kissing his precious daughter over and over again.

Deborah allowed him all the time he needed to let this all sink in, and she needed time to process it as well. For starters, her father was alive, and that was a tremendous blessing.

But wait, what about Barak?

And mother, where was she?

Haran finally released her, and the look on his face told her everything. "Miriam..."

"No, no, no, no..." Deborah teared up, and a torrent of grief overtook her. If only she could have passed on better terms. The past year was so hard, they seldom if ever spoke, never seeing eye-to-eye about her training.

Miriam's accusation, saying she looked like the pagan goddess Asherah, haunted her memories. The fuming and constant discontent, pained her now more than ever before. She brought shame on their home and family honor.

After the incident with Caleb, there was a brief acknowledgement that the dangerous world they lived in was less abstract than before.

The luxury of living in an obscure southern town, sheltered from war chariots by their rocky terrain, was no longer the comfort it once was.

And when those men barged into their home, groping at Deborah;

Miriam saw what they did, and she had great difficulty coping with that wretched feeling of helplessness.

Later that evening, Deborah tried to capitalize on that brief spell of clarity, explaining to her that she felt that same exact helplessness when they were attacked by bandits.

But Miriam was stubborn, and quickly rebounded her position, insisting that a woman's place was not on a battlefield. So their dispute on the matter of Deborah's training was never settled.

As Deborah broke down, she couldn't help but express her regrets

"I could never please her," she wept bitterly.

"She is with Him now," her father explained to her while cupping her cheek in his hand and motioning to the Tent of Meeting. "No one can explain your heart to her better than He can."

"Maybe. She's probably yelling at Him right now," Deborah giggled for an instant, then continued her sobbing.

Harran chuckled briefly. "You're probably right."

A little while later, Deborah finally found Barak, still unconscious. He had a ghastly wound on his leg. She was still in tears, reflecting on her mother, as well as the carnage around them, when Barak woke up and smiled at her in wonder.

"Abraham's Bosom?" he whispered, confused to see her. "So I didn't make it? Why are we still here?"

Needless to say, Barak was very confused, thinking he had to be dead. Whatever rule set he was now operating under, wasn't at all what he was expecting. Dead people shouldn't need bandages, and they shouldn't be feeling intense pain throughout their bodies, either.

Deborah smiled back through her tears, "We're alive."

"What?"

That didn't make any sense either. He recalled far more intensely than he wished, seeing her impaled right in front of him.

He didn't even have any time to experience the onslaught of grief; all he felt was unquenchable fury, but then he was instantly pounded into unconsciousness. The next thing he saw was Deborah's face, and she was apparently just fine.

This had to be a dream, or he was dead.

He looked around. Shiloh was a complete disaster. Weeping echoed near and far, and many were still attending to the dead, wrapping bodies in shredded tents or whatever else they could find. Priests were in prayer, interceding for the people.

"How are you here? I saw you..."

"Something happened...*in there*," Deborah motioned to the Tabernacle. "I, I, I...," she let out a brief wheezing chuckle of astonishment.

"I...was near the Tent of Meeting. I can't explain it," she shook her head. "I don't think you would believe me," she choked, hardly believing the otherworldly memories that flashed in her mind.

"Actually, I probably would," he replied, still shocked that she was alive and well. He gawked at all the blood, then touched the scar on her abdomen with his fingers. In this case, even seeing wasn't believing.

"Let's take care of this leg," she poured heated water on his leg, and ripped some more strips of cloth from her gown to secure two tree branches for a splint.

"How is your family?"

"Mother," Deborah spoke remorsefully. "I was such a disappointment to her."

"Nonsense," Barak rebuked her. "If she saw what I saw, you're so amazing," Barak caressed her face with a level of appreciation he could never articulate, but it emanated from his eyes; in his countenance.

"The only reason she ever wanted you away from the battlefield is because you were more precious to her than life. She couldn't bear the thought of losing you," tears trickled down his cheeks as he recalled seeing Deborah gored on Sisera's sword.

"And neither could I," he gasped. "I understand exactly how she felt," tears now streamed down his face.

"It had nothing to do with disappointment. You never mind what she said; probably told you many hurtful things; anything and everything she could imagine to dissuade you from ever seeing a battle," he gulped.

"Because she loved you with a mother's love. You have to understand that. Please tell me you understand that."

Such words of comfort he spoke, for in them, there was undeniable truth. She recalled seeing it in her mother's eyes.

Through the anger, the pain; through every insult, through every expression of disappointment, there was an underlying fear that she would be the mother of a dead child; cursed with outliving her own child.

Such a death was wholly unnatural. If there was a sword she could fall on to prevent that from happening, even if it cost her the very relationship with her daughter that she so dearly cherished, she would sacrifice it.

"Thank you," Deborah whispered.

Those who witnessed Sisera's attack on Deborah and lived to recall it were shocked and speechless. A few of the warriors with Barak were among them, and they simply stared at her wide eyed, mouths gaping.

She was a living miracle on par with the legends of old, and they couldn't stop whispering among themselves and everyone else they spoke to about her miraculous recovery.

Something was up with her.

The festival was cancelled, and the group from Ramah limped home the next day.

More warriors were summoned to Shiloh to assist with recovery operations, but Barak was ordered to report back to his father immediately and provide a detailed account of what occurred there. Deborah didn't see the point in staying any longer after he departed.

Would they ever have a life together? Only time would tell.

Parting ways again was yet another side-order of sadness to add to the course for this festival. But at least they parted with a growing anticipation that they each wanted nothing more in life than to share their lives together one day.

This attack on Shiloh was the worst anyone had ever seen in Israel, and many wondered what would come of it.

Was Israel going to mount a full scale retaliation? Was there even any unity in Israel to make such a declaration? Did this mean war? What was King Jabin's excuse for this heinous, unprovoked attack?

Rumors later circulated about the attack. Some said it was Sisera's idea, and it wasn't sanctioned by King Jabin. However, Sisera was still in command of King Jabin's forces, so that didn't make any sense.[10]

Others actually argued in Sisera's defense, claiming that he loved the Israelites, and he didn't want to conduct the raid at all. The evil King Jabin ordered Sisera to attack Shiloh, and he gouged out his brother's eye to force him to comply.

With each passing day, accounts of the Shiloh massacre mutated to such an extent, people throughout Israel had a hard time believing what anyone had to say about it.

Sisera was the main reason for all this confusion. He was a master of public relations, well adept at manipulating public opinion. He had his own undercover intelligence agency scattered throughout Israel, doing his bidding and spreading disinformation.

As unbelievable as it was, many Israelites continued to frequent Sisera's ever so popular temple of Baal.

They had their addictions to feed; their love of money and pleasure to attend to. If they didn't witness Sisera slaughtering people with their own eyes, they tended to dismiss the accounts as nothing more than gossip.

Israel was polarized before the attack on Shiloh, and even more so afterward. To some, Sisera was a practically a god worthy of worship; to others, he was the devil.

As far as Jael was concerned, she was with the later crowd, and no longer on the fence. She saw this devil face to face when he nearly killed her.

When Deborah first found Jael, she was still in a state of shock; pale; catatonic. It took some pestering, but she eventually broke through to her.

"You're probably never going to let me borrow another dress. Look what I did to it. But maybe it's not a total loss, maybe you can fix it? Look, hem it up here like this? We can dye it red. Hey, check this out, we can start a new fashion, let's open this hole on the stomach some more so I can sport my scar, and even get my naval in there. What do you think?"

Deborah was relentless, and she finally succeeded in getting Jael to crack a smile. Then on the way home, she continued with the silly comments, as much to distract herself as to help her friend.

At one point during their journey, Jael was self-conscious about two of the gossip girls looking their way. "They're staring at me," she whispered. "They think Sisera had his way with me."

"I don't think so," Deborah replied.

"No one's ever going to want me," Jael moaned.

"That's not true."

"I doubt even Heber will want me."

Deborah put her arm around Jael and gave her shoulder a squeeze. A moment later, one of them, Gavriella, made her way over to them. What now?

"You saved my life," she replied.

Deborah raised an eyebrow. "Want to learn how to fight?"

Gavriella nodded with a small grin. "If you promise not to break my nose?"

Commentary Notes

††

1. See Joshua 5:13-15, the "Captain" or "Commander" of the Lord's host appeared to Joshua as a man with his sword drawn in his hand. On this occasion, He ordered Joshua to take off his sandals, because he was standing on holy ground. This identifies Him as the same God, Yahweh, who appeared to Moses in the burning bush, Exodus 3:5. With His sword drawn and ready for battle, God appeared as a "man of war," referenced in Exodus 15:3 and Isaiah 42:13. Further elements of the pre-incarnate Christ's description were derived from Revelation 1:13-16, "...one like a son of man, clothed with a long robe and with a golden sash around his chest. The hairs of his head were white, like white wool, like snow. His eyes were like a flame of fire...his face was like the sun shining in full strength."
2. See Hebrews 4:12, the Word of God is metaphorically spoken of as sharper than any two-edged/double-edged sword. The Word of God is symbolically depicted as a two-edged sword in Revelation 1:16.
3. Rosemary Ellen Guiley, *Harper's Encyclopedia of Mystical & Paranormal Experience*, (New York, NY: HarperCollins Publishers, 1991), pp. 350-351. See John 20:7, which speaks of Jesus' burial cloth neatly folded in His tomb after Jesus was resurrected from the dead. The Shroud of Turin is purported to be this burial cloth. It is "A yellow strip of linen bearing blood-stains and the brownish image of the body of a bearded man, which for centuries was believed to be the shroud in which Jesus was buried. Measuring about fourteen feet in length and four feet in width, the cloth has been the subject of controversy, debate, and analysis since it came to light in a French church in 1353. It is considered by the Vatican to be the most important relic to Christendom. The shroud takes its name from St. John's Cathedral in Turin, where it has been held, folded, in a locked silver chest since the fifteen century, seldom shown to the public." Many modern artistic renditions of Jesus are based on the image on the Shroud of Turin, which depicts Jesus with long hair, a mustache, and a trimmed beard.

4. Jesus is a fan of scars connected to faith; He retained his own when He visited His disciples following His resurrection, see John 20:25-27.
5. The act of breathing life force into someone can be seen first in Genesis 2:7, with God breathing life into Adam's nostrils. Later in the New Testament, one of Jesus' final acts following His resurrection, was that He breathed on His disciples, and imparted the Holy Spirit to them, John 20:19-22.
6. Haran is familiar with the account of Abraham's question to God in the book of Genesis, Bible Ref Genesis 18:25
7. The Mosaic Law prescribed the death penalty for anyone not in the Tribe of Levi to enter the Holy of Holies, Leviticus 16:2-34; Exodus 40:1-38.
8. For this part of the story, Deborah echo's Moses' sentiments, identifying with the plight of Israel before God chose him to lead Israel, Hebrews 11:24. This story follows that same pattern.
9. God has a track record of choosing the most unlikely heroes for His service. Isaac preferred his warrior son, Esau, but God choose Jacob, the mama's boy, Genesis 25:27-28. When God appointed Moses to lead Israel out of Egypt, Moses repeatedly questioned his own competency for the task, and he tried to dodge the responsibility, Exodus 3:11, paraphrased, "Who am I?," 4:1 "They won't listen to me...," 4:10 "I can't talk...," 4:12, "Please send someone else...." When God selected Gideon as Israel's redeemer in Judges 6:15, Gideon's response was that his clan was the weakest in Manasseh, and he was the least in his father's house. King David is yet another example, when the prophet Samuel identified him, the youngest of his many brothers, as Israel's chosen king, 1 Samuel 16:7. God's response to Samuel was, "Do not look on his appearance or on the height of his stature... the LORD sees not as man sees: man looks on the outward appearance, but the LORD looks on the heart." God's selection of unlikely servants continued in the New Testament as well, with some of Jesus' Disciples being ordinary fishermen, Mark 1:16, and Matthew was even a despised tax collector, Matthew 10:3. Of course, the grand finale of unlikely heroes was Jesus, the Son of God, who lived most of His life as an ordinary man with "no form or majesty or beauty that anyone would desire Him," Isaiah 53:2. He was not a scribe, or known as a religious scholar, or a man wielding governmental authority. Instead, He was a simple carpenter from a small town, Matthew 13:55.

10. In Judges 4:2, Scripture introduces King Jabin, and Sisera is the commander of his Army. The idea that Sisera may have conducted unsanctioned operations on his own is derived from the manner in which Sisera eclipses King Jabin in the narrative. Shortly following King Jabin's introduction, the narrative focuses more on Sisera throughout, and in Judges 5, King Jabin isn't mentioned at all.

Chapter 10:

Scary Delicious

י

Jael, Deborah, Haran, Adonia, and many other villagers stood around Miriam's body, wrapped in linen, covered with flowers. Heber stood near the back of the crowd.

When Jael noticed Heber's presence, she looked away in shame, thinking he had most certainly heard some unsavory rumors about her.

Heber noticed and approached her. He took her hand and pulled her aside, while others were speaking about Miriam in the background.

"I'm sorry I wasn't there. I don't know if I can forgive myself," Heber told her. "Are you okay?"

Upon hearing his kind words, Jael sank into his arms, nearly collapsing with relief.

"I don't know what you've heard, but you must believe me, I am still pure," Jael tried to excuse herself, as if getting attacked by Sisera was a crime.

"Listen, I don't know what sort of man you think I am, but I do not blame victims for being attacked. And unless you willingly give yourself to others, you will always remain pure, do you understand? No one can steal your purity."

Deborah was so relieved for Jael when she observed her nodding silently in tears in Heber's arms.

Miriam was greatly honored in Ramah this day, in spite of her claims of Deborah shaming their family.

While it was true for a time, that many young females in Ramah were dragging Deborah's name through the mud, the mothers of those young females sympathized with Miriam rather than gossiped against her.

They pondered how hard it had to be, seeing her daughter in the spotlight of every young man in town. This was the initial sympathy, but then there was the Caleb incident, which dramatically changed perceptions.

Deborah was serious about her training!

This wasn't a game to her; it had nothing to do with gathering attention to herself.

After all those men were gone, and all the incentive for such attention had departed, she still went after those soldiers and even killed one of them. That was remarkable.

The challenge was issued, and she accepted it, forcing her father and Adonia into the fray. Her neighbor's husband was murdered in cold blood, and Deborah did something about it; she demanded they be held accountable, life for a life.

Following the Caleb incident, there was a period of shame among the young females in town.

Deborah wondered why she was still shunned; why females weren't coming to her and asking for training. The reason why was they were deeply ashamed of themselves.

Shallow, vindictive, and pathetic all their gossip turned out to be, seeing how Deborah risked her life for a neighbor, challenging a brood of vipers. She took a stand against tyranny without even asking for help.

That was Deborah, Miriam's daughter of extraordinary courage, and if Miriam were present at her own funeral, she would have been shocked by what the citizens of Ramah had to say about her.

While Deborah was distracted with Jael, she completely missed all this high praise of her courage, both at Ramah, and also in Shiloh.

Deborah's neighbor Naomi, whose husband was murdered, spoke eloquently, praising Deborah and her mother.

"And we now understand, the events of late, with tyranny at the hands of King Jabin and his vile, disgusting champion, Sisera.

"There has been no leadership in Israel; so very few willing to take a stand against this injustice, but one among us took a stand right here in Ramah!"

"Here, here!" some in the gathering agreed.

"There was slander among some who are here today, speaking against that young lady for a time, but that gossip is over. It has no place here," the woman cleared her throat and rubbed her eyes, still grieving over her husband, and now her good friend Miriam.

"Let it be known, that Miriam's teachings of the law to her daughter have made this entire community a stronghold of justice for all Israel. In this place, we demand...a life for a life!"

"That's right!" another chimed in.

"And from what I hear, that young lady and many of our young men represented well in Shiloh. They were among the few to fight back, driving Sisera's men from our holy Tabernacle.

"The Ark of the Covenant is still with us, thanks to them. So Miriam here, my long-time friend, has much to be proud of, and her legacy lives on!"

There were some claps and words of praise, and many even looked directly at Deborah while clapping, acknowledging her presence with honor.

However, through all this, Deborah was so distracted with Jael, she didn't hear a single word.

Had her name been explicitly mentioned, she might have perked up an ear, but she was too occupied with Jael's distraught predicament to notice anything.

Unkempt and weary with life, Haran was leaning on his rock fence. He stood in the same place as he stood for the funeral a few days earlier, next to his wife's grave. She was buried there in the yard next to

Caleb.

As Haran stared off in the distance, he recognized Adonia from afar, approaching from the east entrance of Ramah. He was greatly pleased to see this man who had since become his very close friend and confidant.

"Adonia! I thought you were never coming back!" Haran spoke in a scratchy voice and coughed, then cleared his throat. "Why have you taken so long?" he held open his arms and embraced him with a kiss on his cheek.

"Hand of Miriam," Adonia lifted his hand. "Haran, my good friend! I most please to see you again!" he spoke in his unusual accent.

"I cannot believe I miss all at Shiloh. So much I hear that day, I know not what true. They want me stay up north," he pointed in a northern direction.

"Yes, that way, they want me stay and train. They like my fight style," he threw a few punches to animate his point. "But I insist, my place here in Ramah with you, Miriam, and the Bee. I give you my words; I have to keep."

"Very good," Haran patted him on the back, but he didn't bother to mention that Miriam was gone. There would be time for that discussion soon enough.

"They say many thing about you family, I even hear amazing thing about Deborah. But before we talk, I have something."

Adonia removed his backpack and another object wrapped in a cloth, which was strapped across his back.

"Barak and his men, they have me bring Deborah gift," he replied, and set the item down on the rock wall. He then untied the bindings and removed the covering to reveal Sisera's jeweled dagger that he almost killed Barak with.

The weapon was a dagger for Sisera, but for a normal person, it was the length of a sword. It also had an extra thick hilt, designed for the hand of a giant; not feasible for a comfortable grip.

It was highly ornate, polished to perfection, and covered with jewels and unusual hieroglyphics.

"This must be Anakim language," Adonia pointed to the symbols. "It not Egyptian, or any language I know, and I know many language. This also light as feather," he held it with one finger, then he handed it to Haran.[1-2]

Haran was amazed, tapping it, analyzing it, puzzled how it could be so thick and made of metal, yet also so light.

"Let me show you this," Adonia reached out his hand for the blade, and Haran returned it. "Most people would say this is from gods. Look how hard the blade."

He then lifted it up, and much to Haran's horror, he took that beautiful dagger and smashed the sharp edge of the blade with a solid whack against the top of the stone wall. Rather than busting it, the sword sank five inches into solid rock.

Haran gasped and jumped back, eyes wide with shock.

"Look, no scratch, no dull," Adonia yanked the blade out of the wall and showed it to him. "This not normal; this not made with human hand; it from gods."

Haran was astonished. "That is...a remarkable weapon," he rasped and coughed again, "but I don't know if I would trust it. You are correct; that is not normal."

Adonia handed the dagger back to Haran, but he refused to take it. "I don't want to mess with that thing."

"But you just had it. It not hurt me; it only serve it master. Sisera no longer master."

"You don't know that," Haran eyed the weapon suspiciously.

"You can always sell. I sure it have good price. But I think you better to keep. I always hear complain about you weapon no good in this land. This weapon better than good; this weapon of gods," Adonia pointed to the sky.

"I'll think about it," Haran replied then coughed again, while Adonia draped a cloth back over it.

"Are you okay? You have the...eh...donkey cough."

"I've been sick the past few days," Haran replied, "That's why I'm outside getting some fresh air; hoping that'll help."

"Have you the elderberry?"[3]

"I'm all out."

"I have," Adonia reached into his backpack on the ground and pulled out a small pouch.

"We make elderberry tea with honey, what say you? Then maybe we come back outside. More fresh the air; go for walk; it beautiful day."

Haran nodded as they both entered the house.

Right as they entered the house, Deborah arrived carrying a large water jar, and interestingly, Gavriella and Sarai were keeping her company, each carrying water jars as well.

Deborah saw the object setting on top of the rock wall, and right next to it, she noticed the groove Adonia just cut into the wall. Was that there before? What could do that?

Just inside the rock wall, Deborah saw Adonia's backpack setting on the ground. Curious, she set her jar down. "What's this?" she questioned while the other two set their jars down next to hers.

Deborah flipped open the covering on the dagger and saw the gleaming blade inside.

Ooh...

She then removed the rest of the covering to reveal the entire dagger. "Wow! Who left this here?" she questioned, then she went to pick it up.

The instant Deborah grabbed the hilt, something quite unexpected happened. She immediately convulsed in a seizure, choking, unable to breathe.

Deborah was no longer in her front yard.[4-6]

Instead, she was back at Shiloh, looking through Sisera's eyes in a flashback so powerful, so vibrant and real, she felt as though she were Sisera himself.

All Sisera's sensory input, all his thoughts, emotions, ambitions; his lust for violence and power; she felt the very essence of the twisted sensual pleasure he experienced when slaughtering innocent people.

Even more shocking, the person she saw him killing was her!

She saw herself lifted into the air on his sword, drooling blood. She threw herself off of his sword, then she blocked Barak's attack and kicked him.

Out of the corner of her eye, she saw herself crawling away, and

then she saw this very dagger in her hand, pulled out of its sheath and thrown at Barak.

The instant the dagger left her hand, the vision vanished.

Deborah dropped the weapon and collapsed to the ground.

From Gavriella and Sarai's perspective, all they witnessed was a convulsing seizure that lasted about ten seconds, then Deborah passed out.

Gavriella immediately ran to the door of the house and pounded on it. "Sir, come outside! Something's happened! Quick, hurry!"

"Very good, you're finally awake," Haran poked his head through Deborah's bedroom door and saw her sleepy eyes open.

It was evening, and Haran entered with an oil lamp. He sat on her bed, took her hand and cleared his throat. "We were very worried, Honey Bee," his voice was even starchier than before.

"We?"

Haran nodded. "Yes, your two friends, and Adonia, he's back in Ramah. You should get up, I made you something to eat."

Food?

A short while later, Deborah entered the kitchen and took a seat at the table while Haran placed a bowl of stew in front of her. "Not as good as your mother's, but I think I did alright," Haran stared at his stew, awaiting Deborah's critique.

"It's good," Deborah started devouring the stew as if the bowl were going to sprout legs and flee from her. She was a barbarian at heart, and spending so much time with Barak and the other men amplified her undomesticated tendencies even more.

Miriam used to think this savage behavior was cute when she was little, but the novelty wore off when she entered her teens. That was the point when Haran thought she was even cuter.

Haran smiled at her, watching her gobble down the entire bowl, then fill it up for another round.

"Are you going to tell me what happened out there?"

Deborah paused before her next bite. "When I touched that weapon, I was back at Shiloh."

Haran lifted his head, as if he knew exactly what happened. "Ah, I've seen this before. It happens with young warriors; the memories will pass."

Deborah shook her head no while taking another bite. Then she replied with her mouth full; something Miriam absolutely abhorred. "This wasn't a memory. I saw through Sisera's eyes, as if I were him. I also felt what it feels like...*to be him*."

Deborah took another bite, but then she suddenly gagged, cheeks puffed up with stew. She nearly vomited with the recollection of being inside of Sisera's twisted head.

By force of will, she swallowed her regurgitated bite with a hard gulp. Smacking her lips after a vulgar burp, she then washed her mouth with a drink, followed by another hard gulp. "Sorry mom," she looked upward sheepishly.

Deborah then pushed her bowl of stew away and raised her hand with a minor declaration.

"I seriously don't want to waste this stew, so let's get some talking out of the way before I keep eating. If there is anything I hate, it's seeing someone lose their appetite over some psychological issue," Deborah waved her hands around her head.

"Then they walk away and leave that perfectly good food just sitting there. That absolutely infuriates me. We have all these laws in Israel, and I am shocked that we don't have at least ten laws to avoid needlessly wasting food.

"People need to eat their food! Some animal died; gave its life for you; you reject that sacrifice, and for what? It's not like you're going to stop eating. We all still need to eat! Get over whatever your stupid problem is and eat!" Deborah slammed her fist on the table.

Haran chuckled; the Bee was back to normal, mostly...

"And you put some serious effort into this stew, father, this is no kidding delicious. I said it was good, but no way, this is scary delicious. Peace on you mother," Deborah looked up again, "but I think father has you beat on this. I mean wow!

"You should stop trading and open a restaurant. We should be offering this in Shiloh. Have the High Priest take this into the holy of holies. Angels will sing over this father. I tell you, this one sacrifice would set us up for ten years at least."

"Okay, enough about the stew!" Haran finally interrupted her babbling. "What happened to you out there?"

So many thoughts were scrolling through Deborah's mind. Where to start?

There was the good stuff; should she tell her father about her vague recollection of that Mysterious Entity that she saw entering the Tent of Meeting? Sure, but first, he asked about the dagger.

"That dagger, it was Sisera's, wasn't it?"

Haran grabbed her hand and squeezed, coughed, then nodded. "Yes, sort of obvious from the hilt, don't you think?"

"Yes, but when I touched it, I was back at Shiloh, seeing through... *that monster's eyes*. I actually know many things about him, and I can't tell you how I know; I just know. But something I don't know is how I'm alive."

Haran squeezed her hand again.

"I thought I lost you in Shiloh," he spoke soberly. "When I saw you there, I cried out to the Lord. I was actually quite demanding with Him; not the normal kind of prayer I have ever prayed. I demanded that He either bring you back, or strike me down."

"You what?" Deborah questioned him, surprised he would admit such a thing. "You shouldn't test the Lord like that."

"Honey Bee, I just lost my wife and my daughter. There was nothing left for me in this world. I wanted to die, and I was honestly hoping He would strike me down. That would've been an act of mercy, the way I was feeling.

"I was actually expecting to die rather than this miracle that happened with you, but now that I see you were spared, I won't question it. You have no idea how grateful I am."

"Father," Deborah spoke quietly, "I think your prayer was answered before you asked it. I saw Him earlier that morning, before sunrise."

An eerie silence passed.

"Saw who?"

Deborah smiled mysteriously.

"I remember dying. I died, right there in the courtyard of the Tabernacle, reaching for the Tent of Meeting. Then the next memory I have, is like a dream.

"There was a cloud of glory around the Tent of Meeting, and I saw someone like an angel, enter that cloud. I think maybe that was...*Yahweh*," she whispered.

When Deborah said the name "Yahweh," a subtle breeze passed through the kitchen, causing the lamp flame to flicker. They both eyed the flame, sensing a presence among them.

"We must return to Shiloh," Haran replied. "We need to speak to the High Priest."

"He won't believe me."

"You want answers, don't you?" Haran then wheezed and coughed a few times.

"You're sick, we shouldn't be going anywhere."

"I'll be fine. Besides, I have to travel north anyway, we have trading to do."

Deborah nodded with agreement, then asked, "So, we're done talking about this now?"

"I think so."

She immediately snatched her bowl before it got away, pulled it in close and resumed her ungracious gobbling.

Wild rabbits zipped into their holes just ahead of them as Deborah, Haran, and Adonia left for Shiloh the next day.

The journey was tedious for Haran. In his stubbornness, he even insisted on taking his extra-large backpack, but that didn't last long. He nearly passed out just a few miles outside of Ramah.

Adonia joined them in case they encountered bandits, but his role also included being a pack mule, along with Deborah. They both split up the contents of Haran's backpack, adding to their own. Needless to say, the trip was grueling on everyone.

Deborah and Adonia were exhausted with the additional weight, and they had no problem going extra slow for Haran to accommodate his fits of coughing.

Fortunately they made it to Shiloh without any incidents. This time they kept very quiet while avoiding the main road. Deborah learned her lesson well on that matter.

The heart of Shiloh was still in shambles, but at least all those who were killed were given proper burials.

The three of them rented a tent for the evening, and Adonia offered to trade or sell some of their goods in the marketplace while Haran and Deborah went to the courtyard of the Tabernacle.

Once they entered the courtyard of the Tabernacle, Haran cleared his throat and asked one of the temple workers, "Sir, we are looking for the High Priest, do you know where we may find him?"

"Why?" asked the man.

"We need him to go before the Ark of the Covenant and inquire of the Lord."[7]

The man huffed and replied, "No one goes before the ark."

"What? Why?"

"No one goes before the ark," he repeated himself.

"What do you mean?" Haran persisted.

"The last High Priest died in the presence of the ark."[8]

"Really! He died? Why?" Haran looked at Deborah with a shocked expression, then he looked back at the temple worker.

While Haran was engaged in his conversation, Deborah was captivated with the Tent of Meeting ever since they entered the courtyard of the Tabernacle.

Even when the temple worker intermittently blocked her view, she stared right through him, as if he were transparent; she couldn't take her eyes off of that badger skin tent. The temple worker noticed and eyed her suspiciously, but said nothing.

"Oh, he was really old, his heart probably just gave out. But because of where he happened to be when it happened, no one has entered the Tent of Meeting ever since, not even the new High Priest."

"How are you atoning for the people?" Haran questioned him, concerned.[9]

The temple worker scoffed at the statement; intellectual superiority oozed from his pores. “Life goes on without such rituals,” he spoke in a smug, condescending tone.

“If you call that living,” the High Priest spoke from behind.

Commentary Notes

++

1. Emil G. Hirch, “Goliath,” Jewish Encyclopedia, https://www.jewishencyclopedia.com/articles/6779-goliath, (Last accessed February 13, 2021). Scripture makes no mention of Deborah or Sisera wielding an exotic sword. However, Scripture records an interesting string of events that follow the sword of another giant, Goliath, whom King David slew. King David originally took Goliath’s weapons back to his tent, 1 Samuel 17:51-53. Goliath’s massive sword weighed 600 shekels, which is about fifteen pounds, in contrast to a normal long sword, usually weighing between 2 ½ to 4 ½ lbs. A 15 pound sword is far too heavy to use in battle. Later, Scripture records in 1 Samuel 21:8-10 that Goliath’s sword mysteriously ended up in the Tabernacle behind the ephod. How did it get there, unless David took it there, either before or after he became king? And why did David take Goliath’s sword to the Tabernacle, of all places? Could it be that David had a metal worker re-forge its metal into a smaller, usable sword? In 1 Samuel 21:8-10, King David went to fetch this sword from the Tabernacle, and he stated that “there is none like it.” This is an indication that it may have been composed of an exotic, meteoric iron. Additionally, there is an interesting Hebrew Midrash to add a touch of mystique to Goliath’s sword. “The sword of David (probably Goliath’s) had miraculous powers (Midrash Golyat, Jellinek, “B. H.” iv. 140-141).” It is this mysterious tale that follows Goliath’s sword that inspires the otherworldly origins of Sisera’s sword, speculating that the weapons of the Nephilim giants may have had extraordinary properties because of their angelic origins. Scripture also mentions another exotic sword associated with an angel; a flaming sword in Genesis 3:24 was used by a Cherub to guard the entrance to the Tree of Life.
2. Tom Metcalfe, “King Tut’s Dagger Is ‘Out of This World,’” https://www.livescience.com/61214-king-tut-dagger-outer-space.html, (Last accessed February 21, 2021). History has a neatly defined timeline when weapons were forged with different materials; the Neolithic Age, Bronze Age, Iron Age, but then some strange artifacts surface from time to time, and they break all the rules. Egypt’s most

famous King Tut, for example, was buried with an exotic iron dagger composed of meteoric iron. "Some archaeologists have proposed that these early iron objects could have been created by 'precocious' smelting of iron ore nearly 2,000 years before the technology became widespread in the early Iron Age — perhaps by accident, or through experimentation... analysis also showed that Tutankhamun's dagger, bracelet and headrest were made from the iron of at least two different meteorites, suggesting that an active search was carried out for valuable iron meteorites in ancient times..."

3. David Brinn, "Israel's Elderberry Remedy Sambucol Provides Solution to U.S. Flu Vaccine Shortage", Israel21c, https://www.israel21c.org/study-shows-israeli-elderberry-extract-effective-against-avian-flu/, (Last Accessed December 22, 2020). (Bracketed comments added) "World renowned Israeli virologist, Dr. Madeleine Mumcuoglu, developed Sambucol, derived from the black elder tree [native to Israel], Sambucus Nigra L. Beginning in the 1970s, Mumcuoglu began research that led to her discovery of the key active ingredient in elderberry."
4. Rosemary Ellen Guiley, *Harper's Encyclopedia of Mystical & Paranormal Experience*, (New York, NY: HarperCollins Publishers, 1991). p. 470. This story operates under the speculation that psychic abilities like psychometry may be God given gifts. "Psychics generally acquire their talent in one of two ways: They are born with it and manifest their abilities in childhood; or they suffer a severe or life-threatening emotional or physical trauma that triggers the ability. The subsequent experiences can be unsettling, even frightening, especially when they are precognitive dreams or visions of death and disaster. Some psychics who fall into the second category at first fear they are suffering insanity. Most, however, find that they cannot rid themselves of their gifts and thus learn to live with them and use them. Every psychic develops a unique method of accessing and controlling his/her power. Throughout history psychics have filled various roles: priest or priestess, prophet, soothsayer, seer, diviner, fortuneteller, healer, shaman, wizard, and witch. In some societies psychics have occupied high positions in state or religion." This story fits perfectly with the basic definition of a psychic who obtained her power following a traumatic Near Death Experience. A scientific explanation might focus on the possibility that a dormant portion of the brain could awaken following such an experience. A theological explanation might speculate that the departure of a person's spirit from the body, and into the close proximity of God, might imbue that person with glory. Then, upon returning to the body, supernatural abilities might manifest. A third speculation might include the idea that increased glory might awaken dormant parts of the brain. Whatever the case, Scripture is clear that Deborah was a prophetess who had the ability to tell the future. She was also a judge, which is highly unusual for a woman in the time and place she lived. The two roles of prophetess and judge combined, suggest Deborah might have had powerful psychic abilities, and she used them while trying cases.

5. Rosemary Ellen Guiley, *Harper's Encyclopedia of Mystical & Paranormal Experience*, (New York, NY: HarperCollins Publishers, 1991). p. 487. "Psychometry. A psychic skill in which information about people, places, and events is obtained-by handling objects associated with them. The percipient receives impressions through clairvoyance, telepathy, retrorecognition, and precognition. The act of reading an object in this manner is called 'psychometrizing.' Psychics say the information is conveyed to them through vibrations imbued into the objects by emotions and actions in the past. The term 'psychometry' comes from the Greek word *psyche*, 'soul,' and *metron*, 'measure.' It was coined in 1840 by Joseph R. Buchanan, an American professor of physiology who saw psychometry as a means to measure the 'soul' of objects. Buchanan conducted experiments in which students could identify drugs in vials by holding the vials. He kept his research quiet out of fear of ridicule, and did not publish his findings until 1849 in his book, *Journal of Man*." Psychometry is a specific example of a psychic ability that would be particularly useful for a judge to determine the guilty party in a case.
6. While psychic phenomenon is commonly associated with the occult, and labeled as demonic, this story postulates the idea that "spiritual gifts" are defined by their origins, motivations, and uses. Spiritual gifts, like intelligence, are neutral; it is the alignment, beliefs, and uses of those wielding such gifts that determines whether they are from God, or from the devil. 1 Corinthians 12 enumerates a list of spiritual gifts, many of which have identical descriptions with their occult counterparts. For example, prophecy is giving words of knowledge and telling the future. Divination also involves words of knowledge and telling the future. Working miracles can include many items commonly associated with sorcery. In short, there are God given spiritual gifts, yet when those gifts are abused, or obtained through any other means than reaching out to God, they can become demonically energized and perverted. This appears to be what happened to Balaam, a man who God used to bless the nation of Israel in Numbers 22-23, but he abused his gifts, Numbers 31:16; Joshua 13:22, and he was killed by the sword because of that abuse, Numbers 31:8; 2 Peter 2:15.
7. Unlike the surrounding nations who made inquiries to fortune tellers and those using divination, the Israelites made inquiries to the Lord through the High Priest, Exodus 18:15; Numbers 27:21; Judges 18:5; 1 Samuel 9:9, etc.
8. Scripture does not state that a High Priest died in the presence of the ark. This speculation, as well as the notion that no one inquired of the Lord following that fictional incident, is derived from the Judges 4:1, which states that the people of Israel did what was evil in the sight of the LORD after Ehud died. This repetitive pattern of Israel's disobedience actually predates Ehud as well, for it began shortly after Joshua, Moses' apprentice, died. Judges 2:8-13, "And Joshua the son of Nun, the servant of the LORD, died at the age of 110 years. And they buried him within the boundaries of his inheritance in Timnath-heres, in the hill country of Ephraim, north of the mountain of Gaash. And all that generation also were gathered to their fathers. And there arose another generation after them who did not know the LORD or the work that he had done for Israel. And the people of Israel did what was evil in the sight of the LORD and served the Baals. And they abandoned the LORD, the God of their fathers, who had brought them out of the land of Egypt. They went after other gods, from among the gods of the peoples who were around them, and bowed down to them. And they provoked the LORD to anger. They abandoned the LORD and served the Baals and the Ashtaroth."

During Deborah's time, the general statement of "doing evil in the sight of the LORD" indicates an advanced state of apostasy throughout Israel. If a high level of complacency leaked into the Tabernacle duties among the Levites and within the Priesthood, it could have been fatal for the High Priest.

9. It was the High Priest's responsibility to make atonement for the people of Israel on an annual basis, Exodus 30:10.

Chapter 11:

Terrifying and Irresistible

כ

"Keen sense of style you have," the High Priest, Elias, replied to Haran. "You got that cloak here in Shiloh, from Tailor Seth, didn't you?"

"Yes, he makes the finest cloaks, and your staff, that's cedar from Lebanon, isn't it, just like mine?"

"Indeed it is," the High Priest replied while smiling at his staff.

"I like this man," Haran pointed at the High Priest while looking at Deborah, but she was still in her own world, staring at the Tent of Meeting.

"Deborah?"

Even when Haran stated her name explicitly, it didn't break her spell. Haran looked back at the High Priest with raised eyebrows. "Never mind her, she's somewhere else. Could you tell me where we might find the High Priest?"

Elias noticed how distracted Deborah was, and also how Deborah's mesmerized state was irritating the temple worker. He turned to the temple worker, "Thomas, you may go."

Thomas nodded and walked away.

"Are you…the High Priest?" Haran asked him.

Elias nodded, "I am. Sorry, I'm not wearing my priestly attire at the moment."

"Ah. We came..." Haran coughed some more, and while he was coughing, Elias ventured a question to Deborah.

"What exactly are you looking at?"

"Can I go in there?" Deborah asked.

"No," Elias curtly responded.

Deborah finally looked at Elias, pointed to the Tent of Meeting, then opened her mouth, but nothing came out. She bit her bottom lip, then finally spoke. "During the attack here, I was...*killed*."

"You don't look dead to me," Elias replied with a grin.

"But I should be." Deborah opened a button in her blouse, just enough to reveal the scar in her abdomen. "See that? I have one in the middle of my back to match it. Sisera rammed his sword right through me, lifted me off the ground, then he threw me.

"I had just enough strength to crawl in here, and I died right here on this spot," Deborah pointed at the ground. Elias looked at the damp spot, then he stared back at her without speaking. His pause invited additional commentary.

"I'm not making this up. People saw this happen to me. The next morning I woke up here in the courtyard, like nothing happened. But something happened," Deborah looked back at the Tent of Meeting. "*Something*," she nodded, eyes bulging.

"Then yesterday, I had a vision of Sisera when I touched a weapon that belonged to him. That was...*freaky*. I feel like something changed with me. So that's why we're here. We want to know what all this means."

Elias continued to stare at her, perhaps waiting for her to add additional information, but Deborah was done talking, so she simply stared back at him.

Was his dramatic pause and intense, scrutinizing gaze, an expression of doubt, or did he know something?

"Please," Haran hacked a verbal slice through their staring match.

"I'm telling you the truth," Deborah reiterated herself.

"I know," Elias slowly nodded.

"You know?" questioned Deborah.

"I heard rumors of a miracle; a woman who was healed. I figured if there was any truth to those accounts, I'd be seeing that woman sooner or later. And...aside from that, the Lord had mercy, even on a failure as I.[1] He spoke to me last night."

"What did He say?" Deborah's eyes lit up.

"Since Joshua, we have seen the Lord's hand on Othniel, son of Kenaz, Caleb's younger brother. Then there was Ehud, and then Shamgar.[2]

"But the days of the Lord's manifestations have waned. Even the last High Priest died in the presence of the Lord not long ago, and I have been fearful of entering the Tent of Meeting ever since I became the new High Priest."

"That doesn't mean you're a failure," Haran interjected. "It just means you have a healthy respect, which is maybe something the last High Priest lacked."

"Only the Lord knows such things," Elias humbly replied to Haran, then he started ranting about Israel's sin.

"That which is obvious is our nation has fallen away, and I have been fearful of going before the Lord. I just...I don't know what to say to Him. How do I intercede when so many don't care?

"Even now, Israel suffers under the yoke of Sisera, yet some among us still worship him as a god. Why? How can our people be so lost, that they would worship a devil who has nothing but contempt for them?

"And how can they enter this courtyard of the Tabernacle at day, and a temple of Baal at night? Sisera was allowed to do what he did here in Shiloh, because Israel opened the door and invited him in."

The High Priest then turned from Haran and finally addressed Deborah.

"Fortunately, there is still a remnant among us who have been faithful, crying out, especially since this attack on Shiloh. The Lord has heard their cries, and He has spoken."

The suspense was killing Deborah. “Please, what did He say?”

“Young lady, would you happen to be from the village of Ramah?”

Haran nodded while Deborah answered, “Yes.”

“Prophecy comes in many forms,” the High Priest spoke enigmatically. “Let me show you something.” Elias felt as though he was reading from a script. He spoke these words before. He dreamt this encounter.

Elias turned and walked over to the fountain, washed his face and hands, then stood up and faced the Tent of Meeting. After a few deep breaths, he proceeded toward the tent.

Priests and temple workers stopped praying and a silence fell over the entire courtyard as Elias walked into no-man’s land past the fountain. This was a place of holy ground, reserved only for select Levites and the priesthood.[3-5]

“He’s going in there,” Deborah replied to her father. Slightly incensed that she was prohibited from going into that area, she impulsively proceeded to march toward the Tent of Meeting, but Haran quickly snatched her arm.

“Do you want to die?” he snapped at her.

“Already did that,” Deborah responded dryly.

“Show some respect!” he snapped at her again. “Remember the last High Priest? Remember the laws of the Tabernacle?”

“I’m...I’m sorry father,” Deborah nodded. Stinking impulses. He was right.

When Elias reached the opening to the Tent of Meeting, he took another deep breath, accompanied with whispered prayers for mercy, and then he finally entered the tent. The priests and temple workers exchanged surprised glances.

A minute later, Elias emerged with another staff. The priests and temple workers gave a collective sigh, and hushed murmuring resumed in the courtyard.

Something major was going down.

"You see this staff?" Elias presented a staff to Deborah. "Grab it."

"What's going to happen?"

"I don't know. Take it and see."

Deborah reached out, but then halted just an inch away, trembling. "I feel something...intense."

"Take it," Elias smiled, motioning the staff toward her again.

As one might leap off a cliff, Deborah cleared her mind, then quickly snatched the staff. In that very instant, her head whipped back as if electrocuted.

As she shook violently, she was transported back in time, finding herself on the shore of the Red Sea at the break of dawn, witnessing the most breathtaking miracle she could ever imagine.

Before her was a chasm of inverted waterfalls; the water at the bottom of the Red Sea cascaded upward in vertical walls of water on the left and right.

She was standing directly in the center of this spectacle, with her right hand held up high. A most extraordinary sensation of power rushed through her body and flowed out of her hand.

What was this?

And in the sky directly above her, was yet another most unusual wonder. A billowing, dark cloud, geometrically precise, formed in a column, aligned with the chasm before her. This was a cloud of glory, and within it, a familiar presence.

As omniscience emerged from eternity, Deborah was overcome with this mysterious Ancient One. He was beyond time; beyond human understanding, yet simultaneously, profoundly relatable, and indescribably personal.[6-7]

He was the purely exquisite personification of all that is good in humanity.

From what Deborah could perceive, she felt His tenderness, and boundless joy, as new parents overcome with love and affection for their newborn child. But on this day, on this occasion, this eternal being of pure love was also fearfully protective, as a mother bear with her cubs.

People streamed past Deborah on both sides. About fifty people remained in the chasm, all stragglers, mostly elders moving toward her as fast as they could manage.

Not too far behind them, an army of chariots was racing forward. This menacing hoard was hell bent on slaughter.

Deborah turned to look behind her, and she saw a great multitude of Israelites on the seashore. Thousands upon thousands gawked a

t this unbelievable manifestation.

Looking upward, she noticed that her hand was not her hand. It was larger than hers, similar to her father's hands; elderly, yet virile and strong. She also noticed a beard draping down her chest. She was... *Moses*![8]

As the remaining stragglers moved up the embankment, she dropped her hand, as if issuing a command to the Red Sea to close this massive divide. Suddenly the upward cascade ceased just behind the remaining Israelites.

The entire channel instantly collapsed on top of Pharaoh's army of chariots. A swirling chaos engulfed them, immediately silencing their screams of terror in a muted death, drowned by a thunderous clap of clashing tides.

As Deborah witnessed the collapse of the Red Sea, she was blasted out of her vision, dropped the staff and feinted. Haran caught her and carefully sat her down on the ground. Her head was drooped forward, mouth gaping.

"Deborah? Honey Bee, are you okay?" Haran revived her. She finally blinked a few times and lifted her head, wobbly; groggy.

"What did you see?" Elias asked her.

Deborah finally spoke as if heavily intoxicated. "I know why you fear...going before the ark."

Elias laughed and stroked his beard. "Yes," he smiled, "terrifying, isn't He? And...*irresistible*."

Deborah smiled at that description.

"Well what happened, what did you see?" Haran reiterated Elias' question.

Deborah collected herself and answered, though tears streamed from her eyes as she spoke. "I was there, father, looking through Moses' eyes. The Lord's arm was resting in the midst of the Red Sea, splitting the waters. I saw it."

Deborah sighed, overcome with the memory. "It was...unlike anything you could imagine."

Deborah wiped her tears and continued. "I felt what Moses felt, the

power of the Lord, flowing through me. He's real, father, He's so..." Deborah fell silent, staring into a heavenly realm, caught up in a dreamy, catatonic euphoria.

"This is the staff of Moses," Elias replied to Haran. "The prophecy is true."

"Prophecy?" questioned Haran.[9]

"I declare this day," Elias raised his staff while shouting to everyone in the Tabernacle courtyard, "a prophetess is among us! The Lord has spoken!"[10]

Deborah's eyes bulged. *Wait, what? Eh...*

Everyone in the courtyard of the Tabernacle, and even some outside the courtyard that heard Elias' declaration, rushed toward them, fascinated, excited, and asking what happened. The atmosphere was electric.

Elias helped Deborah to her feet, then he pulled Haran and Deborah into a huddle. "You have given me hope," he replied, rejuvenated with inexhaustible exhilaration.

"When the last high priest died on Yom Kippur, I did not complete the task he started. When Yom Kippur comes again, I will most certainly go before the ark and make supplication for the people."[11]

The priests near enough to hear this looked at each other with dread, as if Elias going before the ark was a death sentence to all of them. Some were even going so far as to *cancel their temple of Baal vacation plans...*

Within the hour, a celebration erupted from the courtyard of the Tabernacle, and spread throughout the village of Shiloh. Message boys sprinted around the town, shouting the news, "A prophetess is among us, the Lord has spoken!"

Elias and other priests and temple workers left the temple and spread throughout Shiloh, shouting excitedly about the glory of God returning to Israel.

In the midst of all this commotion, some of the residents of Shiloh were confused, still grieving, thinking the priests had gone mad.

Elias strode up to an elderly woman, grieving the loss of her husband.

"Dear woman, the kingdom of God is at hand!" he announced with hope in his eyes. "The Lord has heard you. He is here among us. He spoke to me in a dream last night. Pick up that table, let's clean this place up, we have something to celebrate."

Musicians assembled and starting playing while the clean-up activities amped up. Make-shift tables were pushed together, grills and skewers were prepped with various meats, and baskets of remaining food were spread back on the tables.

Excited villagers poured in from all around, and amazingly, the festival was resurrected in spite of the horrific terror just days earlier.

For those suffering loss, only a wonder of this magnitude was able to lift the veil for them, giving them a foretaste of celestial glory that transcended understanding.[12]

Yelling out instructions, priests and temple workers corralled observers into the courtyard of the Tabernacle in the late afternoon, making sure no one passed the point of the fountain.

In the center of the gathering, temple workers were dressed in their white robes, standing before the altar in a symmetrical pattern.

Following instructions from one of the priests, Deborah knelt on the ground in the center of the formation, and a hush fell over the gathering as Elias exited the Tent of Meeting.

He was wearing his priestly garb, complete with the ephod, which was an ornate apron-girdle, covered with a golden engraved breastplate with twelve large, inlaid jewels.

Upon his head was a mitre/turban and a crown; the words "Holiness to the Lord," were inscribed across the front.[13]

When Elias reached Deborah, he asked her to please stand. He then used his thumb to anoint her forehead with oil from a horn flask.[14] After that, he laid his hands on her head and drew her into an intimate hug, praying quietly.

"The things you see, you must seek to discern. This is your calling." Elias then released her and took a step backward.

"Whatsoever you shall bind on Earth, shall be bound in Heaven, and whatsoever you shall loose on Earth, shall be loosed in heaven.[15] Go forth this day, a judge to all Israel!"

Several temple workers then raised their shofars and blew them loudly at the conclusion of this announcement,[16] and a frenzy of celebration immediately followed.

People were speaking excitedly everywhere Deborah turned; she couldn't have been more self-conscious, just wanting to go away to some quiet place. This audacious response was not the answer she had in mind when they went to Shiloh with questions.

As the spectators proceeded out of the courtyard of the Tabernacle at the conclusion of the ceremony, priests and temple workers continued to observe Elias, Deborah, and Haran with interest.

"The Spirit of the Lord is moving. His hand is upon us. I sensed His presence with you when I first saw you," Elias informed Deborah in a semi-private huddle.

"This is strange," Deborah replied, "I always felt I was meant for battle."

"Battle? You're a prophetess, you should be protected from battle," Elias replied, concerned.

"But my mother was just killed, and so was I for that matter. They have to pay for what they did, life for a life! You said I was a judge, right?" Deborah was confused.

"Deborah, enough," Haran interjected.

"We can provide you with protection," Elias offered. "I don't think you should endanger yourself to battle."

"Are you kidding me? I don't need to be coddled in a corner. You don't know me very well," Deborah was painfully blunt.

"Didn't you say Sisera killed you? Sounds to me like you need protection," Elias countered.

"But I'm here aren't I? I'd say that's some pretty powerful protection I already got, don't you think?"

"Deborah!" Haran interrupted her again. "This is the High Priest of Israel, you show some respect!"

"I'm sorry father, and I'm terribly sorry sir, you're priestly...ness high something, sir. I don't mean any disrespect, seriously.

"I'm just very confused by the mixed messages I'm receiving. You just made this grand announcement that I'm a judge, but then you immediately imply that I'm lacking judgement. How does that make any sense?"

Elias smiled, completely unoffended, delighted with Deborah's candor. "I have a feeling you'll do just fine. You must remember, we are all human. No one has all the answers.

"You just seek the truth, and you will find it.[17] My first prayer for you is to learn how to use your gifts.[18] I pray wisdom and discernment for you."[19]

As Elias was about to begin his prayer, a young priest approached and interrupted them. "High Priest, I have something urgent to tell you."

"Excuse me a moment," Elias excused himself, then he stepped aside while the young man whispered something in his ear. He then thanked the man and returned to address Deborah.

"The Lord is indeed moving, because your first lesson in discernment may have just arrived.[20] Now based on what I saw earlier, your visions seem to occur when you touch things, is this correct?" Elias asked her.

"Yes, so far. And dreams."

"Then your gift may be exactly what someone needs right now. The work of a prophetess is to reveal the truth, is it not? Come," Elias motioned her to accompany him.

The young priest led Deborah to a mother, father, and their son, who was an armed warrior about Deborah's age. "Tell her," the young priest spoke to the father.

"Our daughter went missing two moons ago. We searched everywhere. All we found was this," he explained while holding up a piece of broken pottery.

The mother added, "I sent her to the well in the evening. She never returned. We found this fragment; we know it's a piece of our water jar."

"Someone must have taken her," the father continued. "We don't know why, but we've both been feeling there is something significant about this fragment, like the Lord was telling us to hold onto it and bring it to Shiloh. That didn't make any sense to either of us, but what else could we do?[21]

"It's like we've both been obsessing over this thing," the father shook the piece of pottery. "Now that we're here in Shiloh, we hear all this shouting about some prophetess, and well..." the father shrugged.

"I have to be honest with you," Deborah explained to them, "I don't know what's happening to me. I came here with questions of my own, because I'm confused. I don't know how this works.

"I can only tell you what I experience, if anything at all.[22] If nothing happens, I will not just make something up so you can get your hopes up. And then there's the possibility that I might see something that you would rather not know about. What then?"

"Not knowing anything is the worst of all. We understand, she may no longer be alive. If that's the case, we would rather know about it than remain in the dark," the mother replied.

"Please don't make anything up; just tell us what you see is all, even if...even it's bad. We just need to know."

Deborah gulped. "Then there's the possibility I could see something wrong, something that isn't even true. That would make me a false prophet." Deborah swiped her hand over her throat, illustrating her execution. "I hope that doesn't happen," Deborah spoke to the High Priest.

"Have faith. You'll be fine," Elias reassured her.

Deborah gulped again, then held out her hand for the broken pottery.

Chills shot up her arm the instant the piece of pottery touched her hand. Unlike the other two occasions, this object did not have such a dramatic physical effect on her. Perhaps she was getting used to this unusual experience?

Or maybe there was less energy absorbed into this object compared to the other two objects that gave her flashbacks. If only Deborah knew, yet questions like these remained unanswered in this uncharted territory.

On this third flashback event, Deborah was humming to herself while walking alone in the evening, making her way to a well to draw water.

As she experienced the vision, she hummed the tune out loud, which shocked the father, mother, and brother of the young girl in question. This was a tune their daughter frequently hummed.

She was carrying a water jar on top of her head, as was her usual custom, but on this evening, her routine was disrupted.

Two men rushed from behind and grabbed her; one of them covered her mouth. Deborah jerked and twisted her head as if the abduction were physically happening to her.

The jar fell and broke. One of the men continued to struggle with the girl while the other picked up the broken pieces of pottery and threw them down the well.

At this point, the vision flashed to another location. Deborah found herself hovering in the sky, above Sisera's temple of Baal, in the middle of the night.

Her awareness then rushed passed the temple toward the back of the mountain, flowing like the wind. At the base of the mountain, she saw a small, obscure crack in the rocks, covered by brush.

Passing through the brush and into the crack, Deborah entered a torch-lit catacomb of tunnels littered with bones of all types. Some were obviously human, seeing several distinctive human skulls of varying size.

Deborah silently drifted, carried through the windswept tunnels. Like a hunting dog tracking a scent, she was following the energy embedded in the fragment of pottery in her hand, and it led her to a guarded dungeon beneath Sisera's temple.

Deborah passed the guards undetected, and merged through the door of the dungeon. Before her was the teenage girl she saw carrying the jar, now unconscious, chained to a wall in the dungeon.[23]

A rat scurried over to the girl's hand and took a nibble on her finger. Deborah felt the sting of its bite on her own finger and snapped out of the vision.

"She's alive," Deborah spoke to them.

The mother gasped.

"I know where she is."

Commentary Notes

++

1. Elias considered himself a failure, because he had not yet atoned for Israel's sins per the annual requirement outlined in Exodus 30:10.
2. The judges of Israel appointed by God after Joshua were Othniel, Judges 3:9, Ehud, Judges 3:15, and Shamgar, Judges 3:31. Deborah was the fourth judge.
3. Only select Levites and the priesthood were allowed in the Tabernacle for specific duties, such as maintaining the burning oil lamps, burning incense, and placing bread, Leviticus 24. Two sons of Aaron were complacent in their temple duties, Nadam and Abihu. They made up their own rules about how to complete their Tabernacle duties, and they died because of their disobedience, Leviticus 10:1-2. Then there was the rebellion of Korah, the great grandson of Levi. In Numbers 16, he and his followers rebelled against Moses and Aaron regarding the duties of the Levites in their service to the Lord. He and his 250 followers were belligerent and insisted that they also be part of the priesthood. When they issued their demands to Moses and Aaron, God executed them. Following their execution, thousands of Israelites had the audacity to protest God's judgement directly at the Tent of Meeting, Numbers 16:41. A plague broke out among them, killing 14,700 Israelites, Numbers 16:47.
4. Bible History Online, "The Outer Court", https://www.bible-history.com/tabernacle/tab4the_outer_court.htm, (Last Accessed December 24, 2020). (Bracketed comments added) "Any common Israelite could enter the courts [courtyard of the Tabernacle] but only the priestly tribe could go beyond and into the Tabernacle and only the high priest could go beyond still into the holy of holies once per year on Yom Kippur, The Day of Atonement."
5. NeverThirsty, "Were the Israelites allowed to enter the Tent of Meeting?" https://www.neverthirsty.org/bible-qa/qa-archives/question/were-the-israelites-allowed-to-enter-the-tent-of-meeting/, (Last Accessed 24 December, 2020). "Numbers 3:25-26 indicates that the terms Tabernacle and Tent of Meeting were used interchangeably on occasions, but Exodus 40:6, 24, and 26 seems to indicate that the Tabernacle sometimes referred to the Holy of

Holies. The court outside the Tent of Meeting included the altar and the laver (Exodus 30:18). This background was important in order

6. to understand Numbers 18:21-22 where the Israelites were warned not to enter the Tent of Meeting."
7. Carol R. Ember & Melvin Ember, *Cultural Anthropology, 6th Ed.*, (Englewood Cliffs, NJ: Prentice Hall, Inc. 1990), pp. 282, 286. "Social theories suggest that religion steams from society and societal needs. Emile Durkeim recognized that it is the society, not the individual that distinguishes between sacred and profane things. There is nothing in an object — a piece of wood, a stone, a statue — to make it automatically sacred. It must, therefore, be a symbol."
8. Clifford Geertz, "Religion as a Cultural System." In Michael Banton, ed., *Anthropological Approaches to the Study of Religion*. Association of Social Anthropologists of the Commonwealth, Monograph no. 3. (New York: Prager, 1966) p. 46. "It is when faced with ignorance, pain, and the unjustness of life that a person explains events by the intervention of the gods." This anthropological theory that all religions originated from social and psychological sources can explain many of the oddities found in the mythos of ancient Palestine, Egypt, Babylon, India, and elsewhere. For example, The Egyptian god Seth ripped out Horus' eye, which removed the moon from the night; the Greek god Atlas held up the Earth on his back, and a Heliopolitan myth describes the sun initially rising in the form of a sacred bird called the benu, which was later associated with the phoenix. Countless ancient myths are filled with such fictional accounts that are easily dismissed as scientifically inaccurate. However, what this anthropological theory fails to account for are legends derived from actual events, and/or real entities or people, validated by science. In many instances, mythologies include components of historical narrative verified by archeological research, such as the Trojan War and the city of Troy mentioned in Homer's Odyssey, and the Epic of Gilgamesh. A great deal of archeological research also validates many ancient accounts in the Bible. Gilgamesh, for example, is most likely Nimrod in Genesis 11. These ancient accounts include legends that originated from real people and events. In this story, the descriptions of Yahweh, the Creator, as an entity who is beyond human understanding, yet profoundly relatable and personal, was derived from a historical context and Israel's personal interaction with Yahweh. The books of the Old Testament, the Levitical priesthood, and the time of the judges which concluded with

kings, describe the relationship of a people associated with an extremely powerful being who used signs and wonders witnessed by hundreds of thousands of people, to free them from slavery. The-Hebrew God Yahweh is completely imbedded in a historic context; He intervened on behalf of Israel to keep His promise to their ancestor Abraham. Furthermore, one of Yahweh's primary concerns is that He is the one true God, yet there were many rebellious entities that He created at an earlier time, which were at war with Him. The account of Genesis 6, and the book of Enoch, actually explain the primary source of most ancient legends throughout the world. Therefore, from the Jewish and Christian perspectives, many ancient mythologies stemmed from real entities, and not imaginary explanations derived out of ignorance to explain the "pain and unjustness of life."

9. The staff of Moses is used here in this story, to illustrate connections between Deborah and Moses. In many ways, Deborah was the female counterpart to Moses. Moses was a prophet and the original law giver; Deborah was a prophet and Judge of Mosaic laws. Through Moses, God claimed victory over an army of chariots using water to destroy them. Through Deborah, God also claimed victory over an army of chariots using the water of the Kishon River to destroy them. Moses led Israel for forty years; Deborah also led Israel for forty years.
10. There is no known prophecy about Deborah, but that does not mean that such a prophecy could not have existed. Scripture simply does not say so. In a similar manner, in the New Testament, the magi from the east came to see Jesus based on a prophecy that we have no record of. It could be that many prophecies exist all throughout history, which served their purpose for the times they were meant for, and they have since been lost in antiquity.
11. Scripture has no record of an official declaration from a High Priest, for any of the judges listed in the Book of Judges. However, it is worth considering that something of this magnitude would have given Deborah her credibility and official title as a prophetess and judge throughout Israel.
12. Yom Kippur is the Day of Atonement, the tenth day of the seventh month.
13. See Philippians 4:7, "And the peace of God, which surpasses all understanding..."
14. Jesse Lyman Hurlbut, *Hurlbut's Handy Bible Encyclopedia*, (Philadel-

phia, PA: The John C. Winston Co., 1908), pp. 233-234. Mitre (something rolled around the head), the turban or headdress of the high priest, made of fine linen cloth, eight yards long, folded around the head. On the front was a gold plate on which was inscribed, 'Holiness to the Lord.' Exodus 28:4, 37, 39:28, 30; Leviticus 8:9.

15. Jack Kelley, "Is Anointing With Oil Proper?" Grace thru Faith, https://gracethrufaith.com/ask-a-bible-teacher/is-anointing-with-oil-proper/, (Last Accessed December 25, 2020). There is no Scriptural record of Deborah being anointed by a High Priest, however, anointing with oil had a precedent in Exodus 29:7. "It is meant to demonstrate that the person we're praying for is being set apart for a divine purpose. The Lord had Moses anoint Aaron to set him apart as the High Priest (Exodus 29:7). Later He had Samuel anoint David as the King of Israel (1 Samuel 16:13)." In the New Testament, "Mark 6:13 tells of the disciples anointing many sick people with oil and healing them. In this case, the anointing was to set the person apart for divine healing. Using oil to anoint a person being prayed for is a proper application of James 5:14."
16. Truth or Tradition? "Binding and Loosing", https://www.truthortradition.com/articles/binding-and-loosing, (Last Accessed December 25, 2020). The act of binding and loosing carries with it legal connotations, which would be directly applicable to a judge. "FAQ: What is the 'binding' and 'loosing' that Jesus referred to in Matthew 16:19 and 18:18, and does it refer to binding and loosing demons? 'Binding' and 'loosing' were common terms used by the Rabbis in biblical times. When the rabbis 'bound' something, they 'forbade' it, and when they 'loosed' something, they 'permitted' it. In spite of the fact that the terms were commonly used at the time of Christ, many Christians today are confused about what these terms mean... The Greek scholar, A. T. Robertson, wrote about binding and loosing: To 'bind' (dêsêis) in rabbinical language is to forbid; to 'loose' (lusêis) is to 'permit' [emphasis ours]. [1] The well-respected Bible commentator, Adam Clarke, agrees with Robertson, and writes: 'It is as plain as the sun, by what occurs in numberless places dispersed throughout the Mishna, and from thence commonly used by the later rabbins [rabbis] when they treat of ritual subjects, that binding signified, and was commonly understood by the Jews at that time to be, a declaration that anything was unlawful to be done; and loosing signified, on the contrary, a declaration that anything may be lawfully done. Our Savior spoke to his disciples in a

language which they understood.... [2]'"

17. Shofarot-Israel, "Barsheshet — Ribak, Shofarot Israel", http://www.shofarot-israel.com/index.php/the-shofar/biblicaltime/, (Last Accessed December 25, 2020). "The Shofar is mentioned seventy two times in the bible in various contexts and functions."
18. When Jesus said "Seek and you shall find," Matthew 7:7; Luke 11:9, He was likely quoting Moses in Deuteronomy 4:29, who was also quoted by Jeremiah, Jeremiah 29:13.
19. Is it possible to have spiritual gifts, but not know how to use them yet? Does one learn to use a spiritual gift? Is there such a thing as practicing faith or spiritual gifts? One possible example of someone learning to use his prophetic gift of interpreting dreams is Joseph in the Old Testament. As a child, when Joseph told of his brothers about a prophetic dream regarding his brother's sheaves falling before him, it did nothing but anger them. Then later, he told his parents and brothers about another prophetic dream where the sun, moon, and stars bowed before him. This created an uproar in the family, and his father rebuked him. His brothers were so jealous and filled with rage, they later conspired to sell him as a slave just to get rid of him, Genesis 37:5-11. Years in slavery and then prison, for a crime he didn't commit, humbled Joseph. He continued to exercise his gifts, and when he interpreted Pharaoh's dream to him, he didn't promote himself as part of the interpretation. Instead, he described only what he saw, and nothing more, and it was Pharaoh's decision to put him in charge of Egypt, second only to Pharaoh. When a famine later struck the land, and he faced his brothers once again, he could have gloated that his dreams were correct, but he didn't. He also had the power to execute them if he wanted to, or make them his slaves, but instead, he tested them to see if they repented of what they did to him. When they passed his tests, he forgave them, and declared that all the hardship he endured because of them was part of God's plan to rescue Egypt, Genesis 50:20. This illustrates the issue of how Joseph chose to use his gift. When he was young, there is a hint of pride in the narrative. Joseph was the "favorite," and he may have used prophecy to elevate himself, telling his brothers about his dream to brag about how special he was. That is not a loving way to use a God given gift. The wisdom he garnered from years of hardship, thus, helped him to learn and practice his gifting more in line with the will of God.
20. See James 1:5, paraphrased, ask for wisdom to receive it...

21. See Isaiah 65:24, paraphrased, before they call, I will answer, and while they are yet speaking, I will hear...
22. See 1 Corinthians 13:9-12, paraphrased, knowing in part, see dim reflection... Prophecy sometimes works for a church body to put the pieces together, like pieces of a broken jar.
23. Deborah is careful to only reveal something she sees, considering that a revelation of the Lord. Perhaps this is how Daniel and Joseph learned to interpret their dreams? They would have them, and in Joseph's case, he didn't fully know what they meant until much later. In Daniel's case, he interpreted King Nimrod's dream in Daniel 2, but how he learned to do this is unknown. Other spiritual gifts, such as Samuel's ability to hear the Lord's voice, was simply hearing the Lord's voice like a regular person. Samuel didn't know this was the Lord at first, but the High Priest Eli suspected this was the Lord.
24. Eli therefore established a plan to see if that was the case, 1 Samuel 3:7-9. This plan taught Samuel that it was the Lord who was speaking to him, so the process of discovering spiritual gifts and using them is not always a clear cut operation.
25. Rosemary Ellen Gulley, *Harper's Encyclopedia of Mystical & Paranormal Experience*, (New York, NY: HarperCollins Publishers, 1991), pp. 474-475. "Psychic criminology. Since antiquity, seers and dowsers have been sought out to help locate missing persons and solve crimes. The field of modern psychic criminology began taking shape in the mid-nineteenth century, when Joseph R. Buchanan, an American physiologist, coined the term 'psychometry' and said it could be used to measure the 'soul' of all things... Techniques: Most psychic detection involves psychometry of personal items belonging to the victim. Undergarments often are preferred because they seem to yield the strongest 'vibrations,' or items found at the crime scene. By handling these, psychics say they see images or receive information pertaining to the crime. For example, they may see a reenactment of the crime, or the location of a body or murder weapon, or the location of a suspect's whereabouts. Some feel as though they have entered the perpetrator's mind. Some also receive information through intuitive flashes, dreams, auras, automatic writing, channeling, hypnosis, dowsing, and graphology. Psychics often visit crime scenes to pick up additional information... Sometimes the information is cryptic - numbers, letters, and vague descriptions-and cannot immediately be deciphered. Psychically obtained information is not always reliable and does not

always lead to a solution of a case. Most psychics who work in this field have not been tested scientifically; thus no baseline exists by which to measure the effectiveness of psychic detection work. At the least, however, it provides psychological solace to individuals and can provide law enforcement agencies with more latitude in pursuing leads." In Deborah's case, if she had this ability, she was required to be 100% accurate, else she would have been deemed a false prophet or diviner, and possibly facing the death penalty, Deuteronomy 18:20.

Chapter 12:

Enough is Enough!

ל

Lost in thought, Deborah wasn't sure what to think about all the activity she just experienced.

"That was quite a ceremony yesterday, don't you think?" Haran asked as they traveled on the return trip to Ramah, along with Adonia and three warriors, Ruben, Ezra, and Joash. Elias insisted these warriors accompany them for additional protection.

"I don't like public gatherings," Deborah replied. "All we wanted was a few answers, but all we got were more questions."

"When is anything what we expect?" Haran mused.

"I just wish I could've gone with them to help that girl. Here I am, a prophetess, a judge, whatever that even is, and I'm not doing anything at all."[1]

"You did plenty!" Haran rebutted. "Their daughter is alive; they have hope now. And they also know exactly where to go to get her back. If King Jabin isn't behind this abduction, maybe it will even be enough to put an end to that tyrant Sisera."

The group of them eventually stopped at some ruins to break for camp. Later that evening, they sat around the campfire eating.

"How long will you guys stay with us?" Deborah questioned one of the men when he set his plate down.

"The High Priest sent word to General Abinoam. You'll have a detachment in Ramah from now on."

"You mean like the one that left?" Deborah snickered.

"We appreciate that," Haran replied to the man, glossing over her jab.

"I didn't ask for a detachment. He wasn't listening to me," Deborah fumed.

Haran was about to interject with a rebuke, but he instead unleashed a fit of coughing and gagging. Deborah scowled at him.

"You shouldn't have come on this trip father."

"Hush," he grimaced back at her while wheezing.

"You two have much disagreement. I miss this. You both have the... eh...*banner*...they call it? Is like you have *'word battle,'* no?" Adonia smiled at both of them while illustrating a punch with his fist.

"Banter," Ezra corrected Adonia.

"Ah yes, I close, is the banter. I miss the 'T' sound. Yes, ban-Ter."

Something about Adonia's commentary threw a wet blanket on their conversation; both Haran and Deborah sighed and looked away from each other.

Deborah then noticed a most unsettling sight. One of the men didn't eat his full plate of food. He left two pristine quail legs untouched. "Hey, you going to eat that?"

"Maybe."

"What do you mean maybe? Eat it, it's getting cold."

"Maybe I don't want to eat it all right now."

"Are you kidding me? You better eat that right now, because I'm starving."

"Well, you can have..."

Deborah immediately snatched the plate and started devouring the bird before he finished his sentence. Joash grinned at her, trying not to laugh.

"She does that," Haran nodded.

"I know, I was testing her. The guys said..."

Deborah lifted her head and paused in her bite, staring at Joash.

"Uh, *never mind*," Joash muttered.

Deborah threw the bone of the quail leg at him and hit him in the head.

"What was that for?" Joash questioned her.

"Tell them I said shut up," she chuckled and bit into the other leg.

Later that night, Deborah was groaning and twitching in her sleep. Her wrestles antics increased until one of her arms flailed out and thumped her father's chest, sending him into a fit of coughing again.

Once Haran regained his composure, he was sitting up and saw that Deborah was still asleep, possibly stuck in the middle of a nightmare.

He nudged her shoulder to break the spell, and she suddenly bolted upright, jerking her head around until she realized she just woke up from a dream.

"It's okay, you were just dreaming," Haran calmly replied in his raspy voice.

"Wow, that was so real," Deborah caught her breath. "There was this mass of chariots down in a valley, and I was with thousands of warriors on a mountain. We were preparing to go down to fight them. Why would we do that? Seems like a suicide mission, but it was weird, because I wasn't afraid at all."

Haran reflected on the recent events surrounding Deborah and tried to suppress any expression of alarm.

"Dreams are like that; probably all that quail you ate. Try to go back to sleep, we have a long day of travel tomorrow."

On the following day, as they neared the entrance to Ramah, Gavriella spotted them in the distance and sprung to life, shouting to some other villagers. "They're back!"

A group of villagers rushed out to greet them as they approached Ramah. What was this all about?

They were all filled with excitement, and they led Deborah and Haran to the two palm trees marking the entrance to Ramah. Between the two palms, they built a large bench, the center of which featured back support and arm rests.

"Sit here," Sarai, one of the repentant gossip girls directed Deborah to this seat of honor. "Please tell us a story like your father; tell us what happened."

"A girl from the Tribe of Asher was rescued because of you!" Gavriella reported, hoping Deborah would add the backstory to this news.

"They saved her? How do you even know about it? We just got back."

"It happened yesterday, our messenger bird came home just before you got here," Gavriella explained.

"Even General Abinoam was impressed," Tamar, another former gossip girl added.

"Glory to the Lord! He delivers!" Deborah was overjoyed that something was done about the horrendous situation with that girl.

Perhaps there really was something to this prophetess thing, because this was a tangible result of epic proportions. Who would have ever foreseen such strange experiences actually resulting in an amazing deliverance?

"I told you!" Haran gripped Deborah's shoulders. "This must be your calling! You can do so much good without even leaving Ramah. If you think about it, what you did has the potential to save just as many lives as any fighter on a battlefield; probably even more!

"Fighters are a dime a dozen, but your ability to report on what happened with that girl, and where she was at; only you have that gifting."

"Is that girl alright?" Deborah asked Gavriella, recalling how she looked; emaciated, near death.

"She's alive, and free of that place. That's all we know. And there were others. They would've been caught if they tried to free them all."

"Others?"

What initiated as wonderful news quickly morphed into terrible news. This abduction was not an isolated incident. How hopeless was this?[2-3]

The girl Deborah saw was abused to the brink of death, getting chewed on by a rat, and she was keeping company with others in the same situation. Exactly how many? How wide spread was this activity? How could Israel allow this to continue?

Later that evening, Haran's condition worsened, while Deborah's conscience continued to gnaw at her just like that rat she saw.

A judge's primary concern was justice, and the goings on up north were at the height of injustice. Did Israel have representation to make appeals for justice to King Jabin? Was this her job now?

Regarding her authority, she was endorsed by the High Priest of Israel, but what did that mean to the people of Israel, much less the surrounding nations?[4]

Then there was the fact that she was a woman. Young women in Israel were often regarded as property, and sometimes had little say in who they would marry. As for neighboring nations, their view of women was even worse than Israel.[5]

At least Israel had some ethical laws woven into the fabric of their community. Neighboring nations, in contrast, were a coin toss when it came to ethics and the treatment of women.

With all this in mind, Deborah couldn't fathom the notion of confronting King Jabin about these atrocities taking place. He would never take her seriously, but still, someone had to do something.

According to Haran's knowledge of Israel's political affairs, meetings between General Abinoam and King Jabin were rare and fruitless.[6]

General Abinoam's complaints were treated as unfounded accusations, all the while, skirmishes were common between Israeli troops and King Jubin's forces, and weapon confiscations were routine.[7-8]

King Jabin presented himself as amicable to General Abinoam, always reiterating he would get to the bottom of so-called unsanctioned activities, but nothing ever came of it.

At best, King Jabin was a laissez-faire ruler content to allow his military commanders call the shots, then he played the ignorance card when problems were brought to his attention.[9]

How far was Israel going to allow this ignorance card to be played? Didn't the attack on Shiloh warrant an all-out declaration of war?

Would Israel actually accept a pathetic "Sorry about that, terribly sorry, maybe Sisera got a little carried away," as the response to Sisera's psychotic bloodbath in Shiloh?

As for this new matter of abducting Israelites and subjecting them to protracted executions by means of torturous sexual abuse, how could this be tolerated on any count?

Enough was enough!

Deborah entered her father's bedroom and wiped his sweaty brow with a damp cloth. "I know the routes and all our customers. I can make this round."

Haran lifted his shaky hand and gripped her arm. "Take Adonia with you," he rasped.

"I was planning on it," Deborah whispered, "please rest."

"Don't do anything foolish," Haran warned her, familiar with that defiant, restless look in her eyes.

"Don't worry father, everything will be fine."

The next day, Deborah and Adonia prepared to set off on foot when Ruben, the top ranking warrior sent by the High Priest to protect Deborah, noticed them leaving and he tried to stop them.

"I can't allow you to leave, it's too dangerous out there!"

"Well we have a business to run. These goods aren't going to sell themselves," Deborah argued. "You can't make us stay, that's ridiculous. We're leaving."

"Then I have to go with you," he insisted.

"Suit yourself."

"You know what, please just give me a moment to prepare, and I will make it worth your while, I promise."

A short while later, Ruben returned with three horses he acquired from a neighbor, paying for them out of an allowance the men received to cover their expenses.

Horses were perhaps the most welcome token of appreciation Deborah had seen thus far, regarding her new role of prophetess.

Ruben told Ezra and Joash they didn't need to join them because this was going to be a brief trip and they would be back the same day.

The three rode out of town, and soon they parted from the main road and traveled cross-country through dry, rocky hills. About an hour later, Adonia finally voiced his opinion that they were veering in the wrong direction.

"Ataroth this way," he pointed.

"We're going to Nazareth."

"Nazareth? Your father no approve!

"Nazareth?" Ruben piped up. "That's too far! I thought we were going to be back the same day!"

"I never said how long this would take. You don't have to come. Yah!"

Deborah gave her horse a jab, and poof, a cloud of dirt and rocks kicked up behind her as her jittery young stud, itching for a sprint ever since she hopped on his back, finally cut loose.

"Deborah!"

Adonia and Ruben bolted after her, and now they realized why she insisted on riding that one particular horse. He was the fastest.

Late afternoon of the next day, Deborah slowed to a trot near the entrance of Nazareth, dismounted, and made her way into the bustling marketplace.

Unlike Ramah, where Haran's home served as a focal point trading post with a mixture of goods, Nazareth was filled with tents and open trading stands where goods were sold by specialized tradesmen.

As Deborah wandered through the streets with her horse in tow, she sensed that the overall mood was grim. Merchants and their customers eyed each other with suspicion. Thievery was common, and Sisera's attack on Shiloh was still fresh on everyone's minds.

"Just who I was hoping to find," Deborah replied to Heber as she approached his stand and eyed one of his bows.

"Ah, long time no see," Heber was delighted. "You have an eye for my finest work, as always. Very nice bows here, seven silver."

"Five."

"Just like your father," Heber smiled. Deborah then pulled out Sisera's dagger, wrapped in a sheet, bound with a leather strap, and set it on the counter. Adonia and Ruben finally caught up to her.

"There she is," Adonia grunted as he approached.

"What's this?" Heber questioned the obscured object Deborah set on the counter.

She uncovered a small portion of it for only a few seconds, then she covered it back up. Heber's eyes lit up; he was pretty sure he knew exactly what it was the instant he saw it.

Heber wasn't the only one to see it, either.

A few young lads saw Deborah pull out the curious object bound in a sheet, and their eyes were zeroed on target waiting for her to reveal it to Heber. One of three boys elbowed another, then the younger sprinted off.

Adonia spotted this suspicious activity right away and he suddenly whipped around and shuffled toward them like a lunatic. "What?" He growled.

The two remaining boys jumped back, quickly spun around and perused a neighboring stand. Meanwhile, Heber put two and two together regarding Deborah's latest acquisition.

"So you're the one!" he blurted out, saucer-eyed with shock. "I should've known it was you!"

Deborah's eyes bulged in response, paranoid of drawing undue attention. "If I wanted an announcement, I would've asked you to blow that shofar," she pointed to a ram's horn hanging on the wall of his stand.

"Sorry," Heber was embarrassed. He then picked up the dagger and verified it was indeed the ultra-light blade he heard Sisera was inquiring about.

"Do you mind if I get a closer look at it behind the counter? I've seen it before, but never up close like this."

"Go ahead."

Heber lowered the blade to an obscured shelf behind the counter and completely unwrapped it. His mouth fell open as he gasped a quivered breath, practically drooling on the ornate object.

This artifact was the most magnificent work of art he had ever seen. He marveled at its exquisite workmanship; his hands trembled as he touched it. It was priceless.

The level of detail in the designs and mysterious writing that covered it was well beyond his eyesight. However, the true value of this sword was its composition; such a weapon was not known to exist.[10]

He carefully bound it back up and returned it to Deborah. "Put it away, we can't do this here," he whispered and swiped his thumb past his throat. "Sisera's men are everywhere. Two weeks south, you'll get a good price. Or..."

"Or what?"

"This piece is...*amazing*. It weighs next to nothing, but it's incredibly strong. There are legends about it; I heard it will snap any blade it touches like a twig. Are you really who I think you are...that *prophetess*?"

Deborah wobbled her head with a confused affirmative. Just then, a sparrow dropped from the sky and landed on her shoulder.

What was this? Deborah glanced over at the bird, much surprised.[11-13] She always had a way with animals, but this was taking it to the next level. The small creature emitted a single chirp, then sprung to flight and disappeared.

Heber cupped his chin and searched the sky a few seconds, slightly distracted. "Did that...*just happen*?" He pointed toward the sky.

"Have you ever heard of signs and wonders? Well, that was probably a wonder," Deborah replied.

Adonia and Ruben were shocked as well, staring at Deborah as if she were the main attraction of a freak show. "Yes, that happen," Adonia answered Heber. "Probably tame bird, belong to someone round here," he tried to explain it away.

"Well, if your feathered friend is correct about you, it would seem fitting for such a blade as this to be in your possession, because it would have no equal if there is a smith that can refashion the handle for you.

"The only problem is, that metal is not...*normal*. Canaanites would say it is the craftsmanship of the gods. It might not be possible to melt it down, I don't know. It's not...*from this world*."

"Doesn't matter, I won't touch it," Deborah replied.

"Why? It's just an object; it's not like it's alive."

"Oh, but I think it is," Deborah explained. "When I say I won't touch it, I mean I can't. I already did, and it made me sick," Deborah gulped at the horrendous memory.

"You're probably right about it not being from this world; forged in unholy fires, and a piece of its owner resides within it."

"Then perhaps the holy fires of the altar within the courtyard of the Tabernacle of your God can purify it? Consider this," Heber held out his hands in animated fashion.

"Israel's most sacred object is the Ark of the Covenant, and on top of it, the Mercy Seat. The very throne of your God was forged from

Egyptian gold that was most likely a mixture of idols at one time," he voiced his pondering.

"If your God is the Creator of all things as you Israelites claim, then does He not have the power to purify that which is unholy?"

"He does, and nothing short of that would suffice before I ever touch it again," Deborah considered the proposal. "What would it take to make that happen?"

"I happen to know Shelah, a world renowned metalworker. If anyone is capable of redeeming this artifact, he can. He is a direct descendent of the famous Bezalel.[14] Surely you know who Bezalel was?" Heber's eyes were bulging at the mention of Bezalel's name.

Deborah shrugged.

Heber's eyes nearly popped out of his skull. He was profoundly shocked that Deborah didn't know this elementary piece of knowledge.

"Oh my, your father led me to believe you were a gifted student of the Torah. Do you even know who Moses was?"

"Please. What does metalworking have to do with the law?"

Heber was dumfounded. As far as he was concerned, the legend of Bezalel was the most important part of the Torah.

"Surely you jest!" Heber gripped his skull and briefly looked away. "I must have a word with your father! According to your Moses, Bezalel was specially gifted by your God in many crafts. Legend has it, it was he who made your Ark of the Covenant, and the ephod of your High Priest. His hands were gifted by your God to create sacred, holy artifacts."[15]

"Okay okay, so what would it take for you to fix this thing so I could use it? You know we're not wallowing in wealth like you."

"For you...a simple request. Put in a good word for me with Jael's father, and I'll see what I can do."

Deborah paused. No money?

"Do you love her?" Deborah questioned him with a suspicious glare. "Remember who I am? You don't want to lie to me." Deborah had no idea if she could detect a lie, but why not capitalize on the possibility?

Heber chuckled. "Why ask me if you already know?"

"Why avoid my question when you could just answer it?"

Heber scratched his head, thinking of how to give an honest answer. Did he love her?

He didn't know her well enough to claim a powerful emotional connection, but he was lonely, and the thought of spontaneously marrying a young, attractive girl kept him up at night.

"I can see myself a very happy man with Jael. We're just getting to know each other, and I think we would make each other very happy. I care about her, and I would be faithful to her and take good care of her. It's just, I don't think her father likes me that much."

"But do you love her?"

"Well I wouldn't want to take her as my wife unless she willingly accepted me if that's what you think. A lot of men don't care you know.

"I've had many father's offer their daughters to me over the years, in exchange for a dowry, but I turned them all down when I learned that their daughters found me...*repulsive*. I totally get it," Heber shrugged and lifted his hands in a helpless surrender.

Deborah suddenly realized why Jael liked him so much. His self-effacing comment was charming.

He was wealthy, and because of that, he was fully capable of getting almost any female he wanted, but he was purposely restraining himself, and willfully accepting rejection after rejection for years.

A twinge of guilt pricked Deborah's memory when she recalled humiliating Heber herself, in that rather curt, public rejection of her own.

"Now I know among you Israelites, it's a big deal gaining the approval of the father. In most cases, that's even more important than the approval of the bride, but not with me. However, I want to be in her father's good graces as well.

"I offered him a handsome dowry, but he wasn't impressed, and he eyed me with suspicion. Jael is the first girl to finally take an interest in me, but I don't want to create a rift in her family. That's why I think a good word from you would go a long way."

Heber didn't claim to be in love with Jael, but at least he gave an honest answer. If he wanted to lie, he would've just taken the easy route and said that he loved her.

Also, his answer gave details about the actions of love rather than the emotion of love. This was related to an important life lesson Deborah learned from her parents.

Heber stressed the importance of respecting Jael's wishes, taking care of her, being faithful to her, and wanting her to be at peace with her family regarding their relationship.

Those were concrete examples of a loving person, regardless of an emotional context.

Deborah was taught from a young age, that the actions of love were far more important than the emotion of love. In many cases, one expresses love the most when feeling it the least. The actions of love rule the emotions of love; actions take the lead, and emotions follow.

Budding relationships will often explode with an intoxicating emotion, but without the substance of love in action, the honeymoon is over.

Aside from Heber's intentions, Deborah knew Jael liked him, so who was she to sabotage their obvious chemistry? She still couldn't fathom Jael's attraction to him, but that was Jael's distorted perception, not hers.

Deborah nodded, but interestingly, aside from Heber's request, she detected a hint of guilt from him. He was hiding something; she could see it in his eyes, but she didn't think it had anything to do with Jael. Only time would tell what it was.

"Okay, you got a deal. If this can be done, then go ahead and do it. If not, just return it and I'll sell it down south as you suggest."

Heber took off one of his sandals and handed it to Deborah to seal the deal.[16] "Here, and take this bow while you're at it, you look strong enough to use it," he handed it to her along with a quiver of twenty arrows.

Deborah set seven silver rings on the counter.[17] "Thank you, and here you go, it's worth the seven you mentioned."

Heber was mildly shocked. "Really? Now that's your mother talking," he smiled. "Haran wouldn't pay the asking price to save his life."

Commentary Notes

++

1. What must it have been like to be one of these people of faith in the Bible, informed in a ceremony that they were chosen by God for a special purpose like being a prophet, judge, or king? Did these chosen ones automatically know what to do? Most likely they bumbled like a bee on occasion, uncertain of what they were doing. In 1 Samuel 16:2, the Old Testament prophet Samuel was tasked with anointing a new king to replace King Saul, but doing this publicly carried with it a death sentence. Therefore the Lord planned a low-key event disguised as simply a "sacrifice to the Lord," 1 Samuel 16:5. As part of the invitation to this sacrifice, Samuel asked for the sons of Jessie to come forth, and 1 Samuel 16:13 states that Samuel anointed David with oil. However, he only referred to David as being chosen by the Lord; he didn't say that he was chosen to be Israel's next king. Following this event, the Spirit of the Lord rushed upon David, but David had no idea what his anointing was all about. For all we know, David simply returned to watching his sheep, and his head was probably swimming with questions, wondering what this was all about. Samuel was Israel's most famous prophet; what did he want with an obscure sheep herder? What did he mean when he said he was chosen by the Lord? In this story, Deborah also experienced a ceremony with an official anointing, but her life wasn't immediately changing. There was no official rule book for prophets; no training from a supervisor or personal trainer in most cases. Moses did a good job setting up Joshua, and Elijah did a solid job of mentoring Elisha, but most of the other prophets started out on the ground floor. Ehud, Israel's judge before Deborah, was dead, so there was no instruction in leadership or judging for Deborah. Her instructions came directly from God, and they may not have been crystal clear. For Deborah, the priesthood is not even mentioned in Judges 4-5, so the High Priest's part in this story is pure conjecture. God's chosen throughout the millennia may have felt as though they were stumbling around in the dark half the time. Consider John the Baptist, perhaps the greatest prophet of all time. He stands on the dividing line of the Old Testament and New Testament, and Jesus referred to him as the greatest man on Earth, Luke

7:28; Matthew 11:11. However, during his time in prison, he suffered in such despair, that even he was wondering if Jesus was the Messiah, Luke 7:19; Matthew 11:3. He apparently didn't know one hundred percent, which is quite an admission, for being the one person appointed by God even when he was still in the womb, who would pave the way for the Messiah. If any human being was going to know who Jesus was, it would have been John the Baptist, and yet we read in Scripture that he wanted a confirmation from Jesus. After all, even John the Baptist was only human. Jesus graciously provided that confirmation, so John could have that peace of mind, yet there was a period of time when John's head was swimming. His logical brain was probably trying to connect dots to make sense out of a spiritual reality he knew was the truth, but his external circumstances were probably not adding up.

2. The idea of kidnapping and human trafficking is not explicitly mentioned in Judges 4-5, but it would have fallen in line with activities of an oppressive nation, so it is possible that it could have been going on. Judges 4:2 speaks of God selling the Israelites into the hands of King Jabin; this could be a reference to slavery.
3. J. P. Millar, *The Preacher's Complete Homiletic Commentary on the Book of Judges, Vol 6,* (New York: NY, Funk & Wagnalls Company, 1974), p. 187. It might be possible that some Israelites were slaves working as woodcutters for King Jabin. "'Harosheth' signifies arsenal or workmanship - cutting and carving, whether in stone or wood (Exodi:5), and so it might be applied to the place where such works were carried on. The conjecture is, that this being a great timber district, rich in cedars and fir trees, and near Great Zidon (Josh xi:8), Jabin kept a large number of oppressed Israelites at work in hewing and preparing it at Harosheth for transport to Zidon; and that these wood cutters, armed with axes and hatchets, formed the soldiers of Barak's army... Their task work in hewing timber was like that of their ancestors in making bricks."
4. According to the narrative in Judges 4-5, at the height of her career, Deborah not only tried cases as a judge, but she may have also exercised executive power as a governor, because she summoned General Barak, and he reported to her, Judges 4:6-8.
5. Lawrence O. Richards, *Bible Teacher's Commentary,* (Colorado Springs, CO: Cook Communications Ministries, 2004). pp 182-183. "Ancient civilizations were patriarchal in structure. In such societies, the role of men was emphasized. In many cultures, women were

viewed as nothing more than property, and were not permitted to inherit the possessions of their husbands, much less given authority. Israel too was patriarchal, but women were not oppressed there as in other lands. Women are even among the Old Testament prophets, who were called by God to be His spokeswomen. Deborah was one of these special women. Even before the military victory over the Canaanites, she was 'judging' Israel from Ramah. The term 'judging' is important if we are to understand this woman's importance. A judge was more than a person who settled disputes (which Deborah did: see Judges 4:5). A judge in Israel exercised all of the functions of a governor: he or she held executive and legislative authority as well. We can sense Deborah's authority as she 'sends for" Barak, and he comes...'

6. Ken Anderson, *Where To Find It In The Bible, The Ultimate A to Z Resource*, (Nashville, TN: Thomas Nelson Publishers, 1996), p. 428, Representatives. "Upon the advice of his father-in-law, Moses adopted the policy of working through representatives for many of his administrative decisions, Exodus 18:14-27." Scripture says nothing about any meetings or negotiations between General Abinoam and King Jabin. However, the notion that Israel may have had meetings with King Jabin is derived from the ancient practice of organizations and/or governmental structures appointing representatives for the masses, to address grievances, discuss agreements or treaties, matters of trade or commerce, or simply to disseminate information. This practice even holds true in prisoner of war camps, so it would likely be used in cases of conscripted labor. Israel in particular was already using this established precedent of representatives with Moses, and it worked very effectively, so it is possible the practice may have continued between the Israelites and King Jabin.
7. Arthur E. Cundall & Leon Morris, *Judges & Ruth: An Introduction & Commentary*, (Downers Grove, IL: Inter-Varsity Press Leicester, England, 1968), p. 95. "They had been deprived of their weapons, similar to events in 1 Samuel 13:22, although it may be unwise to accept this as an absolute statement. If it fwere, the battle at the Kishon could hardly have been undertaken. Probably the meaning is that these weapons dared not be displayed publicly."
8. J. P. Millar, *The Preacher's Complete Homiletic Commentary on the Book of Judges, Vol 6*, (New York: NY, Funk & Wagnalls Company, 1974), p. 187. It is suspected that a large number of oppressed Israelites may have worked as wood cutters, and they used their axes and hatchets in battle. Just as this story describes throughout,

there were weapons confiscations, as suggested in Judges 5:8, "not a spear or shield." However, in this story, the Israelites were careful to conceal any weapons they acquired, and they were creative with improvising new weapons.

9. Arthur E. Cundall & Leon Morris, *Judges & Ruth: An Introduction & Commentary*, (Downers Grove, IL: Inter-Varsity Press Leicester, England, 1968). p 82. The description of King Jabin as laissez-fair, allowing Sisera a long leash, is derived from Judges 4 mentioning King Jabin, but Sisera is the bad guy running around doing all the fighting. Judges 5 focuses entirely on Sisera. "It is possible that there was a coalition of Canaanite city-states, under the nominal leadership of the king of the most important city, Hazor, but under the military leadership of Sisera, its most able captain. Sisera may have been a petty king of Harosheth, but his principal role in the narrative is that of the military leader of the combined armies. These facts explain the infrequency with which Jabin, who may have been an old man, is mentioned (not at all in chapter 5 [of Judges] not in connection with the actual combat), and the prominence of Sisera in these records."
10. William G. Denver, *Who Were the Early Israelites and Where Did They Come From?* (Grand Rapids, MI, William B. Eerdmans Publishing Co., 2003), p. 66. Deborah lived during the Bronze Age; bronze swords would have been the norm. Sisera's dagger in this story is a work of fiction. It is unique because it is from the Nephilim, who were sired by fallen angels, making the weapon otherworldly in origin.
11. The scene with this bird is fiction, however, the Bible speaks of "signs and wonders" in many places, and Deborah may have been surrounded by such wonders, testifying of God's anointing upon her. Animals across the globe came to Noah and entered the Ark under God's command, Genesis 7:14-16, and the prophet Elijah was fed by wild birds, 1 Kings 17:2-16. A more recent example of a servant of God having a way with animals can include Saint Francis of Assisi.
12. Carolyn Trickey-Bapty, *Martyrs & Miracles: The Inspiring Lives of Saints & Martyrs*, (Owings Mills, MD: Ottenheimer Publishers, Inc, 1994). p. 117. Saint Francis of Assissi was born in Italy in 1181, and is known as the patron saint of animals and ecology, because of "... his love of all living things. He could talk with the animals."
13. Thomas of Celano, *The Treatise on the Miracle of Saint Francis*, (1250-1252), ed. Regis J. Armstorng, OFM Cap, J.A. Wayne Hell-

moann, OFM Cov, William J. Short, OFM, *The Francis Trilogy of Thomas of Celano* (Hyde Park: New City Press, 2004), 329-330. "One time as [Francis] was passing through the Spoleto valley, he came upon a place near Bevagna, in which a great multitude of birds of various kinds had assembled. When the holy one of God saw them, because of the outstanding love of the Creator with which he loved all creatures, he ran swiftly to the place. He greeted them in his usual way, as if they shared in reason. As the birds did not take flight, he went to them, going to and fro among them, touching their heads and bodies with his tunic. Meanwhile his joy and wonder increased as he carefully admonished them to listen to the Word of God: 'My brother birds, you should greatly praise your Creator and love Him always. He clothed you with feathers and gave you wings for flying. Among all His creatures, He made you free and gave you the purity of the air. You neither sow nor reap, He nevertheless governs you without your least care.' At these words, the birds gestured a great deal, in their own way. They stretched their necks, spread their wings, opened their beaks and looked at him. They did not leave the place until, having made the sign of the cross, he blessed them and gave them permission. On returning to the brothers he began to accuse himself of negligence because he had not preached to the birds before. From that day on, he carefully exhorted birds and beasts and even insensible creatures to praise and love the Creator."

14. The Bible makes no mention of Shelah, a direct descendent of Bezalel, however, Bezalel is mentioned in Scripture. Heber was a Kenite, and the Kenites were associated with metalworking. Because of this, if Heber had connections in the metalworking industry as many Kenites did, he might have heard of a master craftsman of Israel.
15. Bezalel was gifted by God as a prodigy master craftsman mentioned in Exodus 31:1-5. He created the Ark of the Covenant and the Breast piece of the High Priest.
16. The custom of removing one's sandal to confirm a transaction is described in Ruth 4:7.
17. Jesse Lyman Hurlbut, *Hurlbut's Handy Bible Encyclopedia*, (Philadelphia, PA: The John C. Winston Co., 1908). p. 235, "Un-coined Money. It is well known that ancient nations that were without a coinage weighed the precious metals, a practice represented on the Egyptian monuments, on which gold and silver are shown to have been kept in the form of rings. We have no evidence of the use

of 'coined money' before the return from the Babylonian captivity; but silver was used for money, in quantities determined by weight, at least as early as the time of Abraham; and its earliest mention is in the generic sense of the price paid for a slave, Genesis 17:13. The 1000 'pieces of silver' paid by Abimelech to Abraham, Genesis 20:16, and the 20 'pieces of silver' for which Joseph was sold to the Ishmaelites, Genesis 37:28, were probably rings such as we see on the Egyptian monuments in the act of being weighed. The shekel weight of silver was the unit of value through the whole age of Hebrew history, down to the Babylonian captivity."

Chapter 13:

This Cat is a Lion!

מ

"My prayers are answered! Salvation has come!" uttered a woman out of breath as she ran up to Deborah. At her side was the boy who sprinted off earlier when his brother nudged him.

"You've come to deliver us," she pleaded, "my little girl..."

Two more villagers quickly joined her, Shem and Kanaz, both men in their mid-twenties. "You helped save my friend's daughter," Shem replied, "but they have my sister too, and others."

"Many others, both children and adults," replied Kenaz. "They take us at night, some for slaves, others, worse. His sister is my fiancé."

"They cage them like animals," Shem pleaded. "We were going to try and break them out ourselves but we couldn't get anyone to help. Everyone is afraid."

Deborah already knew about these others. Providing information so only one girl could be saved was not enough; it never was. All they did was place a tiny patch on a festering wound infecting the entire nation of Israel.

"Aren't the men around here doing anything about this? What about General Abinoam?" Deborah found herself echoing her father's words, wondering what these villagers would have to offer as a response.

"Nothing!" Kenaz retorted with disgust.

"That's not true," Heber replied.

"We're in this mess because of you merchants trading with the enemy," Kenaz shot back at Heber. "Not you," he nodded toward Deborah,

"but him and others like him. They sell their best weapons to Sisera and his men."

"If you think we're in a bad situation right now, stir up trouble and see what happens," Heber responded. "I am in a very delicate situation

here, just trying to survive. You have to know where to draw the line."

"If you traded places with my daughter you wouldn't say that!" Ruth interjected.

"Look, I don't know what you have in mind with what you're asking her," Heber addressed Ruth and Kenaz, "but I don't have a good feeling about it at all. You all know what happened in Shiloh. Deborah," Heber looked at her intensely. "If you're father were here..."

"You don't speak for my father," Deborah cut him off, "and you don't either," she eyed Adonia, who was about to speak up, but he refrained.

"This...is none of your concern," Deborah spoke to Heber sternly. Now she knew what that hint of guilt was that she detected earlier. Heber was straddling the fence between Israel and King Jabin, possibly selling his best weapons to Sisera's men. This was likely the primary source of his wealth.

However, he seemed genuine about Jael, and he was having an amazing sword of unmatched craftsmanship fashioned for Deborah.[1]

The verdict was still out on Heber.

"We're done here, I'll see you in a few weeks," Deborah replied to Heber, then she turned to go.

Heber quickly blurted out, "Wait, before you go, give this to Jael." He scurried to his stand, then returned to Deborah with a beautiful gold bracelet in his hand.

"Okay, I will when I speak with her father," she nodded, then she turned to Ruth, Kenaz and Shem. "Can we go somewhere private?"

"What you do?" Adonia questioned her.

"What I should've already done."

Not long after the private meeting with Ruth, Kenaz and Shem, Deborah was no longer doing her father's bidding as a merchant.

Adonia would have voiced more opposition to this mad impulse guiding Deborah's next stop, but Kenaz and Shem were tagging along now, both fired up that someone was finally going to do something about this wretched situation.

As for Ruben, he was caught up in the moment, invigorated by Deborah's intense sense of justice.[2-3]

What were they going to do? Only Deborah knew, and she wasn't saying anything...*yet*.

The small band traversed the arid landscape under a setting sun. The terrain was mostly flat where they were, with a few scattered trees and sparse vegetation. Adonia finally couldn't hold his tongue any longer.

"You no listen, Deborah. You father not happy with this business you do here, you up to. I think you need plan, eh...shaggy, shaggery. You can no..."

"Strategy!" Deborah interrupted him. "I have all the strategy I need up here," Deborah tapped her head, recalling the mental blueprint of Sisera's tunnels from her vision.

"Talk, that's all anyone ever does and I'm sick of it. We have to act!"

"It no matter, General Abinoam, he no accept you idea, whatever crazy thing you up to."

"Who said we're going to him?" Deborah raised an eyebrow.

The group approached a wadi and followed it until Deborah spotted horse tracks, then they started following them. They eventually led to a trail that entered the wadi.

A few minutes later, a voice whispered from the darkness ahead of them.

"Halt! Cat vomit."

"Worm skin," Deborah replied.

"Is that Deborah, or...uh, the Prophetess of Israel?"

"When are you going to change that stupid call sign?"

"It is you!" he whispered excitedly. "Come in."

As Deborah dismounted and proceeded forward, the wadi opened up slightly, revealing a contingent of men.

The men were sharpening weapons, making arrows, and cooking a few meals on tiny fires shielded by rocks.

The wadi provided perfect cover from Sisera's mountain in the distance, overlooking the flat terrain. They were deep enough in the trench to conceal their horses.

On the distant end of the wadi, Barak was huddled in a meeting with his squad leaders. When he spotted Deborah, he was both elated, and disturbed. She was here! *Why was she here*?

Seeing Barak again, Deborah leaked out a subtle lip biting sigh.

With all his men around and no place for privacy, she had to keep the discussion light, but it was difficult to suppress her passions simmering beneath the surface.

The best way to suppress passion is to redirect it to yet another passion.

For Deborah, that was seeking justice for those prisoners in Sisera's hell hole. Laser focused on that objective, it didn't take long before Deborah cut to the chase. Controversy soon followed.

"King Jabin's built so many chariots, even conquering all of this land is not enough. Now he intends to take the seas."

"So what!" Deborah retorted. "How can we allow this? Their stories made me sick to my stomach," she pleaded. "For the sake of Yahweh, we cannot allow this to continue!"[4]

Deborah's passion for justice was contagious, but at the same time, everyone sensed the enormity of the consequences of what she was proposing. She was chipping away at a crack at the base of a dam.

"I've heard, I know, but my father won't listen. He even blames you for that attack on Shiloh."

"Me? How is that? I..." Deborah never connected the dots of her attack on those troops in Ramah with the attack on Shiloh, but the instant she heard this accusation, an overwhelming sense of dread engulfed her.

Her own mother was murdered in Shiloh. Did she inadvertently kill her own mother?

Miriam never let up about her disappointment in Deborah's battle scarred warrior ambitions, no doubt sick with fear for her daughter, but maybe she feared for her own life as well. Did Miriam suffer from premonitions?

Deborah cupped her mouth, staring at the ground, silenced. Barak suddenly realized he verbally sucker punched her in the gut; it might have hurt even worse than that physical punch he once delivered. He gently grabbed her by the shoulders and tried to get her attention.

"Deborah. Deborah, look at me. Deborah..."

She finally looked into his eyes, tears welling up in her own, recalling her mother's disappointment. Barak's soothing touch, ever familiar, was a magic salve, but even so, she was focused on the mission at hand.

A sense of clarity quietly washed over her after a few deep breaths, and she returned to her senses as Barak embraced her.

Deep within, the law spoke to her. Its unquestionable logic, beautiful in its perfection, absolved her of guilt, and redirected her focus to where it belonged.

As much as she simply wanted to run away with Barak, further intimacy would have to wait for another day. She gently broke from the embrace and returned to their conversation.

"Evil lies in the hands of the doer," she replied.

For no reason whatsoever, Sisera's men attacked Caleb, a member of her family. They were wrong for doing that, and they were wrong for murdering her neighbor's husband.

The law demanded, life for a life.[5] It was their hands that committed those unprovoked crimes, and they paid for those crimes.

As for Shiloh, that was a massive criminal enterprise, perpetrated at the hands of Sisera and his men. Whether or not it was a retaliation for Ramah was entirely irrelevant.

The attack on Shiloh was pure evil, it had no justification, and it was their hands alone that perpetrated that attack.

Thus far, no one was held accountable for those crimes, nor for these abductions that were taking place on a regular basis.

"What you mean?" Adonia questioned Barak, still processing his opening statement that his father made. "We hear you father in the press by what we did in Ramah." Adonia was confused.

"Impressed," Deborah corrected him.

"Yes, that what I say, in the press," Adonia nodded.

Barak ignored the grammar lesson. "Sure he was, but he was also furious," he replied. "I agree with you, Deborah, I don't blame you for anything," he touched her cheek and gazed into her pretty, mesmerizing eyes.

Barak would've given anything to spend a few hours with her alone. It was taking all his concentration just to talk with her.

"Those sick bastards deserved what they got," he continued, "and suggesting the attack on Shiloh was retaliation for Ramah, is pure speculation.

"Honestly, if Sisera was pissed about what happened in Ramah, then why didn't he attack Ramah? Please don't blame yourself for any of that."

"I don't," Deborah replied, her conscience now clear on the matter, and already reverted to her prior train of thought.

"If I feel guilty about anything right now, it's for not doing enough to help free those other prisoners trapped in Sisera's dungeon. Why do we even have warriors in Israel?

What's the point of knowing how to fight, and all this stupid training you do, when you don't do anything with it? Really, what's the point, why are you even out here? Why don't you just go home?"

"You of all people know, we serve a purpose. You must realize how much worse it would have been in Shiloh if none of us were there to

defend it. We..." Barak pointed to her, then motioned to the rest of his men, "stopped that attack and drove them out of there."

"Okay, well that's a start, but it doesn't end there," Deborah replied.

Barak was baffled with Deborah's lack of comprehension over the gravitas of Israel's predicament. Did she have no idea exactly how vast of a military empire King Jabin wielded?

He knew he discussed those details with her in the past, and so did Adonia and her father. Israel was a miniscule speck in King Jabin's eye. Did she get hit on the head during Shiloh and forget all of that?

"Don't you realize," Barak questioned her, "we are in a delicate situation here? We can't afford a full scale war with Jabin. We play cat and mouse to sustain a fragile peace, but this cat is a lion!"

"Delicate situation, you sound like jelly ball Heber," Deborah fired back.

She then stood up and paced back and forth, waiting for the words.

"Shem and Kenaz here," Deborah motioned to them, "they don't even have any battle training like you guys, but here they are." At the mention of their names, Shem and Kenaz puffed up, nostrils flared.

"She's the only one who would listen to us," Kenaz spoke up. "She's the only one in all Israel who cares!"

"Shem's sister, Kenaz's fiancé, is in that demonic cesspool as we speak," Deborah continued. "They were pleading all over Nazareth for help to rescue her. All they found were a bunch of cowards.

"So let me ask you again..." Deborah scanned the men and spotted an older man to approach; a man she thought might have children.

"Why are we here, when our brothers, our sisters, and even our children, perhaps even your children, sir, are being raped and tortured to death, just right over there," she pointed at Sisera's temple in the distance.[6]

"Guess what? I know exactly where they are. I know a back entrance into Sisera's twisted labyrinth. I know where his guards are posted; I have it all mapped out," Deborah tapped her skull.

"Less than a dozen of us can do this. A small contingent can quietly slip in and out of there, and they wouldn't even know what happened until the next day.

"What's the worst that could happen? You think they might do something like, gee, kidnap our children and torture them to death? Oh wait, *they're already doing that...*"

Deborah then strutted back over to Barak and stood defiantly before him. "What say you to the Prophetess of Israel, man? Are you with us? If not, then fine, it'll be just the five of us," Deborah motioned to Kenaz, Shem, Adonia, and Ruben.[7]

Adonia cleared his throat, saucer eyed, now fully aware that he was just enlisted into Deborah's suicide mission, which could potentially result in a full scale declaration of war by King Jabin.

Abducting strays from the herd is bad, but a full scale war could escalate to a mass slaughter; Shiloh times ten.

A handful of chariots wrought destruction on Shiloh. King Jabin had over nine hundred such chariots in his arsenal,[8] more than enough to destroy every single town in all Israel.

Nonetheless, Deborah was caught up in the heat of the moment, hyper-focused on this rescue mission. As for the aftermath, that was another bridge to cross on another day.

Speaking of Shem and Kenaz, Deborah continued.

"What they lack in training, they overcome with heart. Might even be better this way, the five of us is probably all we need, but the glory of this battle could be yours," Deborah pointed at Barak while uttering her familiar phrase.

"You're incorrigible," Barak moaned.

"Well?" she reiterated.

"Sir, we have to do this," Ruben pleaded with Barak. "It's the right thing to do, and you know it. I...I'm obligated to follow her orders. I was instructed to protect her at all cost. How can I protect her unless I'm with her?

"And how can I prevent her from doing this? I don't outrank a prophetess, anointed by the High Priest of Israel. She and Elias, they don't answer to the words of men. They answer to the Lord."

"I'm in," spoke a voice from behind. Jethro, one of Barak's best warriors, stepped forward with a smile.

"Me too," another chimed in. Several men stood up and a chatter started spreading among Barak's men.

"Sir," Jethro replied, "we follow your command, and we respect your word. But you have to admit, what's the point of our training if not for missions like this?

"We already know about that small group that rescued that girl," Jethro continued. "I still don't know why they didn't get everyone else out of there while they had the chance. They said they would've got caught, but I still think that was a mistake, and we have to make it right."

Barak stared at the ground, brooding with a deep sigh. "I'm probably going to regret this..."

With small band of a dozen warriors, Deborah led the way to the secret entrance she saw in her vision. They left their horses with a dozen more men roughly one mile back.

The flat terrain became rockier as they approached Sisera's mountain, and soon they were standing before a pile of boulders and brush.

Deborah removed a large tumbleweed covering the crack she saw in her vision. The crack was barely large enough to accommodate them.

Adonia scratched his bald cranium, wondering if his barrel-chested frame could squish through it. "I no fit in there," he shook his head negatively while thumping on his chest.

"Nonsense," Deborah replied. "You just need to suck in your gut," she punched him in the stomach. Thump. Adonia grunted.

"Don't worry, this is the narrowest part, it opens up once we get past it. Out of the way," she pushed him aside, dropped to her knees and immediately squirmed her way into the crevice.

Barak felt as though he were in a dream, seeing Deborah out of the blue, and now he was defying his father's orders, sneaking into Sisera's slimy pit in the middle of the night. This couldn't possibly be happening.

"She's insane," Barak finally confided to Jethro and Ruben.

"How can we do this without torches? Where is my head, what are we doing? We have no plan, no tactics, no nothing! We're just blindly following her, and I think she's finally lost her mind! It is pitch black in there!"

Adonia declared with a raised finger, "You right, but we more crazy, because we follow." He then he dropped down and started to squirm his way through the crack.

Half way through, just as he predicted, he became stuck and started grunting.

Jethro grabbed his legs and tried to push him forward. The roller pin effect squished gas through Adonia's abdomen like a squeaking balloon, and a blast of flatulence erupted from his rear end.

"Ah!" Jethro fell backward and writhed in the dirt while the other men stepped away gagging.

Nathan turned back toward Deborah. "What I heard about you is true. Wait until the High Priest hears about this. Like he said," Nathan pointed at the young man, "none of us want to appease the bidding of liars and thieves, even if they're family.

"I should've known better. James here has done questionable things in the past, but nothing this bad. I just don't know what to say.

"At least with your help, we can have true justice in this land. And Saul," Nathan looked at the young man, "I'm sorry for not believing you."[10]

Nathan bowed slightly to Deborah, and the three of them departed. Deborah stood silently, staring at them as they left.

"Well done," Adonia smiled.

"What just happened?" Deborah scratched her head.

When she turned around to return home, she discovered there were several citizens of Ramah who were watching them the entire time.

"Look, here come some more. Word spread quick," Adonia pointed to some other travelers in the distance.

"Where's Ruben?" Deborah quipped. "We need to send a messenger to Shiloh to tell Elias to stop it!"

"Oy vey iz mir, that's foul!" Ruben coughed and nearly vomited.

"Nice," Barak sighed. "Better get it all out now, doing that inside there could kill us all," he berated Adonia.

"Holishkez," Adonia moaned. "They make butt talk."

Some of the men started giggling, trying to keep quiet. Life and death rescue missions were no place for comedy relief.

"Shut up!" Barak reprimanded them, then immediately coughed and gagged, catching another whiff of the stench. He waved his hand to disperse the rancid fumes. "Serious, stay alert, stay alive," he forced a sternness to his voice.

Deborah already squirmed through the narrowest portion of the entrance. She could hear some commotion behind her, but she had no idea what was going on.

Realizing Adonia's presence was not forthcoming and the tiny fragment of light entering through the opening was completely extinguished, she turned around and crawled back his direction.

She didn't stop until he gouged her in the eye with his groping, fidgeting fingers.

"I'm stuck," he reiterated, out of breath.

"Oy, I told you to suck in your gut. Here," she grabbed one of his hands, straddled the opening with both her feet, bent in a squat and pulled.

Course gravel carved into Adonia's flesh as she yanked him through the slim cavity. Finally free of the orifice, Adonia gasped with relief in the bowels of Sisera's mountain.

"I give this mountain hemorrhoid," he replied.

"I think so," Deborah smiled at the metaphor, "you big knobby turd." Adonia started laughing and cupped his mouth, trying to keep quiet. A few more farts squeaked out while he laughed.

"You can't do that in here," Deborah replied and scooted away.

"It your fault," Adonia pointed at her. "You prophesy over me, call me turd, what you expect?"

Soon afterward, the entire crew was crawling on their hands and knees on rough gravel through the crack beyond the narrow entrance.

While the others were feeling their way completely blind, Deborah was guided by her recollection of her vision.

The crack eventually intersected with a very large, well-defined catacomb of tunnels carved out of solid rock. Once inside this large area, a feint glimmer of light provided just enough illumination to see that someone even Sisera's size could stand upright.

"We need to go this way," Deborah whispered while pointing to the right.

"There's two guards right around that corner. Get your two best archers up front. We need precision. There's a torch next to the door, so there's plenty of light."

Barak motioned two men forward, then tapped his throat, indicating the stealth shot they needed to keep the noise down. The men nodded and snuck forward while the rest of them remained in place.

Thump!

As one of the guards gagged, the other turned to see, but before he had a chance to react, thump!

As the two of them stumbled, Barak and Jethro rushed forward and quietly finished them off, muzzling their cries for help.

The rest of the group scurried around the corner, investigating the door the guards were standing in front of, but then they heard more guards approaching from further down the tunnel.

"Quick, get these out of here," Deborah pointed to the corner they just came from. The group scurried back around the corner, carrying the two guards they just took out.

"Did you hear something?" one of the guards questioned another as they approached the unguarded door.

"What the... Did they both leave their post? Damn it, I don't know how many times I tell that stupid Abi..." Thump! An arrow in the chest interrupted his sentence.

"Ah!" the guard roared in agony, and Ruben quickly jutted forward with a dagger to his throat, instantly silencing him.

Deborah and several others rushed forward, ambushing two other guards and quickly finishing them off, though that initial roar of agony echoed throughout the tunnels briefly.

Adonia snatched the torch off the wall next to the door, and Kenaz started fumbling with the door handle trying to open the door. "Bring that torch over here," he commented, but Deborah interjected.

"They're not in there, we need to go this way, quick," Deborah re-directed their attention and started jogging ahead of them into the darkness.

Commentary Notes

++

1. Scripture makes no reference of Deborah having an amazing sword.
2. Arthur E. Cundall & Leon Morris, *Judges & Ruth: An Introduction & Commentary*, (Downers Grove, IL: Inter-Varsity Press Leicester, England, 1968), p. 83. (Bracketed comments added) "At the time of the crisis [mentioned in Judges 4] Deborah was already established as a prophetess and a judge in the non-military sphere. Indeed, it was the demonstration of charismatic qualities in this realm, in all probability, that led the tribes to seek her assistance." It is this charismatic quality captured in the narrative of Judges 4 that we see displayed in this scene; her energy and sense of purpose caused the people of Israel to rally behind her.
3. David M. Howard & Gary Burge, *Fascinating Bible Facts: People, Places, and Events*, (Lincolnwood, IL: Publications International, Ltd., 1999), p. 273-274. "Deborah is called 'a mother in Israel' (Judges 5:7). In this context, it refers to her leadership over Israel. Israel had been quietly submitting to its enemies in those days, and it was not until Deborah arose as 'a mother in Israel' that Israel began to have hope again. She provided the impetus and leadership for action and eventual victory." In this particular scene of the story, Deborah identifies with the young girl as if she were a family member; she is compelled by an unquenchable motherly instinct to rescue these helpless Israelites.
4. Arthur E. Cundall & Leon Morris, *Judges & Ruth: An Introduction & Commentary*, (Downers Grove, IL: Inter-Varsity Press Leicester, England, 1968), p. 93. (Bracketed comments added). "It was formerly thought that the religion of Israel evolved gradually over many centuries, culminating in the insights of the eighth-century prophets, Amos, Hosea, Isaiah and Micah. Scant attention was paid to the literature purporting to have come from an earlier period and the idea of the covenant-relationship existing in this early period was regarded as unlikely. The Song of Deborah, originating from the last decades of the twelfth century BC, is important because of its incidental allusions to the relationship between the nation and its God. The Lord (note the use of the name of God of the covenant) is shown intervening on behalf of His people and fighting their bat-

tles, a theme which may be paralleled in the Pentateuch, the Historical Books of the Psalms. And despite the almost savage spirit of exultation that obtrudes itself [in Deborah's Song, Judges 5], the writer is concerned for His [God's] glory. The covenant-relationship was clearly in existence at this time, and within that relationship the tribes have responsibilities to each other. Those not responding to the summons of Deborah were censured in terms that suggest an *ought* rather than a *must*. The principal point of the censure is not that they failed to come to the help of the other tribes, but that they failed to come to the assistance of the Lord Himself, the covenant God." In this scene, Deborah makes her appeal for unity, for the sake of Yahweh; she connects all Israel as brothers and sisters in a common struggle. This is their united covenant with their God.

5. See Exodus 21:23-24; Leviticus 24:18-20; Deuteronomy 19:21, "life for life..."
6. Arthur E. Cundall & Leon Morris, *Judges & Ruth: An Introduction & Commentary*, (Downers Grove, IL: Inter-Varsity Press Leicester, England, 1968), p. 83. (Bracketed comments added) "There are discrepancies with the listed tribes involved [in Judges 4 and 5]. First, it just says Zebulun and Naphtali, (Judges 4:7, 10), but then it includes Ephraim, Benjamin, Machir, and Issachar. One suggestion is that there were two phases of the campaign, but an initial one in which only two tribes took part, and a second one when they were joined by contingents from neighboring tribes." This story follows this commentator's suggestion, describing several incidents that lead up to full scale war.
7. Scripture records no mention of a rescue mission. However, it would not be unreasonable to consider the possibility of a steady escalation of events that led to a full scale war. One example of a violent incident that led to a full scale war is listed in Judges 19, and another example when Israel was provoked to battle is listed in 2 Samuel 10.
8. See Judges 4:3, "900 chariots of iron."

Chapter 14:

Encounter on Mount Precipice

ב

Nimbly weaving their way through the shadows of Sheol, in some places they passed rotting carcasses of various animals mixed with human remains. There were a few corpses of various ages, but most of the human remains were aborted fetuses.[1-3]

Deborah pointed to a skull with a magic symbol carved into its forehead; the product of human sacrifice.

Another skeleton was clutching a sword and a shield; most likely another Israelite who tried to rescue his family members. One of Barak's men fetched the sword for himself. "Better than the one I got," he whispered.

As they passed a large opening, a fetid gust of wind with the sound of an eerie, raspy breath, nearly blew out their torch. "Let me see that," Deborah reached for the torch. When Ruben handed it to her, she aimed it toward the opening.

They saw a massive cavern containing the ruins of an abandoned subterranean city. Monolithic columns spanned throughout, with countless crumbling structures, and a black slime infested creek oozed down the center of it.[4]

Was that whispers they were hearing, or trickling water mixed with swirling wind in the echoing tunnels playing tricks on their ears?

"Cozy little place, eh?" Deborah whispered to Barak.

"Tell me we're not going in there," Adonia looked at her, voicing what everyone else was thinking. Guards could be shot, but whatever lurked in the darkness of that cavern could care less about arrows. Deborah shook her head, and the small group sighed in relief.

They continued past the cavern and soon spotted another flickering torch in the distance. Deborah dropped their torch and tamped it out, to which Ruben protested. "Don't do that!"

"Shhh, all it does is illuminate our presence. The light up there is all we need to make it there."

Following similar tactics they used with the other guards, they took out two more guards in front of a barred door next to the torch they saw. After opening the door, they found some twenty prisoners, abducted from several settlements throughout Israel. Most of them were naked.

The majority of them were women and children, but there were also a few men. All were sitting in the darkness, covered in mud, slime, and spatters of blood.

They were shivering, terrified, and whimpering, thinking their rescuers were a group of guards coming to take them for another round of whatever they were being subjected to down there.

"We're getting you out of here," Deborah whispered to them.

Shem and Kenaz searched for their loved one, as Jethro reached down to help a child up. She shrieked and fell into a complete psychological melt down, kicking and squirming.

"You're Tabitha, remember me?" he asked her. "I'm Jethro, remember?"

Tabitha gasped with recognition as the torchlight came near.

At the same time, Kenaz spotted his beloved, fell to his knees and embraced her, sobbing quietly. "Rachael," he whispered, stroking her mud slick hair, and seconds later another pair of arms wrapped around the two of them. Shem hugged them both, adding to their sobs.

"Let's go, quick!" Deborah called them to action, and they finally came to their senses. "Save that for when you get home," Deborah tapped Kenaz on the back of his head, "else you might not get home."

Adonia frowned at her in disapproval for being too harsh, but Deborah didn't care. They were still in the belly of this beast, and this was not the time or the place for revelry.

Trembling hands reached for help from the pitch black crevice extending to Sisera's maze of madness. Deborah grabbed them and pulled out an emaciated, naked old man.

He flopped on the ground outside, curled into a fetal position and started convulsing in gut wrenching sobs. "I tried to warn them, I tried to warn..." he kept chanting repeatedly.

"You're okay, get it together, we still need to get out of here," Deborah whispered to him and patted him on the shoulder. She then shivered briefly. "Sir, the Lord has big plans for you," she smiled at the old man.[5]

Barak was the last to squish out of the narrow entrance, and once he stood up, he saw Deborah's grin illuminated in the moonlight. "Maybe you'll be back at your post before your dad ever knows you left."

"I doubt that."

Some of the men split off to travel south, for the captives that lived down south, while others traveled north; one from Jericho, two from Jerusalem, a few from Shechem, another from Jaffa. Sisera's men were snatching Israelites from all over Israel.

Deborah's band made their way back to Nazareth before dawn. They quietly snuck through the sleeping village, releasing their mostly naked captives to various tents as they went.

Ruth was awake when Shem returned his sister, and Ruth dropped to her knees with unspeakable joy. She trembled with her face buried into her daughter's abdomen.

The poor girl was mostly catatonic, the same as most of the others, but seeing her mother ignited signs of hope. Tears trickled down her cheeks as her mother hugged her.

"Thank you so, so much, praise be to the Lord! You are indeed Israel's prophetess," she declared to Deborah. When she turned around, Deborah had already quietly slipped away into the shadows.

After the last of them were stealthily returned home, Deborah, Barak, and Adonia paused on the outskirts of town. Adonia gave them a moment alone before Barak returned to his post.

"We make a good team. I think we should do this more often," Deborah replied, overcome with relief of the burden she carried ever since she had that vision of Sisera's prisoners.

"Part of me agrees, but a bigger part of me doesn't want...doesn't want my wife mixed up in this sort of thing."

"Wife?" Deborah questioned.

Barak cupped his chin and kissed her with his eyes.

She placed her hands on his chest and smiled. "If that's true, then you must understand, the Lord has put something in me...*that insists on being mixed up in this sort of thing.*"

"I figure that much," Barak sighed and gritted his teeth. "What am I going to do with you?"

"What is anybody going to do with me? My father is going to lose his mind."

"Mine too."

A few hours later, as Barak was riding home, he spotted unusual brownish red clouds on the distant horizon.

He broke from the main road and returned to the wadi where his men were hiding out. As he neared the wadi, he spotted a faint line of glimmering lights strung across the barren landscape. What was that?

This line of flickering lights was streaming from Sisera's Temple of Baal, and moving toward the direction of Nazareth, where he just came from.

Barak suddenly realized, those flickering lights were torches! He quickly returned to his men, called them to arms, and they immediately sped off toward Nazareth.

Meanwhile, as Deborah, Adonia and Ruben rode silently through the wilderness back toward Ramah, they heard galloping from behind.

This was unexpected, because they were off the beaten path out in the middle of nowhere.

"I think that's Abijah," Ruben replied, deeply concerned. "Yes, it's him."

Abijah was in a blind panic as he galloped up to them. "Go! Get help! Nazareth!" he cried, panicked and shaken to his core. "It's too late," he sobbed.

Deborah immediately spun her horse around and blasted full speed back toward Nazareth.

"Deborah, wait!" Adonia called out, while Ruben instantly bolted after her. Adonia fidgeted, torn about not returning to Ramah. Would Haran ever forgive him for willfully tagging along with all of Deborah's rebellious plans?

By the time Deborah made it to Nazareth, Sisera's men had already laid waste to much of the town. This was well beyond even the horrors of Shiloh. Dead bodies of men, women, and children, were everywhere, burnt, beaten, and butchered.

Cries of horror and inconsolable screams of agony were all that were left in the wake of Sisera's rampage.

Deborah dismounted and ambled through the ruins. She trembled, mouth gaping, now resembling the prisoners she freed earlier that evening.

When Ruben arrived behind her, he quickly dismounted and tended to Ezra, a fellow warrior. Ezra was groaning in anguish, gripping a seeping wound on his leg. "Here, I got ya," Ruben replied while fetching his first aid kit.

A short distance ahead, Deborah came upon Ruth, Shem, Kenaz, and Rachael, all dead. Barak was with them, holding Ruth on his lap. His fists were clenched with rage.

Deborah shook her head, trying to deny the reality of this horrific nightmare. This wasn't happening. Where was her triumphant grin now?

Nothing less than the humility of Hades etched into her countenance, a level of shame beyond her comprehension.

If the question remained about Shiloh's attack being a response to Deborah's clash with Sisera's men at Ramah, this was the answer. Sisera's pattern of punishment was a show of force, a level of retaliation designed to immediately cease and desist any and all efforts to resist him.

Heber, of all people, was right. Barak was too, but Deborah seduced him with her wily ways. She blinded him with her short sighted vision, the so-called prophetess who wrought destruction on Israel. The High Priest would hear of this, and likely pray a well-deserved plague upon her.

How could she not see this?[6]

Deborah turned away from Barak, unable to look at him in the face ever again. When she turned around, there stood Adonia, a cold statue amidst the smoldering embers around them.

Shame upon shame, yet her father remained at home, trusting her all this time. Would she ever be able to look at him in the face again, either?

Deborah couldn't walk past Adonia, so she turned to leave Nazareth in another direction. On her way out of town, she passed more mutilated corpses, a few of which were more of the prisoners they freed.

Some rescue operation that was.

"All for nothing," she heard Adonia mumble as she walked away. Deborah didn't get too far before Heber spotted her.

"There you are! You stupid girl! Look at this! This is your fault, all of this, it's your fault!" he bellowed at her in tears. "First Shiloh, and now this, curse you! May your God blot you out, curse be on the day you were born!"

Midway through Heber's ranting, Barak stood up and walked over to him. "And why are you still alive?" he yelled at him. "Huh? You want to answer me that? You consort with that evil son of a bitch! You forge weapons for his men!"

Heber fell silent, still angrily scowling at Deborah.

"Don't you look at her, or I swear I'll cut you down right where you stand," Barak growled at him and pulled out his sword. Heber faced Barak and took a step back, suddenly realizing he was in mortal danger.

"I bet they slew women and children on your left and right, and skipped right over you, you piece of shit, so shut your damn mouth!" Barak choked up on his sword, on the verge of taking a swing, but Adonia stepped in.

"Barak!"

Heber stood silent and stared at the ground. A second later, Barak's sword swished past him, narrowly missing him by less than an inch, then pierced the ground. Barak gripped his skull, groaning, consumed with guilt.

Heber pissed his pants.

The ruins of Nazareth was that nagging in his gut Barak decided to ignore. There were so many things they could have done differently to either prevent this, or at least reduce the degree of devastation.

How could he be so foolish, thinking Sisera wouldn't retaliate? For crying out loud, entering his temple that first time was a major risk, but twice? Of course he was going to retaliate!

Deborah was simply ignorant with regard to Sisera and his tactics, but Barak was well aware of Sisera's propensity for retaliation.

He was also fairly convinced that his father was right, and the attack on Shiloh was in response to Deborah's attack on Sisera's men in Ramah. However, he didn't dare lay that guilt on Deborah's conscience. Perhaps he should have; it might have tempered her impetuous behavior.

"You want to blame someone, blame me!" Barak roared at Heber. "Blame your damn self, but leave her alone!"

As Barak was yelling, Deborah backed away, then suddenly screamed an unearthly shrill, scaring off Adonia's horse. She then spun and quickly mounted her frightened steed and galloped full speed out of Nazareth.

"Wait, stop!" Adonia called out, then ran after his panic stricken horse.

As Deborah sprinted out of Nazareth, she rode straight for Mount Precipice,[7]which featured a high cliff that beckoned her presence. Quickly arriving, she dismounted and strode to the crest of the cliff and took a few deep breaths, preparing to jump.

She was so profoundly undone by the devastation in Nazareth, an incomprehensible atrocity she had to answer for, there would be no forgiveness for it.

Her shame was too great; in fact, leaping from this cliff was too merciful, but it would put a quick end to her, and that's what the people of Israel needed.

The only reason Deborah didn't jump right away, was the thought that she wasn't worthy of such a quick and easy death, but the delay was fleeting and Deborah leaned forward to step off the cliff.

In the exact instant she stepped forward, a massive gust of wind blasted into her face and shoved her backward.

What was this annoying hindrance? Why would the wind care? Surely this wasn't the Lord stopping her. Where was Yahweh, anyway?

Never mind, far be it from her to start blaming God for her own stupidity. The Lord opened her eyes to people trapped under Sisera's temple of Baal, but nothing more.

It was she who interpreted that vision as a call to immediate action without any strategy whatsoever. It was she who casually dismissed her father's concerns, ignored Heber's warnings, and refuted and argued with Barak until she bent his will.

Now that poor man she loved so dearly, was saddled with guilt that he would harbor for the rest of his life, all because of her. His soul would contain the smoldering fumes of that burning flesh, and all those cries of agony.

The very best thing she could do for him, was to blot herself out of his life, and everyone else's, once and for all. Life for a life, but in this case, even that wasn't justice. She was only one life, whereas many lives perished in Nazareth.

Resolved to terminate her existence, Deborah proceeded toward the cliff again, but then a voice suddenly interrupted her from behind.

"Stop!" yelled an old man.

Deborah turned around and was quite surprised to see Elias, the High Priest, completely out of place in this deserted location.

Deborah wiped her tears but couldn't stop crying. Now the additional shame of suicide, exposed in the presence of the High Priest. Would it even matter if she just turned and ran off that cliff?

A strange, soothing energy emanated from Elias, and Deborah immediately dropped to her knees, sapped of her strength. She withered and heaved in agony before him as he approached.

"What are you doing here?" she sobbed.

"Should one who was raised from the dead attempt to return? I do not think He would allow you."

Deborah screamed again, not holding back. "I killed them! I killed them all!" she yelled in anguish. "I deserve to die, just let me die..."

Elias gripped her arm and she jolted with his touch, as if electrocuted.

"No!" Elias reprimanded her.

When Elias removed his hand, Deborah swayed, then feinted.

Upon awaking, Deborah's vision slowly came into focus, and she found herself in her bedroom back home in Ramah. She was disoriented and emotionless, suffering from amnesia.

A pigeon kept her company, sitting on the bottom corner of her bed, intently staring at her. When Haran peeked in and saw her awake, he entered with a plate of food, brushed the pigeon aside and sat down. She stared with a blank expression, catatonic.

"You're awake Honey Bee. I made Holishkez," he showed her the plate of stuffed cabbage. No response. "It's okay, I'll just leave it here, eat when you're hungry."

After Haran left the room, Deborah's pigeon returned to his post and helped himself to her cabbage.

The next morning, when Haran peeked into Deborah's room, she looked exactly the same. She didn't move an inch all night, simply staring at the wall, catatonic.

Her food was eaten, but did she eat it, or was it her pigeon? "This is too much of a burden for you to carry. You need to eat. Here, drink," Haran handed her some water, but Deborah sat motionless.

Haran then lifted the cup to her face and poured it down her throat. She sat like a mannequin, water dribbling out of her mouth and down her chin.

"What is this? What's wrong with you, snap out of it. Honey Bee!" Haran grabbed her jaw and turned her head to face him, but she stared right through him as if he wasn't there.

The next day, Deborah showed only the slightest fragment of improvement, breaking from her catatonic spell in brief episodes. She made eye contact on day two, but refused to speak.

Then on day three, Haran couldn't take it anymore, and he threatened to take her outside if she didn't start talking. "Fine, have it your way," he ranted, then he grabbed her arms, pulled her forward yanked her out of bed.

She fell on the floor, and Haran proceeded to drag her out of the bedroom by her ankles. As she passed through the door, she grabbed the door jamb.

"Ah ha!" Haran declared. "There you are Honey Bee, I know you're in there somewhere!"

Deborah's memories returned by now. She wondered why her father wasn't saying a word about the disaster she wrought in Nazareth, and possibly other villages as well. His only concern seemed to be her catatonic condition. Why?

Why was he trying to drag her outside? It was already bad enough for him, having this curse of a child. Her mother thought Deborah brought shame on their family name before, but sparing with the men of Ramah was nothing compared to the rampant slaughter she brought upon Nazareth.

And now her father wanted to expose her to Ramah, which would only invite more shame upon him. He didn't deserve that! He had no idea what he was doing! This thought impelled her to resist, latching onto the doorjamb.

Haran tugged all the more, until Deborah finally moaned a beat down, haggard plea. "Stop," she cried. Haran released her foot and quickly jumped to her side.

She spoke! It was only a single word, but it was a word, nonetheless! She expressed herself, and so Haran gripped tightly to that spark of hope and embraced his daughter on the floor, sobbing along with her.

Deborah's quiet weeping slowly grew in amplitude, and the comforting embrace of her father's love was so undeserved, and so overwhelming, she finally released a torrent of sorrow.

They cried together for a considerable time there on the floor, but as soon as the sponge was squeezed on that grief, Deborah slowly crawled back into her room and back into bed.

Day by day, Deborah's stunted vocabulary grew, but she still refused to leave her bedroom. Haran thought she might have been feeding her food to the pigeons, but he was wrong.

She was eating, but only when she was alone. Even in this decrepit state, her fractured reasoning concluded that none of that bedlam destruction in Nazareth was her food's fault.

Friends from Ramah came by, hoping to visit her, but she refused to see any of them. When Haran pushed her and invited Jael into her bedroom one day, she fell silent and turned away, staring at the wall. She refused to speak to anyone but her father.

Haran tried to reason with her, telling her that the people of Ramah did not blame her for what happened. She was only trying to do the right thing, saving those helpless victims.

1. other job, 1 Corinthians 9.
2. See Leviticus 19:13; Luke 10:7; Matthew 10:10; 1 Timothy 5:18. Paraphrased, "The worker is worthy of his/her wages."
3. See note 8 for Chapter 26.
4. Matthew Tingblad, "How Do We Count the Number of Fulfilled Biblical Prophecy?" Josh McDowell Ministry, https://www.josh.org/how-do-we-count-fulfilled-prophecy/, (Last accessed January 29, 2021). "...a lot of prophecies in the Bible have been fulfilled, with some of the clearest ones about the life and ministry of Jesus. The number of fulfilled messianic (Jesus-related) prophecies is over 300." Regarding all these prophecies, is it possible that the writers who wrote them, might not have been consciously aware that they were prophesying? In this story, Deborah prophesies over her friend Jael, and over Sisera's temple, without even realizing it. Inspiration for this idea comes from King David. He wrote a number of prophecies about Jesus in the Psalms that he may not have been consciously aware of when he was writing them.
5. Dr. Leonard Sweet, "The Greatest Song Ever Sung," Marble Collegiate Church sermon, https://vimeo.com/20343071, (Last accessed February 1, 2021). One of the most amazing prophecies of King David is Psalm 22, and it is very likely that he had no idea that his grandson many generations later, Jesus, would quote, or rather sing this Psalm about His crucifixion, during His crucifixion. Psalm 22 initiates with "My God, my God, why have you forsaken me?" Jesus said these exact words while on the cross, Matthew 27:46. Hearing the initiation of this song, any Jew of Jesus' day would immediately identify it with Psalm 22. Then from that song which had been around for hundreds of years, they would see the lyrics of this song literally played out right in front of them, while the Romans played their parts, oblivious that they were fulfilling prophecy. Consider the details of this song, which initiates with a word for word quote to set it in motion. Within the song, onlookers would see Jesus' crucifixion details in Psalm 22:14-16. Jesus' bones were out of joint, He was sapped of strength, His tongue stuck to his jaws, and life was draining out of Him. He was encircled by a company of evildoers, with His hands and feet pierced. If that weren't enough, the Roman soldiers divided His garments by casting lots, Psalm 22:18, fulfilled in Matthew 27:35. They also saw those around Jesus mocking Him for not being able to save Himself, Psalm 22:8, fulfilled in Matthew 27:40, 42. And to add weight to Dr. Sweet's argument that Jesus

While it was true that some people in Israel blamed Deborah for what happened in Nazareth, it was generally those of unsavory character who favored the activities of Sisera's temple.

It was also people on the fence who benefited financially from the commerce generated by King Jabin's empire; people like Heber.

Most Israelites, however, were repulsed by Sisera now more than ever. They saw their situation for what it was. Sisera was a bully tyrant, and he severely punished those who stood up to him.

That is what Haran tried to explain to Deborah, that the people in their village still looked up to her for having the courage to do what she did, regardless of the consequences.

But Deborah couldn't understand how anyone could forgive her for what happened. All those innocent people died, and they might still be alive if she just let it go.

But then those prisoners would still be down there. Would she have ever felt any peace about that? Probably not. For them, getting killed in Nazareth was more merciful than torture in Sisera's pit, but still, she should have devised a better strategy than doing what she did.

And if these conflicting thoughts and emotions weren't enough, Deborah was now having recurring dreams of a great battle. When she awoke, she recalled bits and pieces, almost as if she were recovering from amnesia.

There was the mass of chariots at the base of a mountain, then the rain, the mud, and quick clips of battle. A dagger thrown straight toward her head woke her up on several occasions.

She also dreamt of arguments with Barak and other men. In these dreams, she was back to being passionate about confronting the evils of Sisera and his men, but then when she awoke, she returned to her shame over Nazareth.

A loud noise outside would blast her back into that horrific sight in Nazareth, or Sisera's sword plunging into her chest and lifting her off the ground.

Deborah was going mad with insomnia, and whether she recalled the vision of those prisoners, or the recollection of burnt, mutilated bodies in Nazareth, there was no escaping the psychological anguish.

Nathan suddenly stopped ranting and took a deep breath, holding out his hand in front of him in a halting gesture. "Listen, we're not here to talk about all that. We're here because the High Priest told us you will help us settle this dispute. I'm just sick and tired of this stupid little war between my brother and his neighbor, so we're here to settle it once and for all."

Now Deborah was hearing for herself, from this complete stranger from another town, that there was no hint of anger, malice, or blame aimed in her direction about the events of Nazareth. He was actually coming to her for justice, as the Judge of Israel.

This was utterly astonishing. How could the people of Israel be so forgiving? How could they overlook her part in the atrocities of those attacks?

But what the man said made perfect sense. Her father spoke similar words, but she filtered him out. Why was that?

Why is it the words spoken by strangers can sometimes break through, when the words of dearly loved ones are translated as ambient noise? This can be a frustrating fact, but in this case, at least the end result helped turn Deborah around.

For the first time in months, she was able to break her thoughts away from a constant recycling of blame and guilt, and finally think about something else for a change.

"So... refresh me then, what's this problem you have? I'm sorry, I have no idea if I can even help you, but what's this all about?"

"I said this man," Nathan motioned to the young man in his custody, "was caught stealing a sheep from my brother," Nathan pointed at the bearded man. "The High Priest directed us to you; you're a judge, so what's his penalty?"

"Okay, I...uh, I actually know this one. I never in ten thousand years thought I'd ever need to know it, but my mother made sure, Lord knows why..." Deborah looked upward, feeling her mother's presence, then she glanced at Adonia.

Commentary Notes

++

1. Henry B. Smith Jr, "Canaanite Child Sacrifice, Abortion, and the Bible," 90-125 *The Journal of Ministry and Theology*, https://biblearchaeology.org/images/Child-Sacrifice-and-Abortion/4---Canaanite-Child-Sacrifice---Smith-90-125.pdf., (last accessed January 24, 2021), p. 112. "*Sexual Promiscuity*. Leviticus 20:1-5 prohibits child sacrifice and the immediate context also deals explicitly with sexual immorality, (Leviticus 19:20, 29; 20:10-21), connecting the two closely together. The results of such illicit unions would inevitably bring about pregnancies, and the unwanted child could easily be disposed of through sacrificial rituals. Cultic temple prostitution was an integral part of Canaanite religion and closely tied to child sacrifice. The Canaanites dramatized their mythologies through ritualized enactments..."
2. J. D. Douglas and Merrill Tenney, *Zondervan Illustrated Bible Dictionary*, ed. Moises Silva (Grand Rapids, MI: Zondervan, 2011), pp. 149-152. (Bracketed comments added), "The ritual [of child sacrifices is] centered in sexual activity, since the rainfall attributed to Baal was thought to represent his semen dropping to earth to fertilize and impregnate the earth with life just as he impregnated Asherah, the goddess of fertility, in the myth. Canaanite religion was thus grossly sensual and even perverse because it required both the services of both male and female cultic prostitutes as the principal actors in the drama.
3. Lawrence Stager and Samuel Wolff, "Child Sacrifice at Carthage: Religious Rite or Population Control?" *BAR 10, no. 1* (January-February 1984), pp. 50-51. "Like contemporary rationales for abortion, socio-economic concerns also played a role in the decision to sacrifice a child at Carthage."
4. Robert Fitzgerald, *The Odyssey, Homer*, (New York, NY: Vintage Books, Random House, Inc., 1990), pp. 83, 181-182. "Here you shall find the crumbling homes of Death. Here, toward the Sorrowing Water, run the streams of Wailing, out of Styx, and quenchless Burning—torrents that join in thunder at the Rock...You shall see, now souls of the buried dead in shadowy hosts... Meanwhile draw sword from hip, crouch down, ward off the surging phantoms from

the bloody pit..." The above description of the surroundings of the River Styx given in Homer's Odyssey, inspires the description of the river beneath Sisera's temple of Baal; it is symbolic of the River Styx. This is a representation of death coursing its way through the underworld. The cursed River Styx is the antithesis of the River of Life that flows from the throne of God in New Jerusalem, (Revelation 22:1-2).

5. See 1 Corinthians 12:8, spiritual gifts, such as a "word of knowledge."
6. See 1 Corinthians 13:12, we "see through a glass darkly," our knowledge is incomplete, i.e. we "know in part."
7. Mount Precipice, Jesus Trail, https://jesustrail.com/hike-the-jesus-trail/points-of-interest/mount-precipice, (last accessed January 24, 2021). "Just south of Nazareth in the cliffs of Mt Kedumim is Mount Precipice, the traditional site of the cliff that an angry mob attempted to throw Jesus off of after His bold proclamation in the Nazareth synagogue (Luke 4:16-30). The site offers a panoramic view of the patchwork Jezreel Valley and Mount Tabor, especially nice at sunrise."

Chapter 15:

Something About a Sheep

ע

One month had passed since the events of Nazareth, and Haran entered Deborah's bedroom one morning with a reserved, yet hopeful smile. "Someone is here to see you Honey Bee."

"Make them leave," Deborah turned away.

"He's an old man like me, come a long way. Please?"

Elias hobbled into the bedroom and sat down on Deborah's bed. This was an unusual sight. Elias was well into his eighties; a jaunt from Shiloh all the way to Ramah was potentially life threatening for him.

Knowing that he took a considerable risk to see her, Deborah felt an obligation to at least acknowledge him, though all she had to offer was a confession of sin and shame.

He was yet another who undoubtedly incurred a marred reputation by endorsing her as a prophetess.

She rolled over and faced him, tears streaming down her cheeks. "You're everywhere," she replied, recalling his unusual presence on Mount Precipice.

Elias glanced up at Haran with a curious expression, then back over at Deborah. "Your father tells me you claim I paid you visit on Mount Precipice. Is this true?"

Deborah stared at him, silent.

Claim? No, that's not the word she was expecting...

"I haven't left Shiloh in years," Elias replied flatly.

Deborah finally broke from her emotionless void and displayed an intense expression of confusion. Then who was that on Mount Precipice? No, no, she saw Elias with her own eyes, and there was no mis

taking him.

"Are you familiar with the story of Job, when he declared that the morning stars shouted for joy?" Elias asked.

Deborah nodded.

"Perhaps you encountered one among those stars. They can look like any one of us. We usually never find out. We never suspect it. They're really sneaky, but sometimes...on rare occasion, we catch them."[1]

A glint of mystery sparked in Elias' eyes. "Whatever that fellow said to you, it was probably important. Don't take it lightly."

Elias grunted with effort to stand up.

"When I anointed you the Prophetess of Israel, I knew you would fearlessly charge into the darkest depths. You would underestimate your enemy. Kids are like that," Elias frowned.

"That's why my first prayer for you was for wisdom," Elias continued.

"I apologize for that prayer, because pain is often the price we pay for wisdom. You have the most powerful anointing I have ever seen. Now you have some wisdom to compliment it, if you don't allow your grief to consume you."[2]

Elias leaned forward and placed his hand on Deborah's head. "I pray your heart returns to you. You were not wrong for what you did. Your motives were pure."

Elias then grabbed one of Deborah's hands. "And your hands are clean, Deborah. Do not be deceived into blaming yourself for the sins of others."[3]

Elias released her hand and shuffled to the door, then he turned around.

"May the Lord cause His face to shine upon you; may He be gracious to you, may He give you peace,"[4] he pronounced a final blessing with his hands raised, then he quietly parted.

Elias' words brought some comfort, but the wound was still fresh.

When he told her that her hands were clean, Deborah recalled what she told Barak when she spoke of the atrocities of Shiloh. Evil lies in the hands of the doer.

That simple platitude made such profound sense back then. Her conscience was clear, and the thought of Shiloh's attack being the result of a retaliation against her was merely an abstract concept.

Now, the attack on Nazareth was clearly a direct result of the rescue operation she spearheaded, using all of her newfound influence as the Prophetess of Israel. There was nothing abstract about it. With that said, was her ethical calculation, evil lies in the hands of the doer, still accurate?

Elias seemed to think so.

But Deborah's conscience was not as clear as it once was. She contemplated the law, and concluded that her crime was more like willful negligence leading to manslaughter, rather than premeditated murder. Unfortunately, there wasn't much comfort in that.

However, no one from Nazareth was compelled to send an avenger of blood after her. If they did, she would have accepted their judgement rather than flee to Shechem for refuge.[5]

She almost hoped something like that would happen. She imagined an avenger of blood showing up unannounced, battle axe in hand, sent by the victims of Nazareth to execute her.

Recalling that Adonia was once an avenger of blood, she wondered where had went off to since that day in Nazareth. Was he giving her time to heal?

The seasons changed. Winter months set in, and Deborah was still hesitant to leave the house, though she finally ventured out of her bedroom during the daytime. The people of Ramah were merciful and respected her wishes for isolation.

Haran bought Deborah a new goat to cheer her up. Little Evie was a joy to have around, but rather than take her outside, Deborah joined Evie in her pen. Sometimes she slept there, using Evie as her pillow.

The family business would have been in peril, but fortunately their expenses were covered by the Priesthood, curtesy of Elias.

Deborah was becoming a complete recluse, shuffling around the home in her slippers, wearing a blanket for most of the day. Haran periodically urged her to accompany him outside, but she rarely ventured beyond the doorjamb.

Then one brisk morning while Haran was away...

Deborah was on the top of a mountain, staring at the Ark of the Covenant. Why was this sacred relic unveiled before her? Who was she to behold the Mercy Seat, hidden within the holy of holies? Why was it exposed like this?

This was Yahweh's throne, and she sensed His presence was manifesting directly above it. The ark began to shimmer, contrasting against the twilight of a thick overcast of dark clouds above.

Then bam, bam, bam!

Deborah immediately jolted upright in her bed; her teeth clenched, hands gripped into fists dug into the sheets.

"Deborah, I know you there, open door!" Adonia shouted from outside.

Deborah rubbed her eyes, wishing more than ever that she remained in that dream, on the cusp of witnessing the mystery of Yahweh's glory. Instead, she awoke to a lingering bleak reality of shame and discontent.

Bam, bam, bam! Adonia persisted with pounding on the door. Begrudgingly, she left her room and approached the door.

"Go away," she moaned, too ashamed to be seen in public.

"Ah good, I hear you in there, you must open door. Look, I have Hand of Miriam to greet you."

"What do you want?"

"Is matter import bee's nest," Adonia replied.

That was an odd response. Deborah pondered if the reaper was finally coming to collect.

She finally opened the door, and the sight of Adonia with his hand lifted up took her back to her last memory of him on the top of Mount Precipice. The infamy of that day swarmed around her vividly.

"Haven't seen you in a while, where you been?"

"Nazareth. I help them rebuild," Adonia nodded. "But now I here, and everyone ask me about you. Everyone worry, it been many moon. They say you rabbit in hole."

Deborah had no intention of going outside. "I'm tired," she replied, then she started to shut the door, but Adonia stopped it with his foot. Now what?

"Move your foot."

"I not move foot."

"You better move it."

"No."

Deborah opened the door wide, then slammed it shut on his foot.

"Ah! What wrong with you!" Adonia yelped, and Deborah couldn't help but giggle slightly, but then she was immediately overcome with guilt for laughing. She didn't deserve to laugh about anything.

Tears immediately followed, and Adonia stepped inside, hugged her briefly and gave her a pat on the back. Then he gripped her shoulders and eyed her with a fierce glare.

"Here, you get better now, you tough girl!" Adonia shook her slightly. "Deborah, you take punch from Barak, you remember that? You even take sword from Sisera, remember?

"The enemy try to crush you body," Adonia smacked his fist in his palm, "but you survive. So then he try to crush you spirit. But you stronger than this, too," Adonia pointed at her.

"You tough girl, you stop this, feeling sorry for self. There no pointy this. You have people depend on you."

"No one depends on me."

"No true! Group of people ask for you. One was avenger of blood, like I was. I know him. They out at your palm tree waiting."

"My palm tree?"

"Yes, they call it Deborah Palm.[6] They wait for you."

"Avenger of blood?" Deborah was roused at the mention of an avenger of blood. Perhaps it was true, the people of Nazareth sent an executioner after all.

The thought of suddenly departing from the world she had so miserably failed, was truly uplifting. Justice would be served. This was the answer to her sorrow.

Those butchered souls of Nazareth would be at peace, knowing someone paid the ultimate price for the injustice that happened there.

Life for a life!

Actually it was life for lives in this case, but better than nothing.

Without delay, Deborah searched for something appropriate to wear. This was not a day for battle attire. She tried serving justice as a warrior, but she failed. Ah, an ordinary, brown hooded cloak was quite fitting.

This plain outfit would declare her final act of justice with an air of regality, and legality. She would peacefully resign her life to this avenger of blood, and the people of Nazareth would have their justice.

When Deborah parted her home, she had her hood draped over her head to obscure her identity. Nonetheless, the people of Ramah took notice, and a few left their homes to tag along at a distance.

Shortly after Deborah arrived at the bench built between the two palms at the entrance of Ramah, three people were waiting for her.

A short, muscular man in his thirties had his hand firmly gripped on the shoulder of a younger man, as if he was his prisoner. Standing in front of those two was a bearded man in his forties. He was staring at Deborah skeptically, annoyed that their business had to involve her.

"What's this?" Deborah questioned, not at all expecting this odd situation.

Adonia motioned Deborah to sit on the bench.

"What?" she asked him.

"Ramah build bench to you. Sit. This you court," Adonia opened his arms and presented their outdoor location with a grand display.

Deborah sighed, confused and too sapped of energy to argue. Would sitting on this bench be her last act before this avenger of blood executed her? Perhaps he would provide her with sudden relief, and make everything leading up to this point irrelevant.

Deborah slogged over to the bench and sat down. "So you're an avenger of blood?" she asked the muscular man.

"Uh, no, that was two years ago."

"This Nathan," Adonia chimed in, motioning to the muscular man, "and this his brother," he pointed at the bearded man. "They think you help settle dispute; something about a sheep."

"A...what? A sheep? You're not here from Nazareth?" Deborah asked the muscular man.

Nathan shook his head. "No, we're here from Gilgal."

Deborah was thoroughly confused. "Gilgal? So are you here to kill me, or what?"

At this question, everyone was dumbfounded. Clearly no one had any idea whatsoever, she was expecting an avenger of blood to execute her.

"What?" Adonia questioned, and Nathan blurted out questions as well.

"Execute you? What are you talking about?" He asked her, then he looked at Adonia. "I thought you said this was the Prophetess of Israel, the Lord's anointed?"

"She is!" Adonia answered him, then he turned to Deborah. "Deborah, you know law, you Prophetess of Israel. Tell him. I was there, I saw High Priest boney. I there..."

"Boney?" Deborah stopped him with her hand raised. "High Priest boney?"

"Yes, they say boney. I not know, it was big party. You remember? They say High Priest, eh, Sarah...boney?"

"You mean...*ceremony*?"

"Ah, I think you right, it sound like Sarah boney, but High Priest not name Sarah, so I confuse... the eh, High Priest ceremony you say, yes?

Deborah nodded, restraining herself.

"So these men," Adonia pointed to the three men, "go to Tabor knuckle for help, but High Priest send them here to you. He say..."

"Did you mean to say Tabernacle?"

"Yes, that what I say, Tabor knuckle. They name it after Mount Tabor, right? That the place. And High Priest say you judge, you give them help. You have gift, you see truth he say. So they travel all this way for you help."

Deborah dropped her face in her palm and sighed. This was Elias forcing a comfortably numb rabbit out of its hole. Why?

Nathan now spoke up. "This young man was caught stealing a sheep from my brother," he pointed at the bearded man. "We heard you are a judge. What is his penalty?"

Deborah glanced at Adonia and rolled her eyes. "I don't know. It's just a sheep, who cares?"

"Deborah!" Adonia chastised her.

"That sheep is all I have," the young man mumbled.

"All you have? It was my sheep you stole!" the bearded man yelled at him. The young man clenched his teeth, but refrained from responding to the accusation.

"Sir, don't you know who I am, what I did?" Deborah clarified herself to the muscular man. "You know what happened in Shiloh? That was... *me*," Deborah gulped. "I caused that. And if that wasn't enough, I'm to blame for what happened in Nazareth, too."

Everyone stood silent a beat.

"You don't look like one of Sisera's men to me," Nathan replied.

"No, of course not, but I'm the one that instigated him to attack those towns."

Nathan's mouth fell open. Was that a sparkle of drool on the corner of his bottom lip, accentuated with a twitch?

"Are you joking? You must know, Sisera and his men abduct our children, torture, rape, and kill Israelites all the time. They don't need a reason; they do it for fun! It's only a matter of time before he murders King Jabin and sets out to slaughter us all.

"You've seen him up close and personal from what I heard. He's a descendent of the Anakim. They're not natural. They're filled with hate. They think only of evil continually![7] How could you possibly..."

"But what I did was short sighted and inexcusable," Deborah interrupted him, doubling down on her mantra. "How can I be a judge, making decisions like that? The people of Nazareth were defenseless. We could have..."

"Could've, should've, would've..." Nathan interrupted her again. "Ma'am, you can play 'what if' all day long, but until Israel unites, we're all defenseless, all the time.

"I apologize for interrupting you, but you can't go around blaming yourself for what Sisera's men do. Those men are sick!" Nathan started getting worked up.

"They shouldn't be taking our children in the night! They started this! One, just one child," he held up a finger, "is worth going to war! Why are we allowing this? You saw it for yourself. It's happening all over Israel! At least you did something. That's exactly what a judge should do, and that was an amazing rescue.

"But why haven't the northern forces launched a counter attack? And why didn't anyone from Nazareth rally behind you for that rescue? I heard all about it. Two men, just two men out of that entire town joined your party. Really? That's downright despicable! We should be retaliating, not Sisera!"

The accuser, Nathan's brother, who was initially glaring at Deborah skeptically, was no longer disgruntled. Now he appeared delighted. But something about his sudden change of demeanor annoyed Deborah. Something wasn't right about him.

"Wait," Deborah lifted her hand.

She then stood up and approached the captive young man, lifted her arm and placed her hand on the young man's shoulder. For an instant, she sucked in a stuttered breath, then she let go of him. She then whipped an aggravated glare toward his accuser.

"So you say he stole your sheep?"

"Yes," the man replied.

"The part you left out is, that was his sheep to begin with. You swindled him out of it, so he took it back."

The young man's accuser was made; his eyes were wide with shock, nostrils flared. "Well...he owed me," the bearded man stammered, trying to make an excuse. "I gave him that..."

"It's always about *that cheese*, isn't it?" Deborah interrupted him, recalling a series of visions she received when she touched the young man. "You stole his sheep, and now you're lying to cover it up."

The bearded man suddenly doubled over, gripping his stomach in agony. He looked at Deborah with fearful eyes. "What are you doing to me?"

"I'm not doing anything," Deborah replied.[9]

"I'm sorry," the accuser apologized to the young man, ashamed that he was caught, more than anything else. He was also terrified about the sudden pain that gripped his abdomen; this had to be a physical manifestation of God's judgement.

Nathan released the young man from his grip. He then glared angrily at his brother who convinced him to help in this scheme.

"I told you!" the young man shouted at Nathan. "I told you he was lying, but you didn't believe me. Is that what you do, just go around helping your brother steal from people? Heck, did he pay you to help him? I bet he paid you more than my sheep is even worth. He's like that!"

"And you," the young man turned toward Deborah. "You really are a Prophetess! You saw what he did, didn't you? I can see it in your eyes, you know!" The young man was thrilled to be vindicated.

"I said I'm sorry," the bearded man groaned again and dropped to his knees, still gripping his stomach.

"It's going to take more than an apology," Deborah replied. "You owe this young man four sheep."

"Okay, whatever you say, please, just make it stop..." he grunted.

"I said I'm not doing anything," Deborah replied. "Maybe you ate too much holishkez. But hey, it's good to hear that you're going to make amends for this. I just hope it's genuine."

"It is," he replied, then he suddenly gasped and sighed with relief, released from the pain.

"Thank you so much," the young man thanked Deborah again. "He's been after my sheep since the first day he saw it. You have no idea the ordeal..."

"Oh actually I do," Deborah nodded.

Nathan pulled out a small sack of coins and handed them to Deborah. She stared at his hand but didn't take the coins.

"Take it."

"No."

Nathan tossed the coins onto her bench, then he addressed his brother. "I can't believe you convinced me to go along with this. This is pathetic. You must do as she says. You owe him four sheep."

"Make it seven for lying," Deborah replied. "See mom, it's seven after all," Deborah looked up with a smile.

"You heard her," Nathan added.

"I will. I'm sorry, it won't happen again."

Commentary Notes

++

1. Robert Fitzgerald, *The Odyssey, Homer,* (New York, NY: Vintage Books, Random House, Inc., 1990), pp. 4-5, etc. Homer's Odyssey initiates with the goddess Athena appearing in disguise, assuming the identity of a family friend, Captain Taphian. She appears to Odysseus' son, Telemakhos. All throughout the Odyssey, she continues to assume various human identities when she interferes in the affairs of humanity. The Bible describes a redeemed version of this same activity in the Old Testament. In the book of Job, did Job's friend Elihu, who was speaking praises to God in Job 37, suddenly reveal Himself as God in Job 38? The transition between Elihu's praise and God's manifestation, speaking from a whirlwind, is instantaneous. The mysterious Priest-King Melchizedek, king of Salem, may be another example of the pre-incarnate Christ, living in disguise as a flesh and blood human in the Old Testament. The New Testament also states plainly, that we should treat strangers with hospitality, because they just might be angels in disguise, Hebrews 13:2. That Scripture can refer to Jesus as well; after He was resurrected from the dead, He appeared in disguise as an average citizen to men walking along the road to Emmaus, Luke 24:15-16.
2. See Ecclesiastes 1:18, paraphrased: sources of grief can lead to wisdom.
3. See Psalm 24:1-6, Elias prays for Deborah's heart, and speaks cleansing over her hands.
4. See Numbers 6:24-26, famous Jewish blessing.
5. See Deuteronomy 19:6-12; Joshua 20:1-9. According to Israel's laws, avengers of blood enforced the law. They were the next of kin for family members; their primary purpose was to ensure justice in cases of murder. According to Israel's laws, if a murder was committed on accident, i.e. manslaughter, a person could flee to a city of refuge and claim the right of asylum. Shechem was the nearest town to Ramah that was a city of refuge.
6. John H. Walton, Victor H. Matthews & Mark W. Chavalas, *The IVP Bible Background Commentary, Old Testament,* (Downers IL: Inter Varsity Press, 2000), p. 150. Judges 4:5. "Holding court. Deborah is the only figure portrayed in the book of Judges as actually

   functioning in a judicial position. She hears and decides cases and provides answers to oracular inquiry under a palm tree which served as a landmark for that region... The description of her 'court' is similar to that found in the Ugaritic epic of Aqhat (1500 BC), which depicts King Danil sitting on a threshing floor before the city gates, judging the cases of the windows and orphans (Aqhat III.i.20-15)." Note, Samuel was also a judge, though he is not listed in the Book of Judges. Samuel most likely held court, 1 Samuel 7:15-17, and the era of the judges ended with Samuel, because his sons were corrupt, and Israel

transitioned into a kingdom during Samuel's lifetime.

7. landmark for that region... The description of her 'court' is similar to that found in the Ugaritic epic of Aqhat (1500 BC), which depicts King Danil sitting on a threshing floor before the city gates, judging the cases of the windows and orphans (Aqhat III.i.20-15)." Note, Samuel was also a judge, though he is not listed in the Book of Judges. Samuel most likely held court, 1 Samuel 7:15-17, and the era of the judges ended with Samuel, because his sons were corrupt, and Israel transitioned into a kingdom during Samuel's lifetime.
8. See Genesis 6, "think only of evil continually..."
9. See Exodus 22:1.
10. Inspiration for this scene comes from the story of Ananias and Sapphira in the New Testament, Acts 5.
11. This arrangement proposed by Nathan answers multiple questions: 1. It connects Deborah's prophetic gifting with her ability to settle disputes. 2. It firmly establishes her as both a prophetess and a judge throughout Israel. 3. It establishes a baseline of how her fame and popularity with the people would have grown over time.

Chapter 16:

Another Satisfied Customer

פ

Patiently listening to once case after another, a few years passed for Deborah sitting on that bench at her palm, resigned to the life of a judge. The seasons changed from winter to spring, and now into summer.

Bam, bam, bam! Adonia thumped on Deborah's front door as usual. Sweat dripped from his brow, and a pesky mosquito buzzed his ear, taunting him incessantly.

Why do they love those ears?

Adonia swiped at the bug, so infuriated with it that he stepped away from the door and tracked its movements, swinging at it wildly. Eventually he turned to see Deborah's door was open and she was staring at him.

"Why not you come out yet? People wait for you in heat!"

"It's hot," Deborah moaned, fatigued.

"I know! We go now."

Word spread among the people of Israel, first from Elias, but then from those who went to Deborah for help. She was indeed the Prophetess of Israel, a seer gifted with words of knowledge.[1]

In the beginning, she touched objects or people to have visions, but her gifting had since grown much more powerful. Now her visions were spontaneously invading her optics without touching anything at all.

Her ability to read people like books was becoming legendary, and many people started confessing to crimes before she ever spoke. Standing before her was unnerving. They didn't want to be read, and more often than not, Deborah knew why.

A strange side effect of her visions is that they often included tidbits from people's lives that they were the most ashamed of. Fetishes, secret sins, or temptations people fanaticize about, flitted before her, but these were also juxtaposed with good deeds no one knew about.

Everything was jumbled together with a complex texture of conflicting emotions and character attributes. Darkness and light; pleasure and pain; courage and fear; love and hate; all coexisted within the same people.

What made the darkness of some of these visions bearable was that they also included formative events from childhood.

Sexual deviance, for example, was often coupled with events from childhood revealing where these behaviors spawned. Seeing people as the innocent children they once were helped Deborah view them in a merciful light the way God saw them.[2]

And much to Deborah's surprise, all those lessons of the law, mostly taught to her by her mother, came in very handy.

Deborah was uniquely qualified for this role she fell into, though she was not very enthusiastic about it. There was always a lot to take in, and on days like this one, she needed to detox.

But the needs of Israel were great, so she said her prayers while walking to her bench, asking Yahweh for strength and wisdom to help His children.[3]

The entrance to Ramah was improved. A four foot wall now surrounded the entire village. Haran sold most of his wares, and converted most of his trading business to a new outdoor café with tables and chairs near Deborah's palms.

With a café near the court, visitors could eat and refresh themselves in the shade while waiting their turn for an audience with Deborah.

By now, Deborah sat confidently on her bench, and she no longer wallowed in guilt and shame. She heard many testimonies that agreed with her first case, when Nathan enlightened her with many important points to consider.

She still owned up to her flawed rescue plan lacking a strategy to counter Sisera's retaliation, but the need for Israel to unite against King Jabin was becoming increasingly evident every day.

Many people throughout Israel frequently came to see her, simply to make that plea.

Just as Nathan said, Sisera and his men routinely abducted children. They tortured, raped, and killed Israelites all the time. They didn't need a reason.

Deborah encountered more family members of these victims, just like before, but rather than mounting a rescue, she reported these cases through messengers sent to Mount Tabor. This pleased Haran's wishes, but tension mounted in Deborah as the years scrolled by.[4]

Unfortunately, because of what happened in Nazareth, these events were left completely unchecked. Israel was living in fear of reprisal, allowing Sisera to get away with murder.

On this day, a dozen people were formed in line in front of Deborah. A dozen more were off to the sides, observing. Jael was among the observers. She was escorted by the warrior, Jethro.

Deborah met her end of the bargain with Heber, and put in a good word for him with Jael's parents, in spite of her knowledge about his making weapons for Sisera's men. Jael married Heber shortly after that.

Heber used to live in Judah, south of the Wilderness of Zin, but after marrying Jael, he desired the comforts offered by King Jabin. He wanted Jael to enjoy a life of luxury, so he pitched his tent up north, much closer to the city of Hazor.[5-6]

Jael came to surprise Deborah with her visit. She was purposely hiding behind the crowd of people, hoping to see if the rumors about her friend were true.

"You know that's mine!" one woman yelled at another.

"No, it's mine!" the other woman yelled back, greedily clutching a stone figurine idol that bore Sisera's likeness.

"There's an engraving on the bottom of it, it has my initials on it!" the first woman now shouted at Deborah to argue her case. "If you look at it, it'll prove she's a thief and a liar."

The woman clutching the statue grew silent. Her eyes darted down to the idol she was holding. Everyone could tell she wanted to look at the bottom of it, but she refrained from doing so.

Deborah glared at the idol and clenched her fists repeatedly, popping her knuckles. The corner of her lip quivered.

"So you're both here arguing over who owns this idol that looks like Sisera?" Deborah questioned the women.

"My...idol," the first woman reiterated.

"Mine," the second woman doubled down.

"Do either of you know who I am?" Deborah asked them.

"Of course, everyone knows you. You're the Oracle of Ramah, Judge of Israel."

"Who made me Judge?" Deborah asked her.

"Well...you did."

"No."

A moment of pure, unfettered silence transpired.

Bam! Deborah slammed her fist down on the arm of her bench while roaring out, "Yahweh!"

At this declaration, the idol suddenly exploded into dust. A collective gasp issued among the onlookers. Both the women shuttered, staring at the floating dust particles.[7]

"That idol came from that filthy temple where your sons have been spending time with prostitutes, and you both know it. How dare you bring that disgusting thing to this court!" she slammed down her fist again, and both the women stumbled backward, trembling.

"Here's what you don't know," Deborah continued. "The disappearance of your niece is a plot between them. They plan to sell her as a temple prostitute, so her corpse can rot with the rest of them beneath that cesspool. Why didn't you ask me about your niece? Do you actually care more about that stupid statue?"

The two women gasped and looked at each other in horror.

"In fact, those two boys have taken other young girls. I know of one in particular, just last year. She's dead now. Sisera rules this land because of people like you. And yet you argue with each other over who owned that vile object. How could you bear to look at it, much less own it?"

Deborah sighed, looked at Adonia, then over to Ruben.

"Tell your sons to return your niece before it's too late. Then tell them if they want to live, they better move to the nearest city of refuge, because I know the next of kin of that other girl who was tortured and killed because of them. Now get out of my sight."

The two women left in tears and shame.

Those next in line stood silently, waiting for Deborah to motion them forward. She was distracted, distraught, collecting her thoughts. She then looked at Adonia and brushed off the episode with a light hearted smile.

"Another satisfied customer."

"They not look satisfy to me," Adonia replied.

"Adonia, don't they have sarcasm is Phoenicia?"

"What sarcas?"

"That's like when you say something is the opposite of what it is."

"So sarcas is lying?"

"No, not really."

"Are you sarcas now?"

"It's sarcas-m, sarcasm, and no, I'm not being sarcastic."

"I thought you say sarcas-m? Now you say sarcas-teek. Why you keep change word?"

Deborah rolled her eyes; this was getting nowhere. Adonia rubbed his bald head, confused. "No, we no sarcas-m or sarcas-teek in Phoenicia."

While Deborah and Adonia were trying to lighten the mood with meaningless conversation, Jael was still collecting herself from what she just witnessed.

She heard the rumors, but she was almost certain everything she heard was one exaggeration on top of another. Now she knew, the stories were true.

After the two women departed, the murmuring among the spectators grew in amplitude, which annoyed Adonia.

What on earth made that idol explode like that? One man was babbling about a possible hoax. Deborah was a trickster, paying off plants among the customers, complete with fake side show stunts. This was all a scam for money.

This accusation was common, but Deborah didn't care. If anyone wanted to challenger her abilities, they were free to confront her about it, but those who did so were soon silenced.

Deborah was merciful, and rather than exposing these people bare, she drew small pictures in the dirt with a stick, made a symbol with her hands, or gave a small gesture.[8]

They knew what she meant, but no one else would.

Other times she would make obscure comments, like "It's always about the cheese," and only a select few would know what she was talking about.

These were words of knowledge, authenticating her anointing as the Prophetess and Judge of Israel. Detractors quickly learned to shut their mouths, for she had the ability to completely expose them if she wanted to, though she seldom did.

Most left donations, but she ignored the money.

At first, she told the warriors to give everything they offered and deliver it to the High Priest, but Elias, in turn, told them to hang on to it as living expenses for anything they needed to support themselves and Deborah's ministry.[9]

Elias insisted, if Deborah was going to be the Prophetess and Judge of Israel full time, she shouldn't be trying to run her father's business at the same time.[10]

Haran was pleased with that arrangement, because a steady allowance was dependable enough to allow him to transition into the new café business. Once the café was established, the business thrived, and Haran gave generously to all in need.

While Deborah was chatting briefly with Adonia, she spotted Jael amidst the spectators, immediately stood up and held out her hands for a hug. "Jael!

"Everyone, it's time for me to take a lunch break. I would like you all to enjoy yourselves to a full meal and refreshments, on the house." With that announcement, even those who were waiting patiently for quite some time were very content.

"Wow, I hardly recognized you!" Deborah remarked on Jael's transformation. In the relatively short amount of time she was away with Heber, she continued to mature and fill out. "Look at that muscle on those arms!"

"Moving tents a lot will do that," Jael flexed both her arms while gripping her fits. "You know Heber; I've been doing all the heavy lifting, but I don't mind. If I still lived here, I'd be training to fight with you."

"I have a feeling you're getting plenty of training just setting up and tearing down tents," Deborah smiled with a nod.[11-13]

"Queen of Israel, that's what you are!" Jael marveled over the earlier proceedings as they walked to the local water well. "I've heard, but now I've seen. The tales are no exaggeration!"

"You're the one that's exaggerating. I'm still the same person I've always been," Deborah tried to calm her down. "Israel has no queen.

We have the Lord; He is our King."

Jael froze, gawking at Gavriella, now a skilled warrior leading a group of females in martial arts training in front of her home. Tamar was also among them.

"So she was serious about that?"

"Definitely," Deborah replied. "She's a quick study, already teaching others what she knows. It's a good thing, too, because I haven't had much time to train lately. It's mostly settling these cases."

Sarai jogged up from behind, giving Jael a start. "Jael, good to see you," she replied. "Wow, you're all grown up!" She then jogged past and joined the group in their routine of katas.

"I can't believe it."

"It shouldn't be too hard to believe, when you know what our choices are. Who wants to end up a war trophy? Ramah girls aren't keen on the idea of taking up residence in Sisera's temple, either. Someone's going to get hurt trying to take one of us."

"It's just the females?" Jael asked, noting that the group in Gavriella's yard were only females.

"Training with them, yes. Just like my mother, their mothers didn't want them training with men, either, but at least they let them train with me.

"I broke the mold on that one, so now they can do their training without men. That's not too hard around here. Most of our men left with Barak.

"But forget what's going on around here, what about you and Heber? How is it you live up there in view of Sisera's temple, yet remain untouched?"

"Heber claims that his alliance with King Jabin is all that stands between Israel and Sisera."[14]

"Is that so?" Deborah subtly scoffed.

"Since the attack on Nazareth, the king stripped Sisera of his command, but it was only temporary. I heard he was recently reinstated," Jael explained.

"That makes sense. After Nazareth, things settled down for a season, but now it's back to normal. They're confiscating weapons, imposing heavy taxes, and villagers are disappearing again. They're targeting young boys now."

Jael closed her eyes, disgusted with the depravity of Sisera and his men. What did she get herself into, marrying Heber, who bartered with these same men? Was she a traitor, a sell-out to her own people? Was there anything she could ever do to atone for her situation?

Yes, there was the guilt offering, which she sacrificed regularly. However, sacrificing a goat without blemish seemed hardly fitting for being married to an agent who assisted the enemies of Yahweh's people on a regular basis.[15]

"Are you ready to go back?" Adonia jogged up, reminding Deborah that a crowd was waiting for her.

"On my way," Deborah nodded, leaving Jael to her thoughts.

Later that afternoon, after Deborah helped settle disputes among the remaining people that were waiting for her, she and Jael were sitting with Haran around the kitchen table.

"Serpent of serpents!" Jael fumed. "Heber says Sisera summoned him, and me, to that cursed temple of his. I told him to leave me out of it, but now I'm stuck!"

"I wouldn't go if I were you," Haran replied.

"He says we don't have a choice," Jael lamented.

"I wish he didn't drag you so far up north. You're practically Sisera's neighbor," Haran replied. Meanwhile, Deborah was lost in thought, staring at a pigeon wandering aimlessly throughout the house.

"Are you listening?" Jael asked her.

"Sorry, I...I have a lot on my mind."

"Thinking about Barak? He wanted me to tell you his father passed away, and he's in charge now. He was promoted to General. It means something to him that you know, that's why he hasn't stopped by to visit you in a while."

"General...Barak?" questioned Deborah.

Jael nodded.

Deborah looked at her father with a somber expression. In response, he stood up and left the room.

"What's wrong with him?"

"He gets like that whenever he thinks I'm going to leave. And he might be right."

"What?"

"I need to deliver a message to Barak."

"About what?"

"Israel must unite; all of the tribes. That way, if we perish, we all perish together."

"I hate it when you talk like that!" Jael fumed. "You know what happens. They're ruthless."

"Yes, you know I'm well aware of what they do, and I'm sure Heber has filled your head with his perspective on it. But where do you think he gets all of his wealth from?

"Doesn't that bother you? He arms these twisted bastards that are abducting and torturing us; prostituting our children; murdering our brothers and sisters..."

Jael was clearly distraught hearing this, and couldn't think of anything to say other than to respond with a weak defense. "He doesn't only make weapons for King Jabin."

"Oh, I know, he just makes his *best* weapons for them, and leaves the scrap metal for us."

"Not true! He'll sell anything he makes to anyone who pays the price."

"I don't think so," Deborah rebutted. "I saw what he was selling in Nazareth. His bows were alright, but the best he had were his spears, which can get hacked in half with one of King Jabin's swords in a single swipe."

"Well he obviously didn't take all of his inventory that time. I shouldn't be telling you, but he's worked out a deal with a famous metal worker in Shiloh. Eh, what's his name..."

"Shelah," Deborah replied. "Well good, at least that *one sword*. I was wondering if he was going to come through on his end of the bargain. I just might be needing that weapon."

"There you go again..."

"We can't be living in fear!" Deborah hammered her fist on the table. "Then we blame each other for what Sisera and his men do. I made that mistake, and I don't intend to make it again."

"You still don't realize how powerful King Jabin's forces are. They'll wipe us out!" Jael insisted.

Deborah stared at her, flat, emotionless.

"Israel must unite," she reiterated. "It doesn't matter how powerful his forces are, have you forgotten who we serve?"

"You've been sheltered here in the south too long," Jael continued. "You don't know what it's like where I live."

"Oh I know alright, and I'm getting sick and tired of hearing about it. Almost every day I receive reports about that cursed temple of Baal, and Sisera's temple guards they call the Sacred Order.

"A bunch of sick pedophiles is what they are, sneaking around capturing fresh slaves for Sisera's pleasure pavilion. Most of his Sacred Order are actually Israelites who were cut off. They should've been stoned to death.[16]

Yahweh is going to crush that entire temple complex under his heel," Deborah seethed.[17]

Haran reentered the room in the middle of Deborah's diatribe. When Deborah saw him, she stopped talking and the atmosphere suddenly grew tense.

"Is that why you came here, to get her all worked up again?" Haran scowled at Jael.

"I...uh..." Jael stammered.

"Shut up!" Haran yelled at her uncharacteristically, then he shouted at Deborah, "Well go then! Leave!"

He was trembling with intense emotion; sorrow over losing his wife and possibly his daughter; enraged about the injustice throughout Israel; frustrated that his daughter, of all people, held the key to unlock Israel's future.

Teary eyed, Haran spun around and stormed out again.

"I'm sorry. Maybe I should leave."

"No." Deborah clasped Jael's hand. "Stay the night. We'll be okay."

1. Professor Wolfgang Rollig of the University of Tubingen, speaks of Og as a Phoenician deity and the protector of tombs: [...and if anyone seeks to open] this sarcophagus and to disturb my bones, the Og will seek him out, the strong one, and with all the assembly [of the gods]."
2. See Matthew 12:22-32, Luke 11:14-23. A common characteristic of Satan and his manipulated minions, is to accuse God's chosen of blasphemy while they themselves are committing it.
3. J. P. Millar, *The Preacher's Complete Homiletic Commentary on the Book of Judges, Vol 6*, (New York: NY, Funk & Wagnalls Company, 1974), pp. 232-307. Location of Deborah's Palm. "She sat in judgement (ps ix:4) under the Deborah palm - so called because Rebekah's nurse was here buried (Genv:8) in Mount Ephraim, between Ramah and Bethel. Ramah was built on a round hill, five miles east of Gibeon; and a little north of it, in the deep hot valley between Ramah and Bethel, was the palm-tree of Deborah. The ordinary place for giving judgement was the gate (Ruth iv:1, 2), but this retired spot was suitable to the unsettled times." This commentary was used to establish the initial location of Deborah's court at the entrance of Ramah. See note 1 for Chapter 19 for further details.
4. Chapter 18 of this book is reserved for this detailed snapshot of Sisera's so-called glory, seated on his twisted throne, overseeing all his evil activities. Note that 6 * 6 * 6 = 18, and Sisera specifically calls out the number 6 three times in this chapter, consistent with the mark of the Beast, Revelation 13:18.
5. See Genesis 4:11, God heard Abel's blood cry from the Earth. According to Hebrews 11:4, it was by faith that Able was able to speak from beyond the grave. Could it be that others are gifted with this same ability?
6. B.C.E. Phoenician tomb inscription (Byblos 13), published by

Commentary Notes

††

1. See John 4:18, Jesus spoke a "word of knowledge" to a woman who had five husbands. On this occasion, Jesus didn't rub this woman's sin in her face; instead, He used His word of knowledge to get her attention, then He offered her living water, i.e. salvation. In this story, Deborah uses her gift of knowledge in a similar manner, exercising mercy and restraint.
2. In this story, Jesus is the inspiration for Deborah's character and the manner in which she uses her gifting in her court proceedings. Jesus was known as a friend of sinners, because He saw the whole picture, and He placed His focus on reconciliation, forgiveness and healing, rather than condemnation. Jesus often knew people's sins, but He also saw past them to offer forgiveness. Jesus is the Judge of Judges, for He will render all verdicts on Judgement Day. Fortunately He is kind and merciful, and He demonstrated mercy on many occasions. In the New Testament, John 8:3-11, Jesus used His spiritual gifting of knowledge in the role of a judge when He saved a woman from public stoning. Everyone knew about the woman's sin of adultery, but Jesus saw much more than that. He saw the sins of her hypocrite accusers. On other occasions, Jesus spoke of actions that people needed to take. He told the adulterous woman, "Go, and sin no more," John 8:11. He said that brothers should be reconciled with each other before making offerings to the Lord, Matthew 5:24, and He chastised religious leaders for caring more about tithing than fairness, compassion, and commitment, Matthew 23:23. Being an Old Testament judge, Deborah would have followed the Mosaic Law in her judgements, and some of those judgements may have been harsh, but she was undoubtedly a fair judge, guided by God in her actions.
3. Jesus also had times when He would have preferred to take a break. However, He set His own needs aside when He saw that the needs of the people were great, Mark 6:30-34.
4. Arthur E. Cundall & Leon Morris, *Judges & Ruth: An Introduction & Commentary*, (Downers Grove, IL: Inter-Varsity Press Leicester, England, 1968). p. 97. (Bracketed comments added), "The direct address to Deborah, (Judges 5:12, 'Awake, awake, Deborah!'), is not necessarily incompatible with her authorship of the poem (in

Judges 5). Before the tribes could be aroused to action, she herlike any connection of Jesus' crucifixion with Psalm 22 is easily identified, but something commonly missed is that Jesus most likely sang this song, and it concludes with a declaration of victory. Psalm 22 begins on a dark note, but ends with an incredible triumph, Psalm 22:31 (italic emphasis added), "they shall come and proclaim his righteousness to a people yet unborn, that *he has done it*." In summation, Jesus' song quote about being forsaken by God was not Jesus thinking His Father was rejecting Him, but rather a queue to all who had an ear to hear, "Name That Tune!" Imagine those who heard the hum of a familiar tune, and their brains started playing along with that song, then they suddenly realized they were looking at the physical manifestation of those lyrics happening right before their eyes. What an astounding epiphany that must have been for so many onlookers that day. Psalm 22 is an amazingly prophetic song, yet it may very well be that King David had no idea that his song, written in poetic, symbolic fashion, was in fact a prophecy where all the symbolic details of the song were actually literal elements about a real event in the future. In a similar fashion, many of the prophets of old may have prophesied constantly, even in their daily conversations, and had no idea they were doing it, just as Deborah demonstrates throughout this story.

5. See Judges 4:17; there was an alliance between Heber and King Jabin.
6. See Leviticus 6:1-7, Guilt offerings.
7. In the Old Testament, there are several references to sins and violations of the Mosaic Law that demanded the death penalty, or being "cut off," i.e. cast out, Exodus 12;15, 19, 30:33, 38, 31:14; Leviticus 7:20, 21, 25, 27, 17:4, 9-10, 14, etc. While these sentences sound harsh by today's standards, a civilization lacking basic government infrastructure to accommodate prison systems, among other things, would have to rely on a primitive legal system to keep society from collapsing into complete anarchy. Failure to enforce such laws would eventually lead to a society overrun by criminals. In this story, Israel's criminal element seek a type of asylum among their oppressive enemies. This might have been a likely scenario for those who were cut off.
8. See note 1 for Chapter 25.

Chapter 17:

A Word from the Lord

ק

Quietly scratching a clay jar with his dagger, Adonia looked up to see Deborah's approach. "What are you working on?" she asked.

"I practice language," Adonia replied, pointing to another jar he was trying to copy.[1]

"That looks Hebrew," Deborah pointed to the word for Lord, "but I have no idea what that is."[2]

"Is Phoenician. I want to you language learn, read, write. May a bee you help?"

"That sounds like a fantastic idea! I practice a little myself, based on what I know from our family scroll mother used to teach me with. Now that she's gone, I like writing; it is a good way to remember things.

"Even the Lord must think it's important, else He wouldn't have given Moses the Ten Commandments.

"And now we have our laws, but I think we should have more. Imagine this, we can even write things like songs! I think songs would be so much easier to teach and remember."[3]

"I never thought that," Adonia agreed, delighted with the idea. "Yes, you teach more me you language, we must work together. I much very like that song idea!"

"You have a deal, but first, I have a favor to ask. Have you ever heard of the Oak of Zaanaim?"

"Yes, Sisera travel near there all time. Harrosheth here," Adonia illustrated a map with his hands.

"Hazor over here," he pointed up and to the right of Harrosheth, "and Oak of Zaanaim right here, middle. I avoid that place," he replied. "Too close to Harrosheth, Sisera temple."

"Well Jael lives right near that oak.[4] I would like you to accompany her back home if you're willing," Deborah asked. "If you've been around there, you should at least know the safest route."[5]

"That man, Jethro. She come here with him. Why not he take? That is long trip."

"He wants to stay here a little longer."

"Why?"

"It probably has something to do with Ramah being full of females, and not many men around," Deborah offered her conjecture.

Adonia grunted. "Okay, I go."

"One more thing. Find Barak. He's probably still hanging around Mount Tabor. Tell him...*this Word from the Lord*." Deborah paused, took a deep breath, and silenced her thoughts. She then placed her hands on her hips and spoke in a commanding tone.

"Gather ten thousand men from Naphtali and Zebulun, near the Kishon River. The Lord will draw Sisera there, and deliver him into your hands."[6]

A chill shot down Adonia's spine. He felt that sensation before, at times when Deborah was holding court.

Sometimes when she said things that she had no natural means of knowing, there was a breathtaking stillness in the air; a profound mystery and overwhelming since of wonder.

Adonia gulped. "Just like that?"

Deborah nodded.

"Your father right, you like the bee. You bounce around," Adonia waved his hand around, mimicking a bee in flight. "You bumble like bee. One extreme to next."

"Maybe. Are you going to go?"

Adonia flared his nostrils. "What you father say of this?"

"I don't know yet."

Adonia shook his head. Would Haran ever know peace in his final days?

A short while later, Adonia escorted Jael home, and Deborah went hunting for few hours. Her little goat Evie tagged along.

When Deborah finally returned home late in the evening, she found her father sitting at the kitchen table, brooding in thought.

"You're still here?" He questioned, slightly surprised to see her.

"Where else would I be?"

"You know where."

"Father, this battle is coming whether we like it or not. I keep telling you about these visions the Lord is giving me, but you don't want to listen. I'm telling you, the time is near."

"Don't do this again!" Haran shouted back. "The day we fight is the day they arrive at Ramah and there's no other choice!"

"Trust me father, that's a vision I hope to avoid, if that's even possible."

"You must avoid battle as long as possible, because your visions are helping all of Israel, with you as a judge. But you're visions won't be helping anybody if you're dead."

It was pointless arguing, because Deborah knew the real reason her father didn't want her going to any battlefield. His fearless demand to Yahweh that day in the courtyard of the Tabernacle rang clear in her memory. He would rather die than go through that again.

Late the next evening, Adonia and Jael approached Jael's home under cover of darkness.

They dropped down into a wadi when they neared the route between Hazor, and Harrosheth Haggoyim, the small town nestled in a forested region near Sisera's temple of Baal.

The entire town of Harrosheth Haggoyim was mostly dedicated to the construction and maintenance of hundreds of war chariots. Surprisingly, many of the woodcutters in that area were Israelites working for Sisera.[7]

These workers earned temple credit for their wages. Most of them were living in perpetual debt, spending their meager income on work supplies, and what little remained they spent on drugs and prostitution in Sisera's temple.

Adonia learned of this dismal arrangement when he encountered some of these woodcutters years before. Recalling their stories, and the ghastly images of his rescue mission with Deborah, he didn't want to be anywhere near Sisera's temple.

"Why you pitch tent here?" he asked Jael, lost as to why anyone would pitch their tent so close to Sisera's temple.

"Heber, it's his work. Most trading is near-by."

"I no understand how you can be safe here."

"Heber says he has powerful allies."

Adonia grunted, but kept his comments to himself. After dropping Jael off at her tent, he disappeared into the darkness, navigating by the stars.

Jael stared at the entrance of her tent, arrested by the aroma of exotic incense seeping out.

Jael and Heber's massive tent was a gaudy display, packed with plush silks, drapery, pillows, Persian carpets, gold vases, statues, and other ornate decorations, many from distant lands.

A monkey added to the meretricious ambiance, casually sprawled on a cushion, resting his head on his hand while he gnawed on a date.

The kitschy little creature threw a partially chewed date at Jael when she entered. Had she known he was so unruly, she would've told Heber not to purchase him.

"So how was your visit?" Heber cheerfully greeted her, delighted to see her.

"Okay."

"Just okay? You've been looking forward to this for months."

"I think I peeled the scab off an old wound between her and her father."

Heber chuckled lightheartedly.

"She's itching to charge into battle again? You'd think she'd learn. What's she up to these days?"

"Oh you should have seen it, Deborah is...amazing! People come from miles around. She's...when she speaks, it's like the *Word of the Lord*."

"Really? Like what?"

"Well, there were these two women arguing over who owned an idol. Can you imagine that? How stupid can some people be? What profound idiocy."

"People steal idols all the time, what's so unusual?" Heber was puzzled.

"You have to be an Israelite to understand. Only a lunatic would ask the Lord's anointed for help to return a stolen idol."

"Why?" Heber was still confused.

Jael laughed.

"Why? Why? The Lord is powerful! Our ancestors were led across the Red Sea on dry ground, with walls of water on the left and right," Jael waved her arms in animated fashion.

"What's that have to do with anything?" Heber was still clueless.

"Yahweh...hates...idols!"[8]

Boom! An explosion erupted near the back of their tent, causing both Jael and Heber to jump. The monkey screeched and scrambled out of the tent.

"What was that?" Heber asked, wide eyed and snatching a dagger from a shelf.

They both crept to the back of the tent where they heard the noise. On the ground was a pile of dust. "My idol!" Heber yelled.

Jael gasped, mouth gaping. "That's what happened...when Deborah ...oh, even here, the Lord's will be known. I shouldn't have spoken his name so casually."[9]

Jael's eyes were wide with shock. An electric chill swirled in the tent; *they were not alone*.

"I told you to get rid of that hideous thing! And you're not going to make me go to that cursed temple!"

"We went over this already," Heber lifted his hands defensively. "We have no choice. This is the price we must pay for the fragile peace in this land."

"There's always a choice. And we have no peace."

One of Barak's men awoke him up from a deep sleep. "Adonia is here from Ramah," he replied.

Barak tried to shake off his fatigue as he yawned and stretched while wandering toward the entrance of their encampment at the base of Mount Tabor.

Roughly one thousand men were scattered in positions throughout the area. Most were sleeping at this time, but a few were huddled around camp fires, cooking food, mending armor and clothes, sharpening weapons, and tending livestock.

As Adonia delivered Deborah's message to Barak, a group of soldiers stared at him, not believing what they were hearing.

"Yes, that exactly what she said, ten thousand."

"I don't understand, the last time I saw her... She's not ignorant. She knows what'll happen. Damn, she nearly lost her mind, how can she flip flop like that?"

"I know, I say she bumble like the bee, but now I regret. General, with the respect say I, she see thing you I no see. She is prophetess, and she say this message from Lord," Adonia explained.

"Anyone can say that!" Barak shouted back.

"But you know she not anyone. She Prophetess of Israel. She see," Adonia poked the side of his head near his eyes.

"She know. You should come watch her hold court. Crazy thing happen all time. I not know how she know thing. People listen her to, many fear her. She have power. Very power!

"She eh..." Adonia shook his hands and licked his lips, searching for the words. "I feel it, you know? When she speak, eh, *that not her*. She... she do prophetess thing. I sorry, no explain good. Is... There no argue to her. Would be... *wrong*."

"I respect her courage, and all the strangeness about her," Barak replied. "I love her! I want to marry her! But all of her confrontations with Sisera end in disaster! No, no, no, no, no!"

Adonia's eyes widened with deep concern.

"Okay. She not like this. I tell you, she not like this at all. I pray for you sir. I pray you not the satisfy customer, as she say."

"A what?"

"Eh, never the mind," Adonia replied.

Barak sensed that further requests for clarification might send him down a rabbit hole. But that didn't matter, he understood enough. Deborah would be upset, but he wasn't going to allow her to cajole him into anything this time. Nope, not going there.

"Sir," one of the warriors, Abijah, spoke up. "Perhaps she had one of her premonitions. Remember what you said about safe passage? Maybe it's time? She might accept it. Should I mention it to her?"

"Safe passage?" Adonia questioned. "What you talk about?"

"It's a private matter," Barak responded curtly to Adonia, then he turned to Abijah. "Yes, go now, and like we said, make sure nothing reaches Heber."

Abijah quickly sprinted to his horse, mounted and darted out of the camp.

Annoyed that he was kept out of the loop, Adonia was about to mount his horse and speed off after him, but his horse shook his head and whinnied, snorting and stomping his hoof in the sand.

"Okay, okay, you rest friend," Adonia patted his horse on the neck.

"I know, you work hard all day long and I just sit there," Adonia conversed with his horse. "It this man," he pointed at Barak.

"You see him, right there? He make angry me, no tell me thing," Adonia eyed Barak suspiciously. His horse was listening intently, and gave a soft whinny in response.

"I even teach him many fighting skill, but now he big man, oh General say they. General this, General that. He tell his messenger, go now, but he keep secret from me. Oy vey iz mir, I fight giant when he was baby shitting self, cry for mama milk."

Barak's men tried not to laugh hearing Adonia's rambling.

"Are you done?" Barak questioned him.

"No, I sure to think more."

"Look, we just have a plan is all. If Deborah has some premonition about Ramah coming under attack, we can help."

"Ah, but I think he say safe passage. That not sound like help in Ramah. That sound like run scare. You think she run like coward? I thought you know Deborah."

"Don't think we wouldn't leave troops to defend them," Barak replied.

"Deborah would never leave her village before attack," Adonia returned. "Private matter say you, more like stupid matter. You not know her at all."

"Look, what she is asking from me is an all-out war. Who am I to make that determination? I'm no king; Israel has no king! Do you know how many of us will die if this happens? Do you have any idea the size of King Jabin's forces?

"They have almost a thousand chariots! A war of this magnitude could take years to plan, all while keeping it a secret. How can we do that, when Deborah's best friend is married to a spy?"

"Yes, I know this all, and she too."

"Well where did her foreknowledge go when Nazareth was attacked? Why didn't she see that? No, when it comes to retaliation, she's completely blind!" Barak ranted.

"If Sisera hears about this *'Word of the Lord,'* if he doesn't already know about it, that might be all it takes. He'll go off in a fit of rage that'll make Nazareth look like child's play! Is that what you want?

"She might be a warrior, but she knows nothing about strategy," Barak continued.

"That area she wants us to go, near the Kishon, is an open plain. How do you think we'll fare on foot against a thousand armored war chariots?[10]

"A thousand. Let that sink in. They'll simply crush us, then proceed from one village after another, slaughtering every man, woman, and child, until we're *all dead*."

Adonia had no desire to continue a debate with Barak. Deborah's plan did sound completely insane, but at the same time, Adonia knew Deborah's gift was genuine. However, something Barak just said greatly troubled him.

Deborah was taken by surprise concerning the events in Nazareth.

She didn't see that coming at all. Could she be making the same mistake, except this time on a much grander scale?[11]

Seeing that Adonia had no further response, Barak settled down and offered his hospitality.

"We shouldn't be arguing; you're just giving a message. You indeed have taught me a great deal, and I greatly respect you.

You're welcome to stay the night. Get your horse watered and fed, and eat something yourself, we have provisions. As for me, I'm going back to sleep."

The next morning, Adonia departed for Ramah, but not before Barak warned him about Heber. He wasn't to hear a peep about Deborah's Word from the Lord.

As for Heber and Jael, they were reporting to Sisera's temple, precisely as Barak's intelligence reports had informed him.

"No, I'm not going in there!" Jael shouted at Heber.

Their heated argument echoed across the barren landscape sprawling the valley floor below Sisera's temple of Baal.

Contrasting with the surrounding desert were the myriad displays of abundant water within Sisera's temple high above. While excavating the mountain, Sisera tapped into an underground spring deep within the mountain.

He then engineered an ingenious system of water transportation.[12] A fresh supply of water was available throughout the temple complex, and the front balcony featured a prominent fountain.

Far below this balcony, Heber and Jael's heated argument ensued.

"Shhh," Heber tried to quiet her down. "You have to. Think of this as a service to your people. Think how you can best represent them."

"That monster almost killed me! Don't you care?"

"Calm down, we'll be alright."

Overhearing some of this commotion echoing faintly in his chamber, Sisera dispatched some of his guards of the Sacred Order to escort them up.

They parted out the grand balcony and down a stone stairway that wound down the mountain. The stairs were carved out of solid rock, and they led to the base of the mountain, opening to the vast Megiddo Valley.

General Arad of King Jabin's eastern division, escorted by four of King Jabin's elite guards, arrived on horseback and dismounted.

When Sisera's guards arrived at the bottom of the stairs, Heber motioned General Arad to come near.

"Uh, after you," Heber motioned to the stairs.

"Let's get this over with," General Arad replied, annoyed, then he and his men proceeded up the stairs.

"We'll be up in a moment," Heber replied to Sisera's guards.

Arad's personal bodyguard, Tartan, spoke to General Arad excitedly. "You won't regret this sir. You won't believe it until you see it for yourself."

"You're right about that," General Arad replied.

General Arad was the first to reach the balcony opening with his four elite guards. He skeptically observed the opulent decor of Sisera's palace.

The usual characters were present.

Just inside the balcony opening, Sisera sat enthroned like a king in the most prominent location within the main temple chamber.

Sisera's one-eyed brother, Lahmi, stood next to Sisera's throne wearing his silver plated ox-skull helmet. As usual, his six fingered hands rested on the hilt of his massive battle axe.

Malchus, along with a few of his underling priests, stood nearby.[13]

Other servants attended to various menial tasks, maintaining candles and incense, pumping a water wheel to supply continuous running water, and walking around with trays of beverages and disturbing hors d'oeuvres. A musician played something akin to a pan flute.

"What's this?" Arad questioned, pointing to the far side of the chamber facing Sisera's throne. Mounted high up on the wall was a circular star chart carved into the rock wall.[14]

The star chart contained symbols, lines, and impaled skeletal remains of animals, humans, and some unidentifiable species.[15] These impaled corpses resembled a macabre dartboard for Sisera's literal man-cave.

Before responding to General Arad's question, Sisera eyed his musician and lifted one of his six fingers,[16] giving a subtle cue for spooky music.

The tune suddenly changed to a slower, deeper, mystical melody. Sisera nodded with a thumbs up; that's the tune. Now for a savory, cryptic comment.

"Surely you've heard, the Anakim descended from the gods," Sisera spoke in his charismatic, unusually cavernous voice.

In this chamber, the rich depth and texture of Sisera's vocal cords rumbled with the vibrations of the mountain itself. The tune of the flute bled into Sisera's voice. Getting those sound vibrations just right was a big deal to Sisera.[17]

His main chamber was jam packed with subliminal messages of all types, from the music, to the patterns on the floor, the furniture, the subtle symbols carved into the walls in myriad languages; everything in this chamber directed praise to Sisera.

"Yes, I've heard plenty, claims your kind once ruled the world," General Arad shrugged.

"More than that, but your primitive mind cannot fathom such," Sisera replied with a knowing gaze.

The Chief Hooded Figure hissed with delight, marveling at Sisera as he spoke. He worshipped Sisera, literally, as one of his gods.

"Primitive? Right. Let's just get on with it," General Arad replied, dismissing the theatrics of Sisera and his stupid temple. He was warned by friends to not get taken in by Sisera's mesmerizing ways.

"The hosts choose willingly?" Malchus questioned Tartan.

"Yes, we accept the risk," Tartan replied. The other four guards nodded in agreement, very excited about something they were on the verge of receiving.

Sisera pointed to four human-shaped diagrams on the floor of the temple. Each of the shapes were surrounded by symbols, candles, blood, entrails...

"Proceed," Sisera replied.

Meanwhile, about one hundred fifty feet below, two of Sisera's guards finally put an end to Heber and Jael's bickering by forcefully shoving them toward the stairs. "Go," one of the guards commanded them.

As they slowly ascended, prodded by the two guards, they could hear a steady crescendo of chanting from the main chamber above. Echoing above the chants, one man started screaming like he was on fire.

"Make it stop! Make it stop!" Tartan screeched in agony.

Heber and Jael paused and looked at each other, disturbed.

A moment later, two of General Arad's elite guards sprinted out of the entrance of the temple and leapt off the balcony, plummeting past Heber and Jael. They smashed into the ground below with a sickening thud of crushed bones and flesh.

Jael was utterly mortified, shivering with fright, and Heber quickly grabbed her and steadied her. "Stupid rituals," he mumbled under his breath. "That's them, not us," he tried to comfort Jael, but it wasn't working.

"I shouldn't be here," she whimpered with a tear trickling down her cheek.

"Move it," one of the guards prodded Heber again, and they continued up the steps.

"I'm very sorry about this sweetie, just let me do the talking. We'll get through this, trust me," Heber whispered to Jael.

Back in the temple chamber, Arad's two remaining guards were still lying within the confines of the symbols drawn on the floor. As for the other two, they were the ones that jumped to their deaths.

Malchus was standing over the remaining two. His hands were dripping with blood. "Arise," he hissed at them. They both slowly stood up and looked around, as if viewing the world through new eyes.

At this point, Heber and Jael finally arrived on the balcony within visual range of Sisera sitting on his throne.

Jael's mind immediately flashed back in time to that wretched evening in Shiloh. Sisera's hand was gripped around her upper body. His hand was so large, he had her throat pinched between his thumb and index finger, on the verge of crushing her windpipe.

Now here Sisera was, relaxed on his throne, and she was reporting to him. How did she get herself into this situation?

Commentary Notes

++

1. "Ancient Ostracon Records Ark's Wanderings" Ministry International Journal for Pastors, https://www.ministrymagazine.org/archive/1991/07/ancient-ostracon-records-arks-wanderings, (Last accessed January 30, 2021). Just for fun, in this story, this scene of Adonia scratching some alphabet practice on a clay jar identifies Adonia as the famous "student" of antiquity, author of the oldest and arguably most famous pottery fragment (ostracon), titled the Izbet Sartah ostracon. "The Izbet Sartah ostracon may be the earliest extra-biblical source that names a biblical personality and supplements the Bible's account of a historical event... The ostracon may have been the result of an exercise of a student practicing writing."
2. Brian E. Colless, "abgadary, The Izbet Sartah Ostrakon, Musings of a Student Scribe", https://sites.google.com/site/collesseum/abgadary, (Last accessed January 30, 2021). "The message obtained from the proposed interpretation for lines 1-3 seems fairly plausible: a student (apparently of mature age) has been learning to write with the alphabet, and muses over the art of writing on ostracon-tablets. If line 4 is a continuation of this, we might suppose that the scribe's name is embedded in the long uninterrupted sequence of signs (bnh.g could be 'son of Haggi'), and the writer is saying that he will be remembered forever, because he has written something that will endure; but the translation 'I am seeing' does not convey this idea. However, if we understand the first 'ayin not as a vocative noun ('Eye!') but as an imperative verb ('See!'), and regard the 'alep-'ayin combination as a Qal passive or Nifal ('I shall be seen'), then the expected meaning emerges before our very eyes: 'See, I shall be seen in perpetuity'." This element of academia was included in this story, because Deborah was clearly interested in academics. Her song in Judges 5 is among the earliest examples of ancient Hebrew songs, and it is touted by some as the work of a "creative genius."
3. H. Franklin Paschall & Herschel H. Hobbs, *The Teacher's Bible Commentary*, (Nashville, TN: Broadman Press, 1972), p. 153. "The lit-

erary quality of the Song of Deborah marks it as an outstanding example of Semitic poetic forms in the late second millennium B.C. The author's portrayal of the oppression under Jabin (5:6-9), her sarcastic rebuke of Israel's reluctant warriors (15-17), and her account of battle (19-27) attest to her creative genius. Her portrayal of a distraught mother awaiting the return of her dead son (28-30) evokes the sympathy of the reader and serves to balance triumphal glee of the remainder of the poem."

4. See Judges 4:11, Heber's tent near Oak of Zaanannim.
5. John H. Walton, Victor H. Matthews & Mark W. Chavalas, *The IVP Bible Background Commentary, Old Testament*, (Downers IL: InterVarsity Press, 2000), pp. 249-250. "Harosheth Haggoyim. It is uncertain whether this place name, translated "forests of the nations" in the Septuagint, is a city site or a forested region in Galilee. Archeological evidence is not conclusive to identify it. From the description of the text, Harosheth Haggoyim appears to be either a staging area or a rallying point within the Jezreel Valley, perhaps within a zone under the control of Philistines."
6. See Judges 4:6-7.
7. See Note 3 of Chapter 12; many Israelites may have been slaves working as woodcutters to build King Jabin's chariots.
8. See Exodus 20:4, Yahweh indeed hates idols! The second of the Ten Commandments addresses the prohibition against making idols, "Thou shalt have no engraved images before me."
9. Rick Meyers, "Equipping Ministries Foundation, e-Sword Bible software, version 12.2.0," downloaded Nov 20, 2020, http://www.e-sword.net; *Hastings Bible Dictionary*, definition for God: "f) Jehovah, properly Yahweh (usually written Jahweh), perhaps a pre-historic name... 'Jehovah' is a modern and hybrid form, dating only from A.D. 1518. The name 'Jahweh' was so sacred that it was not, in later Jewish times, pronounced at all, perhaps owing to an over-literal interpretation of the Third Commandment. In reading 'Adonai' was substituted for it; hence the vowels of that name were in MSS attached to the consonants of 'Jahweh' for a guide to the reader, and the result, when the MSS are read as written (as they were never meant by Jewish scribes to be read), is 'Jehovah.' Thus this modern form has the consonants of one word and the vowels of another. The Hellenistic Jews, in Greek, substituted 'Kyrios' (Lord) for the sacred name, and it is thus rendered in LXX and NT. This explains why in EV 'the Lord' is the usual rendering of 'Jahweh.'

The expression 'Tetragrammaton' is used for the four consonants of the sacred name, YHWH, which appears in Greek capital letters as Pipi, owing to the similarity of the Greek capital p to the Hebrew h, and the Greek capital i to the Hebrew y and w [thus, Heb. יהוָה = Gr. וחוה]."

10. H. Franklin Paschall & Herschel H. Hobbs, *The Teacher's Bible Commentary*, (Nashville, TN: Broadman Press, 1972), p. 152, "In the lowlands around Mount Tabor, the Canaanite war machines (chariots) provided a marked advantage over the Israelite foot soldiers."
11. An Old Testament Prophet's conundrum. In Deuteronomy 18:9-14, we see the Old Testament prohibitions against divination, fortune telling, interpreting omens, sorcery, charmers, mediums, and necromancy. Then in Deuteronomy 18:15, God declares that He will raise up a prophet among the people of Israel, and that the people must listen to that prophet. Regarding prophecy and divination, they both operate in the supernatural, with words of knowledge, and telling the future. The same goes for miracles and magic; they both operate in the supernatural, producing signs and wonders. Something many prophets may have struggled with, is the issue of whether or not they were genuine prophets, because of the harsh warning in Deuteronomy 18:20-22, "But the prophet who presumes to speak a word in my name that I have not commanded him to speak, or who speaks in the name of other gods, that same prophet shall die. And if you say in your heart, 'How may we know the word that the LORD has not spoken?'— When a prophet speaks in the name of the LORD, if the word does not come to pass or come true, that is a word that the LORD has not spoken; the prophet has spoken it presumptuously. You need not be afraid of him." Regarding this issue, what if the prophecy in question simply has not come to pass yet? Consider the prophecy that God gave to Abraham when he was 75 years old. He was told in Genesis 12:7 that his descendants would inherit the Promised Land, yet 10 years passed with no child. That is why in Genesis 16:2, he went along with Sarah's plan to have sex with Hagar, thinking that was how God's plan was going to unfold. Abraham and Sarah both miscalculated on that issue, so the revelation was true, but the manner in which they interpreted it was off-base, because the prophecy had not come to pass yet. Therefore the most reliable means of determining if someone was a false prophet was if they were speaking in the name of other gods, because killing someone due to a prophecy not coming to pass could be a mistake, if the prophecy simply had not happened yet.

Chapter 18:

Six Points!

ר

Run, just run! That's what Jael was thinking to do, but Sisera's guards were everywhere.

More than anything, Heber wanted to get his wife out of this place. Why did Sisera even call him there? Why didn't King Jabin spare him of this summoning?

Or did King Jabin even know what Sisera was up to? Did he realize that the majority of his elite guards were now reporting directly to Sisera?

Heber's eyes bounced around, trying not to fixate on anything in particular. Sisera's dartboard, for example, was a gruesome sight.

What were some of those creatures stuck on there? Some appeared to be freakish creatures of legend; part human, part something else.

Really weird.

Perhaps this was some ghoulish art project the temple workers assembled, attaching bulls' heads to human bodies and such. Profoundly disturbing.[1]

Heber and Jael approached quietly, not sure of what was going to happen next. Jael's skin was crawling.

This place reeked of an evil presence, even beyond Sisera. Something deep within this mountain was resonating with a hideous wickedness, as if the entire mountain were alive; its blood, a fiery, bubbling magma, eager to erupt.

Jeptha, one of Arad's elite guards who just survived whatever demonic ritual they conducted inside those shapes on the floor, lifted his hand toward Sisera's guard who just escorted Heber and Jael up the steps.

Sisera's guard was surprised to see his sword suddenly fly out of its scabbard and across the chamber. Smack! The sword slapped into the palm of Jeptha's hand.

Telekinesis was an excellent ability to add to the resume of any elite guard, provided he was fortunate enough to survive the required ritual.[2]

But then there was an additional cost beyond the risk of surviving a ritual. That cost was their souls, which they willingly surrendered, not realizing they would no longer be themselves.[3-5]

Upon seeing this telekinetic stunt, Heber and Jael jumped away from Sisera's guard.

Jeptha then swung the newly acquired sword, testing it out.

"Well done," Sisera nodded to Malchus, who then nodded back at him.

Sisera greeted Arad's two elite guards with an unusual familiarity.

"Og, Gath, welcome back my brothers."

Arad's two elite guards responded to these names by bowing toward Sisera.

"That's not your names. Tartan, Jeptha, what's wrong with you two?" General Arad reprimanded them.

Arad then unsheathed his own sword and challenged them, believing that the telekinesis stunt was a parlor trick arranged in advance with Sisera's guard. As for the two suicides, they obviously couldn't handle the drugs involved in this ritual.

"Nice trick, now how about you, Tartan, try it with my sword?"

To General Arad's surprise, Tartan performed the same trick as Jeptha, ripping Arad's sword out of his hand with a powerful telekinetic jolt.

Smack, right into Tartan's hand. He then smiled at General Arad while waving around his sword, admiring it.

Dropping his gaze, he replied with a sinister, deeper voice, "I am no longer Tartan. I am Og, supreme ruler of Bashan."

"What?" General Arad was truly puzzled, now thinking Tartan's hype about Sisera's temple was taken to the next level. "How did you do that?" General Arad scanned the area, looking for some hidden means he achieved this trick.

"Who is this?" Tartan, now Og, asked Sisera while pointing his sword at General Arad.

"Who am I?" General Arad bellowed with an outburst. "You know who I am!"

Tartan, now Og, stepped toward him and instantly swung his sword with such force, General Arad's head was cut clean off in a single swipe. It plopped onto the ground sounding like a cracked pot.

"Not anymore," Sisera replied, then he burst into a cackle and slammed his fist on the arm of his throne, joined by the wheezing of Malchus.

Jael gasped, speechless, incapable of breathing. Heber steadied her again. "Easy," he whispered.

Seeing Sisera in good spirits, Sisera's musician suddenly pipped up with a jovial party tune to liven the atmosphere. A few other musicians grabbed instruments and joined in.

Sisera waved his hand at Arad's body, and temple slaves scurried over, snatched it, then dragged it past Jael to the balcony and heaved it over the edge.

Og then kicked Arad's head like a soccer ball, scoring a goal off the balcony, making sure to keep Arad's head somewhere in the vicinity of the body it used to be attached to.

"Keep all his bones together," Og replied to the temple servants that threw Arad's body off the balcony. "We shall give him a warrior's burial among the dead in Bashan. He shall serve me there. I will be his king and protector."[6-7]

Jael swayed, queasy, not sure what would come first; vomiting, or losing consciousness.

"Ah, Heber, please come in. So this is your Israelite wife? Pretty," he smiled at Jael.

As Heber and Jael stepped forward, a temple slave approached Sisera from the side, offering him a snack; gelatinous entrails crawlin with insects.

Heber dropped to his knees, bowing low to Sisera. He then tugged on Jael's arm to do the same, but she refused.

Just a moment before, she was about to feint, but seeing Heber bow before this disgusting monster mustered a rage deep within her. She stood defiantly, royally pissed off.

The musicians took this queue, and started whining their instruments to build the suspense. What was Sisera going to do about this?

Heber yanked on her arm again, but she ripped her arm away from him. "I'm not bowing to this abomination," she spit back.

After she spoke, one of the musicians plucked his chords violently a few times.

As far as Jael was concerned, if she lost her head in the next instant, it was a worthy cause, because she would then be free of this complete sellout she married, and standing before the throne of her God, dead because she refused to bow to a devil.

"Jael, please," Heber whimpered, begging her.

Sisera chucked, then he scrutinized Jael while tilting his head sideways.

"Ah, I remember you, except...you looked more like..." Sisera then suddenly grabbed the timid slave girl standing next to him by her throat and lifted her from the ground.

Musicians added emphasis with their background music...

Right there in front of them, he choked the life out of her, then he quickly pinched her neck between his thumb and index finger, snapping her neck.

The platter in her hands clanked to the floor as her body twitched. "...this," he completed his sentence while staring at the girl's lifeless corpse.

Once again, Jael was about the feint, never having seen such a profoundly wicked, heartless, evil display in all her life.

Sisera suddenly pulled his arm back, then flung the dead body in his hand across the room, and up toward that massive mosaic of corpses hanging on the wall.

Whack! The girl's dead body stuck to a massive spike in the center of the star chart.

"Six points!" Sisera cheered while raising his hands, and all the temple servants jumped, cheered and clapped. The music returned to a festive carnival melody.

Jael finally couldn't take any more of this satanic celebration, and she collapsed on the floor. Heber was too distracted to catch her this time.

"Another six points!" Sisera howled with delight at Jael fainting, and more clapping and cheering ensued.

"If you want your wife to live, from now on the only thing you say to Jabin is what I tell you. Do you understand?" Sisera replied to Heber.

Heber gulped, nodded, then he pulled Jael to his side.

"Lahmi tells me rumors of a famous oracle down south, one who speaks for the gods," Sisera replied to Heber.

"Deborah?" Heber answered. "They say she wields a power from the God of the Israelites, one they call...*Yahweh*.

At the mention of God's name, a draft fluttered all of the candles in the chamber, and a string busted on one of the musical instruments, throwing the music into chaos.

Sisera glowered at the musicians, immediately silencing their attempt to rescue the spooky vibe.

The silence was even spookier, but only to Sisera and his allies, for this was a holy silence in the midst of an evil temple.

Sisera repositioned himself on his throne, stirring with discomfort while Lahmi lifted his battle axe and tightened his grip.

Malchus stepped forward and spoke with a spiteful hiss. "You defile this temple with that name! Speak it again, I shall slit your throat!"

Heber frowned and shrugged. "Sorry." Heber didn't hold any degree of reverence or contempt for speaking the name of Yahweh.

"What sort of...*power*?" Sisera continued his queries about Deborah.

Heber cleared his throat. "Well, uh, legend has it she survived a fatal attack from you my lord, at Shiloh."

Lahmi instantly darted a contemptuous glare toward his brother, then back at Heber. "She lives?" Lahmi was shocked.

"Your liege," Malchus interjected, "she's that infidel I warned you about. The scarred woman you encountered in Shiloh, and the oracle of the south we've heard rumors of, are one in the same. She is a festering larva contaminating your realm with words of blasphemy!"[8]

"Is this true?" Sisera asked Heber. "Where in dwells this...*oracle*? Is it Ramah?"

Heber shrugged again. "I think so," Heber was reluctant to pinpoint Deborah's exact location.

"She counsels the people of Israel from Mount Ephraim, somewhere between the villages of Ramah and Bethel."[9]

"So the scarred virgin lives," Sisera replied with a grin, perplexed with Deborah's resilience. He knew that probably even he couldn't survive an attack like the one he inflicted on her.

Deborah was clearly in possession of the source of supernatural power that enabled the Israelites to overcome Sisera's ancestors.

"That witch took my eye!" Lahmi growled. "Brother, grant me her head!"

"Lord Sisera," Heber hoped to speak some reason into this violent development, "you were just reinstated. Ramah is too far south for..."

"Silence!" Sisera slammed his fist down on the arm of his throne with a quaking thud. "As you can see, Jabin is not here."

"Brother," Lahmi persisted, "no need to lose your command over this. I act alone until the appointed time you shed Jabin like an old skin."

"Very well," Sisera was pleased with his brother's proposal.

"Select a few men and swat this bee. Make an example of Ramah while you're at it, and I will grant you the southern portion of my kingdom as your reward."

Lahmi bowed, then left Sisera's throne room. Malchus then motioned to Heber.

"Lord, I believe this one sides with the infidels. I sense in him a conflict of interest. Say the word, and I shall cut out his heart and serve it to you."

Heber cringed, then looked away at the balcony.

"Jabin trusts him," Sisera replied while staring at Heber. When Heber turned to look at him, Sisera continued.

"You and I shall dine with Jabin tomorrow, and all is well. Say nothing of Ramah, or Arad," Sisera eyed General Arad's smeared blood on the floor.

Heber gulped and nodded.

"Or...go ahead and tell Jabin whatever you want, I don't care," Sisera shrugged.

"I wouldn't mind seeing her as a centerpiece," he nodded toward Jael's limp body, then he held up his hands and framed them around the center of his corpse-laden star chart.

"That would make another six points, and I win," Sisera winked.[10]

King Jabin's charioteers rode through a village, shooting their arrows in all directions. This was going to be fun, *so they thought...*

Tents and structures caught on fire, and villagers all over were shouting orders.

"Now!" a warrior bellowed from behind a stone wall with two other women holding a thick cord. The two women quickly jerked the cord taught and looped it around a tree stump.

"Fire!" Another warrior yelled at some archers on top of a building. An instant later, a haze of arrows and rocks rained down on a gaggle of soldiers below.

In a bizarre, disorienting flash, Deborah was running toward a group of warriors huddled around her father. They were attempting to administer first aid, but they were too late.

Haran was pale and gasping for breath. The moment Deborah set eyes on him, he coughed a spurt of blood on his beard.

Deborah dropped to her knees next to him. Her vision blurred with tears. In the next instant, she found herself on a battlefield in the middle of the night.

A tidal wave of water smashed through a line of chariots. Sisera was roaring in a violent rage in the back, whipping his horses with one hand, and swinging his sword in the other hand.

Fierce gales blasted rain horizontally in a ferocious storm. Cracks of thunder and flashes of lightning blazed above. Mud grew so thick in some areas, the chariots were losing momentum.

"Move it!" Sisera whipped his horses mercilessly, but even with four horses pulling his chariot, his chariot was slowing down. Sisera's enormous weight was simply too much for those horses.

Sisera's face then suddenly morphed into his brother Lahmi's face.

Now it was back to daytime, and Lahmi roared out a battle cry, coming straight toward Deborah with a blind, murderous vengeance.

But now it was back to nighttime yet again, with the fierce rain, thunder and lightning raging in the sky above. One of those flashes of light illuminated the glint of a sword slashing Sisera's arm with a deep gash.

High above, overlooking the plains below, Israeli troops poured down the side of a mountain. There was an ear shattering scream from behind.

When Deborah turned around, she suddenly saw a dagger flying straight toward her face.

Time slowed, and Deborah was paralyzed while the dagger spun toward her. She tried to dodge it, but she was frozen with the same temporal delay that affected this flying dagger of death.

Fighting to dodge this twirling menace with all her might, Deborah was finally released from paralysis, but then the scenery chaotically changed yet again.

Deborah's entire body spun out of her bed and she plummeted to the floor with a thud. A sheet was wrapped around her neck, choking her. She eventually wrangled the malicious linen from her throat and gasped for breath.

Deborah's chaotic dreams were increasing with intensity every night.

As she started to dress, she heard horse hooves approach outside. A moment later, she exited her home, fatigued with dark circles under bloodshot eyes.

"You look tired," Abijah replied.

"Where's Adonia?"

"He delivered your message. He is returning as I speak."

"What did Barak say?"

Abijah tossed Deborah a gold tent peg. Upon inspection, Deborah saw that it had Hebrew writing engraved on it. "The Glory of this Battle is Yours."

Deborah stared at the tent peg momentarily and smirked. She then looked up at Abijah. "You can tell him I said thank you for this. Did he say anything?"

"General Barak sent me ahead for swift reply. He answers thus: 'I admire your courage, but an offensive attack is...*out of the question*.'"

"Is that all?" Deborah asked, not surprised at Barak's response.

"He is aware of Sisera's ambition to push south, and he offers you and your father safe passage to the east."

"Ah," Deborah nodded. "Thank you for the offer, but I pass. My father won't go either. No one from Ramah will leave for that matter. This is our Promised Land, and we're not the ones to be driven out of it."

Abijah nodded, then he started to leave.

"Are you content with his reply?" Deborah questioned Abijah. Abijah turned around to face her.

"It's not for me to say."

"It's exactly for you to say. Barak sent you to deliver his reply, because he believes you agree with him. I know about your little brother, Abishai, among those lost that day in Nazareth."

Deborah stepped closer to Abijah. "Don't think I haven't heard his blood cry from the Earth."[11]

Abijah stared at her contemplatively, but he remained silent.

"If you blame me for what happened, I understand," Deborah replied, willing to accept whatever verdict Abijah was ready to deliver.

"General Barak thinks I blame you," Abijah replied. "He thinks I hold him and you personally responsible for that day...*but I don't*."

Deborah sensed Abijah was holding back. "But something is still bothering you?"

Abijah proceeded, "Well, you seem to know a lot, but why didn't you know what was going to happen in Nazareth? Are you sure your visions are from the Lord?"

"Good question. I've asked that myself," Deborah replied while scanning the skies for inspiration.

"I've had these visions ever since Shiloh, and I believe I had an encounter with Yahweh. Since then, I just see and know certain things.

"Now if I had a false vision, or if any of my words of knowledge were deception, they would be easy to dismiss, but I have been given only the truth so far.

"My visions aren't the problem," Deborah paced while she spoke.

"My response to what I have been given; that is where I have failed your brother and the people of Nazareth. I lacked strategy, and many paid the price. For that, I will never be able to apologize enough."

Deborah stared at the ground, still humbled by her failure.

After a lengthy pause, Abijah finally replied. "That makes sense. General Barak has a saying. 'The ultimate price for experience is making others pay for our mistakes.'"

"This is true," Deborah nodded. "I'm sure I'm the inspiration for that. But now that I have experience, I intend to use it. It all started with delivering the message that the Lord revealed to me.

"Without a shadow of a doubt, the Lord calls Israel to unite, and take a stand against King Jabin. I have seen it many times, and I know what we must do. Our strategy is uniting as one."

Abijah gulped, seeing the intensity in Deborah's countenance. "I don't know how to persuade him."

"We will. We must. If Israel does not unite, Sisera will slaughter us all, one city at a time, while we are all scattered, and our hearts divided.

"But if we turn to the Lord as one, we will be invincible. We will be as we were when we first entered this Promised Land and drove out the Anakim."

Abijah nodded in agreement.

"Return to Barak with this message. Sisera wants me more than he wants the ark in Shiloh. Ramah's next."

Commentary Notes

††

1. C. Scott Littleton, *Mythology: The Illustrated Anthology of World Myth and Storytelling*, (London: Duncan Baird Publishers, 2002), p. 176. Canaanite idols of Baal took the form of a Minotaur; a creature with a man's body, and the head of a bull. The ancient Greeks also featured Minotaur's in their art and legends, but rather than worshipping the Minotaur as a god, they regarded it as a ferocious monster. According to Greek mythology, one of Zeus' sons, Theseus, became the king of Athens after slaying a Minotaur.
2. Colin Wilson and Dr. Christopher Evans, *The Book of Great Mysteries*, (New York, NY: Dorset Press, 1990), pp 209-213. Telekinesis is a type of Psi power that "makes objects or bodies move without visible force. Many experiments on this subject have been carried out by Soviet Researchers... Louis Jacolliot, an eminent French lawyer and later a chief justice, went to India in the early 1860s. He was a free-thinker with a profound skepticism about religion. However, when his servant announced one morning that a fakir (Hindu holy man) wished to see him, his curiosity got the better of him... Jacolliot opened the conversation by saying that he had heard that fakiers possess the power to move objects without touching them — a power that is now called psychokinesis. The fakier — a thin bony little man — replied that he himself possessed no such power, but that spirits lent him their aid." Jacolliot later witnessed and documented numerous demonstrations of psychokinetic power conducted by the fakiers. He witnessed leaves levitating up and down, and the ability to hold down a small table so firmly that Jacolliot's attempts to move it only tore off one of its folding leaves. He witnessed a fakir drop a papaw seed into a pot with damp earth, and make it to grow into an eight-inch-tall plant in just two hours. "A fakir named Covindasamy caused a phosphorescent cloud to form in the air. After a moment, white hands appeared in the cloud. One of them held Jacolliot's hand for a moment. At his request, it plucked a flower from a bowl and dropped it at his feet." These spirit beings spelled out glowing letters in the air when answering questions. On another occasion, a "fakier materialized another shade that moved around the room playing a flute. When the apparition vanished, it left the flute on the ground. It was a flute that Jacolliot had borrowed from Rajah and that he had locked in his house. An impres-

sive element about these stories is that Jacolliot did not write them as an occultist. The book in which they appear is a sober study of Hinduism, and these stories of his experiments were added almost as an afterthought. He was merely interested in recording inexplicable events to which he attached no undue importance."

3. See Matthew 16:26.
4. Wade Cox, "Mysticism, chapter 1 Spreading the Babylonian Mysteries," Christian Churches of God, http://www.ccg.org/english/s/b7_1.html (Last accessed February 8, 2021). Shamanism is one of the oldest religions in the world, dating back to ancient Babylon.
5. Carlos Castaneda, *The Teachings of Don Juan: A Yaqui Way of Knowledge*, (New York, NY: Washington Square Press, 1998). A modern example of sorcery can be found in the works of anthropologist Carlos Castaneda, who wrote of his claims of performing numerous supernatural feats. He studied under the apprenticeship of Iroquois sorcerer don Juan Matus. According to Castaneda, one of the primary means of sorcerers acquiring supernatural power was to battle demonic entities and force them into servitude. Castaneda described with many details that the life of a sorcerer was filled with danger, and going insane with demonic possession was one of the risks involved.
6. See Numbers 21:33. King Og of Bashan, the last of the Raphaim giants, was slain along with his army by Moses and his men at the battle of Edrei.
7. Laura Quick, "Og, King of Bashan: Underworld Ruler or Ancient Giant?" The Torah, https://www.thetorah.com/article/og-king-of-bashan-underworld-ruler-or-ancient-giant, (Last accessed February 8, 2021). Many ancient texts speak of King Og of Bashan, some referring to a living king that the Israelites killed while Moses was still alive. Other texts speak of King Og as a shade, or spirit, because the context of the same word used for giant, also translates as shade or spirit. The land of Bashan also translates as both a real place, as well as a mythical place. Taking all of these accounts into consideration, one clear explanation as to how they can all be true, is that the Nephilim were once real, physical beings of flesh and blood. Then when they were killed or died, they became these shades/spirits. This dual translated meaning for the word Nephilim, is where the origin of demons/devils is derived. Demons/devils are the ghosts of the Nephilim; they are one in the same. As for the land of Bashan, it was a real place, but when everyone there was killed, it ceased to exist as it was. Now, perhaps it still exists in a portion of Sheol/

Hades, along with the lost souls that once lived there. "A fifth-century B.C.E. Phoenician tomb inscription (Byblos 13), published by Professor Wolfgang Rollig of the University of Tubingen, speaks of Og as a Phoenician deity and the protector of tombs: [...and if anyone seeks to open] this sarcophagus and to disturb my bones, the Og will seek him out, the strong one, and with all the assembly [of the gods]."

8. 8. See Matthew 12:22-32, Luke 11:14-23. A common characteristic of Satan and his manipulated minions, is to accuse God's chosen of blasphemy while they themselves are committing it.

9. 9. J. P. Millar, The Preacher's Complete Homiletic Commentary on the Book of Judges, Vol 6, (New York: NY, Funk & Wagnalls Company, 1974), pp. 232-307. Location of Deborah's Palm. "She sat in judgement (ps ix:4) under the Deborah palm - so called because Rebekah's nurse was here buried (Genv:8) in Mount Ephraim, between Ramah and Bethel. Ramah was built on a round hill, five miles east of Gibeon; and a little north of it, in the deep hot valley between Ramah and Bethel, was the palm-tree of Deborah. The ordinary place for giving judgement was the gate (Ruth iv:1, 2), but this retired spot was suitable to the unsettled times." This commentary was used to establish the initial location of Deborah's court at the entrance of Ramah. See note 1 for Chapter 19 for further details.

10. 10. Chapter 18 of this book is reserved for this detailed snapshot of Sisera's so-called glory, seated on his twisted throne, overseeing all his evil activities. Note that 6 * 6 * 6 = 18, and Sisera specifically calls out the number 6 three times in this chapter, consistent with the mark of the Beast, Revelation 13:18.

11. 11. See Genesis 4:11, God heard Abel's blood cry from the Earth. According to Hebrews 11:4, it was by faith that Able was able to speak from beyond the grave. Could it be that others are gifted with this same abi

12.

Chapter 19:

Operation Beehive

ש

Spotting Deborah in the early morning as she left her home, Adonia joined her and replied, “You look tire. Did you take sleep herb I give you?”

“Nah, Evie ate it.”

“That little goat eat everything. You should hide herb better.”

Deborah agreed. “She does eat a lot. She’s also good at finding my hiding spots. She jumped up on my dresser to get it.”

“Why you let goat in house?”

“She keeps the pigeons out. They were crapping on my bed.”

“Why you let bird in bedroom?”

“They’re my buddies,” Deborah smiled, “until they started crapping on my bed. But now Evie crapped in my room.”

“Oh? So now you kick her out too, yes?”

“Nah,” Deborah replied. “It was that herb that did it. It knocked her out so hard, she crapped and pissed on my floor without waking up; just all dribbled out. So it’s probably a good thing I didn’t eat that herb, eh?”

Adonia pursed his lips while averting his eyes. “That not happen with most people.”

“Right,” Deborah nodded.

“At least it work. Goat still sleeping, yes?”

When they reached Deborah's bench, a large gathering of people stood in line waiting for her. "Wow, large crowd today. Ramah shouldn't be the only town reaping the benefits of all these travelers. We need to relocate my court between here and Bethel."

"There is large palm not far that way," Adonia pointed north. "They say it mark someone grave, long time ago."

"I know that place," Deborah replied. "Rebecca's nurse was buried there. That would work."[1] Just before sitting down, Deborah spotted something out of the corner of her eye.

The palm tree on her left was the same tree she struck with a tent peg a few years back, the night Barak left Ramah. For some odd reason, the wound in the tree from that tent peg started leaking sap again. It was the sparkling amber of the sap that caught her eye.

Deborah touched the sap, recalling the sorrow of that night, when the man of her dreams walked out of her life. As she examined her fingers, the blood of this tree seemed to be speaking to her. Another loss perhaps?

Deborah turned to Adonia and spoke with a hushed tone. "I think it's today. Remember, once the battle begins, find my father, and don't let him out of your sight."

"But Ruben..."

"I know, Ruben," Deborah cut him off, "but I'd rather have both of you with him."

"Are you sure about this? The last time we went through this..."

"No, I'm not sure," Deborah interrupted him again.

"I always tell you, I don't control what the Lord reveals. It's just I know Ramah will come under attack any day now. Yes, I had a false alarm the other day, but today, that feeling is stronger than ever. We can't afford to ignore it. *Operation Beehive—go.*"

Adonia motioned to Gavriella, who was standing nearby. After a brief word with her, the two sprinted into town, activating phase one of their well-prepared defense plan.

Deborah addressed the crowd of people. "Nobody brought any idols today I hope?"

Everyone shook their heads—*nope*.

"That's good. Just checking..." Deborah replied, then paused before proceeding, wondering how much time she had before this pending attack would be upon them. Her gut told her there was no time to waste.

"People of Israel," Deborah addressed them, "I don't know how much time we're going to have today. Some of you may know, we've been hearing reports..."

Meanwhile, Operation Beehive was in full swing.

The former gossip girls of Ramah were now promoted to Ramah Security Squad Leaders under Adonia's direction. Adonia took the eastern quadrant of Ramah, Gavriella took the north, Tamar the south, and Sarai the west.

Sarai meticulously positioned a massive wooden lance, fashioned from a weaver's beam, inside a groove carved into the ground near the center of town.[2-3] Next to it, she placed Deborah's bow along with a quiver of arrows.

Gavriella worked with a team, pulling back spiked posts and hooking them to triggers designed to activate from concealed locations.

Tamar directed villagers to light hidden fire pits throughout Ramah. Next to them, quivers full of arrows, jars of oil, and jars of water were set in place.

Clubs, sharpened poles, sharpened rocks, and improvised weapons of all types, most of which were modified garden tools, were stashed throughout Ramah.

As for Adonia, he pre-positioned a concealed rope, lightly buried in a groove trenched across the central road just inside the eastern entrance to Ramah. This would hopefully trip a chariot horse.

If the charioteers were riding as fast and close together as their first attack on Ramah, this one trap could create a cataclysmic chain reaction on those chariots.

Adonia also instructed villagers to pile up rocks of various sizes for slings or throwing by hand, stashed behind the parapets on all the rooftops. They furthermore added bows and quivers full of arrows.

Ideally, if the chariots were bottlenecked in a crash as they entered Ramah, they would receive an onslaught of rocks and arrows immediately afterward.

With most of the permanent structures consolidated in the eastern quadrant of Ramah, the eastern entrance was perfect for this ambush. However, what would guarantee the chariots were going to enter from the east?

Deborah debated this issue with Adonia, and neither conceded to the other.

"But you're just wasting your time creating obstacles outside our walls, because I already know they're coming in from the east. I've had that vision at least a dozen times," Deborah argued.

"And the reason they come from east is because I put Ostridge...eh, you know, the thing in way..."

"Obstacles?" Deborah questioned.

"Yes, those. They make terrain flow east, so I make it natural. I part of you vision, I make it true."

"Whether you do anything or not, they will come in from the east, because I've already seen it," Deborah insisted.

"I know, because I block north," Adonia wouldn't budge.

Thus, the debate of freewill versus predestination would rage on another day.

Adonia spent the last several weeks evenly dispersing large rocks along the northern side of Ramah, and also digging a few trenches, then working to make them look natural.

He also fortified the northern and western walls. Lastly, he cleared rocks away from the path leading to the main entrance from the east, making it wide and inviting for charioteers, who generally avoided rocks like the plague.

So Ramah was jam packed with booby traps of all kinds, staged ex

actly where Deborah knew they would be the most effective. These were also combined with ambush focal points, but would all this be enough?

Sisera's troops rode in massive war chariots with spiked wheels, armed to the teeth with the best weaponry. Each chariot had bows, arrows, and a cache of multiple weapons to choose from.

The chariots were pulled by powerful, fully armored war horses, and the charioteers were skilled fighters wearing full plate body armor that would deflect a great many attacks.[4]

Then there was Lahmi, a ten foot tall monstrosity. He was a warrior of mass destruction, capable of killing a half dozen men with a single swing of his battle axe. With a war hammer, he could smash and kick his way through a solid stone wall one foot thick.

In the face of all this, the Israelites had scraps for most of their weapons. The few swords they had were of very low quality, and there wasn't a single shield among them.[5-6] As for body armor, only a few wore studded leather.

The best equipment they had they retrieved from Sisera's men from prior attacks. However, that didn't amount to very much compared to the number of fighters.

But the citizens of Ramah capitalized on everything they had. Deborah's visions were their secret weapon, combined with their home field advantage, and their unified faith.

They were of one mind, determined to defend their homes, and their families, with their lives.

And so it was, as the villagers completed the final touches of their defense plan, Gavriella started shouting from a rooftop, "They're coming! They're coming!"

In the blink of an eye, Deborah leapt up on top of her bench. "Look!"

she pointed to the north, where a dust storm in the distance indicated a contingent of chariots headed their way.

"Citizens of Israel, today is the day, here they come! Those chariots come here for one reason only, to kill, steal, and destroy![7] I have seen this in my visions, but fear not! We have prepared!

"For any who are not able to fight, we have shelter for you. Ruben will take you there right now," Deborah pointed to Ruben.

"Where is my father?" Deborah questioned Ruben.

"He's locking down the café, but don't worry, I'll come back for him."

"The rest of you," Deborah addressed the crowd, "now is not the time to hide. Repent, all of you, and turn to the Lord. He is our salvation! Today, we unite as one with the Lord!"

"Hallelujah!" a burly man called out from the crowd. "Let's let 'em have it!"

"They're why I'm here!" a woman yelled. "They took my daughter!" she bellowed in a rage. "This has to stop!"

"Life for a life!" rang out a familiar phrase, from the same woman who made that declaration the last time Ramah was attacked.

"Take heart, Israel, the God of Abraham, Isaac, and Jacob will deliver this enemy into our hands! Believe it!"

"Yes!" the Israelites roared out with righteous indignation, ready to take up arms.

Except none of them had any arms.

"We have weapons for you!" Joash, one of the warriors assigned to protect Deborah yelled out.

"Whoever's really good with a bow or a sling, follow me!" He then spun around and sprinted into Ramah, immediately followed by some of the travelers.

"The rest of you, follow me!" Ezra, the other warrior called out, and the remaining crowd ran after him, except for a few stragglers. They stared at Deborah, overwhelmed by what was happening.

Deborah approached one of the women. "Who are you kidding? You're an expert with a bow, why didn't you go with Joash?"

"I've never killed anyone before. I don't know if I can do that," the woman replied.

"You don't have to fight if it's not in you, but they're fighting us whether we defend ourselves or not," Deborah pointed at the quickly approaching dust cloud.

"You have the choice to go with Ruben if you must, but you're really good with a bow. You may very well save lives today if you're over there," Deborah pointed to one of the nearby rooftops.

"There's a reason you're as good with a bow as you are," Deborah nodded at her.

The woman deliberated briefly, looking toward the impending attack. She then turned and bolted to the area where Deborah pointed.

Haran was just finishing up, consolidating all his supplies in an underground hidden storage area accessible from inside his café. He emerged just in time to see some people sprinting into town.

"Now it's time for you to fight," Haran replied to his daughter.

"What, you're still here? Where's Ruben?"

"Ah!" Haran scowled and swiped his arm at her. "I'm not hiding from this!"

"We ready!" Adonia jogged up to them. "Ruben busy, but I here. Hurry, we must go now, they almost here," he grabbed Haran's arm and tugged him to leave.

"I don't need an escort!" Haran yanked his arm away from Adonia.

"Don't fight them father, please," Deborah plead with him. Now the shoe was on the other foot. The day finally arrived when he unleashed her to battle, yet it was now her that didn't want him to fight.

Unfortunately for Deborah, Haran was intent to give her a taste of her own medicine. He grinned while staring at the approaching attack.

"I never wanted you on the battlefield, but now that the battle is here, I'm not going to let you fight alone any more than you ever let me fight alone." He then jogged away with Adonia, fully intent to avoid Ruben's shelter.

"Stay with him!" Deborah yelled at Adonia with gut wrenching concern. She then took a deep breath, centering herself,[8] and channeling that raw, agonizing energy toward the task at hand.

"You two," Deborah addressed the remaining stragglers, "come with me." She then sprinted past Haran and Adonia and headed toward the middle of town with the stragglers trailing after her.

This was going to be the first southern village attack defended entirely by villagers rather than trained warriors officially under General Barak's command.

Moreover, the majority of these villagers were women.

Only a few of General Barak's trained warriors were still among them, at the request of the High Priest. Their purpose was specifically to protect Deborah. However, the way Deborah saw it, protecting Ramah was protecting her, so they were part of her defense plan.

While Ruben rushed elderly and disabled travelers to a fortified shelter, Joash and Ezra equipped and positioned travelers alongside the citizens of Ramah, all throughout Ramah.

Shortly after everyone was in place, Lahmi lead the way with his massive four-horse war chariot, commanding twenty of Sisera's mounted charioteers, and some additional horseback troops behind them.

They poured into Ramah's eastern entrance, single file, bottlenecked by the walled entrance, just as Deborah predicted.

Arrogant and predictable, that's how Deborah described them. They lacked strategy, they lacked discipline; they were over confident, and far too reliant on their numbers and weaponry.

This description brought comfort to those listening to her during their battle preparation meetings.

Nevertheless, Sisera's forces had a massive advantage at face value if they didn't take it for granted. Israel could afford no mistakes. Deborah used every weakness of Sisera's men in her strategy, and she capitalized on every facet of Israel's strengths.

As the first wave of charioteers glided into Ramah, they gleefully torched the first structures they saw, shouting and laughing as they went. These were a depraved lot, craving the lust and carnage of raping and pillaging defenseless people.

Some of them fired flaming arrows at every combustible structure they saw. They all searched for people to shoot, but there was no one in sight. No one except for Deborah.

To anyone with a mustard seed of common sense, Deborah standing in the center of town, in the center of the main road, was obviously bait for a trap.[9]

Lahmi considered this possibility as he charged toward her, but in his mind, no trap could possibly stop him.

These Israelites were too puny and feeble to actually do any damage. Whatever weapon came toward him, he would surely deflect or destroy it.

This was the woman who took his eye, and unlike his brother, he wouldn't be content with simply impaling her. No, first, he was going to chop off her head, then stomp it into mush, then chop her body into small pieces and take those pulverized remnants back to his temple of Baal and burn them on his altar.

After all that, he would then mock the God of the Hebrews, and challenge Him to bring her back so he could do it again.

Deborah was indeed the bait of her own trap, and it was only going to work if Lahmi's four-horse chariot was in the lead. It was exactly as she foresaw. Deborah held fast, defiant, chin raised, holding her ground.

Wait for it...

Following her instructions to the letter, right after Lahmi's chariot passed over the concealed rope, Joash roared out, "Now!" Two women sprung the first trap, yanking that rope up and spinning it around a tree stump.

The first horses directly behind Lahmi tripped and collapsed, precisely as planned, and a quagmire of chariots instantly piled up, killing two charioteers. The first half dozen chariots directly behind Lahmi were completely immobilized.

Sisera's forces instantly realized that they were in an ambush when they heard someone shout, "Fire!"

A volley of arrows and rocks immediately rained down on top of them, but Sisera's men whipped out their shields just in time, deflecting the majority of the first volley.

However, right after that, they discovered that the first structures they set fire to were decoys, which were now knocked over behind them, closing them in.

Another volley of arrows and slingshots rained down, and finally a few arrows penetrated seams in their armor.

A large rock also made its way to a helmet, knocking one of the men unconscious. As for the war horses, they were rearing up in a panic because of the fire behind them.

The remaining charioteers snatched their best weapons and abandoned their chariots, then spread into the town, searching for victims.

The most courageous fighters leapt out and engaged them right away. Other villagers wasted no time snatching weapons from dead soldiers, or weapons abandoned in chariots.

They then redistributed them to the best fighters.

For a number of Israelis, they had no propensity for hand to hand combat, and they weren't much good with projectile weapons, either.

However, anyone could activate a trap, or throw buckets of water to put out fires. Anyone could bandage wounds, or act as battle assistants, fetching and redistributing weapons to the best fighters.

Everyone played their part.

The chariots behind the first six peeled off when they were blocked by collapsing, burning structures. They then discovered additional booby-traps wherever they turned.

Poles were flung into the spokes of two chariots, and a few of the poles were sturdy enough not to snap. They shredded the spokes of those wheels, throwing the charioteers to the ground.

Israelites swarmed in like bees, piercing injured charioteers with their spears.[10]

The best weapons among the Israelis were the few spears that remained from those that Heber sold to them a few years back. They also made a few more, repurposing the spikes on the war chariots abandoned by Sisera's men on their first attack in Ramah.

Other chariots were dowsed with oil and struck with flaming arrows, setting them ablaze.

In less than five minutes, almost every one of those twenty chariots was either destroyed, or damaged beyond use, forcing the charioteers to abandon them.

Heading directly toward the center of Ramah, Lahmi's chariot was isolated from the rest of them after the first trap tripped the horses of the second chariot.

While all the mayhem ensued on the six chariots behind him, Lahmi had Deborah in his sights; he was oblivious of everything else.

Deborah's defiant stance taunted his rage to the extent that he abandoned all manner of reason.

Infuriated, he whipped his horses mercilessly, then he held up his colossal battle axe, preparing to throw it.

In response, Deborah calmly reached down and picked up her bow from the ground. She then fired a well-placed shot at the eye of this raging Cyclopes.

Using the flat blade of his axe, Lahmi expertly deflected the arrow. No way was he going to make that same mistake twice and underestimate this little woman's skill with a projectile.

The arrow pinged off his axe with an insignificant spark, missing its mark.

Lahmi roared with amusement, then he pulled back his axe to throw it, but his howling was suddenly drowned out by ear shattering screams on his left and right.

The two stragglers Deborah asked to join her were screaming with unfettered zeal. In the instant Lahmi turned to look at them, the ground in front of his chariot suddenly vanished.

An enormous pit was concealed beneath goat skins covered by a thin layer of dirt.

The pit was about six feet deep, and the first two horses dropped inside of it and flipped Lahmi's war chariot vertical, catapulting Lahmi into the air.

While the women were screaming, and Lahmi's horses dropped into the pit, Deborah dropped her bow and snatched up the front end of the lance hidden in a groove cut into the road. She had the back end of the lance braced against a notch.

Lahmi's monstrous form glided through the air, and time froze as he sailed helplessly toward his fate. Lahmi met with the business end of Deborah's lance, piercing directly into his chest.

Deborah stood her ground, yelling with ferocity, holding that lance firmly in place.

Lahmi's titanic body rammed down the full length of that lance, snapping it near the base.

Deborah leapt out of the way in the last instant, but Lahmi collapsed on top of her legs.

The two straggler women were still screaming hysterically until Deborah lifted up her head. "Okay already, help me get out of here!" she yelled at them.

They quickly ran over to her and struggled to move Lahmi's hulking corpse.

Deborah finally squirmed lose, then she quickly snatched up her bow.

One of the women tossed her a quiver of arrows just as another charioteer whirled around the corner after weaving its way around the blockade.

Deborah dodged the blades of its wheels, then spun around just in time to smack a dagger out of the air with her bow.

The soldier who threw it at her was shocked, because she smacked that dagger away without even looking.

Forget this!

He suddenly spun and sprinted away.

Commentary Notes

++

1. J. P. Millar, *The Preacher's Complete Homiletic Commentary on the Book of Judges, Vol 6*, (New York: NY, Funk & Wagnalls Company, 1974), p. 187. "She sat in judgement (ps ix:4) under the Deborah palm - so called because Rebekah's nurse was here buried (Genv:8) in Mount Ephraim, between Ramah and Bethel. Ramah was built on a round hill, five miles east of Gibeon; and a little north of it, in the deep hot valley between Ramah and Bethel, was the palm-tree of Deborah. The ordinary place for giving judgement was the gate (Ruth iv:1, 2), but this retired spot was suitable to the unsettled times."
2. "Goliath's Spear, Giants are no match for my God!," https://www.goliathsspear.com/weavers-beam, (Last Accessed February 13, 2021). This website was created by a church that funded the research and recreation of enormous massive spear, which is compared to a "weaver's beam," 1 Samuel 17:7. "Based off the looms used in that time period, it would be common for a weaver's beam to be 2 to 2 1/2" inches thick and more than 5 feet long... For the physics of our Goliath's spear beam to work properly with a 16lb 11oz spear head and the height of Goliath, we choose a 10' length 2in diameter pole, including a 6lb 1.2oz counterweight, giving our spear a total length of 12 ft 7in. This is not to say the spear could not have been even longer. The Bible doesn't give us the exact length. However, the length we calculated for our replica would allow Goliath to have a center of balance to hold the spear easily with one hand about 62 inches from the tip. This would allow him to thrust it directly at the enemy to achieve the best leverage and killing force."
3. How much did Goliath's spear head weigh? FindAnyAnswer, https://findanyanswer.com/how-much-did-goliathaposs-spear-head-weigh, (Last accessed February 13, 2021). The comparison of a weaver's beam helps to provide an estimate for the size of Goliath's spear, but the spearhead also helps to estimate the size of his spear. "A normal spear head from this period would have been eight inches, maybe a foot long and weigh about a pound, roughly half a kilogram at most. No satisfactory theory has yet to explain such gigantic spears, which are approaching the size of Goliath's

spearhead made of Iron and reportedly 600 shekels (15 lbs.)."

4. Jesse Lyman Hurlbut, *Hurlbut's Handy Bible Encyclopedia*, (Philadelphia, PA: The John C. Winston Co., 1908), p. 22, Armor. "The Breastplate, enumerated in the description of the arms of Goliath, a "coat of mail," literally a "breastplate of scale," 1 Samuel 17:5... The Helmet is referred to in 1 Samuel 17:5, 2 Chronicles 26:14; Ezekiel 27:10. Greaves or defenses for the feet, made of brass, are named in 1 Samuel 17:6 only. Two kinds of shield are distinguishable. (a) the large shield, encompassing, Ps. 5:12, the whole person. When not in actual conflict it was carried before the warrior, 1 Samuel 17:7, 4i. (B) Of smaller dimensions was the 'buckler' or 'target,' probably for use in hand-to-hand fight, 1 Kings 10:16; 2 Chronicles 9:15-16."
5. J. P. Millar, *The Preacher's Complete Homiletic Commentary on the Book of Judges, Vol 6*, (New York: NY, Funk & Wagnalls Company, 1974), p. 252. "Was there a shield or spear seen among forty thousand in Israel? Not that the people had not any such weapons (as in 1 Sa_13:22), for if so, the battle of Kishon could not have been fought. The reference is not to Barak's army, which consisted of 10,000 men. The meaning seems to be, that a spirit of trembling had so generally seized the people of Israel, that not a single man among so many as 40,000 had the courage to stand forth to fight his country's battle in the field. There were three kinds of spears, as referred to in the Old Testament. The first was a long slender lance; the second a javelin; and the third—that referred to here (romach), a heavier weapon."
6. Arthur E. Cundall & Leon Morris, *Judges & Ruth: An Introduction & Commentary*, (Downers Grove, IL: Inter-Varsity Press Leicester, England, 1968), p. 95. "They had been deprived of their weapons (1 Samuel 13:22), although it may be unwise to accept this as an absolute statement. If it were, the battle at the Kishon could hardly have been undertaken. Probably the meaning is that these weapons dared not be displayed publicly."
7. See John 10:10, "The thief cometh not, but for to steal, and to kill, and to destroy..."
8. Richard J. Foster, *Celebration of Discipline: The Path to Spiritual Growth*, (New York, NY: HarperSanfrancisco, 1988), p. 30, "A form of meditation is what the contemplatives of the Middle Ages called "re-collection," and what the Quakers have often called 'centering down.' It is a time to become still, to enter into the recreating silence, to allow the fragmentation of our minds to become cen-

tered."

9. See Luke 17:6, faith of a mustard seed
10. Hence the name of Deborah's defense plan, Operation Beehive, inspired by Deborah, the queen bee.

Chapter 20:

About my Soup

ת

There was no mistaking that overwhelming presence of evil Deborah felt moving toward her from behind.

When she turned to her left, she saw one of Sisera's men, Og, striding confidently toward her with a determined countenance.

He was not right, definitely not right.

Deborah lifted her bow to fire a shot, but the second she did, Og whipped out his arm to the left, and her bow suddenly flew out of her hand and landed on the ground.

Okay, confirmed, something definitely not right with this guy.

Deborah took a fighting stance, but Og unsheathed his sword while striding toward her.

"So you don't think you can beat an unarmed woman, you have to use a sword?" Deborah hoped a play on his ego might get him to re-sheath his sword for a more even fight.

Nope, he continued his stride unabated.

Deborah closed her eyes briefly and said a quick prayer to the Lord.

She then pulled out two tent pegs; one in each hand. With dazzling speed, she flung one of the tent pegs at Og's chest.

The same as before, he whipped his free hand to the left, deflecting the tent peg telekinetically.

However, a half second after throwing the first tent peg, Deborah let fly the second tent peg with her left hand, striking it directly in the center of Og's chest.

Bullseye!

"Ah!" Og roared out and froze in his tracks, taken by complete surprise by that immediate second tent peg.

"Tribe of Benjamin; we train with both hands," Deborah replied with raised eyebrows.

Still fueled with demonic endurance, Og ripped the peg out of his chest while tightening his grip on his sword.

He then started to walk toward Deborah again, but she wasn't fooled by this show of force. When Og finally reached her, he swayed and collapsed to the ground, lifeless.

"Back to the pit of hell where you belong," Deborah spoke over his dead body while raising her hand in a prayer over him.

One of the women keeping company with Deborah went to pull Deborah's tent peg out of Og's chest, but Deborah stopped her. "Leave it," she replied. "That gets buried with him."

Boom! An explosion suddenly erupted on the north side of town. A horse peeled out of the area, turned on the main road and bolted out of town, dragging remnants of a burning chariot behind it.

Deborah sprinted in that direction, passing her home on the way there. Haran was nowhere in sight. Where was he?

Deborah soon joined Sarai and Gavriella. While they were firing arrows from rooftops, Deborah snatched a sword tossed in her direction by a villager, and she immediately rushed into battle, hoping to find her father.

Some of the more aggressive villagers were slugging it out with kicks and punches, because they were either out of arrows, or their makeshift weapons were busted. Nevertheless, they continued to fight, seemingly fearless to face their armed adversaries.

Sisera's troops were not accustomed to fighting villagers like this. These citizens of Ramah, mostly women, fought with incredible skill, and unyielding ferocity. A number of Sisera's men were killed primarily because they underestimated these women.

"Get some more weapons over here!" Deborah ordered the two women with her, and off they went.

Deborah then leapt into the fray, swinging wildly, and her sword busted right away. The soldier who snapped her sword laughed and licked his lips, salivating over what he thought was going to be the spoils of this battle.

He then sheathed his sword. "Oh, I don't want to hurt you. I want you alive," the slimy crustacean of Sisera's cesspool gurgled in his barely human voice.

Cool, a freebie.

Deborah whipped out a tent peg and flung it into the man's throat, killing him instantly. She then pulled out another tent peg and turned to see another one of Sisera's men as he rounded a corner from behind.

When the soldier saw her, he yipped in panic, skidded and tripped over his own feet, falling to the ground next to the soldier Deborah just killed.

He then screamed again, rolling in the dirt, yipping and squealing with a bizarre combination of dog and pig sounds.

Deborah simply stood and watched him as he scrambled back to his feet and ran off, terrified by every woman he saw.

Sisera's men were not expecting anything like this. Some of them finally came to their senses, realizing they were outmatched, and the entire village of Ramah was turning into a death trap.

"Behind you, he's getting up that ladder!" a young boy yelled to Gavriella on the rooftop.

This child was originally forced to shelter in place with Ruben's group, but he broke away in the hustle and bustle, giving his grandparents the slip.

He was determined to fight, whether his grandparents approved or not. His parents were both killed in Nazareth, and he recognized some of these soldiers as the culprits who murdered them.

Gavriella was nearly out of arrows, so she dropped her bow and picked up a spear lying near the ladder behind her.

Just as that soldier reached the rooftop, wham! He met with a Gavriella's spear in his gut, and he fell off the ladder.

"I need more arrows!" Gavriella yelled down to the boy, who was busy yanking out that spear.

Once he pulled out the spear, he saw Deborah was about to fetch it, so it tossed it to her, then he started fetching arrows wherever he saw them.

Sisera's troops were thinning in numbers, and they started falling back toward the eastern entrance to Ramah.

Meanwhile, Adonia and Haran were in the heat of battle protecting the fortified shelter where Ruben took the children, elderly and crippled.

Sisera's men attempted to burn the structure down, but able-bodied villagers extinguished the fire in time while Adonia and Haran fought Sisera's men.

While Sisera's men were fleeing from the north and center of town, they fell back to the eastern entrance and started to regroup where Adonia and Haran were fighting.

In this location, Sisera's men were gaining the upper hand, but Ruben and Tamar joined forces with Adonia and Haran. Even so, the four of them were outnumbered three to one.

Deborah, Gavriella, and others in the north side of town were so exhausted, they gasped to catch their breaths, and Gavriella dropped to her knees, but Deborah couldn't rest until she found her father.

All of Sisera's men retreated in the same direction, which was indicative of a designated rally point where they might be regrouping.

Deborah stumbled off in that direction, and soon discovered about one hundred yards away, the last vestige of battle around the fortified shelter. Once again, Sisera's men were attempting to set the building on fire.

Deborah tripped and fell down, heaving to catch her breath. It was her golden tent peg the she tripped over; the one deflected by Og. "The Glory of this Battle is Yours," the peg was inscribed.

Invigorated, Deborah snatched it up, sheathed it, stood back up and started jogging toward the battle.

Her limbs were moving, but the sensation was odd, because she felt as though she were riding along in someone else's body. She had no energy left to stand up, yet she was jogging.

Adonia, Haran, Ruben and Tamar were successfully fending off the majority of their attacks. The four of them had each other's backs. All were facing outward, completely surrounded by Sisera's men.

While Deborah was making her way to this battle, she spotted a soldier about fifty feet away, standing on top of the wall near the main entrance. His bow string was pulled taut, loaded with an arrow, aiming and waiting for the right moment.

When Deborah saw him, she picked up her speed and lifted her spear, preparing to throw it. This was it!

How many times had she thrown her spear at this pot-bellied man on a rock wall, in a horrific recurring nightmare? She practiced relentlessly to avoid missing this shot.

If she threw her spear too soon, she was going to miss. If she waited too long, she wouldn't prevent him from firing. What to do?

Right on queue just like in her dreams, a panicked horse blasted through the center of the battle and broke up the group.

In that instant, Deborah flung her spear with all her might, but the man was too far away and her spear fell short. The soldier then fired his shot at Adonia from behind.

Haran turned just in time to see that arrow whistling through the air toward Adonia's back, and he dove in front of it. He intended to block the arrow with his arm, but it shot through his arm with such force, it penetrated his ribs from the side. It then sank all the way into his heart.

Deborah was too late.

She already saw this in her dreams as if it were a memory. Her demeanor around her father changed since she started having that vision.

She couldn't love and appreciate him enough. She hoped a preemptive attack up north would prevent an attack on Ramah, but Haran wouldn't have it. Everything she thought of to avoid this battle backfired.

Or maybe she wasn't too late?

Was this perhaps that dream again, and any second, she was going to wake up and find her father smiling at her, offering breakfast?

No, this time it was actually happening.

Deborah's stumbling jog turned into a sprint, and she charged straight for the guy who shot the arrow.

He proceeded to load another arrow, but Deborah snatched out her gold tent peg and continued her charge. The man fired his arrow at her, but Deborah dove to the ground and rolled, successfully dodging it.

As soon as she was on her feet, she closed the distance. The man loaded another arrow, but Deborah threw her tent peg and sank it into his rotund gut before he could fire his shot.

The soldier's knees buckled and he fell, slamming his crotch into the brick wall so hard, he busted his pelvis. He convulsed a few times, bouncing on his belly, until he bounced his way off the wall and fell on the ground, lifeless.

Deborah then skid to a halt, altered course and sprinted toward the battle to help Adonia, Ruben, and Tamar.

But the battle was already over.

Haran was the last casualty.

Haran was the only casualty.

When two of Sisera's remaining soldiers saw Deborah headed their way, they abandoned the fight and left the others to fend for themselves.

In the next few seconds, Adonia, Ruben and Tamar subdued the remaining soldiers.

Only three of Sisera's men managed to escape on foot, out of a contingent of fifty soldiers. The odds against Ramah were staggering, and this resounding victory was monumental. But the cost of this battle was Deborah's father.

Both Sisera and Lahmi were expecting an absolute slaughter, because this same group of men, his Sacred Order, were the same soldiers who destroyed half of Nazareth without even trying. Now all but three of them were dead.

"Go find my bee," Haran gasped, struggling to cling to his life just a little bit longer.

Deborah ran toward Adonia, Ruben, Tamar, and several other villagers huddled around her father. She was screaming, "No! Father!"

One of the villagers experienced with basic medicinal skills was attempting to render first aid, but it was of little use. Pulling that arrow out of his side would probably end his life instantly.

Haran was pale and gasping for breath. The moment Deborah set eyes on him, he coughed a spurt of blood on his beard. "There she..."

Deborah dropped to her knees next to him, wailing inconsolably. "No, no, no, I'm so sorry father, please don't go. Please, Yahweh, don't take him, *please no...*"

Deborah embraced her father, rocking him in a hug, and Adonia knelt beside her as Haran was mustering the sum total of his remaining strength to utter his last words.

"You...were...right...." He meekly lifted his hand to her cheek and wiped her tears with his thumb. *"About my soup. It's really good..."* He coughed more blood, wheezing out a laugh.

Deborah impulsively yelped out a laugh. "Ha! Yes, you bet I am..."

Haran nodded with a smile, barely able to breath. Tears trickled down his cheeks, because he knew he was about to check out.

"You were right...about...Israel too. Go...Barak..." He then sighed his last and drifted to another realm, into the arms of Yahweh.

Deborah fell into a breathless, heaving anguish. Her vision blurred with tears, and in the next instant, she found herself on a battlefield in the middle of the night.

Fierce gales blasted pelting raindrops, stinging her face in the midst of a ferocious storm. Her hair was whipped back and she leaned forward to remain standing.

Peals of thunder and flashes of lightning blazed above, unleashing a magnificent display of divine power. This was not a natural storm; this was supernatural; the storm of a Father with unfettered ferocity coming to rescue His children.

Just over her shoulder, Deborah spied the dark silhouette of a mountain struck by a lightning bolt. Light flared out with an intense explosion, followed by a cloud of billowing fire erupting. As it dissipated, a luminous humanoid form emerged.

The vision of that person on the mountaintop defied normal perception, for this person was very far away, yet He appeared crystal clear, as if up close.

The figure turned toward Deborah and raised His arm toward the sky with His index finger extended upward. He then lowered it to point at Deborah. The instant His finger pointed directly at her, she felt His touch inject His life force into her soul.

The pure, intoxicating essence of His spirit, soaked into her blood and circulated throughout her body. With each breath she took, she felt herself expanding and floating upward toward the stars of heaven.

A chorus of angels hummed in her ears; their voices numbered thousands upon thousands, and ten thousand times ten thousand.[1] Wave upon wave of holy energy emanated throughout the wholeness of her being.

"Deborah?" Adonia placed his hand on her back, instantly snapping her out of the vision. Deborah jerked back violently, falling backward on the ground, shivering and gasping. She then curled into a fetal position.

Ah yes, where was I? Gut wrenching grief was it? Yes, that's it, and yet, that miraculous figure on the mountain, He let Deborah know that things weren't all that bad for her father.

In fact, Haran was dancing with joy, and shouting praise and cheers of celebration, so proud of his daughter's masterful victory.

He was marveling at Lahmi's defeat, and reuniting with the love of his life! The only day to match his joy now, was the day he saw his baby girl for the first time.

In that place where her parents were, they would receive the greatest honor that neither of them ever could have imagined. Their daughter would be memorialized among the heroes of the faith for all eternity.

Haran was doing just fine, but as for Deborah, she was going to miss him. And so she remained in that fetal position on the ground, while the others surrounding Haran let her be.

As Deborah lay, she recalled sharing her father's grief, about how they both missed Miriam so much.

And now Deborah was left alone, with no one in her life that knew her like they did. So many memories, so many long walks, so many lessons and delightful times.

Deborah was often the proxy of her parent's interactions with each other.

Haran taught Deborah to hunt, and on one of those early hunting expeditions, Deborah almost shot her mother with a stray arrow. That didn't go over well. But then Deborah burned her father when Miriam was teaching her to cook.

They couldn't stop laughing about that. Haran knew it was an accident, but he couldn't help taunting Miriam that it was payback for the bow incident.

And as much as Haran nagged Deborah about rough housing with Caleb, she caught him in a wrestling match one evening when he thought no one was watching.

He excused himself, saying he had to teach him a lesson for head butting Miriam in the rump.

As usual, this was Deborah's fault for not properly securing him in his pen for the evening. She also cultivated his devious persona, secretly rewarding him for his successful attacks.

Deborah was the apple of her father's eye, and the essence of pure joy to her mother. When Miriam was an older teen, she was taunted relentlessly by her jealous sister, declaring that she would be barren. For an Israelite woman in those days, that was the capstone of insults.[2-3]

A few years after marrying Haran, Miriam thought this curse was true. One year passed, then two years, then five...

Haran built their four room home with an extensive capacity for future growth; the ample space in the second floor was prepared for a multigenerational family.[4]

For many years, Miriam cried and mourned a child she could not have. Every time a family member or friend was blessed with child, the scab of her wound of barrenness peeled away, until nearly a decade passed.

Even her sister sorely regretted taunting her in their youth, and later begged forgiveness. Miriam forgave her, but the pain remained.

By the time Miriam finally gave up on the notion of ever being a mother, she was thirty years old. When her wound was finally scarred up and numb, that's when this miracle child sprang into her womb.

And so Haran and Miriam delighted over Deborah with profound gratitude, doting and thrilled, absolutely adoring their most beautiful, precious child.

Of course, that delight sometimes took a turn toward fear as Deborah aged, because they couldn't fathom losing her. She was everything to them.

But it was always clear, the love they lavished upon her was the context of their words, their actions, and their hopes and dreams for this child of promise who was their legacy after they would be gone.

And gone they were, both of them. Deborah was alone, though Adonia remained, like an uncle or older brother she never had.

Quite some time had passed while Deborah lay on the ground, before she finally became aware of people cheering in the distance, and excited chatter all around.

While Haran's death was a tragedy, he did not die in vain, nor was his death the only significant event that occurred on this day.

Deborah eventually sat up and saw Gavriella, Tamar, and Sarai all sitting next to Adonia, waiting to speak with her. The first thing she noticed besides them was that her father's body was gone.

"They take him your home," Adonia replied while pointing. "They make rest place next to mother."

Deborah nodded. "I don't blame you, I know you tried to protect him," Deborah replied to Adonia. "It was my fault. I missed with my spear."

Adonia disagreed. "It was fault of man who shoot arrow. It also Sisera fault, he why they come."

"You're right," Deborah nodded. She then addressed all of them. "You all fought very well, so valiant. Such courage. We did it," Deborah smiled with tears still trickling down her cheeks. "Let's go say goodbye to...my father."

By the time Deborah arrived home, Haran was already wrapped in a burial cloth, and a grave was prepared in the yard next to Miriam and Caleb.

After they buried him, Deborah spoke to her father while placing her hand on his grave. "You always believed in me." She then did her best to mutter through a brief eulogy.

The people of Ramah were gathered around, and many joined in, recalling their fond memories of Haran.

He was the heart of Ramah; their home was the first solid structure anyone could recall. Haran's trading post was the primary source of revenue for much of the town.

Then when Deborah was announced a prophetess, Haran was the first to respond to the immediate need for a café for weary travelers.

There were others that joined in a healthy competition for business with the increase of visitors, but rather than trying to corner the market, Haran would help them get started.

Haran had many, many friends, all throughout Israel.

Following Haran's funeral, villagers continued to work throughout the day using their newly acquired chariots, to pile up the bodies and take them to a trash dump south of Ramah.

After salvaging all the usable artifacts for additional weaponry, they burned the remnants of battle. They also washed themselves, their clothes, and anything with blood on it.

Lahmi's corpse posed a bit of an ordeal. His chariot was destroyed, and there were no other chariots big enough to accommodate him, so they strapped him to two horses.

With two horses and five men, they could only drag him to the south edge of town but not beyond the wall.

Since there was so much more work to do with the town clean up, they draped a tent over Lahmi's corpse to keep the flies away, and continued with the mountain of easier tasks at hand.

Adonia snatched up Lahmi's axe and swung it around, amazed at how light it was. "Like bird feather," Adonia went to hand it to Deborah.

"No, no, that's fine, you keep it. In fact, take it to Shiloh and find a metalworker named Shelah. See if he can bless it, cut the handle down, and resize the grip for your hand."

"Oh no, I know him. He cost way much."

"Tell him I sent you."

Adonia nodded excitedly and left right away, riding on his newly acquired horse, with his newly acquired weapon strapped to his back.

Commentary Notes

++

1. See Daniel 7:10; Revelation 5:11, ten thousand times ten thousand is used in both the Old and New Testaments.
2. Janice Pearl Ewurama De-Whyte, *Wom(b)an: A Cultural-Narrative Reading of the Hebrew Bible Barrenness Narratives*, (New York, NY: Brill, 2018). pp. 81-123. The wives of the first three Old Testament Patriarchs, Sarah, Rebekah, and Rachel, all dealt with barrenness. Abraham's wife Sarah was taunted by Hagar, Genesis 16:5, and Jacob's wife Rachel was taunted by her sister Leah, (Genesis 29:31). This taunting was the product of a misconception that infertility was a curse from God.
3. WordSearch Bible, "Birth," https://wordsearchbible.lifeway.com/products/13070-bible-biography-series-jacob/sample_text, (Last accessed February 21, 2021). "In the days of Isaac and Rebekah it was a very painful experience for a woman to be barren. Those who were barren were subject to the cruel taunts of people. Many folk felt that the barren woman was under the curse of God, that she had committed some great sin, and that barrenness was the punishment for her sin."
4. William G. Denver, *Who Were the Early Israelites and Where Did They Come From*, (Grand Rapids, MI, William B. Eerdmans Publishing Co., 2003), p. 103. "The houses were of a distinctive type that we may call 'pillar-courtyard' in style. It is often called, however, the 'four-room' or even 'Israelite' house. In a typical example, three banks of rooms are grouped around a central courtyard, usually set off by a row of pillars. At Raddana (and elsewhere), two or three of these individual houses are usually grouped together to form a sort of 'family compound.' This turns out to be significant because it reflects the biblical ideal of the 'mishpaha,' or 'extended multiple-generation family,' as for instance in the narratives in Judges and Samuel."

Chapter 21:

Prepare the Ark!

ו

Unrelenting visions flashed before Deborah, one after another, seizing her throughout the night and into the early morning.

Recalling her father earlier in the day, she held him in her arms, and this time, rather than saying "You...were...right," he said *"You...must... fight."*

She then found herself standing before a deep chasm sliced through the center of the Red Sea.

A miraculous power surged through her, sustaining towering walls of water on the left and right, while a horde of chariots raced toward her through the center of the chasm.

Moses' staff was in her hand, and in one fatal swoop, she swiped his staff to the ground. The walls of water instantly collapsed on top of the Egyptian army.

Their screams or horror rang out, but then they merged into the screams of other charioteers in the middle of the night.

This second group of charioteers were sideswiped by colossal waves striking their chariots. Most of the chariots were toppled and crushed, ejecting the charioteers, then burying them beneath torrents of jagged debris.[1]

Then again, Deborah saw through Moses' eyes, holding up his staff, but the light of the sun flashed like lightning, and the day became twilight.

Moses' staff transformed into a magnificent sword, and Moses' cloak morphed into Deborah's cape billowing in the wind.

Deborah stood at the precipice of a cliff overlooking a vast valley below. Thousands upon thousands of armed troops and chariots swarmed toward the mountain where she stood; numerous as the sands of the sea.[2]

She turned and beheld the Ark of the Covenant directly behind her. How was she able to set eyes upon this holy artifact, normally housed within the holy of holies of the Tabernacle?

Why was it exposed in this place? Might she fall over dead at any instant?[3-4] A holy fear struck her and she trembled in awe.

Only the High Priest was allowed in the ark's presence in the Tabernacle, yet here it was, directly in front of her. She thought to shield her eyes, but she could not, for it began to sparkle, seizing her with an irresistible captivation.

Just behind the ark, Deborah saw the silhouette of a man with his staff raised high. She heard Elias the High Priest bellowing out prayers into a raging storm. Lightning flashed, and the High Priest was now Moses, then another flash, and he was Elias again.

At the pinnacle of Elias' prayers, a magnificent bolt of lightning struck the top of the Ark of the Covenant, blasting Deborah out of her dream. She sprung upright and immediately tumbled out of bed.

Thinking she was falling off the mountain in her vision, she grasped for a handhold and snatched her bed stand, knocking it down on top of her as she fell to the floor.

As soon as she opened her eyes, a curious pigeon stared at her, cooing.

Then bam, bam, bam!

Gavriella?

Deborah was surprised to see Gavriella rather than Adonia pounding on her front door.

"There's...a lot of people out there," Gavriella informed Deborah, wide eyed, stressing the intensity of the situation.

Just behind Gavriella, Deborah spotted Adonia walking down the main road toward the entrance to Ramah. "Leave her alone, she need break. I take care," he replied to Gavriella while swiping his hand in her direction.

"I don't think they're going to leave," Gavriella mumbled.

"We all need a break...from Sisera!" Deborah replied loudly.

At that, Adonia halted and turned.

"Come over here," she called him.

Adonia sighed, annoyed that Deborah seldom if ever took advice when it came to her own wellbeing. Her father just died, she needed a break! But that was just it; now that Haran was gone, he wasn't there to nag her to take it easy.

As Adonia approached, Gavriella tried to warn him. "Watch out!"

Wham! Too late, Evie, Deborah's new goat, snuck up from behind the rock wall and delivered a solid head butt to his knee, nearly knocking him down.

"Ooh, good one," Deborah complimented the attack while Gavriella covered her mouth. The goat bleated back, lifted her head high and walked away, satisfied with her performance.

"Almost got me too," Gavriella commented.

Even more annoyed now, Adonia rubbed the side of his knee while glaring at Deborah with flared nostrils. "I have something for you, but maybe I not give now. You need to teach goat manner."

"Oh, she's just playing," Deborah excused Evie while walking over to the rock wall where Adonia stood. "Can you please return to Barak? I need you to give him the same message as before. Maybe he'll reconsider after seeing what we did here."

Adonia nodded, then he removed an object that was strapped across his back, covered in sackcloth.

"I see metal man in Shiloh, like you say. He give me this to give you. He work axe too. Thank you. That man, he eh..." Adonia waved out his hand, "he like eh, the mustard."

"Mustard?" questioned Deborah.

"Yes! He mustar, you know, the very skill metal man, very skill. So good, yes, take it, see!" Adonia held out the object covered in sack-cloth.

"Oh, maybe you mean...*master*?"

"Yes, that it, he master! You good to think word I mean. Here," he held out the object to her.

"Set it there," Deborah motioned toward the stone wall. Adonia uncovered and unsheathed the sword, then he set it down. Most of Sisera's ornate dagger was the same; every jewel still perfectly intact.

However, the handle was now resized to fit Deborah's hand, and the strange writing on the blade was replaced with Hebrew writing.

The inscription read: "Consider the voice of the singers at the watering places. They recite the victories of the Lord, the victories of his villagers in Israel."[5]

Deborah nodded with exceeding approval while staring at the blade. She then turned to Gavriella.

"If you see me seize up or start to sway, catch me." She then held her hand over the blade. There was a gentle, warm energy, and nothing of Sisera's presence.

Finally she picked it up, and a pure, peaceful sense of clarity washed over her. Then for a brief instant, the faces of a multitude in the centuries to come flashed before her eyes.[6-7]

She found herself overlooking the Megiddo Valley once again; a familiar place, but an unfamiliar time.[8]

Strange creatures; perhaps they were horseless chariots? They rumbled across the valley below. She couldn't see the horses pulling them, but she could hear them. They were horses of thunder.[9]

And the most peculiar, largest birds she could have ever imagined, flew overhead. Were they birds, or were they flying scorpions? Look at their tails! They hovered as hummingbirds; their wings, a whirl.[10]

Instantly, the scene vanished.

"Whoa, that was...*interesting*," Deborah chuckled.

"What, you see something?" Adonia questioned her.

"I wouldn't even know where to start," Deborah shook her head. "This thing is going to be around for a while," she motioned toward the sword, then swiped it back and forth a few times.

"Wow. He did it! It's pure and clean. And it's so light, like holding a twig, or an arrow." Deborah smiled at Adonia. "You're going to like your axe. Hopefully he finishes it in time."

"In time for what?" Adonia questioned.

Deborah snatched the sackcloth, re-sheathed the sword and covered it up. She then patted Adonia on the shoulder while walking past him, headed toward the entrance to Ramah.

Deborah quietly walked through the center of Ramah with Gavriella at her side. The people of Ramah took notice, and one after another stopped what they were doing. Three villagers repairing their home put down their tools and started following.

Others joined in, including Tamar and Sarai.

By the time Deborah reached the main entrance to Ramah, over half of the citizens of Ramah were behind her, and over one hundred Israelites from surrounding villages were all patiently waiting in front of her bench.

Those present from the day before who fought in Ramah, stayed overnight, and more joined them on this day.

Ruben and Jethro were frying food and serving drinks at the café in Haran's honor, knowing that is exactly what he would be doing if he were still alive. "Shakshuka!" Ruben called out while holding up a dish of eggs poached in tomato sauce.

"Right here," one of the travelers called out and set a silver ring on the counter.[11]

Life was moving so rapidly, there wasn't enough time in each moment to digest it all. Her father was gone. Her mother was gone. Barak was gone...

Israel was on the verge of a war, but what about all these people? All of them were waiting for her, as children reporting to their mother to settle their arguments.[12-13]

And their disputes were so taxing.

All these souls stood bare before her. Each had their own histories, their own personalities, likes and dislikes, friends and enemies, experiences of joy, trauma, hopes, dreams, fears...

The first woman in line wanted her fortune told. Nope, not a fortune teller, *repent, go home, next*.

As the next person stepped forward, Deborah was slightly surprised, for there was no urgent need with this woman. Her request was the first of its kind, because she was not there for herself.

"Judge of Israel," the woman bowed, "you have given everything, yet you come here today to serve us. What can we do for you?"

Deborah shuttered, not expecting this. Her eyes welled up with tears and she quickly wiped them away. A brief silence followed.

"Say the word," Tamar, who was standing nearby, added to the request.

"Your father's death was not in vain. He gave himself for us, just as you have, as long as any of us can remember," Gavriella followed Tamar's comment.

"We're ready to do the same, we wish to serve Israel, by serving you."

The crowd of villagers started getting worked up, adding in stray comments, agreeing with the energy of the moment.

"Yes!" Gavriella declared.

"We saw you fight with the strength of ten men!" Sarai shouted, and villagers and travelers alike started shouting in agreement.

"Sisera's executioner met his match!" a scrawny teen roared out.

"I'm not the only warrior here in Ramah, and neither is my father!" Deborah finally spoke up. As she looked at the mass of people, she sensed a unified energy emanating from them, supercharged with purpose.

Then Deborah suddenly realized, most of these people weren't gathered here for her to settle their disputes. They came for another reason. They came to witness history in the making, to hear what Deborah had to say about the day before.

More tears flowed, and now Deborah decided to ignore them.

For the newcomers who weren't there to experience the previous day's battle, they came to see things for themselves. Were the reports true? Was Sisera's executioner slain? Show me his bloody corpse!

If Israel was going to war, Israel was going to need every ounce of this energy, so Deborah seized the moment and stood on top of her bench.

"Just yesterday, I saw each and every one of you Israelites, citizens of Ramah, Bethel, and other villages near and far.

"You all demonstrated unbreakable, unyielding courage. The power of the Lord surged through you, I saw it for myself! Those chariots were nothing!"

Gavriella echoed Deborah's sentiments, "We need to take what we did here, to Sisera!"

The massive crowd shouted in agreement, then they started a chant, "Wake up, Deborah! Wake up, Deborah!" After a half dozen chants, Deborah added, "Arise, Barak!" between "Wake up, Deborah!"[14]

This became the new chant, and the crowd was getting worked into a frenzy. Deborah then held up her arms to quiet them down so she could continue her speech.

In the crowd, Deborah spotted the Nathan, the man who requested her help on her very first case as a judge, to settle that matter of the stolen sheep a few years back. Seeing him stirred his words to her memory.

"In the past, Sisera deceived me. He made me think his actions were my fault. But you have all given me my heart back; my faith."[15]

A loud applause and cheers erupted, and as Deborah continued to speak, more travelers from distant villages continued to stream in.

Today was the day, Deborah would make a monumental announcement. Hopefully Barak would agree to take up the challenge.

Deborah removed the sackcloth from her new sword, then she unsheathed it and held it aloft. "On the first day of Tammuz, we meet at Mount Tabor! We are going to put an end to this devil once and for all![16]

"I have called on the sword of General Barak, son of Abinoam, to lead this charge. The Lord will go before us, and grant us victory!"

The shouts and cheers were infectious, and the crowd multiplied and chanted, "The Lord goes before us, victory! The Lord goes before us, victory!"

"Even if only this remnant right here is all that stands before Sisera's entire legion, the Lord will grant us victory!" Deborah shouted above their chants. "Israel unite! Prepare for war!"

Deborah then stepped down from her bench and re-sheathed her sword. By now, the crowd was in a wild fervor, and a stream of travelers rushed into Ramah, directed to Lahmi's corpse, demanding to see it for themselves.

Several villagers mounted up and darted out of town to spread the word. Israel was going to war!

Elias was thrilled with the news of Deborah's declaration. He was actually expecting it for quite some time. His fellow priests and temple workers, however, were very distraught and in a complete panic.

"You're in no condition to travel to Mount Tabor!" Thomas, one of the temple workers fumed. "This is preposterous! That last trip to Ramah nearly killed you, and now you think you can climb a mountain?"

"None of us have ever carried the ark," a young priest added.

Yet another priest protested, "We're scared to death of that thing!"

Elias was very disappointed with all of them. "What is this? You should be filled with joy to carry the ark! What an amazing honor, to carry the ark into battle! The things you will witness will astound you."

"But..." Thomas interjected.

"Thomas," Elias cut him off, "great grandson of Korah, you of all the priests should know better than to argue with me in this place. I said prepare the ark!"[17]

"I...I...*we say no*" Thomas put his foot down.

"Silence!" Elias roared back, and when he struck the ground with his staff, an earthquake erupted at exactly the same time.

The entire courtyard of the Tabernacle and everything within it shook for about ten seconds. Following the tremor, a stillness settled over the area and all the temple workers and priests.

"I uh...*I'll get the poles,*" Thomas scrambled away.

The priests and temple workers in the Tabernacle weren't the only ones to experience the earthquake.

About seventy miles to the north, Malchus was in the middle of an incantation when the earth rumbled through his unholy mountain. Jars with potions and powders fell off shelves, breaking and mixing, destroying many of his ingredients.

Malchus scurried for cover, sensing something unusual about this earthquake. Once the shaking ceased, he immediately scrambled out of his chamber to find Sisera.

"Something is happening," he reported in his usual raspy voice. "Those rumblings of the earth...were not natural."

Sisera could care less about the earthquake; he was impatiently brooding, awaiting the report of his brother's attack on Ramah. More than anything, he was looking forward to seeing Deborah's head on a platter.

However, before seeing this most desirable presentation, he was expecting to hear a report on the matter from Malchus first.

What was taking so long?

As it turned out, the incantation Malchus was working on was an attempt at getting that information, but now all the ingredients of his spell were destroyed.

"Where is my brother?" Sisera growled.

"I do not sense him," Malchus replied. "That woman clouds my vision. He may yet live, but if not, he will find us...*below*."

Sisera glared at Malchus with gritted teeth. Was that anger? Wait, that couldn't possibly be a hint of fear, could it? Malchus sensed both, which was terribly unsettling.

Sisera was one of his gods! Malchus worshipped him; he couldn't possibly be afraid of anything!

Sisera bolted upright and strode across his throne room toward the dark corridor on the other side. The Chief Hooded Figure silently glided behind him.

As they wove their way through a maze of tunnels, Sisera made a point to stomp on every human skull he saw scattered throughout the tunnels. He liked that crackling sound they made.

They eventually arrived at the underground city that Deborah and the other warriors witnessed earlier when they rescued Israeli prisoners.

Shadows of demons flited among the ancient ruins. Among them, Lahmi's silhouette loomed forth, whispering barely audible, "Avenge me..." Sisera paused and gazed into the darkness.

"There," Malchus whispered, "I..."

"Shut up!" Sisera growled at him, then he addressed his deceased brother. "How could you allow that puny woman to defeat you? Explain yourself!" Sisera's deep voice echoed throughout the endless cavern.

Lahmi's voice whispered in response, "Bring me back..."

"You had your chance! Now you can rot in hell!" Sisera roared, his voice thundering throughout the entire mountain.

The ground rumbled, and debris trickled from the ceiling. A flurry of angry whispers followed them as they continued their descent, deeper into the depths of the mountain.

Malchus eventually fetched a torch from one of the walls, because they finally reached the point where the darkness was no longer an absence of light.

This was an unnatural darkness; a penetrating, opaque death lingering in the atmosphere. It absorbed ambient illumination to such an extent, Malchus could only see the ground two to three feet in front of his torch.

Malchus started to trail behind Sisera, struggling to keep up, while Sisera strode forward with no need of a torch, because he could see in the dark as if it were daytime.

Eventually they reached the deepest, darkest dungeon in the heart of the mountain. Within the swirling mist of this dungeon was a black pit, wherein the veil was thinnest between this world and Sheol.

Malchus glided up next to Sisera, and Sisera replied to him, "Proceed." Malchus knelt down, reached into a pouch and sprinkled some dust into the pit while reciting the words of a spell.

"Abaddon, we call you forth," Malchus finally uttered. "We beseech your presence; implore the words of my lord..."[18]

Sisera then spoke into the pit, "There's been a disturbance."

After a brief silence, a raspy whisper blew words from the abyss. Even Malchus could barely remain standing when this rancid stench echoed out. "Prepare for battle."

Feeling bold, Malchus figured he'd try to earn a few extra points with Sisera by submitting a request. "Will you grant us signs and wonders? May we call upon your name in battle?"

Sibilations echoed from the depths of the pit, "Call upon me, and I will answer thee. They shall be utterly destroyed..."

The Chief Hooded Figure couldn't have hoped for a better response than this! If Israel was getting big headed and bold about overcoming Lahmi, they had another thing coming!

Nazareth was nothing compared to what was coming next! Who did these pesky Israelites think they were, anyway?

If Deborah were to answer that question, she would declare the Israelites were servants of the one and only true living God, Yahweh! And that is exactly what she was declaring every single day after she issued her declaration of war.

Commentary Notes

++

1. See note 8 of Chapter 11. There are unmistakable links defining Deborah as a female counterpart to Moses.
2. See Genesis 32:13, Isaiah 48:19, numerous as the sands of the sea.
3. See Joshua 3:13-17. When the Israelites entered the Promised Land, they carried the Ark of the Covenant, out in the open. It wasn't until the priests carrying the ark touched the Jordan River, that the river receded, and allowed the Israelites to cross it on dry ground.
4. See Numbers 4:18-20. When the Tabernacle was in place and in use, the Ark of the Covenant was stored within the holy of holies, and simply looking at it, or even the sacred utensils associated with it, could kill someone. Numbers 4:5 states that when the ark was packed up for transport, it was covered with the veil of the curtain for the holy of holies. However, this rule was probably not followed by the Philistines when they captured the ark in battle, because they did not have these instructions. When the Philistines returned the ark to Israel, both Philistines and Israelites looked upon it and they did not die. It is only when the Israelites took this leniency too far and opened it to look inside, that the death penalty was executed upon seventy of them, 1 Samuel 6:19.
5. See Judges 5:11, this inscription is found in Deborah's song.
6. "Fact or fake? The relics of Christ's Easter suffering on cross are.. Shrouded in mystery," https://www.mirror.co.uk/news/uk-news/fact-or-fake-the-relics-of-christs-easter-387558, (Last accessed February 24, 2021). This website provides several examples of significant historical artifacts that have avoided destruction through the centuries. There are multiple speculations about the Ark of the Covenant, and its future return. The Javelin of Calvary, aka, the Spear of Destiny, is the spear that pierced Jesus, and the Shroud of Turn is the purported bury cloth that covered Jesus after he was crucified. The Catholic Church has many such ancient artifacts scattered in churches all over the world. Many of these objects have their own stories to tell, changing hands from one century after another.
7. Peter Lloyd Sheerin, "The Baronial Order of Magna Charta & Military Order of the Crusades," https://www.magnacharta.com/dtk/, (Last accessed February 24, 2021). If there were a sword of power from antiquity, associated with the ancient Israelites, the Knights Templar would have been the likely caretakers of such a relic. Are

there any modern Knights Templar still around? There is currently a group called 'Descendants of the Templar Knights,' whose membership requires proof of lineage."

8. David M. Howard & Gary Burge, *Fascinating Bible Facts: People, Places, and Events*, (Lincolnwood, IL: Publications International, Ltd., 1999), p. 372. (Bracketed comments added) "Where is Armageddon? Revelation 16:16 states that Armageddon is a Hebrew word, but no such word is actually found in Hebrew. Many scholars think it stands for har-megiddo 'mountain of Megiddo.' Megiddo was the site of two decisive battles in the Old Testament between Israelites and foreign forces, [one of them with Deborah and Barak in Judges 4-5]. It might well have served as a symbol for the great and final struggle between the forces of good and evil."
9. See 2 Kings 2:11, Elijah and Elisha witnessed angelic chariots associated with "horses of fire."
10. See Revelation 9:1-11. Some speculate John's visions described in the book of Revelation could be descriptions of modern technology. Flying scorpions, for example, might be an ancient Israelite's description of a helicopter.
11. Jesse Lyman Hurlbut, *Hurlbut's Handy Bible Encyclopedia*, (Philadelphia, PA: The John C. Winston Co., 1908). p. 235, Un-coined Money. It is well known that ancient nations that were without a coinage weighed the precious metals, a practice represented on the Egyptian monuments, on which gold and silver are shown to have been kept in the form of rings. We have no evidence of the use of 'coined money' before the return from the Babylonian captivity; but silver was used for money, in quantities determined by weight, at least as early as the time of Abraham; and its earliest mention is in the generic sense of the price paid for a slave, Genesis 17:13. The 1000 'pieces of silver' paid by Abimelech to Abraham, Genesis 20:16, and the 20 'pieces of silver' for which Joseph was sold to the Ishmaelites, Genesis 37:28, were probably rings such as we see on the Egyptian monuments in the act of being weighed. The shekel weight of silver was the unit of value through the whole age of Hebrew history, down to the Babylonian captivity."
12. Rick Meyers, "Equipping Ministries Foundation, e-Sword Bible software, version 12.2.0," downloaded Nov 20, 2020, http://www.e-sword.net; *Cyclopedia of Biblical, Theological and Ecclesiastical Literature*, (bold emphasis added), "Deborah (2)... She was not so much a judge (a title which belongs rather to Barak, Heb_11:32) as

one gifted with prophetic command (Jdg_4:6; Jdg_4:14; Jdg_5:7), and by virtue of her inspiration '**a mother in Israel**.' Her sex would give her additional weight from the peculiarity of the circumstance, as in the instances of Miriam, Huldah, Anna, Noadiah (2Ki_22:14; - Neh_6:14). Her official designation probably means that she was the organ of communication between God and his people, and probably, on account of the influence and authority of her character, was accounted in some sort as the head of the nation, to whom questions of doubt and difficulty were referred for decision."

13. Rick Meyers, "Equipping Ministries Foundation, e-Sword Bible software, version 12.2.0," downloaded Nov 20, 2020, http://www.e-sword.net; *Hastings*, (bold emphasis added), "Deborah... She was the real deliverer of the Israelites, who had sunk into a state of feebleness and impotence, through the oppression of Jabin, king of Hazor (see Barak). A personality of great power and outstanding character, she was looked up to as a '**mother in Israel**' (Jdg_5:7), and was instant both in word and in deed in fulfilling her calling of 'Judge.' Her role is the more remarkable in that the general position of women in those days was of a distinctly subordinate character."
14. Arthur E. Cundall & Leon Morris, *Judges & Ruth: An Introduction & Commentary*, (Downers Grove, IL: Inter-Varsity Press Leicester, England, 1968). p. 97. (Bracketed comments added), "The direct address to Deborah, [Judges 5:12, 'Awake, awake, Deborah!'], is not necessarily incompatible with her authorship of the poem [in Judges 5]. Before the tribes could be aroused to action, she herself, at the word of the Lord, (Judges 4:6), must be awakened from an apathetic acceptance of the situation." In agreement with this commentator, this story explains a possible backstory as to why Deborah included herself with a subtle rebuke. The phrase, "Awake, awake, Deborah!" implies a period of inactivity that preceded her demand for action. There are multiple reasons in this story explaining Deborah's period of inactivity. After the death of her father, there is finally nothing holding her back; she has the wisdom, the confidence, and a purpose driven by prophetic visions, to see Israel through to victory.
15. Deborah echoes the words of Elias' earlier prayers from Chapter 15, "I pray your heart returns to you," now fulfilled this day.
16. "17th of Tammuz in Israel," https://www.timeanddate.com/holidays/israel/fast-of-shiva-asar-b-tammuz, TimeAndDate.com, (Last accessed February 27, 2021). Deborah picks the Hebrew month of Tammuz for two reasons; this is the month when Moses drew the line, smashing the Ten Commandments because of his anger with the Israelites and their creation and worship of a Golden Calf

idol. This month also falls in the June/July time frame, when no one would ever suspect a severe rain storm.

17. In this story, Elias refers to a precedent mentioned in Numbers 16:19, when a Levite named Korah and 249 co-conspirators instigated a rebellion against Moses in front of the Tent of Meeting. In response to this rebellion, Moses pronounced a judgement from the Lord in Numbers 16:28-32, declaring that the Earth would swallow them up, taking them alive, down into Sheol. That is exactly what happened.
18. Abaddon is mentioned in the Old Testament, Job 26:6, 28:22, 31:12; Psalm 88:11; Proverbs 15:11, 27:20, and in the New Testament, Revelation 9:11. The Book of Revelation describes him as a king of demonic entities residing in the bottomless pit.
19.

Chapter 22:

The Lord is on His Throne

ו

Very soon, Israel would depart for Mount Tabor, but Deborah made it crystal clear, no one was going anywhere without first getting their hearts right with Yahweh. The true battle was always in their hearts, even before King Jabin rose to power.[1]

Israelites throughout the Promised Land held their Sabbath with prayers and fasting. Many sacrifices were made in the courtyard of the Tabernacle.

Then following the Sabbath, many Israelis took to intense training and a frenzy of battle preparation; sharpening blades, making new weapons and arrows, packing rations, discussing battle strategies, forming teams, and so forth.

Those with horses could afford to leave later, but many of those who were walking began their trek the first day following the Sabbath. The distance from Ramah to Mount Tabor was a four to five day journey for most.

Barak finally arrived in Ramah with a half dozen warriors. Abijah, one of the warriors that arrived with him, was the first to speak up. "What's that disgusting stench?"

"How can they take it?" another warrior replied.

"Stop sniveling," Barak reprimanded them.

As they rode through town, no one cared about the stench. Instead, everyone was preparing for war; sparing, shooting arrows and sling-shots at targets, sharpening weapons, etc.

Deborah was decked out in her warrior attire, leading a group in training in front of her home. As soon as she spotted Barak, she exploded with unbridled joy and sprinted up to him, grasping his leg while he still sat on his horse. "Lapi!"

Breathless, a chill shot through Barak's spine. The metal in his marrow met with the magnetic pulse in Deborah's hands. Such a glorious creature, this woman before him! How, and why did he take so long before returning to see her?

Time has a way of slipping by unnoticed. In an instant realization, a wraith of regret struck Barak's heart like a flaming arrow. Her father recently died. Was that not enough to summon his presence?

While Barak was confused, questioning and cursing within for not seeing her sooner, Deborah knew the reason why.

She moved on regarding the events of Nazareth, but Barak had not. His absence all this time was a testament to his prison sentence from that day.

He owned that devastation even beyond Deborah's torment, but through sheer act of will, he blocked it out for the sake of his father and his men. Calloused and scarred, he suffered his life as the no-win situation it had become.

Israelis were beaten and burned, taunted, tortured and tormented; abducted and enslaved; mocked, ridiculed, spat on, humiliated, stripped of their dignity, and murdered.

They endured all this, and like a dog with its tail between its legs, they cowered in fear, refusing to defend themselves. The second they lifted a finger to strike back, they were punished ruthlessly until they screeched and scurried back into their corner.

Thus far, Deborah understood Barak's dilemma more than anyone else. He owned the shame, humiliation, and anguish of Israel's plight, so she respected his space.

Deborah also kept her father's wishes close to her heart, serving her role as Israel's Judge from Ramah.

However, all along, they all knew the clock was ticking on this holding pattern. The day Ramah fell under attack, the waiting was over.

Neither Sisera, nor Deborah, were content with the status quo. The one thing they had in common was the firm belief that their place in the Promised Land was an all or nothing proposition.

As far as Deborah was concerned, she was better at telling time on this ticking clock than Barak was. She already drew a line in the sand, declaring the exact day when things were going to change. Barak, however, was nowhere near settled on this matter.

As soon as their eyes met, an overwhelming longing enveloped them, slicing through all these psychological barriers. Forget Nazareth, forget Sisera, forget a foreboding war; forget every clinging, nagging commitment that restrained them.

Where's a tent? Could we not just duck out for a few hours while everyone looked the other way?

No, privacy was not a privilege either of these two enjoyed. In fact, with the two of them together, the spotlight was amplified all the more.

Villagers stopped what they were doing, caught in that shockwave of vibrational energy that warped time-space the instant Deborah touched Barak's leg.

Yes, there was shockwave, every bit as tangible as the earthquake that rumbled through the Earth about an hour earlier.

Everyone was thinking the same thing. These two deserved each other; a reward for enduring the worst torments life could throw at them. But Israel owned them; their lives were public property, *service before self*.[2]

So back to business. Perhaps after this small matter of a war was settled, Yahweh would spare a few minutes of destiny for these two.

When Deborah left her training session, Adonia took over without skipping a beat, reprimanding the group to direct their attention toward him. Barak's first comment to Deborah was to commend her about the high quality training he noticed.

"You have everyone trained so well. This is amazing, what you've done with so little. Twenty armed chariots. Very impressive," he nodded while looking around, then he lowered his gaze to Deborah.

Yahweh dabbled a glitter of glory upon her this morning, to remind Barak that Deborah's father was gone now. What was he waiting for? Where did they leave off, anyway? Didn't he say something about her being the one?

Perhaps Barak didn't think he deserved a wife after what happened in Nazareth, but that didn't matter at the moment. Simply looking at

Deborah was a conjugal visit during his self-imposed prison sentence.

Barak finally stepped down from his horse and stood in front of her. Before he knew it, his thumb was lightly rubbing the scar on her cheek. The two finally hugged each other and tears streamed down their cheeks.

While they held each other, healing in each other's arms, Barak's troops dispersed, and the villagers resumed their training in Deborah's yard, albeit distracted.

Nazareth; reports of Sisera and his men; angry shouts, accusations, and demands for action met with silence and overwhelming grief and trepidation—all this flowed from their tears.

So much pain, and so many dear loved ones lost, but the time had finally come. This season of wretched sorrow was about to end. The winds of change were upon them, and it was Deborah's challenge to convince Barak of this revelation.

"Very soon," Deborah finally broke their silence, "you'll see something even more amazing than what happened here."

"Listen," Barak tried to reason with her, "what you're talking about, an offensive strike, that's not what happened here. Attacking Sisera in his own backyard, that's suicide."

Deborah's countenance changed. "If just five of us struck at the heart of that devil in his stronghold, think what we can all achieve together."

"We can't do this," Barak insisted. "All our trained men in the north combined have not so much as made a dent in Sisera's armor. I don't inspire them anymore. They've lost their will to fight."

Deborah stared at him; Barak's words bounced off her face. "You were supposed to summon ten thousand troops. What did you do?"

"You have not seen a fraction of Sisera's force. Don't you understand? Even ten thousand is nothing."

"Oh, but it is, it's ten thousand, exactly what the Lord said we need. You must have faith."

"I...*faith*," Barak muttered and stared at the ground, deflated. "There's no way I could convince my men of this plan. Maybe down here in Ramah, where you had this recent victory, everyone's all fired up, but in the north...

"I've seen so many die, and you know, don't act like you don't. Let's not kid ourselves, where was the Lord when Sisera's men rode into Nazareth?"

"The Lord is on His throne," Deborah replied without hesitation, "wondering why only two men out of that entire town cared enough about their neighbors to join us. The Lord...has been waiting on *us*...all this time. It is *Israel* who strayed, not Him."

Barak turned away and stared at the setting sun. "It's nice to hear what faith sounds like again."

He then chuckled, almost mocking, but more sadness than anything else. "I think I forgot. I don't even know anymore, and neither do my men in Naphtali or Zebulun."

"Look around you. We're here, aren't we? You know how many casualties we suffered? One. Even that one would still be here, were it not for the Lord calling my father to be with Him among our ancestors."[3-5]

"Look, there's faith, and then there's common sense. I've tried to unite Israel through the years, but they just don't listen to me." Barak turned to see his men chatting with each other a short distance away. He then whistled at them and motioned them over.

"All of you, go in all directions, to all the towns as far as two days will take you. See what the people say about this declaration of war. Go!"

Barak's men quickly zipped out of town, and Barak watched them leave, believing full well his men would find nothing but dull complacency in the surrounding villages.

"All of this flurry of activity we see here in Ramah," Barak waved his arm, "it's probably only here in Ramah. Up north, I haven't seen anything like this...*ever*."

"Daniel, is that you?" Sarai called out to one of Barak's men as they were leaving Ramah.

"Oh, hey Sarai, wow, it's been so long!" Daniel immediately stopped his horse. "Hey guys, hold up, I just need a moment." Daniel quickly dismounted and marveled at this young beauty, who was only twelve years old the last time he saw her in Shiloh.

"Fantastic! You are absolutely beautiful! And you...why are you dressed like that? All the women around here are, what's..."

"Don't you know anything about what's been going on here in Ramah?" Sarai interrupted him. "Almost all our men in Ramah are up there training with you guys in the north, you should know."

"No, I don't know hardly anyone from Ramah. We're divided into smaller groups, scattered all over Zebulun and Naphtali. It's been...it's been really difficult. We've been fighting in the shadows; no major confrontations since Nazareth."

"Hey Dan, we have to get going," one of the men reminded Daniel.

"Wait, before you leave, I have something to show you," she waved the men to follow her.

Sarai led the men to Lahmi's body, still covered under a tent tarp. "We've all been training and so focused on preparing for battle, we haven't had time to drag this disgusting heap of flesh out of town." Saria pulled back the tent to reveal Lahmi's corpse.

Abijah, the highest ranking warrior among them, was dumbfounded. His eyes were bulging, jaw dropped. "The Anakim were here? I didn't hear about that. Twenty chariots, and one of these guys?"

"Deborah did this, didn't she?" Gabriel questioned.

"You know she did," Daniel answered.

"Yes," Sarai replied, "Deborah executed the executioner, but it was I who was put in charge of building his trap," Sarai proudly announced with her chest puffed out.

"We dug a pit, and prepared a lance hidden in the road. Deborah was the bait, just standing there without so much as a flinch while this towering beast charged straight into her. Before he knew it, Deborah rammed this lance into that sick bastard's chest."

Abijah, Gabriel, Daniel, and the other warriors gawked at Lahmi's corpse, then at each other.

"I can't believe this," Abijah finally exclaimed. "I mean, I'm looking at it," he waved his hand toward Lahmi's corpse, "and I can definitely smell it, but I...I just can't believe what I'm looking at."

"Neither can I" Daniel replied, "but I've heard stories about Deborah. I mean, I never believed a word of any of those stories, but...well... it looks like they're probably *all* true."

"Either way," Gabriel reminded them, "we have to get going. When we get back, we definitely need to show this to Barak."

"Well," Sarai questioned the men, "I was actually going to ask you to help us drag this unclean heap to the burn site outside of town," she pointed in the direction of the burn site.

"Like I said, we've all been preparing for battle, but the six of you big, strong guys and all your horses could probably take care of this pretty quick."

"I'll tell you what," Daniel said, "when we get back, , we'll take care of that, but General Barak needs to see this first before we destroy it."

"Definitely," Abijah agreed, "else he might not believe us."

The six warriors rode out of town, and right outside the main entrance, they paused to discuss their assignments.

"You two go north," Abijah pointed to two of them, "you two go west, and you and I will go east," Abijah pointed to Daniel.

"Wait," Gabriel replied. "What are we even doing? Why is Barak questioning the Prophetess of Israel? I heard her message, we were supposed to summon ten thousand from Naphtali and Zebulun. So what's this errand he's sending us on?"

"It's not for us to question," Abijah answered him.

"Besides, you know as well as I, getting the entire northern forces to unite would be a massive undertaking, and there would probably be a lot of dissention. Barak knows what we're up against, but these people down here in Ramah don't."

"Pretty sure Deborah knows," Gabriel countered.

"Well we're just going to go and see what we're going to see," Abijah answered sternly. "Move out!"

Then men quickly dispersed, two by two, headed toward the nearest towns first.

Abijah and Daniel soon arrived in Jericho, where they witnessed a replica of what they saw in Ramah.

Villagers were gathering improvised weapons, making arrows, conducting target practice, sparring with staffs, boarding up buildings, packing horses for travel—the entire city was on the verge of a mass evacuation.

An old man, easily in his eighties, had a sword strapped to his back. This was the same old man that Deborah rescued from Sisera's dungeons.

Ever since he returned home after that torturous ordeal, Deborah's words about the Lord's big plans for him echoed in his mind.

What did she mean?

Driven with purpose, he began training relentlessly, dusting off the cobwebs of his glory days, for he was once a valiant warrior. And now he concluded, Yahweh wasn't through with him yet.

His family ridiculed him before, treating his warnings about Sisera and his men as if they were paranoid delusions.

After he returned home, they had nothing to offer but apologies, but he wasn't interested in their apologies. Life was all about moving forward, not living in regret.

When they apologized to him, he handed his sons and daughters wooden swords in response. In their humility, they bit their tongues as their grandfather, as old as he was, insisted he train them to fight, following Deborah's example.

And now here he was, walking out of town, followed by his entire family. This must have been what Deborah saw when she touched him, all encapsulated in that amazing message, that the Lord had big plans for him.

"Sir," Abijah asked the old man, "where did you get that sword?"

Seeing that these men bore no insignia associated with Sisera's soldiers, he replied, "Rare sight, eh? Got it from one of Sisera's men a few days ago."

"How's that? They've been confiscating weapons from us, not the other way around," Daniel responded.

The old man started laughing. "Not anymore they aren't!"

"Seriously, sir, where did you get that sword?" Abijah persisted.

"I was fighting in Ramah the other day," the old man halted, unsheathed his sword, then swung it back and forth a few times, demonstrating an unusual virility for a man of his age.

Clearly, his training was doing wonders for his stamina. "Why you keep asking, do you want to take it from me?" he challenged Abijah, pointing his sword at him.

"No sir, I just wanted to know, because it looks like a pretty nice sword. Better than mine."

"You bet it is," the old man re-sheathed his sword. "I can tell that Kenite traitor Heber made this one. Look, has his mark," he pointed to a small mark near the hilt.

"No difference, it's mine now." The old man spun around and proceeded out of town, followed by the rest of his family, mostly armed with staffs and slings.

In the town of Ataroth, Gabriel and Malachi also witnessed a repeat of what they saw in Ramah.

Almost everyone already vacated town, but for those who remained, they were preparing for battle, getting in some last minute target practice, making a few more arrows for their quivers, and packing their backpacks.

The same young boy that tossed a spear to Deborah during the battle in Ramah trotted by with a gardening tool in his hands.

"Hey boy," Gabriel called out to him, "where's your father?" The boy stopped and turned around.

"Who are you?"

"We're from the northern forces at Mount Tabor," Malachi replied.

"Can I ride with you?" the boy asked him, "I don't weigh that much. That's where I'm going."

"Son, you're way too young, this is..."

"You're wrong about that!" the boy interrupted him, then spun around and continued his stride where he left off.

"Hey, wait!" Malachi raised his voice. The boy spun around for an instant. Malachi unstrapped a dagger from his waist and tossed it to him. "Here, at least this."

"Thanks!" the young lad strapped on the dagger then quickly darted away.

"Do you see what's happening here?" Gabriel questioned Malachi. "I wonder how many towns are like this. What if...what if this fever has reached up north?"

And in the town of Shamir, the two remaining warriors rode into town, and the entire town was completely vacated. They dismounted and snooped around, poking into several empty tents and knocking on the doors of a few small houses.

Just when they were about to leave, they heard a scuffle in one of the tents.

"Over there," Jacob replied to Thomas, the other warrior. Expecting a possible confrontation, Jacob pulled out his dagger and quickly whipped back the opening of the tent.

A young teen brandished a sharpened stick at them; it was the best she could do as a spear. A dozen toddlers huddled around her. The moment she realized Jacob wasn't one of Sisera's men, she sighed with relief.

"Thank the Lord! I thought you were..."

"Where is everyone?" Thomas stepped inside and questioned her.

"They all left to Mount Tabor. Don't you know?"

"Whose idea was this, leaving you alone with all these children?"

"Some men from Arumah should be here any minute. When they get here, we're leaving for Ramah.

"Why Ramah?"

"They have good hiding places there," the village girl replied. "They've been preparing longer than anywhere else; that's the home of the Prophetess, Deborah.

"You can come with us," Jacob offered their assistance.

Meanwhile, back in Ramah, Barak was wandering around town, brooding, wondering how he was going to convince Deborah that things were not the same throughout Israel as they were in Ramah.

Almost everything about this day was a flashback to that evening when Deborah met him in the wadi and convinced him to go on that rescue mission.

It felt like the right thing to do. For a brief period, they were heroes, on top of the world. They freed the captives.

Then came the horror that followed; a nightmare he was still living in. The fury and shame his father unleashed on him with a simple glance followed by his deafening silence, still haunted him.

Barak's father never trusted him after that incident. On the day of his death, he surrendered his command to his son, then the last words he uttered to his son were, "Don't do anything stupid."

And Barak meditated over these words many sleepless nights. What did that mean? What was the point of having an army, if Israel refused to fight whenever they were attacked?

Barak always knew, the key was unity.

The only way King Jabin could ever be overcome, was for Israel to unite as a single force, but Israel was polarized unlike ever before.

Perhaps only about half the nation was still faithful to the Lord. Some Israelites lived in such rebellion, they even joined Sisera's elite guards, the Sacred Order. How could a nation so divided, ever unite against an enemy who many of them idolized?

Perhaps there was something about Deborah's renown, her amazing popularity that could unite Israel.

Even in the north, there was widespread popularity regarding the many stories that circulated about her. However, was Israel as an entire nation willing to take this gamble?

Imagine the events of Nazareth visiting every village in the entire nation of Israel. Sisera's response to an all-out attack would be nothing less than genocide. Was Israel prepared for this response?

Commentary Notes

++

1. See Judges 4:1-2. The true battle was in Israel's heart before it ever reached a battlefield. It was because of Israel's apostasy that God allowed them to fall under King Jabin's oppression.
2. "Air Force Vision," https://www.airforce.com/mission/vision, (Last accessed February 27, 2021). Service before self is one of the three core values of the United States Air Force, "Integrity first, service before self, and excellence in all I do."
3. In Deborah's time, there was very little revelation about the afterlife, however, the book of Job existed, which Deborah may have had access to, and Job 19:25 states, "For I know that my Redeemer lives, and at the last he will stand upon the earth." [ESV]. Furthermore, Genesis 12:3 states that all nations on Earth would be blessed through Abraham. While these scriptures speak of redemption and they point to Christ, they do not specifically mention the place of departed spirits. Psalm 16:10 may be the first Old Testament reference to distinguish the righteous dead from the unrighteous dead, where King David states, "For you will not abandon my soul to Sheol, or let your holy one see corruption." By saying this, David was saying that some among the dead will be rescued from death. Much later, around 100 B.C., 4 Maccabees 13:14-17 states, "Let's not fear him who thinks he kills; for great is the trial of soul and danger of eternal torment laid up for those who transgress the commandment of God. Let's arm ourselves, therefore, in the self-control, which is divine reasoning. If we suffer like this, Abraham, Isaac, and Jacob will receive us, and all the fathers will commend us." This is a very clear extra biblical reference to a place of the righteous dead, and Jesus gave validity to this location by calling it Abraham's Bosom, Luke 16:22. While it is unknown what knowledge God may have imparted to Deborah about the places of departed spirits, consider the curious wording at the end of her song in Judges 5:31. "'So may all your enemies perish, O LORD! But your friends be like the sun as he rises in his might.' And the land had rest for forty years." First, the enemies of God perish, which is contrasted with the friends of God, implying that they will not per-

ish. Second, take note of Deborah's unusual metaphor of the sun, ascribing a gender to it. The Hebrew word here, shemesh, means "brilliant," as if to say "He," and "brilliance," and "eternal life" are all intimately connected. In context, she is saying the righteous dead will live on as he who is brilliant forever. Could this be a reference to the Son, rather than the sun?

4. EBible.org, "Book of 4 Maccabees," https://ebible.org/pdf/eng-web/eng-web_4MA.pdf, (Last accessed February 28, 2021). "The Fourth Book of the Maccabees appears in an appendix to the Greek Septuagint. It is considered to be apocrypha by most church traditions."
5. "4 Maccabees," New World Encyclopedia, https://www.newworldencyclopedia.org/entry/4_Maccabees, (Last accessed February 28, 2021). 4 Maccabees "is generally dated between the first century B.C.E. and the first century C.E. It was probably written before the persecution of the Jews under Caligula, and certainly before the fall of Jerusalem in 70 C.E."

Chapter 23:

This the Bee Sting

ו

Wandering throughout Ramah in the late afternoon of the following day, observing everyone's battle preparations, Barak approached a group of mostly females, sparring with staffs.

Seeing Sarai leading the group, he waited for her to take a breather, then he initiated a conversation with the group she was training.

"People of Ramah, you know who I am?"

"General Barak," Sarai replied, "of course we know of you. I remember when you used to train here."

"Has anyone told you the size of the force you plan to attack?" Silence; no one answered his question.

"About forty thousand. Even if we muster ten thousand, they still outnumber us four to one.[1] And do you have any idea what sort of weapons King Jabin has acquired?"

"Does it matter?" Tamar questioned him.

"You tell me. They have highly accurate bows and about nine hundred chariots. We have farm tools, tent pegs, rocks. No swords, no shields, no spears; next to nothing."

"You're wrong!" Gavriella shot back, "we have bows and spears!"

"One spear," one of the trainees corrected her, "and we got that spear from one of Sisera's men just the other day, remember?"

"Well, we're making more spears right now, using spikes from those chariots. All the weapons those men brought here, they're ours now.

We have enough to equip this entire village of Ramah."

"That's nice," Barak replied, "but up north, we only have a hand full of swords for ten thousand men, and forget the spears or shields. Wooden swords, that's what we have; pathetic training weapons. Sisera's men have been confiscating from us a lot more than he has from you."

"We'll take whatever we have, and the Lord will do the rest," Gavriella replied.

"You had victory here in Ramah because you made traps, and you knew exactly where to set them. Beautiful strategy," Barak tried to elaborate.

"Actually, Deborah knew where to set them, we didn't," Gavriella added.

Barak nodded, raising an eyebrow, but then he continued.

"With an ambush, you have the element of surprise. You won't have that where you're going. The plains of Megiddo and Jezreel, offer you no protection whatsoever. You'll all be dead before you can even attack.

"I'll be blunt; this isn't a glorious battle, it's a bloodbath. Have any of you here even seen General Sisera?" Barak prodded them with what he thought was a rhetorical question.

"We saw his brother," Sarai replied.

"You...*you did*?" Barak was puzzled.

This Lahmi-sized detail was missing from the reports he received thus far.

Adonia approached from behind carrying Lahmi's battle axe in his hand. He just returned from Shiloh and he was searching for Deborah to show him the marvelous work Shelah did, refashioning the handle and grip of his new battle axe.

"Greeting," Adonia lifted his hand. Barak spun around and spotted Lahmi's battle axe in Adonia's left hand.

"Hand of Miriam, right?" Barak returned the gesture. "So...uh, that looks like Lahmi's battle axe."

"It is," Adonia replied. "Deborah kill him."

"She killed...*the executioner*?" Barak wasn't sure he heard right. "That...no way." This was obviously a case of mistaken identity. Deborah killed a big guy, but not Lahmi.

"They say she slay him single handed, but no, I saw her use both hand. Still, very pressed. This was his weapon," Adonia tossed the axe in the air, spinning it, then he caught it.

Deborah approached while they were talking. Her arms were full of spears, tipped with spikes repurposed from the chariot wheels. "What are you doing?" she asked Barak.

"I'm trying to talk some sense into your people." Barak then lifted his pants leg to reveal a collection of deformed scars. "This is what happens when you get too close to those chariot wheels. I almost lost this leg."

Deborah dropped the load of spears, then pointed to the south side of Ramah, toward the direction of Lahmi's body. "And that's what you get when you get too close to me."

Curious to see what she was pointing at, Barak made his way to the southern part of town and approached the heap of fly infested flesh covered with a tent tarp. Adonia and all the trainees followed him.

When they arrived at the pile of bodies, Barak whipped back the tarp, witnessing Lahmi's impaled, maggot-ridden corpse.

"Look, this the bee sting," Adonia tapped the busted lance.

"What?" Barak squinted, not believing his eyes. This is...impossible."

"Not for her," Adonia pointed to Deborah. Barak looked back at Deborah, then toward Lahmi again.

While they were staring at this hideous pile of flesh, the six warriors Barak sent on their errand trotted back into Ramah.

Barak turned to hear what Abijah had to say. Sure, this sight of Lahmi's corpse was certainly the most impressive feat he had ever seen as a warrior. But what was going on in the surrounding villages?

Surely, this is when the village of Ramah would learn about some depressing news that only Ramah was preparing for battle. As for the rest of the surrounding villages, he was certain it was business as usual; nothing but stagnant complacency.

"I see you've stumbled upon this," Abijah replied while looking at Lahmi's corpse.

"Indeed," Barak answered, "but the weightier matter is what you have to report about the surrounding villages. Let's have it."

After a brief pause, Abijah continued. "We've never seen anything like this...*ever*.

"We split into three groups, and traveled throughout Benjamin, Dan, Reuben, Gilead, Manasseh, Issachar, and we sent runners to Naphtali, Zebulun, and Asher. Everywhere we went, most of the villagers were already headed to Mount Tabor."

"Judah and Simeon are too far south, and they have enough problem with the Philistines, so we didn't bother with them," Daniel replied.[2-3] "Reuben and Gilead seemed disconnected on the other side of the Jordan, but everywhere else, the people of Israel are on fire."[4]

"Sir," Gabriel replied, "In most villages, those who remained were either preparing to defend themselves or they were wrapping up last minute details.

"We only saw two villages in Dan, and they acted like nothing was going on, but everywhere else, Israel is on the move."[5]

Barak squinted his eyes, having difficulty processing what he was hearing.

"Sir," Jacob chimed in, "I'm wondering if our northern forces will be...*embarrassed*," he shrugged.

"Personal opinion, I think we should move out tonight and start preparing the northern forces as soon as possible. I can't believe I'm saying this, but we might actually have a chance. I've never seen Israel united like this."

"Me neither," Thomas piped up. "Under normal circumstances, this battle is suicide. But this is not normal. *She...*" Thomas nodded toward Deborah, *"is not normal..."*

"In a good way," Gabriel corrected him.

"Of course," Thomas added with a giggle.

Clearing his mind, Barak walked a little distance away and stared out the countryside south of Ramah. He then dismissed his men with a wave of his hand.

What to do?

When he departed for Ramah, he didn't think he would honestly be facing the real possibility of going to war. After everyone was gone, and it was just the two of them, Deborah opened up.

"Look, I understand your reservations. Probably no one knows about the torment you went through following Nazareth as much as I," Deborah explained. "I own what happened there. I had no strategy for defending Nazareth in case there was a reprisal.

"That's why all this time, I've been doing nothing but sending you one report after another, about all the same horrific things happening repeatedly in villages all over Israel.

"Have I once come to you since Nazareth, making demands for justice? No, I haven't. Instead, even when I knew my own village was coming under attack, we took our stand without you."

"But I warned you..." Barak interjected.

"Please..." Deborah sighed. "Safe passage, really? Don't you remember who I am? In case you forgot, you saw what we did here," Deborah pointed to Lahmi's dead body.

"The way I see it, every village in Israel has the potential to do the same thing we did here, but so very much more if we unite."

"I realize you have much to boast about here," Barak countered, "but the battle up north on the pains of Megiddo; why on earth did you choose that as our place to confront Sisera and his men? There is no strategy to that!

"The reason you were so successful here in Ramah is because you ambushed them! This is your home!

"You had a strategic advantage here, but fighting him up there, the advantage is entirely on his side. On those plains, that's where his chariots are the most lethal!"[6]

Deborah smiled, shaking her head in disagreement, then she took on a very serious tone.

"You think I have no strategy, but you're wrong." A gust of wind suddenly blasted Barak in his face, emphasizing Deborah's speech. A chill shot down his spine. This was no longer Deborah speaking; the Lord was speaking to him directly through her.

"The Lord, the God of Israel, commands you: 'Go, take with you ten thousand men of Naphtali and Zebulun and lead them up to Mount Tabor. I will lead Sisera, the commander of Jabin's army, with his chariots and his troops to the Kishon River and give him into your hands.'"[7]

Barak froze, paralyzed by the force he felt emanating from Deborah. Deborah then released a deep breath and blinked a few times, as if regaining control of her consciousness.

Where did she go?

"Look, it's simple, just trust the Lord," Deborah returned to speaking in her casual manner. "The Lord is giving this enemy into your hands. He asked me to give this message to you, specifically," Deborah pointed at him.

"All you have to do is accept it. And if you're still concerned about me being on the battlefield, then I'm fine with that. I don't have to be there. I have peace about it now.

"In fact, I prefer it if I don't go, because the Lord commands *you* to go. The glory of this battle is yours if you accept it. I'll just stay home, as my mother would have it. I did my part defending Ramah. Here, take my sword," Deborah handed Barak her sword.

Barak cupped his chin while staring at Deborah's sword. He then glanced over at Lahmi's corpse.

After a prolonged pause, deep in thought, he smiled in wonder, then reached out and grabbed the sword. He was about to speak, but then he was suddenly distracted by the amazing sword in his hand.

"What the...?" Barak whipped the sword back and forth a few times. "What's this thing made out of?" He tapped it against his boot. "Wait a minute..."

Barak then analyzed the sword with a familiar eye. "This was Sisera's," he replied. "He almost got me with this thing!"

"I knew you'd like it. Now you know what you have to do, right? Are we in agreement?"

Barak signed while looking upward. "My father's last words were not to do anything stupid. Can you believe that? Don't do anything stupid."

"Well disobeying a command from the Lord is stupid," Deborah replied curtly. "So you wouldn't be disobeying him to do this, but you would be stupid if you don't. Besides, my father told me the same thing, more than once."

"Probably not on his death bed," Barak countered.

"True."

"Well, there is only one way Israel is going to war. I have to convince everyone up north that we can achieve the impossible, but I don't think I can do that."

"Why? You're their commander, just order them."

"I already told you, I don't inspire my men anymore, and I don't inspire myself, either, for that matter. However...*if you go with me...*"

"The Lord has commanded you, not me," Deborah replied.

"When we fought together that day in Shiloh, I was invincible. And when we rescued those captives, it was like nothing could stop us. I've never felt alive like that before or since.

"When I'm with you, I can do anything. But the moment I'm away from you, I'm back to second guessing everything I do, think, and say. I'm confused, my father's voice in my mind..." Barak rubbed his forehead and he took a deep sigh.[8]

"You carry the presence of Yahweh with you. That is the only explanation for everything about you. All of Israel knows this, and we need you out there with us. So...*if you go with me, I will go; but if you don't go with me, I won't go*."[9]

Deborah finally responded.

"Very well, *I will go. But because of this course of action, the honor will not be yours, for the Lord will deliver Sisera into the hands of a woman.*"[10]

Barak smiled. "I know. I think I've always known," he humbly acknowledged.

Barak turned around, walked over the Lahmi's corpse, then without warning, he slashed Deborah's sword down and whacked off Lahmi's head.

Deborah observed in disgust as Lahmi's head rolled to the ground, but she refrained from speaking.

Barak proceeded to slash off a chunk of the tent tarp and wrap Lahmi's head in it, but then a strange sizzling sound distracted him. Lahmi's blood on Sisera's sword was burning to a crisp.

"What's this?" he questioned the oddity.

Deborah shrugged. "It was blessed in the Tabernacle; doesn't seem to like Anakim blood now."

Brushing off the incident, Barak picked up the bundle with Lahmi's severed head.

"There's a lot of stories that circulate about you up north. Some believe, some don't. If I tell them you executed the executioner, they'll just laugh. Heck, I didn't believe it until I saw it. But when I show them this, they'll shut up."

Barak returned Deborah's sword with a wink. "Here, you'll need it."

Barak left with his troops shortly after agreeing to Deborah's plan. He split up his men to spread the word ahead of him, ordering all the northern forces to gather at Mount Tabor. There, he planned to have Lahmi's head on display.

Just after he left, Tamar called Deborah to a gathering of warriors assembled at their largest training area.

"Before we move out, we wanted to present you with something," Gavriella called Deborah to the front of the group. She then presented Deborah with black studded leather armor and a cloak.

"This is on behalf of Ramah. We all engraved our names on it. Sharon did these strips, Joshua the silver studs. Ariel and I did the artwork," Gavriella pointed out the contributors among them.

"Thank you...all of you. I will wear this with honor," Deborah bowed and humbly accepted their gift. "I hope everyone is about ready to move out, because we need to leave...*now*."

"Let's go!" cheers and shouts erupted, and everyone scattered to collect their gear and move out.

The mass of Israelites took the shortest route north toward Mount Tabor, where Barak's forces were gathering at the base of the mountain to see Lahmi's head, and listen to a speech from Barak.

Deborah requested Ruben to stay with the main group as the most experienced fighter remaining, while she and Adonia moved ahead on horseback.

Miles ahead, Deborah and Adonia veered east from Mount Tabor, taking a brief detour to visit with Jael, since this battle was going to be fairly near to where she lived.

Jael was busily scrubbing laundry on a washboard when she spotted Deborah and Adonia in the distance. She immediately dropped what she was doing and ran to them, full of excitement.

"You're here!" she shouted exuberantly.

"Jael!" Deborah called out with equal enthusiasm. Deborah dismounted and hugged her friend.

"What are you two doing here? You better be careful, something's happening; something big."

Several miles away, across the flat dusty plain, stood Sisera's temple. Clouds of dust indicated a mass movement. "I've never seen activity like that before. He's summoning a lot of his forces, Lord knows what for."

Adonia dismounted and questioned Jael, "Heber here?"

"No, but he should be back any minute now. Hey, let me get you something to drink."

"Actually, we can't stay," Deborah replied.

"Oh please, just a drink, you must be thirsty."

A moment later, they were standing inside Jael's luxuriously accommodated tent. Deborah was completely smitten with Jael's pet monkey. "Here, give him some dates, he loves those," Jael handed Deborah a few dates.

"I'd love to, but like I said, we don't have much time. Israel is going to strike. That's why I'm here to warn you to keep low."

"I have to go with you!" Jael gasped, shocked with the revelation.

"We need you to do something more important. We're gathering on the east side of Mount Tabor, preparing to move near the Kishon River. Pass this on to Heber, but do it in a way that sounds natural, like you don't realize you're giving away important information."

"But he tells Sisera everything! What kind of strategy is that?"

"Our entire strategy relies on Sisera's forces gathering in the Valley of Megiddo along the Kishon," Deborah responded.

"In a way, I could say I already know he's going to be there, but Adonia here got me all confused about how things like this work.

"Will he be there because I already know he will, or will he be there because of something I do? I don't know," Deborah shrugged.

"No bring me into this!" Adonia protested. "That wrong location, very bad. He easy move all chariot there, wipe us out!"

Deborah glared at Adonia until he backed down. "Okay. No problem, lure him there easy. That exactly where he will want us."

"I hope so," Deborah nodded.

On her way out of the tent, Deborah suddenly froze, then she turned around and stared at a mallet and tent pegs in the corner of Jael's tent. Reaching into her studded leather, she pulled out the gold tent peg that Barak gave her.

"Remember that day I almost made Lapidoth a eunuch?"

"Who could forget?" Jael laughed.

Deborah held up her tent peg. "This is it. Here, take it" she tossed the tent peg to Jael. Jael caught it and read the inscription.

"Why are you giving this to me? This was a personal gift to you."

"You're right, and now it's my personal gift to you," Deborah winked. "Stay vigilant."

Before they left, Deborah couldn't resist feeding Jael's monkey a few dates. The monkey took an instant liking to her and jumped on her shoulders. It took some wrangling to finally peal him off.

After departing Jael, Deborah decided to take another detour. They headed west, and left their horses at the bottom of a wadi. They then quietly snuck toward Sisera's temple, obscured within the wadi.

They eventually found a location close enough to see some activity, but the location was dangerously close. A massive horde assembled at the base of Sisera's temple balcony; the number of troops was staggering.

"Intimidated?" Deborah whispered to Adonia.

"No."

"That an honest answer?"

"No."

"Look, there he is," Deborah spotted Sisera arrogantly striding to the edge of his balcony overlooking forty thousand soldiers in formation. The Chief Hooded Figure hovered behind him.

At the base of the balcony, Sisera had an enormous stone altar piled high with dead bodies. Sisera then bellowed out in a commanding voice for all to hear.

"On my altar, these infidels of Ramah shall pay for the life of my brother!

"Let every kindred, every tongue, every nation know, that I spit on this Israelite God. I am the one true god!" Sisera raised both his arms with clenched fists while making the audacious declaration.[11]

"Blasphemy," Deborah whispered to Adonia. "And I don't know who those poor dead souls are, but they aren't from Ramah."

The horde of soldiers below repeated an unintelligible chant. Sisera then opened his hands and raised them to the sky. "Behold! I call down fire from the heavens, burn! I command you, burn!"

As Sisera roared out, the Chief Hooded Figure wove a spell kneeling next to him. Then a spectacular marvel lit up the evening sky. A house-sized ball of fire streaked down from the heavens and blasted the altar, incinerating the bodies on top of it instantly.[12]

The mass of soldiers roared in excitement.

“Nothing is impossible for me! Who is like me? Who can wage war against me?”[13] Sisera continued to bellow out, facing the sky as if to challenge God Himself.

“No one!” he growled with venom, and all the soldiers below screamed praise in response.

Deborah and Adonia observed quietly; Adonia’s eyes were wide with shock. “How he do that?” questioned Adonia.

“I...don’t know,” Deborah replied.

“But...that...” Adonia was confused, wondering how they could fight against such awesome power as this.

“Why would the Lord allow such power in the hands of someone like Sisera?” Deborah questioned.[14]

“You ask me?” Adonia was confused.

“Remember those spectators that visit my court, the ones that bother you so much?”

“Yes,” Adonia nodded.

“Some of them are down there, marveling at Sisera.”[15] Deborah shook her head, troubled about this development.

The two quietly pulled back and returned to their horses. To keep the noise down, they walked their horses for a few hours before resuming their course to Mount Tabor.

Commentary Notes

††

1. See Judges 5:8, 40,000 is the number referenced in Deborah's song.
2. Kenneth Barker, *The New International Version Study Bible*, (Grand Rapids, MI: Zondervan Bible Publishers, 1985). p 337, study note for Judges 5:13-18, roll call of the tribes, "Judah and Simeon are not even mentioned, perhaps because they were already engaged with the Philistines."
3. Arthur E. Cundall & Leon Morris, *Judges & Ruth: An Introduction & Commentary*, (Downers Grove, IL: Inter-Varsity Press Leicester, England, 1968). p. 99, "Only Judah and Simeon are not mentioned. Their geographical remoteness was accentuated by political factors, notably the barrier caused by an unreduced Jerusalem and other towns on their northern frontier and, possibly, pressure by the Philistines on their western frontier."
4. See Judges 5:15-17, Deborah's song rebukes Reuben and Gilead for not participating.
5. See Judges 5:17, Deborah's song also rebukes the tribes of Dan and Asher, but for this story, only Dan is mentioned. At this point in the story, they would not have learned of Asher's non-participation yet, since Asher was so far to the northwest of Ramah.
6. Rick Meyers, "Equipping Ministries Foundation, e-Sword Bible software, version 12.2.0," downloaded Nov 20, 2020, http://www.e-sword.net; *Commentary of David Guzik*, "They had essentially no weapons to fight with against a technologically advanced army (having 900 chariots of iron), and God led them to fight on a plain, putting them at a big disadvantage."
7. See Judges 4:6-7, The Lord commands Barak through Deborah.
8. J. P. Millar, *The Preacher's Complete Homiletic Commentary on the Book of Judges, Vol 6*, (New York: NY, Funk & Wagnalls Company, 1974), p. 188. (Bracketed comment added), "...we must not underrate [Barak's lack of faith]. He did not look on Deborah so much as a woman, as on one who had the Spirit of God. And this, be it man or woman, meant an all-conquering strength. It did however look a little like the superstitious feeling of the Israelites, when they thought themselves safer by taking the ark into the field, than by

simply trusting in the promise of help assured by their God on their obedience (1 Sam iv: 3-5.). Some class Barak as an illustration of the phrase, 'out of weakness made strong' (Heb xi:34). He needed some visible presence to strengthen his faith in the invisible power. We too often need something of sight to help our weak faith - the touch of our Father's hand in the dark, to show that He is with us."

9. See Judges 4:8.
10. See Judges 4:9.
11. Scripture records multiple instances of God making declarations to every tribe, nation, and language/tongue, Acts 2:5, 10:35, 17:26; Revelation 5:9, 7:9, 14:6. Satan is a copycat, and for a short season, God makes a similar declaration, granting Satan authority over every tribe and people and language and nation, Revelation 13:7. As a type of the Antichrist, Sisera follows this same pattern, adding to it his blasphemous declaration that he is the one true god. In the Old Testament, the Philistine giant Goliath made similar blasphemous declarations, 1 Samuel 17-18.
12. As a type of the Antichrist in this story, Sisera wields the same kind of demonic, supernatural power mentioned of the Antichrist in Revelation 13:11-14.
13. See Revelation 13:4, "Who is like the beast, and who can fight against it?"
14. It is not unusual for God's people, if they are honest, to have questions of this nature. Job had similar questions regarding the prosperity and power of the wicked, Job 21:7-16.
15. See Matthew 16:4, a wicked and perverse generation asks for a sign.

Chapter 24:

Pray Hard

ס

Xerophilous plants were mostly what grew throughout the Megiddo Valley, for the region was barren, and usually dry and hot.

Adonia's mental state was much the same after witnessing what occurred at Sisera's temple.

"What if Sisera call fire on us? What chance have we?" Adonia finally broke the silence.

"I've been wondering that myself," Deborah replied.

"What you mean? How you not know?"

"I can't help but wonder, if I would've got off my high horse and accepted Barak's offer for safe passage, maybe my father would still be alive," Deborah muttered.

"Your horse same tall as mine. Why horse tall you talk? I no understand."

"These visions, they direct me to this battle at the expense of everything, even my father," Deborah expressed her frustration. "Sometimes I wonder, what if I'm all wrong. What if I'm leading Israel to her death?"

"No talk like that!" Adonia rebuked her, terrified at her uncertainty.

"I have seen many things about this battle, but I know nothing about fire from the sky. I've never seen any such thing," Deborah gave her honest assessment.

"Then what do we do?" Adonia was lost, on the verge of complete hopelessness.

"The only thing we can do. Pray. *Pray hard*. Don't put your trust in me; I'm just a woman. You, Lapi, and everybody else, need to put your trust in Yahweh."

After a brief night's sleep in the wilderness, early the next morning, Deborah and Adonia resumed their course. They eventually wove their way up the side of Mount Tabor.

When they reached the summit of the flat toped mountain, Deborah dismounted and stood on a ledge overlooking the Israelites as they ascended from the other side.[1]

Those with horses were already there, but even some who either left early walking, or they were athletic enough to jog for half their journey, were arriving on this third day before the great battle.

Deborah stood in the billowing gales, regal with her purple cloak with golden embroidery, tossed in the wind. Daggers and tent pegs lined her ribs. A thin coil of rope was fastened to her left hip like a whip, secured to a tent peg.

On her right hip, she wore her one of a kind sword; strapped across her back, bow and arrows; in her right hand, her father's staff.

Quietly observing the mass of Israelites ascending the mountain, faith began to well up within her. Barak was successful! Zebulun and Naphtali were faithful to his summoning.

These Israelites were the few standing against many, expressing their profound faith in Yahweh by putting their lives on the line.

Israel was united!

"Slingers over there, there, and there," Barak positioned some of his men while they continued their ascent. "Get those longbows over here, and there," he instructed his men. He then turned and saw Deborah just ahead of him.

"Thank the Lord you're here! I was wondering where you were," Barak approached her and paused to check out her outfit, scanning her up and down.

"Too much?"

"Never," Barak shook his head while giving her the Hand of Miriam. "You've always been a master at dressing for the occasion."

"And you're not so bad yourself, but today you keep your shirt on," Deborah winked.

Barak smiled with the memory; it warmed his heart to remember that the Deborah he used to know was still in there.

But ever since the Lord spoke to him directly through her, he was having difficulty reconciling the young warrior he once knew, with this Judge of Israel; Prophetess of the Living God.

Now for the task at hand.

"Okay, here's the plan," Barak laid out a strategy. "The base teams have the most dangerous assignment. It's their job to lure Sisera's forces up this mountain..."

"That's not the plan," Deborah interrupted him.

"You never mentioned a plan other than getting here."

"Oh but I did. We're not fighting on this mountain. The plan is, we wait here until the High Priest arrives and instructs me to give the signal. Then we charge down this mountain, across Jezreel, and we meet them near the Kishon."

"Look, you got us here. It was you who united Israel, and I get it, the glory of this battle is yours. But I'm the one who knows how to strategize this battle. I learned from the best; my father. We have to stay on this mountain, it's our only chance!"

Deborah lifted her hand to silence him.

Uh oh, the Prophetess is back. Barak held his tongue.

"You're still not listening," Deborah reiterated herself. "First, I said the glory of this battle goes to a woman; I didn't say it was me. Second, it is the Lord who wins our battles; we must never forget that.

"We're not moving until the High Priest arrives and instructs me to give the signal. And last of all, we're initiating this battle near the Kishon River; that is not negotiable. If we chase them all the way down to Taanach, then so be it, but it starts at the Kishon."[2]

"Chase them?" Barak huffed. "Look, they can't bring their chariots on this mountain. The terrain..." Barak tried to argue his point, but Deborah lifted her hand again.

"This is not *my* strategy. I'm telling you the visions the Lord has given me. My visions have *never* been wrong.

"I don't always see everything, and all of your skills have a place in this battle. Perhaps after the battle has begun, then your strategy with this mountain can come into play, but I doubt it. You'll see when the battle starts. We *all must go down* to meet the enemy near the Kishon River. *We must.*"

"You might as well be asking us all to leap off a cliff," Barak stated his opinion bluntly.

"He won't let us to that," Deborah glanced upward with a chuckle.

"What?" Barak was lost on her inside joke with Yahweh.

"Just try to believe. You have to trust me," she placed her hand on his chest. She didn't intent it, but a soothing assurance seeped out of her hand, putting Barak's battle scarred conscience at ease.

"Okay," Barak gave in. Who was he to argue with this woman he witnessed getting impaled by Sisera, yet lived? "When are you going to give this...*signal*?"

Deborah looked up at the clear sky. "Not until the day of the battle. Not everyone is here yet. Elias has to be here. Setup shifts so the men can get some sleep. I'll take the first shift off."

Barak nodded, then motioned to Abijah nearby. "Find out where the High Priest is."

"On it," Abijah trotted off.

Deborah pulled a blanket from her saddlebags, bundled up and sat down. In less than a minute, she was passed out. Barak quietly observed her peaceful disposition with envy. He then pointed his thumb at her and commented to Ruben, "Look."

"Not a care in the world," Ruben replied.

"That funny," Adonia also noticed. "Every time we travel, she never sleep. Alway have night scare. Now she sleep like baby."

Barak nodded. "She needs a war to be at peace."

Throughout the remainder of the day, and all the following day, Israelites continued to flow up Mount Tabor. Every now and then, Deborah continued to request reports, to see if anyone from the tribes of Dan, Reuben, Gilead, and Asher had arrived.

"None yet," Gabriel reported. "I even went to Asher personally; it's pretty shameful. They just don't care."[3]

Just before the first light of dawn on the final day of battle, Elias arrived on foot, hobbling up the mountain.

About every twenty feet, he paused to lean on his staff. Behind him, four priests struggled under the weight of the Ark of the Covenant, covered with a thick blue cloth.

"Change over," one of the ark bearers grunted, and a replacement carrier from the formation directly behind him sprinted up and swapped places with him.

About fifty yards in front and flanking the ark on both sides, several jittery temple workers were spread out, giving instructions to clear the way.

"Clear the way. Show respect, don't stare, and keep your distance," they advised. "You can tell your children and grandchildren all about this someday, just don't think about touching it, or you'll die. Then you won't be telling anybody about anything."[4-5]

All who witnessed the ark stepped back, awed and fearful.

Abijah whispered to Barak, "I thought only the High Priest was allowed in the presence of the ark."

One of the temple workers overheard him and replied, "We've never seen the ark in battle, but Elias says this is how it works. We should be okay if we maintain a safe distance and show respect."

Elias directed the priests carrying the ark to a ledge overlooking the Jezreel Valley to the west, where it bled into the Megiddo Valley, skirted along the Kishon River. Sisera's Temple of Baal was roughly fifteen miles away, on the other side of Megiddo.

A group of warriors stood nearby, casting anxious glances toward Barak, fidgeting, wrestles. Was this battle going down, or what?

"Elias is here," Barak nudged Deborah awake. "One of our scouts have seen Sisera's forces gathering at his temple. I still think we should try to lure them up here."

"Wow," Deborah yawned, "I think that was the best sleep I've had in years." She then looked up at the sky, observing the lightly scattered clouds.

"You heard what I said, right? The High Priest is here," Barak reiterated himself. "We want to kick this off. I have a lead element ready to strike. If they hit from the south, they have an escape route mapped out..."

"Not yet," Deborah cut him off.

"But you said..."

"Don't send anyone down until I give the signal. Our men will die if you don't do exactly as I say. Now please leave me alone until it's my shift." Deborah covered up and laid back down, only to be nudged by Barak again.

"What!" She whipped back her cover, annoyed.

"It's your shift," Barak smiled.

"Oh."

Across the Megiddo Valley, from his temple balcony, Sisera stood next to Malchus, overlooking his legion encamped below.

"Heber is here," Tartan replied from inside the temple.

Sisera turned to see Heber escorted up the stone stairway. When Heber reached him, he bowed low. "My lord, you're going to want to hear this," he replied.

A short while later, Barak and Deborah observed Sisera's vast host of military force slowly advancing toward the Kishon River. Deborah nodded, pleased with this development.

Meanwhile, over near the edge of the cliff near the top of Mount Tabor, the priests held their hands to the sky, praying to Yahweh.

Deborah walked toward them to get a little closer, then she knelt down and bowed her head toward the ark and began to pray quietly.

Adonia nudged Barak, "We should do same. If you saw what we saw, you would."

"What did you see?" Barak asked.

"All that is nothing," Adonia pointed to Sisera's horde of troops moving in the distance.

"Only your God get us through this alive," Adonia replied, then he walked over to the left side of Deborah, knelt down and began praying in his native tongue to this God he had since adopted as his own.

Or was it the other way around?

Taking this advice, Barak turned to his leading warriors.

"Let everyone know, if they want to get through this alive, they better start praying now, and I don't mean that as a joke. Pray like you mean it, even if you've never prayed before."

He gulped, then walked over to flank Deborah on the right, kneeling down and joining her and Adonia in prayer.

Over the next hour, the word spread, and all of Mount Tabor was covered with Israelite warriors humbled in prayer.

They asked for forgiveness for their nation; they asked for deliverance from this powerful enemy who had been ruthlessly crushing the life out of them for the past twenty years.[6]

While everyone's eyes were closed, the wind picked up, and in the span of an hour of prayer, the status of the lightly scattered clouds transformed into a heavy overcast.

Then the wind died down, and a stillness settled over the mountain.

All was quiet, and Elias the High Priest slowly lowered his hands, took a deep breath, grabbed his staff, then he suddenly jabbed it toward the sky.

"I call upon you, All Mighty God! The Great Yahweh, the God of Abraham, Isaac, and Jacob! Deliver us! Deliver us!"

When Elias was shouting at the top of his voice with all of his might, and the prayers of the other priests echoed him, the thick clouds directly above Mount Tabor coalesced into an impenetrable opaque mass.

Boom! A powerful crack of thunder shook the ground as a stream of lightning sparkled in the midst of the looming darkness.

The Ark of the Covenant began to glow, emanating light beneath its cover. A luminescent mist materialized, seeping from the midst of it. This mist continued to flow, seeping down the sides of the mountain.

Elias held his staff high, continuing his prayers, and Deborah opened her eyes to witness the mysterious mist.

Other Israelites also began to open their eyes, and many were stricken with terror. Was this the shadow of death they heard about; that shadow of death that struck down Egypt's first born?[7]

But not all were afraid. A few waved their hands through it, gazing in wonder, and murmuring began to spread among them. Deborah stood up, followed by Barak and Adonia.

A wild excitement beamed from Deborah's eyes.

"*Do you feel...?*" She whispered to Barak.

"What's happening to us?" Barak asked her. "What is this strange feeling...in my body?"

"Shekinah glory," Deborah whispered back. She then looked to the sky and smiled. "Almost time."[8]

Barak saw her looking up, then he was suddenly shocked at how much the sky had changed during that brief period when his eyes were closed in prayer.

Or was he lost in prayer longer than he thought?

Not really, but the content of his prayers made it seem so. His prayers to Yahweh were interlaced with memories of his earthly father.

All his life he dedicated his entire being to trying to please this man, who eclipsed the sum total of his efforts with "Don't do anything stupid."

It was this agonizing phrase that Barak laid as an offering at the feet of his Heavenly Father, and in that place, he found something he wasn't expecting, or even looking for—*peace*.

While it was true that there would be no glory in this battle for him, he could care less now, for the divine, profound peace he was experiencing with God in this moment was all he ever wanted. He just didn't know it, because he never experienced it before.

Israel as a whole was engulfed in this same peace. They were all finally united, both with each other, and with their God. And the justice that they all longed for would soon be theirs.

Or would it?

Was Deborah ever going to give that signal? What was she waiting for?

Instead of giving the signal, she was busy daydreaming, staring intensely at these strange, dark clouds. Why?

And what was going on with these clouds, anyway? Not only did they arrive from out of nowhere almost instantly, but this was in the middle of the summer time.[9]

Deborah then dropped her gaze to scan Sisera's forces below, approaching the Kishon River and spreading out his men, most likely searching the area for them.

As Barak observed Deborah, seeing that she was keeping a close watch over the High Priest, Sisera's forces, and the clouds above, it finally dawned on him what she was waiting for.

"It's going to rain, isn't it?"

"You think so? In the middle of the summer? Nah. It never rains this time of year," Deborah smiled deviously.

Barak's mouth fell open as he marveled at the brilliance of this strategy, imagining the battle unfold with this new master variable introduced into the equation.

In a major storm, the Megiddo Valley turned into an endless quagmire of thick, muddy clay, very difficult, if not impossible to navigate with a chariot.

All of Sisera's chariots were about to be transformed into a worthless, massive maze of confusion.[10]

Then there was the heavy armor that Sisera and his men wore with pride. In almost any battle, they had the advantage, nearly impervious to arrows and slingshots.

Add thick mud all over the ground, and their heavy armor was more trouble than it was worth.

In contrast, most of the Israelites had no armor at all. They could quickly maneuver around all those chariot obstacles with ease, using them to their advantage.

Most of Sisera's men also wore helmets, which offered protection for their heads, at the slight expense of less visibility.

However, adding darkness and rain decreased their visibility even more, whereas the Israelites were completely unencumbered with the advantage of perfect visibility.

This strategy was so ingenious, it initially created the illusion of a suicide mission for the Israelites, serving as the perfect lure for Sisera.

By the time Sisera's forces crossed the valley, they might find themselves in the middle of a trap, where the Israelites would have the ultimate advantage of every facet of the battle.

If it rains...a lot.

Brilliant, absolutely brilliant!

But no one could ever plan such a strategy. Doing that would require both a freak storm in the middle of the summer, and a person who could predict such a freak storm to the exact day.

"The Lord summoned this storm, and you are His lightning," Deborah winked.[11]

Delighted and wildly impressed, Barak gave her a playful shove.

To both of their surprise, his playful shove was much harder than he expected, and she stumbled several feet and fell to the ground.

"I...I'm sorry! I didn't mean to!"

Adonia noticed the shove and he glared at Barak, slightly upset.

"Really, I didn't mean to," Barak tried to explain. "Something...I feel really weird," Barak stretched out his fingers and gripped his fists. His hands were trembling.

Deborah stood up with a rock in her hand, and she handed it to Barak. "Take it."

"What? It's a rock."

"Take it," she shook it toward him. He grabbed it, puzzled about this request.

"Squeeze it," Deborah instructed him.

"Why?" Barak asked her while giving the rock a slight squeeze. Pop! Barak jerked his head back as the rock exploded into dust and bits of rubble.

Deborah yelped with a laugh as Barak's jaw dropped and his eyes bulged with astonishment.[12]

Adonia was equally alarmed and he noticed that his hands were trembling as well.

"I feel too," Adonia was shaking with nervousness.

"I told you; *Shekinah glory—that's the anointing,*" Deborah motioned toward the Ark of the Covenant, now shimmering with a glorious, amber hue emanating so intensely, the ground beneath the ark was illuminating the entire area.[13]

"Yahweh is here, among us" she shivered. "As long as Elias keeps his staff up, we have this anointing." Then she left Barak and approached Elias and the priests, where they prayed encircled around the ark.

Deborah moved around them, keeping a safe distance as they instructed. She eventually made her way over to the edge of the cliff, with the priests and the ark behind her.

From this vista, she witnessed Sisera's chariots surge across the trickling Kishon River, which was currently a small creek.[14]

Sisera was too far away for Deborah to see with her natural vision, but Sisera was up front, pulled by his four-horse chariot.

Deborah then experienced a bizarre flash, where her vision rushed forward, and she now saw with the eyes of an eagle. Sisera was leading his forces up front. She swayed, nearly fainting with a dizzy spell as a chill shot up her spine.

Did her thoughts just traverse a temporal barrier, and transmit those images back in time to the mind of her younger self, tossing and turning in bed?

Wind blew through her hair, and the energy surging through her was one with the storm gathering above.

She whipped back her cloak and unsheathed her sword. Branches of a lightning tree sparkled blue, red, purple, swirling in the midst of a thick, majestic darkness above, followed by roaring cracks of thunder.

As Deborah prepared to give the signal, on the other side of the Megiddo Valley, a summoning of dark forces was underway...

Malchus, the Chief Hooded Figure stood, surrounded by a half dozen priests of Baal. They all stood on the balcony overlooking the battlefield, reciting incantations.

Malchus held up his hands while chanting in a dark language; his eyes were completely black, void of life.

"Master of destruction, grant us this victory you swore!" Malchus called out to one of his gods. "Rain fire on that mountain!" he pointed toward Mount Tabor.

Then it happened.

Commentary Notes

++

1. J. P. Millar, *The Preacher's Complete Homiletic Commentary on the Book of Judges, Vol 6*, (New York: NY, Funk & Wagnalls Company, 1974), p. 188. From the commentary on Judges 4:6 regarding Mount Tabor: "[Mount Tabor]—now called Jebel et Tur—rises on the east from the plain of Esdraelon, where Sisera's chariots would be assembled, and was a convenient rallying point for all in Naphtali and Zebulon on the north, and for Issachar and Manasseh on the south. It stands by itself on the plain, a truncated cone of limestone, with flat top, an area of a quarter of a mile in length, and half that in breadth. Round the circumference are the ruins of a thick wall of masonry, and there are the foundations of private dwellings within. The height is estimated from 1000 to 3000 feet, and it requires an hour to ascend it. The sides to the very top are covered with verdure and clumps of trees, oaks, olives, and sycamores, with many plants and flowers. It overtops all the neighboring hills (Jer_46:18), and commands a magnificent view of Northern Palestine, especially to the west. It may have been the Mount of Transfiguration, as the reasoning to the contrary consists quite as much of strong assertion as of clear evidence."
2. Judges 4:7 mentions the river Kishon, yet Judges 5:19 mentions Taanach, by the waters of Megiddo. Some commentators suggest two battles took place, but a simpler explanation suggests the battle initiated at the river Kishon, then the Canaanites were chased to Taanach.
3. Judges 5:15-17, Deborah keeps a tally on the tribes that participated, and rebukes those who did not.
4. When the ark was carried with Joshua in charge, it was carried in front of Israel with a distance of 2,000 cubits, which is roughly 1,000 yards, Judges 3:4. However, this was before the ark had a permanent home in Shiloh, and Israel was already established throughout the Promised Land. For these later battles with Israel already in the Promised Land, Israelites would have arrived from many directions to a single rally point, which in this case, was established at Mount

Tabor. So this different technique of sending out temple workers to instruct Israelites to keep their distance from the ark is a likely scenario for how the ark may have been brought to a battle location.

5. "Ancient Jewish History: The Ark of the Covenant," https://www.jewishvirtuallibrary.org/the-ark-of-the-convenant, (Last accessed February 22, 2021). (Bracketed comments added), "According to one Midrash, it [the Ark of the Covenant] would clear the path by burning snakes, scorpions, and thorns with two jets of flame that shut from its underside. Another Midrash says that rather than being carried by its bearers, the ark in fact carried its bearers inches above the ground (Satah 35a). When the Israelites went to war in the desert and during the conquering of Canaan, the ark accompanied them; whether its presence was symbolic, to provide motivation for the Jews, or whether it actually aided them in fighting, is debated by commentators."
6. See Judges 4:3.
7. See Exodus 12:12, when the shadow of death passed over the Israelites and struck down the firstborn among the Egyptians.
8. Rick Meyers, "Equipping Ministries Foundation, e-Sword Bible software, version 12.2.0," downloaded Nov 20, 2020, http://www.e-sword.net; *International Standard Bible Encyclopedia*, "Dwell: In order to avoid appearing to localize the Divine Being, wherever God is said to 'dwell' in a place, the Targum renders that He 'causes His Shekinah to dwell there.' The Hebrew word 'Shekinah,' meaning 'to dwell,' is actually not found in the Bible, but there are many allusions to it, such as 2 Chronicles 7:1-3, and Isaiah 60.
9. Arthur E. Cundall & Leon Morris, *Judges & Ruth: An Introduction & Commentary*, (Downers Grove, IL: Inter-Varsity Press Leicester, England, 1968). p. 86. (Bracketed comments added), "It is unlikely that he [Sisera] would be so foolish as to attempt to use his chariots in the rainy season; Judges 5:4-5, 20-21, suggests an unusual torrential downpour, possibly a thunderstorm, which came after the normal season of the later rains in April, and early May. [The June/July time frame for this event in this story agrees with this commentary]. Possibly Deborah gave the order to attack as she saw the storm approaching, knowing that a heavy downpour would nullify the numerical advantage and the superior equipment of the Canaanites and thus make the propitious moment to strike."
10. See Judges 5:21, chariots swept away by the Kishon.
11. Ibid, p. 87. "The Lord was often depicted as the God of the thun-

derstorm, moving in awful splendor and power to the help of His people (Jos 10:11; 1 Sam 7:10; Ps 19:9-15), and this belief may be implied in the words of Deborah, 'Is not the Lord gone out before thee?' It must be realized, however, that the Israelites did not have a monopoly of this conception, for recent discoveries at Ras Shamra (the ancient Ugarit) have shown that the Canaanites looked upon Baal in much the same way. He was the storm-god, the rider upon the clouds (Isaiah 19:1). He is uniformly depicted as wielding a club in one hand and a stylized spear in the other, representing thunder and lightning respectively. A storm at this juncture, however, favored the Israelites and enabled them to extend their advantage from the hill-country (where chariots could not operate effectively) to the valley, where the Canaanites had hitherto been supreme." Note: Something the above commentator overlooks is an obvious foot stomp for the one true God, who sends His lightning, (Barak's literal name), in the midst of an unexpected thunder storm, to defeat the Canaanites, who worship Baal, a false god claiming the same power of thunder and lightning. This is God's poetic way of demonstrating that He is the one true God.

12. The idea of the Israelites fighting with super human strength comes from Exodus 17:8-13, "Then Amalek came and fought with Israel at Rephidim. So Moses said to Joshua, 'Choose for us men, and go out and fight with Amalek. Tomorrow I will stand on the top of the hill with the staff of God in my hand.' So Joshua did as Moses told him, and fought with Amalek, while Moses, Aaron, and Hur went up to the top of the hill. Whenever Moses held up his hand, Israel prevailed, and whenever he lowered his hand, Amalek prevailed. But Moses' hands grew weary, so they took a stone and put it under him, and he sat on it, while Aaron and Hur held up his hands, one on one side, and the other on the other side. So his hands were steady until the going down of the sun. And Joshua overwhelmed Amalek and his people with the sword." [ESV] In this story, Elias follows this precedent established by Moses, holding his staff up high for the duration of the battle, and having designated assistants to help him with this task.
13. "Ancient Jewish History: The Ark of the Covenant," https://www.jewishvirtuallibrary.org/the-ark-of-the-convenant, (Last accessed February 22, 2021). (Bracketed comments added), "According to one Midrash, it [the Ark of the Covenant] would clear the path by burning snakes, scorpions, and thorns with two jets of flame that shut from its underside. Another Midrash says that rather than

being carried by its bearers, the Ark in fact carried its bearers inches above the ground (Satah 35a). When the Israelites went to war in the desert and during the conquering of Canaan, the Ark accompanied them; whether its presence was symbolic, to provide motivation for the Jews, or whether it actually aided them in fighting, is debated by commentators.

14. Arthur E. Cundall & Leon Morris, *Judges & Ruth: An Introduction & Commentary*, (Downers Grove, IL: Inter-Varsity Press Leicester, England, 1968), p. 85. (Bracketed comment added), "The whole of the upper section of the river [Kishon] is seasonal, depending on the rainfall, so that in the dry summer it is little more than a wadi, but when swollen by the rain of the winter and early spring it could become a raging torrent. In such conditions the low-lying areas surrounding the river would be completely waterlogged and the deployment of chariots would be impossible."

Chapter 25:

A Footstep of Divinity

י

Yahweh!

It was He who appeared to Moses in the burning bush, and on the summit of Mount Saini.[1]

He appeared to Joshua, sword in hand, Captain of the Hosts of the Lord. [2]

And on this day, *from heaven the stars fought, from their courses they fought against Sisera...*[3]

On this day, *the earth trembled, and the heavens dropped...The mountains quaked before the Lord...*[4]

Directly above Sisera's temple of Baal, the sky rolled up like a scroll, curling into a swirling vortex.[5]

Then suddenly, a waterfall of multicolored sparkling light fell from out of that vortex, dropping on top of Sisera's mountain, striking the center of the temple balcony.

This was a footstep of divinity; the Mysterious Entity who resurrected Deborah from the dead, set His heel upon the Earth.

At the touch of His heel, the entire mountain jolted, quaking beneath His foot, and a gaping crack split across the grand entrance to the balcony.

Deep below, where all the prisoners were chained in dungeons, every prison door at once exploded into splinters.

Chains fell to the floor,[6] and a mighty wind swept through the tunnels. Cracks formed all throughout the mountain, and a blinding light pierced the darkness, forcing its way into every crevice.[7]

Those among the living, prisoners trapped within the dungeons, fled for their lives, but there were others who fled as well.

The shadows of the dead, who flitted about from chamber to chamber, swarmed in terror as all this light invaded their space.

These shades, many summoned by sorcery, fled into the bottomless pit in the lowest depths of the mountain.[8]

Up on the balcony, bolts of lightning struck the mountain repeatedly, followed by deafening claps of thunder. Malchus and the other priests were blown off their feet, hurled to the edge of the balcony.

From the midst of the cascading light stepped the Mysterious Entity. He wore the same full plate battle armor as before, radiating waves of sparkling, amber light.

His scarlet hooded cape billowed in an ethereal wind. His piercing eyes were flames of fire, gleaming with the essence of life, complimented by shimmering white hair, forming a nimbus of unapproachable brilliance.[9]

The temple priests of Baal would have screamed, but their fear was so profound, all they could do was gasp, weep, and shiver, gnashing their teeth.

A few of them dared to look upon this Mysterious Entity. They sucked in one last breath of air, overtaken with a seizure of instant death.[10]

The darkness in Malchus' eyes drained away and returned to normal. Terror gripped him unlike anything he'd ever experienced in his life.

At the raising of His hand, the Mysterious Entity threw Malchus against the rock wall of the mountain. He then flicked His fingers, and Malchus flew off the balcony, screaming as he plummeted to his death below.

The Mysterious Entity then strolled toward the edge of the balcony, and the balcony with all its remaining inhabitants broke away from the mountain and disappeared beneath Him, amidst the collapsing stone pillars, titanic blocks and debris.

The entire temple complex caved in, imploding behind Him, and the whole mountain disintegrated. Billowing clouds of dust, smoke, and hot ash rippled outward in a plume of destruction.

Yet the Mysterious Entity continued His casual stride in the air, as if the balcony were still there.

Sisera's elaborate temple, with all its vile filth and gaudy luxury, was no more.

However, amazingly, as the whole mountain collapsed to one third its original height, there were still survivors from this devastation.

Prisoners poured out of a tunnel at the base of the mountain, the last of which escaped as the only remaining tunnel collapsed behind her.

Watching from above as this last prisoner escaped, the Mysterious Entity, who stood floating in the sky above, then lifted his foot and stomped it back down.

A crushing force emanated from His heel, having the same destructive force as a meteorite, obliterating the center of the mountain, leaving a crater in its place.

A radius of earth, rocks, monolithic boulders, and clouds of debris erupted outward, followed by an earthquake that rumbled across the valley floor.

This foot stomp pulverized the last remnants of the ancient ruins deep below, and it sealed the pit in the center of the mountain, slamming the door shut on this unnatural portal.[11]

What was once a pit with an unholy portal leading to Sheol, was now a place of holy ground.[12] A fragrant aroma of roses permeated the area.

The Mysterious Entity then looked across the valley toward the dark clouds above Mount Tabor. He calmly adjusted a ruffle in the collar of his cape, then He unsheathed His sword and swiped it toward the clouds.

A blazing bolt of white, brilliant lightning burst out of His sword, arched up into the dark clouds, and then back down on top of the Ark of the Covenant.

Boom!

Ω

A spherical shockwave of divine energy erupted from the ark, exploding outward, blasting all the Israelites to the ground.

Everyone on Mount Tabor already felt the earthquake about a minute earlier, but this blast was even more powerful, aimed directly at their location.

Deborah slammed up against a boulder and bounced off of it. Under normal circumstances, she would have been knocked unconscious, but the same energy that blasted her was also protecting her.

Slightly dazed, the Israelites staggered to their feet, and Deborah stood back up, searching for Elias.

There he was, a bit shaken, but so overwhelmed with excitement, he looked twenty years younger!

"Trumpets, trumpets!" he shouted to one of his priests. Two young priests near him scrambled for two silver trumpets, then they lifted them high and blew them together.[13]

Deborah immediately whipped her sword up high and bellowed out for all to hear, "Fight! Go, go, go! Fight!"

A clap of thunder echoed her command, and a mass of Israelites streamed down Mount Tabor in a screaming rage.

They quickly reached the base of the mountain, and as soon as they started streaming across the Megiddo Valley, Sisera's forces spotted them and started driving toward them.

"Run!" Deborah roared out and she sprinted with amazing speed. "After me, Benjamin!"[14]

Not far behind Deborah, the old man in his eighties was sprinting like a twenty year old, and next to him, the young boy from Ataroth galloped like a gazelle.

The boy tightly gripped his new dagger in one hand, and garden tool in his other hand, fearlessly charging toward an entire army of armored war horses, spiked chariots of death, and fierce warriors.

As the army of chariots drew near, a volley of arrows darkened the sky. A few Israelites, including the young boy, were immediately struck and fell to the ground.

Seeing this, a number of Israelites stopped to aim and fire their bows. However, their primitive weapons did absolutely nothing.

Most of their arrows lacked iron arrowheads, and they were fired from low quality bows. The few arrows that actually reached their marks simply bounced off thick armor.

One woman went to fire her bow, but she wasn't used to this new-found strength surging through her body. She snapped her bowstring when she pulled it back.

Seeing this instant flop on the initial charge, and some of their companions struck with arrows, many Israelites slowed down, and a few came to a complete stop.

The wall of chariots before them was endless. The enemy was screaming and charging like a ghoulish demon horde. Sisera was in the lead; his massive, towering figure in his four-horse chariot, roaring like a devil from the pit of Sheol.

At the sight of Sisera, a few Israelites started to panic, overwhelmed with the supernatural fear that Sisera emanated. Just as one group was about to turn and flee, the old man stood in their way with his sword drawn.

"Where to you think you're going?" he yelled at them.

Then the boy who was struck down with an arrow, who was lying in their midst, suddenly came to. He instantly leapt up and snapped off the front of the arrow that was sticking out of his shoulder.

The boy tossed the busted piece to the ground and then asked the old man for assistance. "Can you pull that out?"

When the boy spun around, the old man saw the tipped point of the arrow protruding from his back, and he quickly snatched it and gave it a yank.

"Ah!" the boy yelped, gritting his teeth. Then he quickly shook it off and burst through the feint hearted group observing him, screaming as he went.

The old man growled at the group of Israelites about to desert. "If you don't turn your asses back around, you'll have more to fear from me than them. *Go*!" he bellowed at them, pointing his sword.

At the exact time he shouted, a bolt of lightning lit up the sky, followed by an explosion of thunder, and torrents of rain immediately gushed down.

The small group rapidly spun around and resumed their charge.

"Fight!" Deborah commanded from the front again. This was it, no more games, no more squeamish back peddling, no more second guessing.

As the gap closed between these two armies, water gushing in from the surrounding mountains carved wadis into the terrain. These outstretched tendrils then fed into the Kishon, promptly transforming it from a small creek into a mighty river.

Those furthest in back saw what was happening, so they turned south, hoping for higher ground near Taanach. But there were so many chariots, a swath of them couldn't get away from the Kishon as it overflowed its banks.

One chariot after another was caught in the Kishon's vicious torrents and swept away. Charioteers who bailed into the waves were crushed by struggling horses and tumbling chariots.

The previously parched, cracked earth of the Megiddo Valley was now a thick, muddy clay. All the remaining chariots on the plain were dramatically slowed, and many were getting stuck, while their horses were slipping and struggling.

Sisera's expectation to roll over the top of the Israelites and trample them down with an anticlimactic bloodbath was no longer an option. Most of the remaining charioteers started abandoning their chariots, and preparing to fight on foot.

Part of the effectiveness of the chariot was that it allowed the charioteers to stockpile more weapons than they could carry on foot.

Many of these weapons were also heavier, such as their metal tipped spears and long swords.

When the charioteers abandoned their chariots, they were forced into the difficult decision of whether or not to abandon some of their advanced weapons.

The few who chose carry all of them paid the price, because they were weighed down with heavy armor and a load of extra weapons. They slipped and stumbled awkwardly, easy pickings for the nimble Israelis.

By the time the Israelites finally clashed with them, they swarmed through their ranks like ferocious leopards, running circles around Sisera's front line with unmatched agility.

Unfortunately, those who had staffs and wooden swords didn't do much damage, but that quickly changed when the first wave of Israelites discovered weapons abandoned in the chariots.

"There's weapons in here!" they started shouting out to each other, and the Israelis started equipping themselves with whatever they could find. For some, all they could get were a few arrows, but they were so fast, they used them with their bare hands.

When the battle initiated, the previously intimidated Israelites that were holding back soon mobilized into action when they realized how fast they were compared to Sisera's troops, who trudged about like a bunch of sloths.

The boy with his dagger and garden tool took on two large men, dodging an attack from one of them, and smashing the other with his garden tool.

Then he threw his dagger into another soldier who was about to impale Malachi with a spear from behind.

His dagger thrust into the soldier with such impact, he flew backward and thudded to the ground, after which he was crushed beneath the wheel of a chariot.

The boy quickly fetched his dagger and displayed it to Malachi, whom he recognized as the person who gave it to him. "Works great!" he yelled to Malachi.

"Excellent! Thank you!" Malachi thanked him for saving his life.

Superb investment on that dagger...

The old man was slaying Sisera's troops left and right, and he quickly acquired another one of their swords.

He was a highly skilled Benjamite swordsman, ambidextrous and untouchable, fighting with all the swiftness, strength, and agility of his youth.

From the summit of Mount Tabor overlooking the battlefield, Elias the High Priest held his staff high; his cloak billowed in the fierce gales and torrential downpour.

He had a team of designated staff bearers taking turns, helping him to keep his staff up in the air. "Hurry up, change over!"

The arrogant, smug temple worker that frequently rubbed Elias the wrong way, Thomas, quickly ran over to Elias and grabbed his arm, switching places with the other staff bearer.

Elias grinned at him with a scrutinizing glare.

"Thomas, you haven't once looked at the ark all this time. Aren't you at least curious to have that privilege for once?"

Thomas didn't know what to say, so he simply frowned and stared at the ground, afraid to speak.

"He forgives you. He told me to tell you that."

As Elias's words sunk in, Thomas started trembling and shaking so much he could barely stand. "Come on now, help me out," Elias was struggling with the staff. "My arm's falling asleep, I need help."

Thomas nodded, sniffling, thankful for the rain hiding his tears. "Why would He care about me," Thomas finally spoke. "I'm just a fool. I should've been stricken dead a dozen times."

"Sixteen actually," Elias nodded with a smile, then he started laughing. Thomas giggled briefly, then he started crying again.

"But then you always do something when no one is looking. You know what He means by that, I don't; He didn't tell me. But you know. He sees something special in you."

Thomas started bawling, now a total wreck.

Struck a nerve.

Another staff bearer came and replaced him, and Thomas backed away, tripped and stumbled toward the ark. Elias gasped as he almost touched it, but spun away in the nick of time and back-flopped in the mud right in front of the ark.

"Seventeen," Elias shouted at him, and Thomas started laughing hysterically, and crying, in the mud in front of the ark.

Elias shook his head and rolled his eyes, then returned to his prayers, focusing on the needs of Israel.

He listened to accounts of Moses, about how he held up his staff for the duration of their battles. Elias wasn't sure if the same thing would apply to him, but he figured he'd at least give it a try.[15]

When he first raised his staff to initiate their prayers before the battle, he was overcome with the overwhelming power of Yahweh surging through him. This must have been what Moses felt, and from that moment, he knew he had to keep his staff raised high.

This was the same power that Moses experienced, and the Israelites were the divine beneficiaries on the battlefield below. All of them felt this anointing, and many were bold enough to experiment with it.

Some leapt in the air and delivered two kicks before landing. Others swatted arrows and slingshots away with their bare hands, having no need for shields or armor. The more they believed in their invincibility, the more invincible they became.

Adonia's multi-opponent techniques were on full display; he fought like a cornered animal with nothing left to lose. With a single swing, his battle axe demolished entire chariots. His blade was wide enough to hack soldiers completely in half at the torso.

The Israelis tore through Sisera's frontline fodder forces with ease in their first wave of battle, and then they found Sisera's more experienced warriors deeper in his ranks.

It was near the middle of Sisera's horde where Adonia finally met his match when he encountered Gath, whose eyes were glowing red.

Adonia blocked Gath's unrelenting barrage of attacks, having no time for an offence, until he finally used one of his blocking maneuvers to snap Gath's sword.

Gath then lifted one of his hands toward Adonia, while he reached out his other hand to a sword he spotted lying on the ground.

Adonia felt his battle axe jerk to the right by an unseen force, and he plunged it into the ground, missing his mark.

The sword Gath was reaching for suddenly flew off the ground and shot over to his hand and he caught it. He then swiped it at Adonia, but Adonia deflected it with his wrist bracelet.

With bow in hand, Deborah was making one throat shot after another, some without even looking. This entire battle was one massive déjà vu for her.

At one point, she sensed it without seeing, a dagger flying toward her head from behind. She immediately spun around and caught it by the handle, right in front of her face.

She then threw it right back at her attacker so hard, it ripped completely through him and stuck into the soldier behind him, killing him as well.

And Barak was so invigorated with power on high, he tackled a horse head on, gripping its neck and body-slamming it to the ground. As the horse went down, the chariot attached to it flipped and threw its rider.

As soon as Barak rolled over, he whipped back his arm to block a sword strike, and he busted the enemy's sword in half using his bare arm against the flat of the blade.

As the soldier gawked at his broken sword, Barak snatched the broken shard of the same sword, and flung through his chest, killing him instantly.

When Barak stood back up, he turned so see Sisera in the distance, towering over everyone around him, still in his war chariot.

Sisera wasn't paying any attention to anyone around him; his glowing red eyes were laser focused on one target—Deborah.

As soon as Barak saw this, he quickly worked his way over to Deborah and braced himself by her side.

"Together," he replied, and Deborah nodded, ready to face Sisera once again. This time, she wouldn't underestimate him.

Deborah pulled out her cord attached tent peg and flung it toward the spear of an enemy soldier. The tent peg whipped around the shaft of the spear, and Deborah yanked it out of the soldier's hands and directly into the spokes of Sisera's chariot.

The spokes of the chariot snapped and collapsed the wheel, flipping Sisera's chariot and slamming Sisera to the ground.

As soon as he was on his feet, Israelis scattered away, keeping their distance. Sisera quickly spotted Deborah and smiled through blood-stained teeth.

Time to swat this bee!

Seeing a dead horse lying on the ground, Sisera squatted down, gripped its head in his hands, then he spun it around a few times like an Olympic hammer throw, and flung it toward Deborah and Barak.

They easily dodged the flying horse, but others did not. The horse smashed through a dozen Israelis and Sisera's own men, clearing a path as it slid, spinning in the mud.

Sisera's eyes began to pulsate red, illuminating sickness, death, and perversion to compliment his twisted smile.

Always the showman, Sisera was putting on a show for his best warriors that he was grooming to replace his Sacred Order. He wanted them to see his prowess on the battlefield, complete with all the bells and whistles.

He actually made a checklist for this. *1. Horse Throw, 2. Glowing Eyes, 3. Fear Projection, 4. Telekinesis...*

The famous horse throw was only for show on this occasion. He knew Deborah and Barak would dodge it, but still, he liked throwing horses, and he knew it impressed his troops.

So what's next? Oh yea, these seasoned warriors would probably be immune to tricks of the mind, but who knows, might get lucky. After all, Abaddon was supposed to be helping, right?

Where was that fire from heaven, anyway? Malchus had some explaining to do...

Sisera stood still a moment and concentrated while staring at Barak and Deborah. He exercised his ability to project the most powerful aura of fear he could muster.

A wave of terror suddenly seized Deborah and Barak. They both shuttered, overcome with the irrational impulse to collapse in a fetal position, as if that would help.

The two of them nearly dropped to their knees, but fortunately the episode only lasted a few seconds. "Shit," Barak muttered, then he shook his head. "You still with me?"

"No kidding," Deborah replied under her breath. "Keep it together. Okay, over there," Deborah coordinated with Barak to spread out.

"That's my sword," Sisera growled while stepping forward and holding up his hand. Deborah's sword suddenly flew out of her hand and landed squarely into Sisera's palm.

A crackling sizzle soon followed, then a spurt of flames shot off the handle of Deborah's sword. Sisera yelped and dropped it in the mud. "Not anymore," Deborah laughed at this face.[16]

He shook his hand, now dripping with blood; all the skin on his palm was bubbling flesh. He reached down and gripped a handful of mud to sooth it.

"How dare you defile my weapon!" he roared and took the first swing of his huge sword.

Deborah dodged, rolled near her sword, snatched it back up then lodged it into Sisera's side. The sword was so deep, she relinquished it and leapt back.

A sword in the gut is bad enough, but this sword was burning Sisera as if it were fresh out of a forge; a glowing hot blade ready for the hammer!

Seizing on Sisera's moment of weakness, Barak lunged, slashing Sisera's right arm. At the same time, a dozen arrows plunged into Sisera, knocking him down.

Barak rushed in, but Sisera pounded him with his fist on a back swing, flinging him through the air about fifteen feet away. Deborah wasn't the only one experiencing déjà vu.

Coming to his defense, Sisera's most experienced warriors immediately swarmed in on Deborah, surrounding her in a semicircle. A wadi full of gushing water was directly behind her.

One of the men with glowing red eyes rushed in so quickly, he slammed into her, propelling her from the edge of the wadi. Before she knew it, they were both underwater.

Adonia's words echoed in her memories, "Attack the throat if underwater."

Deborah reflexively jabbed the red eyed beast with a finger strike to his throat, and off he went, swept away in the currents as she swam back to the edge of the wadi.

Next?

As soon as Deborah climbed out of the wadi, one of Sisera's troops swung his sword at her.

She instantly ducked beneath it, then flung a tent peg into his neck. Another lunged forward with his sword, but she deflected his blade into one of the other soldiers standing too close to her.

Like a wild cat surrounded by a pack of dogs, she kicked, spun, punched, swiped her dagger, and flung out another tent peg, dropping all five men in a scant few seconds.

The delay these troops created for Sisera didn't last long, but it was long enough, because Sisera was no longer lying on the ground where he was before.

Instead, Deborah's sword lie in the mud, sizzling, with Sisera's blood burning to a crisp on its blade.

Severely wounded and utterly humiliated, Sisera escaped on foot, stumbling through the battlefield, ducking behind chariot debris as he went. Things were not going his way at all. Where in the hell was Abaddon?

Abaddon was actually *in hell,* but Sisera didn't know that yet.

Instead, Sisera was hobbling away as fast as he could, reeling this battle through his mind, so infuriated he could vomit with rage.

This was supposed to be the battle of the century, the battle of Anakim glory, where these vile Israelite cretins would finally get wiped out once and for all!

But this glorious battle started out with an unexpected torrential rain, trashing his chariots, rather than a rain of fire on top of Mount Tabor.

Okay, whatever, charge into battle anyway, but then his grand entrance turned out to be a flipped chariot, face plant fiasco.

Brush it off, throw a damn horse!

Nope, took out a half dozen of his own men with that stunt, but never mind, seize them with fear!

No? Immune to fear? Abaddon, what's up?

Then Deborah had the audacity to pull out his own weapon to use it against him. Seriously?

He thought he was going to teach her a lesson with that, freaking her out with his powers to snatch it from her with a wave of his hand. But no, no, no, not even that!

His hand was nearly burned off gripping his own weapon, then she slammed it into his side with the most horrendous, gut wrenching, searing pain he had ever felt in his entire life.

His brother met with this bee sting, and now he did as well, though humility was not in Sisera's nature, so he had no regrets over rebuking his own brother to hell.

Instead, he comforted himself with the thought that he at least survived. That meant he would eventually hunt this bee down and swat it if it was the last thing he would ever do.

Sisera snatched his oversized longbow and a few of its custom mad arrows from his demolished chariot before he escaped the battlefield.

Commentary Notes

++

1. See Exodus 3:2, the Burning Bush.
2. See Joshua 5:14, Captain of the host of the Lord.
3. See Judges 5:20, the stars fought.
4. See Judges 5:3, the earth shook and trembled.
5. See Revelation 6:14, the sky vanished like a scroll that is being rolled up.
6. See Acts 12:7, the Apostle Peter's chains fell to the floor when he was miraculously released from prison. This also happened with the Apostle Paul, Acts 16:26.
7. See Luke 1:79, a light to them that sit in darkness and in the shadow of death.
8. See John 3:19-20, men loved darkness rather than light.
9. See 1 Timothy 6:16, unapproachable light.
10. See Exodus 3:20, simply looking at God can cause death if He deems it so.
11. See Revelation 20:3, speaks of sealing the bottomless pit.
12. See Psalm 130, God redeems.
13. See Numbers 10:2, 9, In addition to blowing shofars, (rams horns), the Israelites also blew two silver trumpets when going to war.
14. See Hosea 5:8, "we follow you, O Benjamin!" war cry.
15. See Exodus 17:11, Moses held up his staff during Israel's battles.
16. Could the gift of prophecy sometimes manifest without the prophesier realizing it? That speculation inspires this scene, where Deborah quotes Sisera's own mocking phrase, "not anymore," from chapter 18, now directed against him.

Chapter 26:

Two Women

ፒ

Zipping back and forth, Adonia and Gath were still in the midst of fierce combat, exchanging blow after blow.

Each of them were experts at defense, meeting most of their attacks with successful blocks and deflections, which resulted in the most prolonged battle Adonia had ever fought.

However, Adonia was struggling through a disadvantage, hindered by an arrow stuck in his right shoulder. Then another arrow plunged into his leg, but he fought his way through it, swing after swing, block after block.

In a moment of vulnerability, as Adonia gasped to catch his breath, Gath's eyes pulsed red, and Adonia's battle axe suddenly flew out of his hand and landed in Gath's hand.

Adonia's axe was blessed the same as Deborah's sword, and just as Deborah's sword burned Sisera, Adonia's battle axe scorched Gath's hand.

Nevertheless, Gath managed to get at least one solid swing with it before relinquishing it.

He swung it down toward the top of Adonia's skull with all his might, but just before it reached Adonia's skull, clank!

Deborah threw her cord attached tent peg and smacked the blade of the axe askew, so the flat of the blade bounced off Adonia's head rather than the sharp edge hacking through his skull.

Deborah then whipped her tent peg back and out again, latching it around Gath's neck. In the instant Gath grabbed the cord, struggling to remove it, Adonia snatched up his battle axe and finally hacked Gath down in one final swipe.

"Where's Sisera!" Deborah yelled out, searching for anyone who saw him leave.

"That way!" a few Israelites pointed, and Deborah immediately sprinted after him, though it was difficult to see in the heavy wind and rain.

While the Israelites pursued Sisera's troops to the south toward Taanach, Sisera escaped to the north, headed toward Hazor, periodically looking behind him to see if he was followed.

No one appeared to be following him, so he paused to yank arrows out of his body. He had so many, he looked like a pin cushion.

However, his leathery skin was thicker than studded leather, and his muscle was so dense, most arrows didn't do much other than sting.

It wasn't long before Deborah found Sisera's tracks; they weren't that hard to follow in the thick mud. Even with the rain gushing down, the clay retained the shape of Sisera's enormous, easily identifiable footprints.

Seeing the warm glow of a tent in the distance, Sisera was desperate for relief of any kind.

With his amazing recovery and healing abilities unique to the Anakim, most of his arrow wounds were quickly healing up, and the gash Barak gave his arm already stopped bleeding.

However, something about Deborah's sword in his gut was worse than any wound he had ever received. He needed bandages, and he was on the verge of passing out because he lost so much blood.

Sisera limped up to the tent, which happened to be Jael's tent. He then dropped to his knees in the mud and began to crawl.

Jael was in the middle of eating her dinner when she heard a noise outside.

Setting her plate down, she peaked out of her tent and saw Sisera gasping for breath on his hands and knees near the opening of her tent. She immediately jerked back inside.

What's this? What to do?

Jael's eyes scanned her tent, then dropped down to the mallet and tent pegs in the corner of her tent. On a shelf near those, set a gold colored tent peg. The words, "Stay vigilant," echoed in her mind.

Jael exited her tent wearing a dark cloak with a hood draped over her head. The fierce storm helped her; it provided low visibility, and a good excuse for wearing a hooded cloak. There was no way she wanted Sisera to know who she was.

Sisera struggled back to his feet, barely able to stand. But even so wounded, he was still a monstrously imposing figure. Jael remained calm and approached him sympathetically.

She noticed he was scanning the area nervously, paranoid. He wasn't used to being afraid like this. The last time he felt like this was over one hundred years ago, when he and his brother fled from their village.

"Sir, are you okay? *Please come in, my lord, fear not*. You need rest."[1-2]Sisera shoved Jael aside, ducked low and stumbled into her tent. When he saw Jael's pet monkey, he tried to kick it, but the creature was far too quick.

The monkey screeched and darted up Sisera's leg, squirting urine as he went. He then leapt for cover, scuttling through myriad decorations and furniture, cramming himself into the most obscured crevice he could find.

Sisera dropped to a rug with a pile of blankets and pillows, out of breath and bleeding profusely. *"I'm thirsty, get me some water,"*[3] he panted.

He then notched and arrow and lay his bow across his waist, aimed at the opening of the tent. Satisfied the location was semi-secure, he fell back on the pillows with labored breathing.

Jael approached with a blanket. "Sir, you must be cold," *she handed him the blanket*[4] and he accepted it and wrapped it around his waist to bandage the wound in his side.

"Please accept this milk."[5] Jael handed Sisera some warm goat's milk in a fancy bowl.[6] He lost so much blood, he was barely conscious, but not so much that he didn't drink the milk she gave him.

As Sisera rested, Jael grabbed another blanket and draped it over him. He didn't object. Instead, he relaxed and replied, *"Don't let anyone know I'm here. Close that opening,"*[7] he pointed to the opening in the tent.

A few deep breaths later, he closed his eyes, though Jael couldn't tell for sure if he was falling asleep or not.

It was a risky move, but she might not get another opportunity, so Jael quietly eased her way over to the mallet and tent pegs.

That gold tent peg was especially appealing, extra sharp as Deborah said it was, so she snatched it up, then slowly crept her way back around Sisera.

Sneaking up to his head from behind, she slowly lowered the tent peg with the spiked edge pointing directly in the center of Sisera's temple.

Her hands were trembling uncontrollably, and it took her all concentration not to drop it.

Just as she pulled back the mallet to swing it, the tent flap whipped open. There Deborah stood with her bow, though she used her hand to open the tent, so an arrow wasn't ready to fire yet.

Sisera instantly whipped up his bow at the same time as Deborah drew her bow.

Sisera then became aware of Jael's tent peg centered directly over his temple.

What's it going to be?

Wham!

Jael was the first to strike, smashing down her mallet on the tent peg Deborah gave her, burying it into Sisera's skull so far, it sank into the ground.[8-9] As Sisera convulsed he fired his bow.

Thump!

Deborah shot her bow as well, but Sisera's oversized metal shaft arrow slammed into the far left side of her ribcage first, flinging her backward out of the tent.

Jael shrieked in anguish, struck by Deborah's misfire.

A moment later, Deborah ripped open the tent flap again and stumbled inside with blood oozing from a hole in her side.

That arrow blasted right through her, but she was so amped up with adrenaline, and an abundance of Shekinah glory, she was ready to resume where she left off.

Fortunately, Sisera was done for, but Jael wasn't getting through this without a scratch.

Deborah's arrow was stuck in Jael's arm.[10] While the pain was intense, she was actually quite pleased with that arrow, and she would later cherish the scar it left behind for the rest of her life.

"You did it," Deborah gasped, the pain in her side finally catching up with her. "Wow, I thought I messed this one up," she replied.

Jael laughed, recalling herself saying the same thing years ago. "No, I'm always the one messing up your shots!"

Deborah giggled at the recollection while bandaging her wound.

"Not this time! But actually, I meant...I never saw the conclusion of this battle in my visions. I..." she looked at the mallet in Jael's hand.

"I just had a feeling when I saw that mallet," Deborah pointed at Jael's mallet. "When Sisera got away, and I saw him headed this way, I didn't...I just didn't know. But you did it, you really did it!"

"I did, didn't I?" Jael was very pleased she was able to contribute in the battle, even though she never set foot on the battlefield.

When Deborah dropped to her knees next to Jael, Jael heard a noise outside. She immediately jumped up and poked her head out of the tent. Fortunately, it was Barak.

Jael stepped outside to address him. "Come, I think I know who you're looking for."[11-12]

When Barak pulled back the tent flap, he was shocked.

"Whoa!" he exclaimed, observing the hideous tent pegged menace before him. "How'd you pull that off? What happened?"

"The glory of this battle went to a woman, that's what happened," Deborah replied while pointing her finger at Jael. "She took out a giant."

"Two women," Barak agreed while pointing at both of them. "You did it. Your plan...worked."[13]

"*Yahweh's plan*," Deborah pointed up. "Without Him, the battle would've ended on Mount Tabor."

"What do you mean?"

"Ask Adonia, he's better at storytelling than me."

Deborah suddenly jerked up her head with a sniff, alarming Barak and Jael.

"What?" They looked at the tent opening nervously; Barak gripped the handle of his sword, ready for action.

No, Deborah wasn't catching the scent of battle. It was Jael's half eaten plate of food setting on a shelf that arrested her attention.

"Oh wow, don't tell me you're not going to eat that," Deborah pointed at the food. Barak rolled his eyes, releasing his sword. Face palm.

"How could you think about food after this?" Jael chastised Deborah. "That's just...*weird*."

"I beg to differ, young lady," Deborah made her way over to the dish of food. "I can't even comprehend how you can just shut off your appetite like this. I mean, who cares...," Deborah motioned to Sisera's corpse.

"He's dead already, it's not like his condition is going to change. Meanwhile, you have this perfectly delicious plate of lamb over here getting cold. What a waste!

"Have you learned anything from me? Out of all my prophecies, teachings of the law, words of knowledge, tips for fighting, and whatever else, *please... please...* don't go wasting food like this! I just...*don't do it*!"

Deborah snatched up the plate, grabbed a chunk of lamb and immediately tore into it, chewing ravenously.

"This is scary delicious," she spoke with her mouth full. "You got any carrots around here?"

"Yes, we have a few. Why, you think I should've added carrots to that?" Jael questioned, still bewildered how Deborah could gobble down a meal with this massive corpse lying right there.

"No, not for me. My horse has been hankering for a carrot. Bugging me every day about it."

Jael fetched a few carrots.

"Hey, by the way," Deborah motioned toward Sisera's body, still speaking with her mouth full.

"You'll need to burn his body, that sheet, destroy everything he bled on, then crush his bones to dust and scatter them at least a hundred furlongs out in the sea. Then move your tent a few furlongs from here."

"Is that all?" Jael questioned, somewhat overwhelmed with this monumental to-to list.

"Probably. I tell you, these Anakim, they don't rest in peace. Some of them manage to squirm out of Sheol. My guess is, it has something to do with their bones, and probably that sorcerer Malchus. I've seen their spirits wandering in desolate places.[14]

"You have?" Barak questioned.

"Yup. Even dead, these Anakim are bad news. I'd say the only one caring about Sisera here would be his mother, but I doubt it. She's probably just looking out the lattice, whining about the plunder. 'Where's my new slaves, son? Where's my dyed embroidery?'"[15-16]

"He was a hideous beast," Jael recalled her visit to his temple.

"If you still want that tent peg," Deborah pointed her lamb bone at the gold tent peg in Sisera's skull, "you're going to have to give it to that metal man, Shelah. He has a unique talent for purifying things."

"Metal man?" Jael questioned.

"That's what Adonia calls him. I like it. Metal man. You know the guy."

"Hey," Barak suddenly noticed something, "I thought I gave that to you," he pointed at the golden tent peg.

"You did," Deborah replied, "and I gave it to her. Looks like she put it to good use, don't you think? And well, what you had written on it also fulfils a prophecy for Jael. Seems I'm not the only prophet around here."

An ornately decorated Hebrew marriage contract inscribed on a vellum scroll, the ketubah they called it, lie unfurled on a table in the courtyard of the Tabernacle.[17-19]

Barak was wearing a white robe, and Deborah was wearing a white gown with a wide sash and a flower pinned on her side covering her bandaged wound. They stood before Elias, dressed in his full priestly garb, beneath a decorated canopy.

Deborah and Barak each stepped forward, taking a turn to sign the ketubah before all the witnesses packed in the courtyard.

Most of these observers were not of noble birth, nor people of exceptional wealth. Most were ordinary people met with extraordinary circumstances, which brought about the extraordinary within them.

A young boy and an old man were given special honor with a prominent view, standing next to Jael, the giant slayer. And Heber stood by Jael's side. He was among the few wealthy attendees, arriving in a grand display, he and Jael both sporting their exotic white donkeys.[20]

Barak initially objected to Heber's presence, but Deborah reminded him about her custom sword, and the fact that Heber was faithful to Jael and did his best to please her. He wasn't all bad, and he finally severed his ties with King Jabin.

Yes, Heber made weapons for Sisera's men for a time, he straddled the fence with Israel, and he was an informant, albeit not entirely by choice. He was a man of tarnished wealth. However, it was only through forgiveness that Israel would ever unite.

Adonia and other prominent warriors were also present.

Abijah, Jethro, Rueben, Ezra, Joash, Daniel, Malachi, Gabriel, Jacob, and Thomas all stood together. Other warriors who trained with Deborah and Barak in their early days also stood with them.

And next to them, the Ramah Security Squad Leaders, Gavriella, Tamar, and Sarai; they stood with their trainees.

Deborah and Adonia's personal friend, Nathan, who was the first to break Deborah out of her downward spiral of self-loathing; he stood proudly next to Deborah's neighbor, Naomi. They were soon to be married.

The two women shamed over their idol dispute beamed with joy. One of them had her arm around her niece who was almost lost to Sisera's temple. Thanks to Deborah's word, they prevented that from happening.

And the young man with his sheep brought his sheep with him to witness this glorious occasion.

His former bearded accuser came as well, also saddled on a white donkey. Where were all these white donkeys coming from?

These two had since reconciled over the sheep issue, but the bearded man still couldn't help coveting that sheep. He kept eyeing its flawless wool; such a beautiful animal—*look away, just look away...*

Metal man Shelah was there, naturally; he lived in Shiloh, and so did Tailor Seth. Who else but Tailor Seth could have made Barak's ornate, white robe, and Deborah's dress?

Those who worked on Deborah's studded leather armor, Sharon, Joshua, and Ariel, were looking forward to some personal tutelage from Tailor Seth.

Haran always complained that Ramah was in need of Seth's tailoring talents, and Deborah was seeing to it that one of his recurring rants was finally addressed.

Even a handful of Sisera's former troops deserted King Jabin's ranks right before the battle. They came to their senses about who they served, and they presented themselves to Deborah, begging for forgiveness.

Of course she forgave them; she of all people knew full well their repentance was genuine.

"To all Israel," Elias announced, "I present to you your General Barak, and your Judge and Prophetess, Deborah, husband and wife!"

An enormous applause, cheers, howls and shouts of joy erupted from the courtyard of the Tabernacle.

Even the wayward temple worker, Thomas, abandoned his usual scowl since that day on top of Mount Tabor. He exchanged it for the good spirits abounding throughout the land.

As dancing and music erupted, initiated with shofar blasts from the priests, Adonia and Jael flanked Barak and Deborah and led them through the jubilant soiree.

The two were intoxicated with profound joy. So long they suffered, but not in vain, for Yahweh was indeed delighted to spare these two a slice of destiny in each other's arms.

Just outside the courtyard of the Tabernacle, the two made their way to a ceremonial tent setup for them. Jael and Adonia were relieved of their escort duties, releasing these newlyweds for the breaking of their marriage fast.

When they entered the tent, they found a delicious meal prepared for them, amidst silk pillows on the floor. They sat, enraptured with each other, and each gave one another a bite to eat.

Barak finally broke the silence while gently stroking his favorite scar upon Deborah's cheek with his thumb.

"I noticed you were distracted during the ceremony."

"Visions have little respect for timing," Deborah muttered.

"Visions? You had visions while we were getting married?"

"Annoying sometimes, yea."

"What did you see?"

"I saw the Angel of the Lord, over by the Tent of Meeting."

"You wha..." Barak was astonished.

"Yea, He was just right there, and my pet goat Caleb was standing next to Him. Can you believe that? I almost passed out," Deborah nodded. "And then...then I saw us taking back the city of Hazor, in another battle to come. Sisera's gone, but Jabin..."

"Oy," Barak sighed.

"And we're going to have a son," Deborah smiled.

"Really? A son? This tent is only a symbolic gesture!" Barak joked. "We're not actually supposed to do anything in here."

Deborah shoved him as they giggled and fell into each other's arms. "We might want to...reconsider the symbolic aspect of this tent."

Perched on poles of the Tabernacle courtyard, a line of doves quietly cooed from above, intently observing the tent.

Were these really doves, or were they the angels of Haran and Miriam visiting from heaven? Perhaps Ruth, Shem, Kenaz, Rachael, and others lost in Nazareth were among them?

"Praise the Lord for the avenging of Israel, when the people willingly offered themselves," Deborah softly sang a tune. *"Hear oh kings, give ear, you princes; I will sing unto the Lord."*[21-24]

Her words then blended into a haunting flute melody, ascending like a fragrant incense to the heavenly spheres.

The festive ceremony within the courtyard of the Tabernacle continued unabated, and Yahweh smiled down from above.

In the years to come, the hand of the people of Israel pressed harder and harder against Jabin, the king of Canaan, until they destroyed Jabin king of Canaan.[25]

And the land had rest for forty years.[26]

The End

Commentary References

1. "17th of Tammuz in Israel," https://www.timeanddate.com/holidays/israel/fast-of-shiva-asar-b-tammuz, TimeAndDate.com, (Last accessed February 27, 2021).
2. "4 Maccabees," New World Encyclopedia, https://www.newworldencyclopedia.org/entry/4_Maccabees, (Last accessed February 28, 2021).
3. "Air Force Vision," https://www.airforce.com/mission/vision, (Last accessed February 27, 2021).
4. Analida, "Moroccan Lamb Tagine with Apricots", https://ethnicspoon.com/traditional-lamb-tagine-with-apricots/, (Last Accessed December 19, 2020).
5. "Ancient Jewish History: The Ark of the Covenant," https://www.jewishvirtuallibrary.org/the-ark-of-the-convenant, (Last accessed February 22, 2021).
6. "Ancient Ostracon Records Ark's Wanderings" Ministry International Journal for Pastors, https://www.ministrymagazine.org/archive/1991/07/ancient-ostracon-records-arks-wanderings, (Last accessed January 30, 2021).
7. Arthur E. Cundall & Leon Morris, *Judges & Ruth: An Introduction & Commentary*, (Downers Grove, IL: Inter-Varsity Press Leicester, England, 1968).
8. Bedford Astronomy Club, "Moving Large Stone blocks in Ancient Times", https://www.astronomyclub.xyz/easter-island/appendix-2-moving-large-stone-blocks-in-ancient-times.html, (Last Accessed December 12, 2020).
9. Bethania Palma, "Did U.S. Special Forces Kill a Giant in Kandahar? False. Snopes.com. "https://www.snopes.com/fact-check/u-s-special-forces-killed-a-giant-in-kandahar/" (Last Accessed December 6, 2020).
10. Bible History Online, "The Outer Court", https://www.bible-history.com/tabernacle/tab4the_outer_court.htm, (Last Accessed December 24, 2020).
11. Brian E. Colless, "abgadary, The Izbet Sartah Ostrakon, Musings of a Student Scribe", https://sites.google.com/site/collesseum/abgadary, (Last accessed January 30, 2021).
12. Bruce Fessier, "Did 14-foot giants exist? Did they differ from humans? Author explores these ancient beings", Desert Sun, "https://www.desertsun.com/story/life/entertainment/people/brucefessier

13. Byod Seevers and Joanna Klein, "Genetics and the Bible: The Curious Case of the Left-Handed Benjamites", Communication, The American Scientific Affiliation, https://www.asa3.org/ASA/PSCF/2012/PSCF9-12Seevers.pdf, (Last Accessed December 2, 2020).
14. C. Scott Littleton, Mythology: The Illustrated Anthology of World Myth and Storytelling, (London: Duncan Baird Publishers, 2002).
15. Carlos Castaneda, The Teachings of Don Juan: A Yaqui Way of Knowledge, (New York, NY: Washington Square Press, 1998).
16. Carol R. Ember & Melvin Ember, Cultural Anthropology, 6th Ed., (Englewood Cliffs, NJ: Prentice Hall, Inc. 1990).
17. Carolyn Trickey-Bapty, Martyrs & Miracles: The Inspiring Lives of Saints & Martyrs, (Owings Mills, MD: Ottenheimer Publishers, Inc,, 1994).
18. Colin Wilson and Dr. Christopher Evans, The Book of Great Mysteries, (New York, NY: Dorset Press, 1990).
19. "Conversation and Debate", My Jewish Learning, (Last Accessed December 17, 2020).
20. Clifford Geertz, "Religion as a Cultural System." In Michael Banton, ed., Anthropological Approaches to the Study of Religion. Association of Social Anthropologists of the Commonwealth, Monograph no. 3. (New York: Prager, 1966).
21. Craig S. Keener, The IVP, Bible Background Commentary, New Testament, (Downers Grove, IL: Intervarsity Press, 1993).
22. David Brinn, "Israel's Elderberry Remedy Sambucol Provides Solution to U.S. Flu Vaccine Shortage", Israel21c, https://www.israel21c.org/study-shows-israeli-elderberry-extract-effective-against-avian-flu/, (Last Accessed December 22, 2020).
23. David M. Howard & Gary Burge, Fascinating Bible Facts: People, Places, and Events, (Lincolnwood, IL: Publications International, Ltd., 1999).
24. EBible.org, "Book of 4 Maccabees," https://ebible.org/pdf/eng-web/eng-web_4MA.pdf, (Last accessed February 28, 2021).
25. Elvio Angeloni, Anthropology, 92/93, 15th Ed., (Guilford CN: The Dushkin Publishing Group, Inc., 1993).
26. Emil G. Hirch, "Goliath," Jewish Encyclopedia, https://www.

jewishencyclopedia.com/articles/6779-goliath, (Last accessed February 13, 2021).
27. "Fact or fake? The relics of Christ's Easter suffering on cross are.. Shrouded in mystery," https://www.mirror.co.uk/news/uk-news/fact-or-fake-the-relics-of-christs-easter-387558, (Last accessed February 24, 2021).
28. "Fake News in Biblical Archeology", Bible Archeology Report, https://biblearchaeologyreport.com/2018/10/11/fake-news-in-biblical-archaeology/ (Last Accessed December 4, 2020).
29. "Golan Heights (Biblical Bashan)", BiblePlaces.com, https://www.bibleplaces.com/golanheights/, (Last Accessed December 12, 2020).
30. "Goliath's Spear, Giants are no match for my God!," https://www.goliathsspear.com/weavers-beam, (Last Accessed February 13, 2021).
11. H. Franklin Paschall & Herschel H. Hobbs, The Teacher's Bible Commentary, (Nashville, TN: Broadman Press, 1972).
31. Hassan Ammar, "Solved! How Ancient Egyptians Moved Massive Pyramid Stones", NBC News, https://www.nbcnews.com/science/science-news/solved-how-ancient-egyptians-moved-massive-pyramid-stones-n95171, (Last Accessed December 12, 2020).
32. Heather Burton, Cannibalism in High Medieval English Literature, (New York, NY: Palgrave Macmillan, 2007). Beowulf is the hero of a 6th century Scandinavian account of a cannibalistic giant known as Grendel.
33. Henry B. Smith Jr, "Canaanite Child Sacrifice, Abortion, and the Bible," 90-125 The Journal of Ministry and Theology, https://biblearchaeology.org/images/Child-Sacrifice-and-Abortion/4---Canaanite-Child-Sacrifice---Smith-90-125.pdf., (last accessed January 24, 2021).
34. History.com Editors, "Petra," https://www.history.com/topics/ancient-middle-east/petra, (Last accessed February 2, 2021).
35. "How much did Goliath's spear head weigh?" FindAnyAnswer, https://findanyanswer.com/how-much-did-goliathaposs-spear-head-weigh, (Last accessed February 13, 2021).

36. "How Tall Was Goliath?" Apologetics, WordPress, https://bibleapologetics.wordpress.com/2011/01/30/how-tall-was-goliath/ (last accessed April 9, 2016).
37. Isidore Singer, George A. Barton, "Moloch (Molech)", JewishEncyclopedia, http://jewishencyclopedia.com/articles/10937-moloch-molech, (Last Accessed December 16, 2020).
38. J. E. Cirlot, A Dictionary of Symbols, (United States: Dorset Press, 1991).
39. J. Pritchard, Ancient Near Eastern Texts and the Old Testament, 3rd Edition (Princeton: University Press, 1969), quoted in Christian Answers Network Bible Encyclopedia, s.v. "Nimrod: Who was he? Was he godly or evil?" by Dr. David P. Livingston, http://www.christiananswers.net/dictionary/nimrod.html, (Last Accessed December 10, 2020).
40. Jack Kelley, "Is Anointing With Oil Proper?" Grace thru Faith, https://gracethrufaith.com/ask-a-bible-teacher/is-anointing-with-oil-proper/, (Last Accessed December 25, 2020).
41. James M. Volo, "Did war chariots ever actually have blades on the wheel hubs?", Quora, https://www.quora.com/Did-war-chariots-ever-actually-have-blades-on-the-wheel-hubs, (Last Accessed December 19, 2020).
42. Jan Cashman, "Origin of Species of Corn, Potatoes, and Tomatoes - and Some Other Interesting History", https://cashmannursery.com/gardening-tips/2012/origin-of-species-of-corn-potatoes-and-tomatoes-and-some-other-interesting-history/#:~:text=Tomatoes%20are%20native%20to%20South,tomato%20was%20small%20and%20yellow, (Last Accessed December 19, 2020).
43. Janice Pearl Ewurama De-Whyte, Wom(b)an: A Cultural-Narrative Reading of the Hebrew Bible Barrenness Narratives, (New York, NY: Brill, 2018).
44. Jeffrey H. King, "Connecting the Dots; The Book of Enoch, Part 7", Jeffrey H. King's Blog, May 27, 2017, https://jeffreyhking.wordpress.com/2017/05/27/connecting-the-dots-the-book-of-enoch-part-7/, (Last Accessed December 8, 2020).
45. Jesse Lyman Hurlbut, Hurlbut's Handy Bible Encyclopedia, (Philadelphia, PA: The John C. Winston Co., 1908).
46. John H. Walton, Victor H. Matthews & Mark W. Chavalas, The

IVP Bible Background Commentary, Old Testament, (Downers IL: InterVarsity Press, 2000).
47. Jonathan M. Golden, Ancient Canaan & Israel, (Santa Barbara, CA: Oxford University Press, 2009).
48. J. P. Millar, The Preacher's Complete Homiletic Commentary on the Book of Judges, Vol 6, (New York: NY, Funk & Wagnalls Company, 1974).
49. Judah David Eisenstein, "Greetings, Forms Of:" Jewish Encyclopedia, http://www.jewishencyclopedia.com/articles/6873-greeting-forms-of, (Last Accessed December 2, 2020).
50. Ken Anderson, Where To Find It In The Bible, The Ultimate A to Z Resource, (Nashville, TN: Thomas Nelson Publishers, 1996).
51. Kenneth Barker, The New International Version Study Bible, (Grand Rapids, MI: Zondervan Bible Publishers, 1985).
52. Krav Maga Worldwide, "The History of Krav Maga", https://www.kravmaga.com/the-history-of-krav-maga/, (Last Accessed December 3, 2020).
53. Land of the Bible, "Hazor", https://www.land-of-the-bible.com/Hazor, (Last Accessed, December 7, 2020).
54. Laura Quick, "Og, King of Bashan: Underworld Ruler or Ancient Giant?" The Torah, https://www.thetorah.com/article/og-king-of-bashan-underworld-ruler-or-ancient-giant, (Last accessed February 8, 2021).
55. Lawrence O. Richards, Bible Reader's Companion, (Colorado Springs, CO: Cook Communications Ministries, 2004).
56. Lawrence Stager and Samuel Wolff, "Child Sacrifice at Carthage: Religious Rite or Population Control?" BAR 10, no. 1 (January-February 1984).
57. Leonard Sweet, "The Greatest Song Ever Sung," Marble Collegiate Church sermon, https://vimeo.com/20343071, (Last accessed February 1, 2021).
58. Linda Heaphy, "The Hasma (Khamsa)", Kashgar Website, https://kashgar.com.au/blogs/ritual-objects/the-hamsa-khamsa, (Last Accessed December 2, 2020).
59. Matthew Tingblad, "How Do We Count the Number of Fulfilled Biblical Prophecy?" Josh McDowell Ministry, https://www.josh.org/how-do-we-count-fulfilled-prophecy/, (Last accessed January 29, 2021).

60. Michael S. Heiser, "Clash of the Manuscripts," Bible Study Magazine, October 31, 2014, http://www.biblestudymagazine.com/extras-1/2014/10/31/clash-of-the-manuscripts-goliath-the-hebrew-text-of-the-old-testament (last accessed December 6, 2020).
61. MJL, "The Ketubah, or Jewish Marriage Contract," My Jewish Learning, https://www.myjewishlearning.com/article/the-ketubah-or-marriage-contract/, (Last accessed March 4, 2021).
62. "Mount Precipice," Jesus Trail, https://jesustrail.com/hike-the-jesus-trail/points-of-interest/mount-precipice, (last accessed January 24, 2021).
63. Robert Fitzgerald, The Odyssey, Homer, (New York, NY: Vintage Books, Random House, Inc., 1990).
64. NeverThirsty, "Were the Israelites allowed to enter the Tent of Meeting?" https://www.neverthirsty.org/bible-qa/qa-archives/question/were-the-israelites-allowed-to-enter-the-tent-of-meeting/, (Last Accessed December 24, 2020).
65. "Olive Oil in Biblical Times and Later", Israel Olive Bond, https://israelolivebond.com/olive-oil/olive-oil-history/, (Last Accessed December 19, 2020).
66. PBS Nova, "Pyramids: How Heavy?" https://www.pbs.org/wgbh/nova/pyramid/geometry/blocks.html#:~:text=How%20Heavy-%3F,metric%20tons%20(2.5%20tons)", (Last Accessed December 12, 2020).
67. Peter Lloyd Sheerin, "The Baronial Order of Magna Charta & Military Order of the Crusades," https://www.magnacharta.com/dtk/, (Last accessed February 24, 2021).
68. Ray Vander Laan, "Fertility Cults of Canaan", That The World May Know, https://www.thattheworldmayknow.com/fertility-cults-of-canaan, (Last Accessed December 12, 2020).
69. Richard J. Foster, Celebration of Discipline: The Path to Spiritual Growth, (New York, NY: HarperSanfrancisco, 1988).
70. Richard Laurence, The Book of Enoch the Prophet, (London: Kegan Paul, Trench & Col, 1883), obtained at https://archive.org/details/bookofenochproph00laur, (Last Accessed December 8, 2020).
71. Rick Meyers, "Equipping Ministries Foundation, e-Sword

Bible software, version 12.2.0," downloaded Nov 20, 2020, http://www.e-sword.net;

– Companion Bible Appendix 25, E. W. Bullinger

– Cyclopedia of Biblical, Theological and Ecclesiastical Literature

– David Guzik Commentary.

– Didache, The Teachings of the Twelve Apostles, Ante-Nicene Fathers, Volume 7, chapter 2.

– Easton Dictionary.

– Fausset Dictionary.

– King James Version (KJV) Bible.

– Hastings Bible Dictionary.

– Hippolytus - Refutation of All Heresies, Book 9, Chapter 7.

– History of the Christian Church (Philp Schaff), Vol. 4, Ch. 13.

– International Standard Bible Encyclopedia.

– International Standard Version (ISV) Bible.

– Jewish Publication Society (JPS) Bible.

– Modern King James Version (MJKV) Bible.

– Preacher's Homiletical.

– Sketches of Jewish Social Life, Synagogues: Their Origin, Structure, and Outward Arrangements.

– Strong's Enhanced Lexicon.

– Young's Literal Translation (YLV) Bible.

72. Robert Fitzgerald, The Odyssey, Homer, (New York, NY: Vintage Books, Random House, Inc., 1990).

73. Ron Wyatt, "Red Sea Crossing" videos, https://anchorstone.com/red-sea-crossing-revealing-gods-treasure/, (Last Accessed December 4, 2020).

74. Rosemary Ellen Guiley, Harper's Encyclopedia of Mystical & Paranormal Experience, (New York, NY: HarperCollins Publishers, 1991).

75. Scott Alan Roberts, The Rise and Fall of the Nephilim, (Pompton Plains, NJ: 2012).

76. Scott Littleton, Mythology: The Illustrated Anthology of World Myth and Storytelling, (London: Duncan Baird Publishers, 2002).

77. Shikha Goyal, "Top 10 most famous Martial Arts in India", https://www.jagranjosh.com/general-knowledge/top-10-most-famous-martial-arts-in-india-1467440667-1 (Last Accessed December 3, 2020).

78. Shofarot-Israel, "Barsheshet ⊠ Ribak, Shofarot Israel", http://

www.shofarot-israel.com/index.php/the-shofar/biblicaltime/, (Last Accessed December 25, 2020).

79. Shoshana Sussman, "Psalm 68: Echoes of the Song of Deborah?" Questia.com, Jewish Bible Quarterly, https://www.questia.com/library/journal/1G1-302403180/psalm-68-echoes-of-the-song-of-deborah, (Last Accessed December 2, 2020).

80. Tamar Kadari, "Deborah 2: Midrash and Aggadah," Jewish Women's Archive Encyclopedia, https://jwa.org/encyclopedia/article/deborah-2-midrash-and-aggadah, (Last accessed March 6, 2021).

81. The Epic of Gilgamesh, trans. Robert Temple, Biblioteca Pleyades website, http://www.bibliotecapleyades.net/serpents_dragons/gilgamesh.htm (Last Accessed December 10, 2020).

82. The Great Courses, Religion, The Old Testament, Part Two, Lecture 13, The Book of Judges, Part 1, DVD Series, Taught By: Professor Amy-Jill Levine, (Chantilly, VA: The Teaching Company Limited Partnership, Vanderbuilt University Divinity School, Copyright 2001).

83. "The Human Weapon, Krav Maga Israel," https://www.youtube.com/watch?v=bt8w92ilbVM, (Last Accessed December 12, 2020).

84. "The Human Weapon, Krav Maga Human Weapon Israel," https://www.youtube.com/watch?v=UpyoYuTW_V8, (Last Accessed December 12, 2020).

85. The Next Faithful Step, "The Self-Emptying of Christ", Fuller Seminary, https://www.fuller.edu/next-faithful-step/resources/kenosis/, (Last Accessed, December 12, 2020).

86. Thomas of Celano, The Treatise on the Miracle of Saint Francis, (1250-1252), ed. Regis J. Armstorng, OFM Cap, J.A. Wayne Hellmoann, OFM Cov, William J. Short, OFM, The Francis Trilogy of Thomas of Celano (Hyde Park: New City Press, 2004).

87. Tim Chaffey, "Giants in the Bible", Answers in Genesis, https://answersingenesis.org/bible-characters/giants-in-the-bible/, (Last Accessed December 12, 2020).

88. Tom Metcalfe, "King Tut's Dagger Is 'Out of This World,'" https://www.livescience.com/61214-king-tut-dagger-outer-space.html, (Last accessed February 21, 2021).

89. Truth or Tradition? "Binding and Loosing", https://www.truthortradition.com/articles/binding-and-loosing, (Last Accessed December 25, 2020).

90. Wade Cox, "Mysticism, chapter 1 Spreading the Babylonian Mysteries," Christian Churches of God, http://www.ccg.org/english/s/b7_1.html (Last accessed February 8, 2021).
91. William G. Dever, What Did the Bible Writers Know & When Did They Know It? What Archeology Can Tell Us about the Reality of Ancient Israel, (Grand Rapids, MI: William B. Eerdmans Publishing Co., 2001).
92. William G. Denver, Who Were the Early Israelites and Where Did They Come From, (Grand Rapids, MI, William B. Eerdmans Publishing Co., 2003).
93. WordSearch Bible, "Birth," https://wordsearchbible.lifeway.com/products/13070-bible-biography-series-jacob/sample_text, (Last accessed February 21, 2021).

CPSIA information can be obtained
at www.ICGtesting.com
Printed in the USA
LVHW050905070921
697192LV00001B/58

9 781955 531184